THE
RESURRECTION
CHRONICLES
BOOKS 1-3

THE
RESURRECTION
CHRONICLES

BOOKS 1-3

M.J. HAAG
BECCA VINCENZA

Shattered Glass
—— PUBLISHING ——

THE RESURRECTION CHRONICLES. Copyright © 2023 by Melissa Haag. All rights reserved.
Published by Shattered Glass Publishing.
Print Cover design by Shattered Glass Publishing
© Depositphotos.com
© Stock.Adobe.com
Editing by Ulva Eldridge
Proofread by The Proof Posse (Jackie, Dawn, Heather, Mirjam, and Roxanne)

ISBN 978-1-63869-043-6 (eBook Edition)
ISBN 978-1-63869-044-3 (Paperback Edition)
ISBN 978-1-63869-045-0 (Paperback Edition)

Version 2023.12.11

THE RESURRECTION CHRONICLES

BOOKS 1 - 3

DEMON EMBER

After a series of earthquakes, deadly animals with glowing red eyes begin attacking people and start the spread of a zombie-like plague. Safety is just a memory as she tries to make her way home. When a different creature attacks the people helping her reach Oklahoma City, Mya is sure she'll never see the light of another day.

Despite his eerie yellow eyes and very sharp teeth, the grey-skinned creature is more intelligent and humanlike than he first appears. He's determined to keep Mya by his side and protect her from the new world's dangers. When his path starts taking her further away from home, she must choose between safety and her family.

DEMON FLAMES

As hellhounds continue to roam and the zombie plague spreads, Drav leads Mya to the source of her troubles—Ernisi, an underground Atlantis and Drav's home. There Mya learns that the shadowy demons, who've helped devastate her world, are not what they seem.

Trapped in Ernisi, Mya tries to convince Drav to return her to the surface so she can continue her search for her family. However, he's determined to keep her where he knows she'll be safe. When Mya falls ill, Drav must choose between her and his people.

DEMON ASH

The world is nothing like Mya remembers. While in Ernisi, cities have been bombed and burned in an attempt to stop the hellhounds and the plague. The survivors are doing everything they can to win back their world from the hell that was unleashed with the first quake.

With Drav's help, Mya reunites with her family, but they are far from safe. Marauders, hellhounds, and the infected are doing their best to destroy what's left of the world, and it's up to Mya and Drav to save it.

DEMON EMBER

CHAPTER ONE

I LEANED BACK IN MY CHAIR AND RUBBED MY EYES.

"What is the point of math?" I asked. My roommate laughed behind me.

"The point is to separate the wheat from the chaff, Mya. The weak give up and drop out."

I spun in my chair to look at her. Our desks occupied a corner of our dorm room just outside the shared bathroom. Not the ideal location, but it freed up the space under our loft beds for a couch and TV.

"I think I proved myself by making it through the first year. I need a break. Do you mind if I turn on the TV?"

As roommates went, Kristin wasn't bad. Our personalities blended well since both of us were fairly mellow.

"Go ahead. I'll put in headphones."

I flopped down on the couch but hesitated to turn on the TV. I didn't think I had the brain power it would take to watch a show. I couldn't wait for winter break, still weeks away. Sure, I would need to deal with the stress of finals first, but it would be worth it to get away from campus. I loved going to OU Tulsa and living in the dorms in Walker. I just missed home and my family.

I picked up my phone and sent a snap to my younger brother. He was no doubt in the middle of a class. But as a senior in high school, he likely wasn't paying much attention, anyway.

This is my math-sucks face, I captioned the selfie.

A minute later my phone beeped. I opened an image of him trying to crawl inside a locker.

This is my escape plan, it read.

I grinned. Ryan was a goof, and I could always count on him to cheer me up.

Feeling a bit better, I stood.

"I'm going to grab something from the cafeteria. Want to come?"

Kristin pulled out one ear bud. "Nah, I'm good. Don't forget your pants."

I made a face. Kristin, like me, usually lounged in a shirt and underwear when in our room. The rooms were warm, and it was comfortable going pantless. Too bad the administration didn't agree. I put on my shorts so I didn't have to listen to another lecture about walking around without pants in public corridors, grabbed my ID, and left.

The halls were fairly quiet as I made my way to the exit. Most students were either in class or still sleeping. Given the option, I would have preferred to sleep in as well on my late start days. I wouldn't call myself a morning person. I just couldn't seem to sleep past eight. It probably had something to do with the fact that I had a hard time keeping my eyes open past midnight. I used the quiet morning time to get assignments done and relax before class.

I shivered slightly when I stepped outside and almost went back in for a hoodie, but I didn't have far to go.

At the Couch, our cafeteria, I helped myself to some eggs, ham, and country potatoes and sat at a table to eat. A morning news show played on the huge TV. They were talking about the protesters at the pipeline.

At the bottom of the screen was a news feed about increasing tremors outside of Rheydt, Germany.

"Crazy, huh?" the guy next to me said. "I was thinking of putting some money together to send some supplies to the protestors."

"I wouldn't. It's just perpetuating the need for the oil line. If the protestors really wanted to stop the pipeline, they would abandon their cars and their consumerism. If people stopped buying too much and using their cars daily or even weekly, we wouldn't need so much oil."

The guy gave me a disbelieving look. "Do you really think that's the solution?"

"No. I think less people is the real solution."

"What do you suggest? The Purge becomes a reality?"

"I'm not suggesting anything. I'm only pointing out that those protests are pointless. Most of the people traveled from distant places, using more fuel than normal to get there. The protest just puts more strain on the supply and demand system they are protesting. Sending them goods, like everyone wants to do, will only add to that demand."

He shook his head, picked up his empty tray, and walked away. I was used to that. I didn't think like other people did. My heart didn't automatically bleed for causes. I was too busy asking myself why a cause was needed in the first place.

Ignoring the protestors on the screen, I read the newsfeed about the earthquakes. The tremors began just after ten a.m. in Germany.

"Two hours ago," I said softly. The tremors started at a 2.1 magnitude that had increased to 3.9 already. Officials were saying the tremors occasionally occurred due to the Garzweiler mine, some miles south of the town. That was something I could relate to. Residences on the outskirts of Oklahoma City, where I grew up, often felt tremors because of fracking.

"You'd think we'd get smarter," I said to myself. I finished breakfast and made my way back to my room.

"Anything decent?" Kristin asked when I entered.

"Same as always," I said.

I took my laptop from my desk and settled on the couch so I could keep an eye on the news while finishing math. Kristin put her earbuds in, and we worked in silence for several minutes before she closed herself in our shared bathroom to get ready for class.

"Hold on, we're getting reports of unusual activity from our source in Germany."

The words caught my attention, and I looked up at the TV. The reporter was frowning and calling someone's name. A second later, a line crackled and the still image of a dark-haired man filled half the screen.

"Garan," the newswoman said. "Tell us what is happening."

"Another tremor just shook the area," the man said with a heavy accent. "Some buildings sustained damage. The results are not confirmed, but we believe this one might be in the sixes. Local residents are being evacuated as a precautionary measure."

"What about the mining?" I asked the TV.

"Were there any injuries?" the reporter asked, instead.

"Minor injuries," Garan said. "The most unusual part of this last tremor is the animal reaction."

"What do you mean?" the news lady asked.

"Everything has gone quiet. I don't hear or see any birds, and the people I've interviewed in the last few moments noted that their pets have run off. One elderly woman said that behavior had decided her evacuation. To quote her, 'The whole place has an ominous feel.' I can't say Rheydt feels very welcoming at the moment."

"Thank you, Garan."

His line disconnected, and the anchor woman promised to keep the viewers up-to-date as news broke.

Kristin came out of the bathroom and opened her closet.

"Geez, it sounds like Germany is being hit by some wicked quakes," I said. "They're evacuating a town."

"Really? It must be a pretty big deal if they're reporting it here," Kristin said as she continued to get dressed.

"Yeah, they just had some news guy on from over there. He made it sound kinda creepy when he mentioned how all the animals have disappeared from the area."

As I spoke, the slightest vibration tickled the bottom of my feet.

"Did you feel that?" Kristin asked.

"Yep. Stupid fracking. You better hurry up," I said, glancing at our large wall clock. "And you might want a coat."

She quickly combed her hair before grabbing her things and rushing out. It wasn't long after that one of the girls from the adjoining dorm room closed our shared bathroom door, and I heard the water run again. We'd really lucked out. Our class schedules worked so we never had to fight for bathroom time in the morning.

I listened to the TV and worked on homework for another hour before I started to get ready for class. The talk of quakes and weird animal behavior had spooked me more than I realized because I jumped a little at the sight of my ghostly reflection in the steamed-up mirror. Shaking my head at myself, I pulled the hair tie from my long brown hair then locked both bathroom doors. Nothing about the news had been significantly disturbing. Yet, as I turned on the shower and stripped, I couldn't shake the disquieting feeling that clung to me. Probably too much stress and the need for a break.

As I washed, my thoughts drifted from the news to possibilities of going home for the weekend. Home was just over an hour away. I didn't have a car here, but Ryan would pick me up.

I turned off the water, dried, and went back to my room.

My phone beeped. It was an actual text from Ryan, not a snap.

Are you watching the news?

Just turned it off. Is it about the tremor that just went through?

I started to get dressed but only managed a bra and fresh underwear when the phone beeped.

No, Germany. Turn on the TV.

Already saw. They've been having quakes for hours.

I finished dressing and read his next text.

A 9.0 just happened. They have it on in school.

Garan was back, but this time live, when I turned on the TV. The scene behind him was a pile of rubble and ruin. His skin was coated with dust, and the air was still thick with it.

"As you can see, this area was hit the hardest. There's still no estimate of how many residents hadn't evacuated in time. Rescue personnel are on their way." The faint sounds of sirens came through the speakers.

"Are you all right, Garan?" As the newswoman said that, something dark zipped across the scene behind him. The camera shifted slightly as if whatever it was had startled the camera man. A smattering of German broke out, silencing whatever response Garan had opened his mouth to say. Garan's gaze shifted from the camera lens to something just off camera.

"Garan?" the newswoman said.

"I'm sorry. It appears some of the pets are returning. Perhaps to look for their owners." The camera shifted to a pile of distant rubble where three dark shapes moved. "They appear to be digging," Garan said.

I stared at the screen, squinting to make out what they were seeing. With the dust still clouding the air, blocking out the already weak sun, it was hard to see the dark shapes they were talking about. The sirens grew louder, and the camera swept away from the rubble as Garan ran toward the vehicle to point to the pile of rubble. Since he switched to German, I wasn't sure what was being said. But the gesturing and concern on Garan's face had me thinking he was trying to get them to go check out where the dogs were searching.

A lone, deep yowl filled the air as the sirens suddenly silenced.

The news woman came back on the screen and again promised to keep the viewers up-to-date on what was happening.

The chilling scene of such devastation stunned me, and I yearned for home even more.

I'm thinking about skipping my next class, I sent to Ryan.

Life of a college kid, he sent back.

I shook my head, knowing I needed to go to class, and grabbed my things. The newswoman tried to contact Garan again but reported he wasn't answering. She speculated that everyone was working together to find survivors as quickly as possible. After expressing that the station's thoughts and prayers were with the community of Rheydt, the newswoman signed off.

I shut off the TV and hurried out the door. Campus was still quiet and chilly on my walk to class.

Arriving early, I took a seat toward the back of the room and set up my laptop, content to stalk social media until the professor arrived. Around me, the few students in the room were talking about parties that had happened the night before.

My phone beeped, and I hurried to turn off the sound before checking the most recent message from Ryan.

Go to YouTube and look up Nachbar von Hund angegriffen.

Is that German? I sent back before typing in exactly what he'd texted.

Yes. The video is just a few hours old and already going viral.

I made sure to turn off my speakers then pulled up the video. It started with a shot of a backyard from an upper window. After a moment, the back door of the neighboring building opened. A man stepped out with a gun. I watched him fire twice prior to something rushing at him and knocking him down. Before the camera could focus, the thing attacking the man darted away. I covered my mouth with my hand as the shaking camera stayed on the fallen man. Spots of crimson grew on his shirt and pants.

The man jerked, and I watched as he continued to spasm then stilled. The video had several seconds left to it. I was half tempted to turn on the volume to see if I was missing anything when the man slowly got to his feet. As soon as he did, he looked straight at the camera. The video stopped there, leaving me staring into his eyes. Something about them sent a shiver of fear through me.

CHAPTER TWO

A DOOR SLAMMED SHUT, STARTLING ME. THE PROFESSOR CONTINUED to the front of the classroom, unaware of my near heart attack. I minimized my browser but kept my laptop out with every intention of taking notes. However, my mind returned to the video as the professor began her lecture.

I gave in to the urge to check social media after another text from Ryan. My feed was exploding with "prayers for Germany" and thoughts going out to them.

When class ended at noon, I started to pack up my bag. The ground trembled beneath my feet again. Not many of the students even paused on their way out of the room. Tremors in Oklahoma weren't a rare occurrence. I shouldered my bag and joined the flow out of the room.

My phone beeped almost immediately after the tremble stopped.

Did you feel that? Ryan sent.

Yeah. Stupid fracking, I sent back.

Tremors were near Irving, Texas. And we're feeling them here, he replied.

My stomach dipped as I continued my walk outside. We

shouldn't have been feeling tremors all the way from Texas. The ones we felt here were usually from fracking to the north of us. Ryan had to be mistaken.

I hurried to my dorm building, eager to turn on the news to learn more when my phone chimed with another text from Ryan. I didn't look at it until I made it to the fourth floor landing.

Are you watching the news? This is insane!

I didn't stop to answer. I was in my room and had clicked the TV on a minute later. The channel was still on the news station from before. Streaming on the bottom bar was an urgent update: "There have been reports of tremors and earthquakes in Irving, Texas."

The door opened and Kristin came in with her bag strapped over her shoulder.

"Did you feel that?" she asked. "I was walking past Gould when I felt the tremor. My professor let us out early."

"Yeah, I was just leaving class when I felt it. The news is saying that it originated from Irving, Texas."

"Texas?"

"Oh, shit. Kristin, I'm sorry. I forgot."

"It's okay. Wichita Falls is about two hours outside of Irving. My parents should be fine." She sent a quick text off before she came to sit next to me on the couch. Only a minute later, her phone chirped. She looked at the screen.

"They're fine," she said. "No damage so it couldn't have been too bad."

We continued to watch the news for updates, but there wasn't much to report. Just a tremor that didn't destroy anything. Yet, I couldn't stop feeling a sliver of unease. First, Germany's tremors, and now, here in the States?

A very quiet rumble started in my stomach, a reminder that I hadn't eaten anything since breakfast.

"You ready to get something from Shades of Brown and some

lunch?" I asked. It was a typical Tuesday run for us. She liked the Bolivian cocoa from Shades of Brown, and I loved the artisan sandwiches from Zoe's Kitchen.

She nodded and grabbed her keys. I took my wallet from my backpack and followed her out the door. We took the stairs to the ground floor level, passing other students coming and going.

"How about I drop you off at Shades of Brown and run to get the food? I need to keep working on my paper," she said.

I agreed, wanting to get back to keep my eye on the news. Little vibrations still rumbled under our feet.

It didn't take too long to get to Shades of Brown. Kristin pulled over to drop me off then left to go a few blocks down for our sandwiches. I walked under the black awning protecting the entrance and into the quaint shop. I inhaled the rich scent of fresh ground coffee and stepped up to the counter.

The tall barista with dark hair brushing over bright blue eyes smiled at me, starting a flutter in my stomach. I was a marshmallow for a gorgeous set of eyes.

"Hey, what can I get ya?" he asked.

"Two Bolivian cocoas please."

"Sure thing," he said with a wink and pushed off the counter to start my order.

I glanced around. I enjoyed coming here when I needed to get away from campus. The distressed wooden counters and small reading nooks made the place feel cozy and homey. There were always open tables, like now, to sit and take in the atmosphere.

"All right, two Bolivian cocoas to go," the Barista said, jarring me from my study.

I smiled and paid.

A tremor rolled under my feet, causing the hot chocolates to ripple. I held my breath as I waited for it to finish. I glanced up, and the Barista's brows were pinched and his lips were tight.

"It's getting really Jurassic Park out there."

He turned to me, his lips parting in a silent question. I forced a smile on my face and walked out. Not everyone got me. Fine, very few people got me.

My phone beeped, and I set the cups on the outdoor seating to check my messages.

Tell me you're seeing the pattern, too. #freaksbyblood

I grinned. Ryan was one of the few who got me.

Creepy coincidence? Anything on the news?

Kristin pulled up. I quickly got in, ready to head back to our dorm building.

Local no. Searching for anything new from Germany.

Once we got back to our room, Kristin and I immediately turned on the TV. We watched the local report, waiting to see if something would come up about the earthquakes in Texas.

Sent you a link, Ryan texted.

"Ryan tagged me in a new video from Germany," I said, moving to get my laptop before sitting back down next to Kristin.

I logged in and tapped the link for the video that had been live-streamed from Germany. Kristin muted the TV and watched with me as a man's face appeared on screen. He was breathing heavily and his eyes were wide. The image was dimly illuminated and bounced around as if the man was running. The angle of the recording changed as he lifted his phone high. I couldn't understand what he was saying and focused on the black he was recording.

For a moment, there was nothing but darkness and his harsh, gasping breaths. Then, I heard it. The clack and clatter of something moving in the void. Kristin and I both leaned forward. A growl started low and grew louder through the speakers.

"Is this live?" Kristin asked softly.

I looked at the time stamp. "No, but it was live."

The jerky aim of the camera caught a flash of movement in the darkness behind the running man. Suddenly, dozens of red dots flashed before the angle changed again.

My phone chimed, but I ignored it.

A blood-curdling scream made Kristin and me jump. We stared at the black screen and listened as the sound of growls and screaming increased. Something moved close enough to the camera light and was caught on video. It looked like a very large dog's leg. An instant later, it moved out of frame. Teeth flashed, and the recording went black.

Kristin and I remained silent. My sandwich felt like lead in my stomach. For a moment, I couldn't process anything beyond the fact that I was certain we'd just watched a man die. Then I picked up my phone.

Are you watching? Ryan had sent.

Why would you send me that? I'm going to dream of that shit now.

That's just one of the reports of animal attacks from Germany since the last tremor. It's like the wildlife freaked out and turned on us. Why aren't we seeing any of this on the news?

I didn't know how to answer Ryan so I turned the volume back up on the TV instead, to try to figure out what was going on.

"There have been reports of aftershocks in Irving, Texas. Viewers are urged to seek shelter."

Kristin jumped from the couch.

"I'm going to call my parents."

I nodded as she walked back into our bathroom. I texted Ryan.

Are you still feeling tremors there?

No. But are you still watching the news?

Yeah.

Did you see they announced communications are down in western Germany?

I hadn't heard that. Earthquakes...bizarre, aggressive animal behavior. I nibbled my bottom lip. What the hell was going on over there? And why was I feeling so creeped out about the tremors we felt here? I glanced over at our bathroom door and heard Kristin speaking to her mom. At least they were still safe.

Once Kristin finished talking, she rejoined me to watch the news. At 5 p.m., I got another text from Ryan.

Just heard from a friend in Wichita Falls. EAS ran a broadcast in Texas to stay indoors.

Without saying anything to Kristin, I changed the channel to see if we could get more local information.

"Due to reports of strange animal activity, people are encouraged to avoid animals showing any unusual traits or seeming unnaturally agitated. In other news..." The news anchor went over other safety precautions for Earthquakes.

"How's your mom holding up?" I asked Kristin.

"Good. They just had dinner. That last quake messed up the storage in the basement so they're cleaning that up."

If her parents weren't mentioning anything about the EAS, neither would I.

The station we were watching cut over to a program in progress. I tried a few other channels, but they similarly were no longer reporting on Europe or the tremors.

Kristin went to her desk and worked on her paper.

What's happening in Germany? Local cable sucks, I sent Ryan.

Reports of lost communication spreading. Friends no longer able to get messages to friends. Saw a message translated from someone in France reporting dog attacks in their neighborhood. Keep you posted.

I settled in to watch a movie. The room was getting warmer, as was usual in the evenings. Kristin opened the window a crack without me asking, and I kicked off my pants and got comfortable with a blanket.

It was around nine when Kristin climbed into her bunk, and I turned off the volume. It didn't do much good. Laughing and loud music faintly reached us. Somewhere nearby, someone was having a good time, and I heard Kristin move restlessly in her bed.

Near eleven, the music finally quieted. Kristin sighed, and I turned off the TV and climbed into my bunk. Someone called a goodbye in the hallway, and I closed my eyes.

All was quiet in our room when an eerie howl sounded from outside. Fear formed a cold ball in my stomach as I glanced over at Kristin, who stared at our partially open window.

The howl came again, sounding closer.

I grabbed my phone and scrambled down from the bunk to get to the window. Outside, the campus lights illuminated the view of the grounds, street, and distant parking lot.

Someone walked into view from the base of our building. He looked back toward the entrance and yelled goodnight just before another howl rent the air. The guy stopped and looked toward the south. Whatever he saw had him turning quickly.

"Get back inside," he shouted as he ran toward the building.

Behind him, in the distance, several shapes were moving fast. Dogs. Really, really big ones. Their thin, black bodies flew through the shadows, their eyes reflected red in the darkness.

"What the fuck is that?" Kristin asked.

The dogs were gaining on the guy fast. One sprang forward and knocked him to the ground. It closed its maw around the man's calf and shook its head viciously. I dialed 911 and lifted the phone to my ear. I listened to an all-circuits-are-busy message as the guy outside screamed and thrashed. Beside me, Kristin began to sob. More dogs converged on the man.

CHAPTER THREE

I STARTED TO SHAKE AND ENDED THE CALL TO TRY AGAIN. SCREAMS echoed from outside and inside the building. Kristin and I weren't the only ones awake and seeing the attack.

Another guy ran from our building, yelling and waving his hands. The dogs stopped their violent assault, lifting their heads as one. In that moment, I saw they weren't really dogs. They had no ears that I could see, and their eyes glowed red. It wasn't a reflection but an actual glow.

"Get out of there. He's not moving," someone yelled from below.

Whoever said that was right. The man on the ground was a bloody mess. I couldn't be sure, but one of his legs looked broken or chewed off.

Behind the dogs, a car beeped and the lights flashed as someone tried using their key fob as a distraction. The dogs didn't even flinch. They remained focused on the new guy who had stopped waving his arms and was slowly backing away. He disappeared from our line of sight and the dogs howled, leaping forward.

The screaming started up again. Beneath those sounds, there

was yelling. There were too many voices at once, but it sounded like there were people at the entrance, trying to hold the door closed.

Kristin turned from the window and opened our room door. She listened in the hall while I kept trying 911 and stared at the fallen man. What the fuck was going on? My mind played that panicked question on repeat until my fifth redial. That's when I saw I had a message.

It was from Ryan from about forty minutes earlier, thirty minutes before the music had turned off.

It's the dogs. Stay inside. Stay safe. Stay away from the infected.

I stared at the words, struggling to think and breathe. The dogs. Did that mean Mom, Dad, and Ryan had seen the same thing Kristin and I had just seen?

Are you safe? Did they come by you? I tried to send back. But the message kept failing. I tried to call and received the same "circuits are busy" message. I turned on the TV, and every damn channel had the damn EAS bars with a message warning everyone to stay indoors to avoid infection.

"Infection from what?" I said.

It took three tries to turn off the TV because my hands shook so badly. When it was off, I still heard the distant screaming and yelling.

"What's going on?" Kristin didn't have any better of an idea than I did, but I couldn't stop myself from asking.

She turned from the door, her face white. Shock. I'd seen it before when Ryan broke his arm. I walked over to her and tugged her back into our room before I closed and locked the door.

"You need to sit down." She vacantly stared straight ahead as I led her to the couch.

"Kristin, you're in shock. We both are. But we need to get past it." Sitting beside her, I took one of her hands in mine and rubbed it aggressively. Doing something helped quell enough of the panic that I could think beyond "what the hell is going on?"

Those things outside were what we'd seen in the video. What was happening here had happened in Germany. Germany had lost communications, too. Why? What were those creatures?

"I don't know what to do," I said. "Ryan said the dogs are infected. The TV is saying to stay away from them."

She exhaled shakily and new tears trailed down her cheeks. I'd take crying over numb silence any day.

I stood up and went to the window to check on the man. I watched in horror as he struggled to pull himself in the direction of the building. Part of his leg dragged behind him, leaving a bloody trail. Chunks were missing from his side. My already racing heart kicked up a notch. He couldn't be alive. Not in that condition.

"Mya," Kristin sobbed. I didn't realize I was making noises until she spoke. I swallowed hard and turned away from the window.

"J-just freaking out. Did you hear what I said about the dogs?"

"Yeah. Infected. Stay away from 'em."

I took a deep breath and tried to calm the shaking. We couldn't both lose it.

"Right." I sat beside Kristin for a moment and rubbed her hand again. "If the dogs are infected and they bite people, then the people they bite might be infected, too. We should stay away from everyone. Stay in our room."

She nodded, and I picked up my phone.

"Just stay here," I said to her before getting up and going back to the window. With my back to her, I slid the window open and got ready to take a picture of the man. He paused in his struggles and looked up, as if searching out the noises coming from our building. There were many. A lot of shouts and crying.

I snapped the picture and then zoomed in on the image to see his face. It was the same creepy, cloudy-eyed look as the man from the German video.

"Are they still out there?" Kristin asked. "The dogs?"

"Not that I can see. But there's a lot of yelling still."

There was a scuff of movement behind me, and I turned in time to see Kristin walk into our shared bathroom. She knocked on the adjoining door.

"Amy? Dawn? Can you guys open up?"

I hurried toward Kristin. "I don't think that's a good idea..."

The door swung open to reveal a very pale Dawn.

"Where's Amy?" Kristin said, looking into their room.

"Nate's dorm," Dawn answered. "I thought I was alone. Did you see outside? Why is he moving?"

"Who's moving?" Kristin asked.

"Never mind. Did you lock your door?" I asked Dawn.

"I don't know. I closed it when I heard the yelling."

I moved into Dawn's room to make sure her door was locked. Once I verified it was, I used the peephole to look out into the hallway. Someone ran past. A door slammed shut further down the hall. The screaming and shouting was getting closer.

"Let's go to our room," I said.

Kristin nodded and led Dawn through the bathroom. I took a moment to push a desk in front of Dawn's door then retreated back the way I'd come. In the bathroom, I locked the door from the inside.

When I joined Kristin and Dawn, Kristin was looking out the window.

"Will you help me move a desk?" I asked her.

She didn't say anything about the man still dragging himself across the parking lot as we moved the desk. In the hallway, the noises grew quiet. I caught Kristin's glance at the peephole.

"Don't look," I said quietly as we eased the desk into place.

She nodded and moved to sit next to Dawn. I stayed near the door, staring at it. None of this seemed real.

A sound at the door made me jump. I held my breath, listening.

The sound came again. A rasp of something against the other side of the panel. Swallowing and struggling to breathe quietly, I leaned forward to check the peephole.

A cloudy, once-blue eye stared back at me. I jerked backwards and covered my mouth. I would not scream. I would not panic. I would not die.

Our doorknob moved slightly. Not a turn. More of a jostle. None of us made a sound.

I waited, holding still and keeping quiet. Screams erupted nearby. The noise outside our door stopped.

I let out a shuttering breath that threatened to turn into hysteric sobs. No. *They'd* hear. I took a steadying breath and then another, working to control the hysteria. When I turned, Kristin and Dawn were staring at me with wide eyes. Their pale faces were a reflection of how I felt.

Outside, a smattering of distant pops broke out. Lifting a finger to my lips, I let them know to remain quiet and moved back toward the window. I couldn't see anything beyond the street lights. The roads were empty of traffic.

"I think we're on our own," I said softly.

I tried to move past the panic fogging my mind. What should we do? Should we stay and wait for help? It was smart. It was what people did when lost. Stay in one spot.

"We can stay here. We have water," I whispered, mostly to myself, "but only enough snack food for a day or two." It could work. Yet, I couldn't get the parallels between what had happened in Germany and here out of my mind. The video of the man being bitten then getting up. Seeing the man outside torn up and then dragging himself toward the building. And the cloudy eye in our peephole. The EAS used the term *infection*. Infections spread. Did staying in one spot make sense?

"Leaving means..." I turned to look at the door. The person

who had been staring back at me wasn't healthy anymore. If we left our room, we would likely end up the same way.

I glanced at Kristin and Dawn and saw the same hopeless defeat in their eyes.

More pops sounded from outside, pulling my attention back to the window. Nothing moved but the guy in front of the building. Even the screams inside had died down. I hoped it was because people were in their rooms hiding, not dead.

In the silence, I could hear the distant whine of several engines.

"Get dressed," I said. I pulled on my pants and yanked the sheets from our beds.

"What are you doing?" Dawn asked quietly, following me.

"There are people out there with guns and vehicles. We have two options. Through the door or the window. There's no way I'm going in that hallway."

Before we finished tying the sheets, Dawn pushed out the screen and waved her arms.

"I see them," she said.

We joined her at the window and exhaled in relief at the sight of several military vehicles followed by a line of cars and trucks.

"If you're not infected, come to your windows," a man yelled from below. His gaze swept up the building and over to the other wings.

He spoke softly to several uniformed men who broke off and moved around the building, out of sight.

"Stay in your rooms. We'll knock when it's clear."

On the far side of the vehicles, people emerged from the shadows, running in an awkward jerking way toward the sound of his voice. Before they got too close, the uniformed men standing in the backs of trucks, shot at them. The runners dropped with a shot to the head.

"It's real, isn't it?" Dawn said. "Zombies. Hellhounds. I'm not going to wake up, am I?"

I didn't say a thing. What could I say?

Instead, I stepped away from the window and helped Kristin move the desk from the door. I watched the halls through our peephole. Gunshots echoed from inside the building.

Several minutes later, a shot rang out on our floor. It wasn't long before a uniformed man knocked on our door.

"It's clear. You have ten seconds to open the door before—"

I opened the door not waiting to hear the rest.

"Stay close and stay behind me," he said.

We joined seven other girls. Behind us, two more military men guarded the hallway from where they'd come. An unmoving body lay on the floor. The hysteria I'd shoved down threatened to bubble back up. I turned away from the sight and followed the lead man.

We made slow progress through the rest of the wing, clearing other healthy people from their rooms, before we reached the stairwell. Our footsteps echoed as we ran down four flights to the ground floor.

Outside, another uniformed man waved us toward the vehicles where other students were hurrying to get into the back of the trucks. Through the chaos of evacuation, more infected ran from the dark. Shots didn't stop ringing. Dawn and Kristin pressed close to me as we waited for our turn.

As soon as everyone was in and the buildings cleared, men with guns jumped onto the backs of the trucks, and the engines started again.

CHAPTER FOUR

"WHERE ARE WE GOING?" I ASKED.

"The stadium for now. We're trying to establish communications to set up an evacuation."

When we arrived a few minutes later, we left the trucks. The uniformed men corralled our group from the university toward the stadium. As we jostled forward with the flow of the crowd, Kristin lifted up on her toes, searching for Dawn. Behind us, the vehicles pulled away.

"Come on, we'll find her inside," I said.

Together, we moved toward Oklahoma Memorial Stadium, our temporary shelter. We followed the herd of people to Gate 14, and the sound of our footsteps almost drowned out the distant shots and howls.

More military people with guns guarded the doors we entered. Inside the entrance, it was chaos, stifling hot and humid with the hysteric and shell-shocked people milling about. Some called out for friends, but most stumbled around looking lost.

Kristin tugged my hand, weaving us through the crush of bodies. The entry was filled with even more students and residents and so were the ramps and halls leading from it. People weren't spreading out or even thinking of the fact that the vehicles had left again, which meant there would be more people coming.

Kristin wedged through two people, pulling me. My sweaty hand started to slip.

"Hold on," I called out, but she kept going. I tugged her hand, stopping her. She looked back to me, her eyes wide and wild.

"We have to find Dawn," she said.

"Breathe. We're not going to find anyone in this mess. Look around."

Kristin took a deep breath and held it before she slowly released it. I did the same while struggling to think what we needed to do next. The frantic look in her eyes drained a little, and the stuttering of my heartbeat slowed.

"I'm okay," she said.

"Let's see if we can find someone who might be able to tell us what's going to happen next."

Kristin and I pushed toward some of the uniformed men inside the building.

"Can you tell us what's going on?" I asked the first one who made eye contact with me.

"Sorry, ma'am. At this point, all we know is that a State of Emergency was declared. Water bottles are being handed out at different concession stands. Our focus is rounding up civilians until we're told something else." He turned away from us to direct a family with a missing child.

Kristin and I moved back and roamed through the hallways, making our way to the rear of the stadium where it was a little less crowded. The gates we passed were either guarded by more military personnel or blockaded with benches and trash cans. The sight of all the men and women dressed in fatigues made it feel safe. Were Mom, Dad, and Ryan safe? I worried my bottom lip and followed Kristin, until the conversation of a group we passed caught my attention.

"Oklahoma City isn't that far. I say we drive there," a guy with a buzz cut said, piquing my interest. I tugged Kristin's hand and stopped walking.

"Who the hell knows what's out there, Josh," the only girl in their group said.

"Fuck this. We can't just sit around and wait," Josh said.

The two other men nodded, one of them pulling his shirt up to reveal the handle of a gun.

"We'll be fine," he said.

"Kevin," the girl said, yanking his shirt down. She fisted her hands and glared at each of them.

Kristin tried to pull me away.

"Hang on." If they were going to Oklahoma City—

A scream rent the air, breaking the tense silence between the friends. We all turned toward the source of the sound. A moment later, shots echoed further down the corridor. People started pushing our direction in their panic to get away from whatever was happening.

I glanced at the small group near us. The girl's eyes were wide. With grim, determined expressions, the trio of men moved toward the blockaded emergency exit.

I gripped Kristin's arms and forced her to look at me.

"Let's leave with those guys."

Kristin shook her head as the crowd began to swarm toward us. Shouts rang out behind them.

"Run!"

"The infected broke through!"

"The army will take care of us," Kristin said.

"The infected have already gotten in."

"And they are shooting them. If you go out there, you'll die."

Further down the hall, more screams and shots echoed. The panicking mass of people rushed toward us. Staying here wasn't any safer than leaving.

"To the field," someone yelled.

I hugged Kristin quickly.

"Run, be safe," I said.

Kristin released me and took off down the hall, away from the mob. I ran over to the group of four trying to clear the exit. The third man struggled with moving one of the heavy trashcans. I helped drag it to the side while Josh and Kevin pulled the last remaining bench from the doorway. Josh pushed the door and it opened a quarter of the way, partially blocked by something from the outside.

"Stay close," Josh shouted before he ran out.

The screams grew deafening before Kevin then the girl hurriedly squeezed out. The third guy pushed me forward as the first wave of the crowd shoved to escape through the open doorway.

I ran after the others. Cool night air brushed my sweaty skin. My heart pounded. I knew what could be out in the dark. However, the waning moon was high, giving us enough light to navigate through the mostly deserted parking lot.

Josh and Kevin were already over halfway to the closest vehicle. The girl had fallen well behind. Panic and running shoes had me gaining on her until something moved to our right. When I looked, I saw nothing but shadows.

The girl ran hard toward Josh and Kevin, who were now at the closest truck to us. Out of the corner of my eye, a shadow blurred into something more, and it darted straight for the girl.

I called out a warning too late and skidded to a halt as a hound knocked her down. Its growls froze the blood in my veins. The hound's back arched as it bit down on her shoulder. My breath caught in my throat at her bloodcurdling scream.

One of the guys grabbed my arm and yanked me toward the truck. I couldn't take my eyes off the large, demon dog hunched over the girl. Her screams stopped by the time we reached the vehicle. Gasping breaths strangled my lungs. The guy shoved me into the backseat of the cab.

While Josh struggled to hotwire the truck, I looked out the windshield toward the building as other hounds ran into the mass of panicked people trying to escape. The hounds weren't the only thing chasing fleeing survivors. Infected people, ones who ran with an odd gait, attacked, too.

The engine finally roared to life, causing the hound, who'd killed the girl, to look up. Its red gaze locked with mine, and its lips peeled back to reveal bloodied teeth.

Military men came around the corner of the building and opened fire on the beasts and infected people. The first hound pivoted and snarled at its attackers. Blood flew with the impact of several bullets into its hide. Instead of fleeing, it charged toward the military men. They continued to shoot, and it kept running.

The truck reversed then jerked around before moving forward. We raced out of the warzone. People ran past. Some scared. Some with cloudy eyes. Then, it all fell behind us.

It's the dogs, Ryan had texted earlier. *Stay away from the infected.*

Was this really the damn zombie apocalypse? When I'd said we needed less people, I hadn't meant this.

"Breathe." The guy sitting next to me grabbed my hand and held it tightly.

I focused on each in and out breath, willing my shaking to stop. The driver swore softly as we sped through town. Once we were on the eerily vacant expressway, he glanced back at me.

"Who are you?"

"Mya."

"I'm Russ," the man gave my hand another squeeze. "That's Josh and Kevin."

"I'm sorry about your friend."

"Thanks," Kevin said.

No one spoke after that. Instead, we watched the roads.

Cars with shattered windshields were abandoned on the shoulders, and several of the infected staggered along the blacktop. When we sped past, they would run after us for a bit before they gave up. The fact that they kept up for even small bursts of time worried me, and I shivered as their dead gazes followed us down the road.

Once, out of the corner of my eye, I saw a flash of shadow running on the side of the road, and I caught a glimpse of glowing eyes. Blood red. Like the girl's blood that had stained the beast's teeth. Another shiver ran down my spine.

The men were tense in their seats as we drove around more abandoned cars on the expressway.

"We are going to have to stop for gas," Josh said from the front. "It's almost empty."

Kevin spotted a gas station near the next exit, not quite halfway to Oklahoma City. Josh took the ramp and pulled into the empty parking lot. The lights flickered inside the building, but I saw no other movement.

"Kevin's got a piece, and I have mine. Mya? I'm guessing you don't have anything on you." Josh looked at me in the mirror again.

I shook my head. I hadn't planned on the apocalypse.

"Stay in the truck, then. Russ, you guard the back, I'll pump and watch my side. Kevin, you watch the front and the other side. Watch everything, Mya. Yell if you see anything."

In the silence after Josh cut the engine, we all waited, watching and listening to see if it was safe for the guys to climb out. Skeletal trees hugged the back of the building. Nothing moved but a few dead leaves in the wind. The whole place felt creepy.

It took a couple of minutes before Josh opened his door and the other two followed, getting out one by one. I rolled down the back passenger window an inch so I could hear them. Kevin's boots crunched on the loose gravel, interrupting the only other sound... the quiet hum of the overhead lights.

I watched Josh open the gas cap and remove the nozzle. He swore and fumbled for his wallet. A beep echoed in the air when he prepaid, and the gas began to flow into the tank.

Russ moved to the end of the truck. I twisted in my seat and stared into the darkness surrounding the gas station. The shadows from the light of the building and the moon casted an eerie half-light. As I stared, the light seemed to bend around a certain spot. I leaned closer to the window and blinked, trying to see better. However, the spot had vanished.

Another gust of wind made the loose leaves on the ground rustle. The branches crackled together, and goosebumps prickled over my skin. I rubbed my arms. The fine hairs on the back of my neck rose.

The truck bounced ever so slightly, and I glanced out the windshield. Kevin stood not far away, staring into the dark. I looked at Josh and rubbed my hands over my jeans, trying to dry the clamminess.

Josh lifted his head. His expression went from impatient to worried as he focused on the back of the truck.

"Russ?" he called.

I turned in my seat again and stared at the back of the truck. The bed was empty.

I scooted over on the bench seat, close to where Josh stood.

"Where did he go?" I asked.

"I don't know." Josh's eyes were wild, and he kept glancing around as he continued to pump gas.

"Something ain't right," he said.

A bitter retort rose, but I swallowed it. Now wasn't the time to piss off the guy with the gun.

"Guys," Kevin said.

With his back to us, he stared out into the darkness near the road. I strained to see what he did, but saw nothing.

From the corner of my eye, something moved. I looked to the

left and caught a dark blur rushing forward. I cried out. Kevin spun toward the incoming shadow.

One second he was standing, the next a blur of something lifted him in the air. I blinked at the sharp cracking sound, and squeaked when Kevin flew at the truck. He landed on the hood, making the truck rock. His neck lay twisted at an odd angle. My hand covered my mouth as I held in the scream lodged in my throat.

Something rattled against the truck. I glanced right, at Josh, as he frantically jerked the pump from the tank then moved toward the hood.

"Kevin?" Josh halted when he realized his friend was dead. He tugged his gun from the waistband of his jeans and held onto it with both hands as he looked around.

"What did that?" he asked.

I had no answer.

The light dimmed as something shattered outside. Glass hit the cab with soft pings. Josh looked at me through the window. A moment later, the remaining light went out.

There was a quiet sound behind the truck, like claws on blacktop. I jumped and twisted around in my seat thinking of the man outside of my dorm room. He'd been the first to die, then the guy's friend. It was happening again, and I would be next. My breaths came in heavy pants, and I frantically searched the darkness, struggling to find the thing that would kill me.

Something moved just in front of the truck. I caught a glimpse of grey skin and thick limbs.

Josh pulled the trigger, and the noise made me flinch. The shadow kept moving. Josh shot again.

Bam.

Bam.

Bam.

Click.

The shadow leapt into the air toward the truck, and Josh let out a shocked grunt-scream.

The metal above me bent inward as the creature landed on top of the cab. I squealed and crouched lower in my seat, unable to take my eyes from Josh. His eyes rounded as he stared up at whatever had landed on the roof of the truck. I could barely breathe past the fear squeezing my chest.

I jolted when something jumped from the top and landed in front of Josh. It rose from a partial crouch to its full height. A man. Impossibly huge. His biceps were as big as my head, but...he wasn't human. His grey skin, and pointed ears that poked out from the long black hair he had pulled into a twisted ponytail hanging down his back, made him very not human.

Josh's face paled further.

"Wh-what...?" he breathed.

The thing reached out, gripped Josh's neck with one hand, and twisted. Josh's face went slack, and the thing released its hold. Josh fell limply out of sight.

I looked at Kevin, who lay draped over the hood, then frantically scrambled across the seat, getting as far away as I could from the thing that had killed everyone else.

It heard me and slowly turned around.

CHAPTER FIVE

Green eyes with reptilian pupils stared at me through the window.

I couldn't breathe. My heart thundered in my ears. I was going to die. I thought of my family and hoped they wouldn't suffer the same fate.

The creature leaned toward the glass. His gaze shifted from my head to my body then back up again. Though I shook uncontrollably, I couldn't look away from his eyes. The black vertical slit of his pupils interrupted the otherwise solid bright green of the rest of his eyes.

Finally, he pulled back from the window to study the glass separating us. Specifically, the one inch gap at the top.

Shit. The leather squeaked under me as I shifted in my seat.

His gaze snapped to mine again. His complete stillness motivated me. He was the hunter. I was the prey. I needed to get my ass moving. Sitting there waiting to die wasn't an option.

I glanced over the front seat at the wires hanging below the dash. A simple connection. I could do it. Start the truck and drive off before that thing figured out the flimsy piece of glass separating us posed no problem.

When I looked back at the window, the creature had vanished. I didn't hesitate. I climbed over the seat and grabbed for the wires. A shock zapped through me, and I yelped. But I didn't stop trying. The engine turned over once then started.

Something thumped on the hood, making the truck bounce slightly. I flinched and looked up, expecting to see the creature. Instead, Kevin's body slowly slid away from the windshield and over the edge. For a horror-filled moment, I could only think about how I would need to drive over him to get away.

Movement next to my window made me jump, and I turned my head. Yellow-green eyes met mine. I froze, afraid to move. My heart felt like it wanted to pound its way out of my chest. He watched me as I watched him. His focus made me very aware that I needed to do something soon. My shaking was only getting worse. If I continued to hesitate, I'd end up dead like the rest.

My knees still pressed against the seat, my feet nowhere near the pedals. I grabbed the wheel and started to swing my legs to the side. He slammed his open hand against the window. The glass splintered and folded in toward me. He reached in, his hand wrapped around my left arm.

I yelped and pulled back, no longer caring about lunging for the pedals. He reached in with his other hand, grabbed me under the right armpit, and dragged me forward. The steering wheel slipped from my grasp. I tried for it once more but missed as he yanked my upper body out the window. I reared back, flailing. His hold under my right arm slipped, and I struggled to pull myself back in. He reached for me again, missed my arm, and grabbed my boob.

He jerked his hand back, and I froze, staring at him with wide-eyes as I hung out the window, pinned in place by his other hand. He reached forward with his free hand, and I put my arm up, trying to protect my neck.

His palm covered my right boob, and he gave it another

tentative squeeze. I lowered my arm in shock and watched him pull back once more. His gaze zeroed in on my left side.

"Hell no," I said, renewing my struggles.

As if his first attempt to remove me had just been a test, he plucked me out of the truck and set me on my feet in front of him. He kept his right hand firmly anchored around my upper arm as he lifted his other hand.

My chest heaved with each panicked breath. When his hand got close to my boob, I swatted it away.

He grunted, lowered his hand to his side, and studied me. When his gaze dropped to my jeans, a new panic surged forth. I pulled hard, willing to yank off my own arm to get away from him. He backed me against the truck, limiting my struggles, and proceeded to pat down the front of my jeans.

"No...no...just kill me already."

He stopped patting and sniffed my hair, my ears, and my face. Shock kept me still for most of it.

Abruptly, he let go and stepped back. We stared at each other as my pulse thundered in my ears. What the hell was going on? Was he toying with me?

The truck still rumbled behind me, a possible means of escape if I could just get inside. With the door handle digging into my back, I edged to the left. He put his hand on the door, stopping my progress. I bolted the other direction. He moved incredibly fast, blocking me by the front tire.

With a growl, he turned toward the hood. He raised his fisted hands and brought them down on the hood. I jumped at the sound of metal crunching on impact. He hit the front of the truck again and again, crushing the metal in until the engine clunked several times then died.

I took an involuntary step back. He'd just smashed a truck with his bare hands. I swallowed hard, and it took a moment to realize he'd killed any means of escape. I stared at him, out of ideas and out of hope.

He wasn't even breathing heavily, just standing there watching me. When he saw he had my attention, he reached up and pulled the cord holding his shirt together at his throat. Within seconds, he had the loose-fitting dark shirt off.

I stared at his heavily muscled torso with increasing despair.

He tilted his head at me, then reached up and patted his chest. First one side, then the other. When he reached for me, I cringed back. It didn't deter him. He followed me and patted first one boob then the other before tugging at my long-sleeved shirt.

My brain struggled to process what was happening.

"I don't want to take off my clothes."

He tilted his head again and waited for a moment. When he reached for the cord at the waist of his pants, I squeaked. My reaction didn't stop him from shoving the dark material down far enough to show me his grey package with a penis longer than any human version I'd ever seen. Not that I'd seen many in person.

He palmed himself as if saying "see, this is what I'm offering you" and watched me expectantly.

"No, thank you."

He shook himself again and, in that moment, I understood he was attempting to communicate.

"I-I don't want to play Tarzan and Jane."

He tilted his head at me again, as if listening to my words.

"Let me go. Please, just let me go."

He slowly pulled the material up around his hips and tied it. When he picked up his shirt, I got ready. Glass crunched under my shoe as I shifted my weight to my right foot. He stopped putting on his shirt and tucked it into the waist of his pants, instead.

Scratching his ear lightly, he continued to watch me like I was some kind of puzzle. I didn't want to be figured out. I wanted to be let go. Like right now.

He looked at my crotch, my boobs, and my hair once more then grabbed his shirt. As soon as he had his head covered, I took off. I only made it a step before he caught me from behind and lifted me off my feet. With one arm wrapped around my waist, he groped me with the other. This time between my legs.

I twisted and kicked, trying to get free. He didn't even seem to notice.

Suddenly, I stood on my own two feet again. I spun around to face him, backing away a step. However, I no longer had his attention. Cringing, I watched him lift his hand to his nose. He sniffed.

A sound of disbelief escaped me, and he met my gaze. If he would have licked his fingers, I would have known he saw me as a walking meat stick. Instead, he slowly lowered his hand.

"What is going on?" I said in a half whisper, half whimper. Did he plan to kill me or not? My chest felt so tight I was pretty sure my stuttering heart would give out any minute. Death by fear or death by...whatever he was. The method didn't change the end result. Death.

Swallowing hard, I closed my eyes and resigned myself to that fact. If I was going to die, I would rather die trying to get away. I opened my eyes, turned, and started walking. Nothing happened. Well, not nothing. Gravel crunched behind me. I glanced back to see him studying my walk as he followed me. I didn't try to guess what that might signify; I just kept going.

At the edge of the road, I hesitated. Infected riddled the not too distant highway, making the easiest route, the most dangerous. That meant hiking through the fields and trees. I crossed the road and started through the field, angling slightly away from the highway.

The crunch of dry grass under my shoes made me cringe. Behind me, a softer footfall echoed each of my own.

Although I felt beyond confused and scared, a sort of numbness had slowly crept in, blanketing me from my current reality. A reality where black, dog-like creatures with red eyes were running around biting people and turning normal humans into things resembling zombies. And, as if that hadn't been a hard enough reality to grip, a man with grey skin, pointy ears, and slitted eyes had just killed the three guys with me. I couldn't even think about the groping that had also taken place.

What the hell was going on? How had life gotten so messed up? For a brief moment, I thought of Kristin and wondered if my fate would have been any better if I'd stayed with her at the stadium. I should have been sleeping now, not trying to figure out how to get to Oklahoma City while avoiding zombie infested roadways.

Suddenly, the creature stood in front of me. I barely stopped in time to avoid colliding with his chest.

"What do you want from me?" I asked, my voice shaking. I was ready to crash hard, mentally and physically. And, I desperately needed my version of reality back.

He opened his mouth and spoke, or at least made sounds, but I didn't hear much. My attention locked onto his very pointed canines. It took me a moment to realize he'd stopped making sounds.

Barely breathing, I took a slow step back from him. He shadowed me, stepping into my retreat. I moved faster. He stalked me. I stopped. He stopped. We stared at each other.

Holding my gaze, he started to lean in.

"Go away," I said softly.

He didn't stop his approach.

"If you try grabbing me again, I'm aiming for your balls." I remembered Kevin's broken neck and the way his body had draped the hood and regretted my words.

When the creature started to bend his knees, my stomach gave a sickening lurch. I moved to step back, and he grabbed both my arms. Instead of breaking my neck or throwing me, he held me in place as he buried his nose in my shirt-covered cleavage. Since I had a decent amount, he had to wiggle a little to really get his face in there. He inhaled deeply, then pulled back to look at me.

Scared shitless but pretending not to be, I glared at him.

"Get a good smell?" Instead of indignant and angry, my voice shook pathetically.

He blinked at me again, and I wondered why I still lived. Despite his groping and weird sniffing, he hadn't been aroused when he'd pulled down his pants. Thank God. However, that left me completely clueless regarding the current staring contest.

CHAPTER SIX

IN THE DIM MOONLIGHT, I TRIED TO SEE PAST HIS LARGE, EERIE EYES and focus on his other features, like his thick black eyebrows and his very strong, stubborn jaw. His pointed ears were longer than normal. Well, longer than a normal human's ears, by about two inches.

He let go of my left arm, reached up to touch the tip of the ear I was studying, then reached out to brush back my hair. It took all my will not to jerk away. His fingers brushed the outer shell of my ear, then he leaned in for a closer look.

He seemed curious. But that didn't make sense. If he was this curious about humans, why did he kill everyone else?

"It's an ear," I said, finally.

His gaze met mine, and he gently touched my ear again.

Hoping that he was curious and not just deciding how to kill me, I reached up and carefully grabbed the wrist of the hand clamped around my right arm. His hold immediately loosened, and he straightened away from me.

Free, I sidestepped him and started walking again. Each footfall thumped in time with my racing heart. While I almost jogged, the creature beside me kept up with long, loose strides. We made it several yards before he stepped in front of me again.

My sanity cracked.

"No," I said, bringing up a finger to scold him as if he were a bad dog. "If you don't quit stopping me, one of those hellhounds is going to find us. We're too close to the highway. I need to keep moving or I'll never make it home."

I couldn't believe what I'd done. Swallowing past the lump of terror in my throat, I went around him once more. He didn't try to block me or get handsy again. But he did stick right to my side and keep studying me. I picked up my pace and tried to out walk him.

One minute I was going along fine, and the next, the ground wasn't where it should have been. I fell face first into dried grass because of some kind of animal hole. The impact felt like a punch to my face. Stunned, I lay there for a moment as the smell of copper filled my nose.

I groaned, rolled onto my back, and yipped at the sight of a grey face right in front of mine. Without thinking, I pushed him away then immediately jerked my hand back and covered my face. Nothing happened. I peeked through my fingers and saw him studying my chest again.

"Enough already. Boobs," I said pointing. "They're boobs. And staring doesn't make them go away. I tried."

He tilted his head and pointed at my chest.

"Boob," he said.

I paused mid-nose wipe and stared. He was talking. English.

"Boobs," he said, reaching for one.

I slapped his hand away and sat up.

"No. No more grabbing."

He flexed his hand as he glanced at it then back at me. Too late, I realized what I'd done and stared at him with round eyes. What was I thinking? He'd snapped necks and tossed bodies right in front of me.

"Grabbing boobs."

He reached forward again, and I blocked his hand before it reached its destination.

"Stop."

He cocked his head, eyes narrowing slightly.

"Stop," he repeated.

I licked my lips, and a copper tang bloomed on the tip of my tongue. With a shaky hand, I wiped under my nose. A smear of blood coated my fingers. Crap. I tugged my sleeve over my hand and brought it up to my nose to staunch the bleeding.

With a frown, the creature pulled my hand away from my face. He lifted my sleeve and looked at my wrist. Then he grabbed the other hand and looked at that wrist too before focusing on my nose...my blood. I couldn't move as he leaned forward, his lips curling back over those massive fangs.

Please don't bite me. Please don't bite me.

My silent plea changed abruptly when, nose to nose, he inhaled deeply.

Please find the smell repulsive. Please. Please. Plleeaase.

He pulled back, his gaze locked on mine. My panicked thoughts were still trying to decipher his lack of distinguishable expression when he jerked his gaze from mine and stared at the darkness to our left.

Nothing good had been coming out of the dark since the sun had set. Zombies. Hellhounds. Him.

A howl sounded from the direction he was looking.

I shivered and debated what to do. Try to run? I glanced at the man-creature squatting beside me. How far would I get? Would it piss him off? Would I fall on my face again?

He stood, and I scooted backwards, trying to get to my feet and failing in my fear. My heart bounced into my throat. I stopped crab crawling backwards, flipped over, and scrambled to my feet.

My captor seemed to have eyes in the back of his head because he'd already moved so he stood in front of me.

"Stop," he said.

Yeah, right. Like I wanted to stay and go toe to toe with one of those hellhounds. Before I could step around him, the sound of paws pounding against the dirt had me pivoting to face the new threat.

Shit. How fast did those beasts move?

A snarl came from the dark ahead and just to the left. Another, slightly to the right, answered the first. I couldn't outrun them. And, I knew what would happen when they found us. My breathing grew choppy, and my muscles wanted to turn to liquid.

My captor stepped around me and crouched low just as I spotted two sets of glowing red eyes speeding toward us. One in front of us and one to the right. The sound of their growls increased. A third rattling growl joined the first two, and I searched the dark, waiting for another set of eyes. When none came, I glanced at the dark back shielding me, realizing the sound was coming from him.

Yards from us, the hounds slowed, their dark bodies just visible in the weak moonlight. Ribs protruded from under their mangy, short fur. Yet, even starved, their long and tall bodies made them look large.

The hellhound in front of us dipped its head low. Saliva dripped from its jowls. The hellhound to the right darted forward, snapping his teeth. I backpedaled and fell. My elbow connected with a rock, and the pain robbed me of air as I watched the hounds make their move.

With its jaws open wide, the hellhound to the right dove straight for my defender's neck. The man lunged forward and caught the hound around the torso. The pair of them fell to the side, struggling. But, I didn't watch their fight. I watched the other hound focused on me. When it tensed, ready to spring, I frantically felt the ground for the rock.

The hound launched itself at me as my fingers closed around my only weapon. Before I could lift my hand, the grey man appeared in front of me with inhuman speed. The hellhound's long, lethal claws tore his shirt as the two collided. With a forearm braced against the beast's throat, he barely avoided the yellowed, snapping teeth. I feared what would happen if the beast bit him.

A noise to my right had me finally scrambling to my feet. The first hellhound was getting up. It looked at the fighting pair then stalked around them as its gaze shifted to me. I shadowed its moves, circling around the opposite way.

I got about a quarter of the way around the fighting pair when the man let out a monstrous bellow. He reached up and caught the snapping hellhound's jaws in his hands. His biceps bulged as he gripped around the beast's mouth and heaved. The lower jaw came away with a spray of blood and wet sound that made me gag.

The other hellhound howled its displeasure. Hefting the weight of the wounded one, the man twisted around and threw one beast into the other. Pinned under the weight of its weakly flailing partner, the hound growled and snapped and struggled to gain its feet.

The man cocked his head at the beast, snarled, then turned toward me.

I backed up as he strode forward. He said a string of words that made no sense. But they sure sounded angry. I kept backing away.

The hellhound was slowly working its way out from under its partner.

"Stop."

My heart almost quit at his command.

"Go," he said.

Before I could figure out what he meant, he grabbed me by my bruised elbow and started walking, pulling me along. I hissed in pain and stumbled as I tried to keep up with him. Although I really wanted to get away from the hellhounds as fast as possible, my legs were definitely not as long as his.

His grip tightened, and he pulled me harder. The throb in my elbow intensified.

"Wait," I panted, trying to tug my arm free.

He grunted and moved in front of me.

I lifted my chin, ready to tell him I was moving as fast as I could when he bent forward, dipped his shoulder, and caught me around the waist. My breath left in a whoosh as his shoulder dug into my soft stomach and he lifted me into the air.

The brute wrapped an arm around my legs and took off running. My hair flew around my head. I opened my mouth to tell him to put me down then reconsidered. The ground whipped past at an incredible speed. Faster than I could ever dream of going. And, there were two hellhounds behind us. Closing my mouth, I grabbed the back of his shirt and hung on.

He ran tirelessly. Around us, the sky began to lighten enough that I could make out the highway in the distance and a few buildings in the other direction.

Eventually, he slowed and then stopped. When he leaned forward to put me on my feet, I groaned with relief. My stomach and head were killing me.

He loosened his hold on me as blood rushed to places it hadn't reached while I rode over his shoulder. Feeling lightheaded, I struggled to find my balance. My legs started to shake, and I began to drop. He caught me by my bruised elbow again. This time I didn't bite back the cry of pain that made my eyes water. He released me slowly and followed my descent down.

He squatted near me and brought his long fingers to rest under my eyes. He dabbed at the wetness and pulled it back to his nose. He closed his eyes as he breathed in.

Exhaustion made me not care that he was sniffing me again.

"Let go," he said suddenly.

"You're going to let me go?"

He frowned then made a bunch of word-sounding noises that were incomprehensible to me.

"Who are you? *What* are you?" I asked.

"Drav."

"I don't know what you're saying."

"Drav," he said, patting his chest again. He didn't try grabbing me. His gaze remained steadily on mine.

"Is that your name?"

"Name Drav."

"Drav," I said slowly. A monster with a name.

He reached forward, clearly aiming for my chest again.

"Boobs."

I crossed my arms over his goals, effectively blocking him.

"No. My name is Mya. Not boobs. And boobs aren't for grabbing."

"My-ah," he repeated

He sat back on his haunches.

"I just want to go home."

Drav's eerie eyes met mine.

"Home," he repeated.

I looked away to the glow on the horizon and hoped the light indicated the direction for Oklahoma City and not someone's yard light. Time to finish this journey, lose my stalker, and get home to my family. I climbed to my feet.

A strong hand wrapped around my bruised elbow. I yelped and tried to pull my arm back. Drav moved in front of me, his large fingers still pressing into my sensitive skin.

"Ow," I said.

Drav trailed his hand down my arm. I winced when he skimmed over my elbow.

"You can't grab me there. It's bruised."

47

"Bruised?" He cocked his head and lifted my arm.

Drav's nostrils flared, and his eyes widened. I didn't like the look on the big brute's face, and my pulse jumped in alarm. His gaze fixated on my sleeve. My dried blood dotted the cuff from where I'd wiped my bloody nose.

He bunched the fabric between his fingers and pulled back hard. I stumbled forward, the sound of tearing fabric cutting through the otherwise quiet world around us. I gaped up at him, as he yanked half my sleeve off my arm and held it up in his hand. He growled at the fabric then paced away.

In stunned silence, I watched him quickly dig a hole and toss my sleeve in. Could my life get any weirder?

Shivering at the cool air on my exposed arm, I turned toward the distant glow of Oklahoma City and started walking. In two steps, he was beside me.

We didn't speak as we moved closer and closer to the outlaying north-eastern portion of the city. Very faintly, I heard a quick succession of pops. The noises grew with each passing step. Worry twisted in my stomach. Shots meant infected, hellhounds, more Dravs or all three. I hoped Mom, Dad, and Ryan would be safe.

When the first houses came into sight, Drav slowed. I kept going until he grabbed my arm again.

"Will you please stop yanking on my arms? They're going to fall off," I said in a harsh whisper.

Drav blinked at me then let go.

"Thank you. Next time try saying stop or wait."

He motioned to a copse of trees and nudged me in that direction when I didn't immediately start moving. I looked at the houses and reluctantly gave into his urging. Some of the lights were on, some weren't. Who knew what lurked inside. Infected? Scared humans with guns? Both would be dangerous.

In the shadow of the trees, he watched the houses. I shifted my weight from foot to foot and yawned until my eyes watered. He kept glancing at me but didn't say anything.

As we stood there, I realized the kind of decisions that lay before me. Life or death ones. I'd always thought the saying, "or die trying" sounded so melodramatic. But now it was my reality.

Sitting heavily, I leaned against the trunk of the nearest tree.

Was I smart to keep trying to get home? I didn't know. I didn't see any safer option. If I stayed in the trees, one of those hounds would find me eventually. Or the infected. I listened to the pop, pop, pop and decided, at least in the city, I might pick up a gun. Or die trying.

I shivered and closed my eyes as I thought about what waited for me.

Hellhounds, zombies, demon looking man-people who liked breaking necks and ripping off jaws...I was so fucked.

CHAPTER SEVEN

SOMETHING TICKLED MY NECK, AND I AWOKE WITH A GASP. THE night sky had lightened with the approaching dawn, and the air no longer rang with distant pops. In fact, an eerie silence blanketed the area, including the vacant space before me where Drav had stood.

I turned my head to check the trees to my left for him and almost screamed. Drav blinked at me, just inches away, then stood from his squatted position.

Taking a deep breath to calm my racing heart, I looked down at myself. I didn't know what I expected. Blood? Wounds? Signs of a recent groping? To my surprise, I found Drav's dark shirt covering me. I touched the warm material and looked up at him as he stepped away to watch the houses once more.

I sat for a moment, confused as hell. Nothing about Drav made sense. Standing, I winced at the pressure on my bladder. How long had I slept? Maybe an hour? Two? And he'd watched over me. Why? I shook my head, unable to believe I'd slept at all.

With his shirt in my hands, I cautiously approached him. He looked down at me, his gaze sweeping over my face and hair as I held out his shirt.

"Thank you," I said.

He studied me for a moment longer before he took the shirt with a grunt of acknowledgement. He tugged the shirt over his head then went back to watching the houses.

Since he didn't show any sign of wanting to leave soon, the need to pee had me glancing back at the trees again. The inky shadows had me questioning how badly I needed to go. Bad enough to seriously consider dropping my pants where I stood. I looked at Drav and knew that wasn't an option, given his previous crotch groping and interest in my boobs.

Scrubbing my hands over my face, I turned toward the trees. He stood in front of me before I took a second step. I looked up at him. He blinked at me.

"I have to pee," I said.

He didn't move.

"If I go stand behind a tree, is something going to attack me? My loose use of 'something' includes you."

He blinked at me again.

"I don't like when you do that."

He didn't blink, which freaked me out more.

"How much of what I say do you understand?"

He turned away from me and walked into the trees a few feet, making me think he didn't understand much at all. He looked back and motioned for me to follow.

"I don't want to leave. I want to go home." I pointed to the nearest house. "I just wanted to pee, first."

"You pee. No attack. Includes me."

My mouth dropped open. When he'd repeated boob and grab, I'd thought he'd just parroted the words.

"No leave. Go home," he said.

He moved toward me, and I backed up a step, my heart hammering. He understood me. Not only understood me, but what he'd just said almost made it sound like he would take me home.

That couldn't be right. Yet, unlike my previous companions, I still lived. I opened my mouth to ask if he really meant that he would help me get home, but that didn't come out.

"Why did you kill Kevin and Josh? And probably Russ? Are you going to kill me? Where did you come from? Why are you here? What is happening?"

He frowned. "No."

"No? Those weren't 'no' questions."

"No leave. Go home. You pee."

"Can you at least tell me what's happening?"

"Pee."

He stood before me, a solid mass of authority. He didn't need to cross his arms to make that point either.

"Yeah, yeah, yeah. I know pee. Fine. But, I can't pee with you staring at me. It's creepy. If it's safe, go back to watching the houses." I didn't trust his perverse curiosity.

He moved back into his watchful position. I hurried to a nearby tree and unbuttoned my pants, but before I tugged my pants down, I debated. Face him to make sure he didn't peek or the woods so I wasn't attacked with my pants down? I scooted over so the tree would hopefully block his view. I faced the woods, squatted, and power peed like my life depended on it.

When I finished, I zipped up and tried not to think about the grossness. The world was ending, and I had bigger problems than no toilet paper.

I turned and found Drav looking my direction. As I joined him, I didn't acknowledge the fact he'd probably tried to sneak a peek. Thankfully, the few houses nearest the trees where we hid had no lights shining.

"My home is on the other side of the city," I said, still unsure what he could understand.

When he didn't answer, I sighed and studied the houses before us.

"What's smarter? Cutting through or going around? Cutting through might mean running into infected. But, it could also mean water, food..." I stopped thinking aloud when I realized the other reason I wanted to cut through instead of going around. I wanted to find the humans with the guns I'd heard. I glanced at Drav, wondering what would happen then, and found him watching me, his head slightly tilted.

Crap. I shouldn't have mentioned food. I really hoped I didn't look like his idea of a steak breakfast.

Pretending like I hadn't just unnerved myself, I made the decision and took a step forward.

"If we see any infected, you have my permission to toss me over your shoulder and run."

He didn't try to stop me as I crept toward another grouping of trees closer to the houses. When I reached them, I checked for the next bit of protective cover. Slowly, dash by mad-dash, I made my way into the first of many subdivisions.

The neighborhood appeared unnaturally quiet. With the sun almost kissing the horizon, there should have been kids up, getting ready for school, parents leaving to go to work. Movement. Noise. Something. Instead, there was the whisper of wind rattling the few dry leaves still clinging to otherwise barren branches and the snap of a sheet that billowed in the wind. I glanced at the white material caught in the window and my stomach tightened with worry. Everything seemed so desolate.

The further we scurried, the quieter it got. Not even the occasional bark of someone's dog reached our ears.

I saw the first infected after three blocks of traveling. Before I could react, Drav pulled me behind a tree. With a hammering heart, I waited as a man in sweatpants and t-shirt shambled up the center of the street, his bare feet dragging on the pavement with a rasp. The sound burrowed into my mind. Crsht. Crsht. The need to cover my ears made me twitch. Drav's hand brushed over my back, a weird comfort that gave me courage to keep watching the infected's progress.

The infected man could have passed as a sleep walker if not for the bites on his arm. He didn't turn his head to look around or veer from his ambling path down the center of the road. Drawing a deep breath after he passed from sight, I prepared to dash to the next tree then saw the bloody trail he'd left behind. A shiver chased through me, and I forced myself to focus on reaching the next area of cover.

Sightings became more frequent as the sun rose to show a beautiful, clear blue November sky. I doubted the sun had anything to do with the amount of infected drifting around. Those numbers likely had everything to do with the increase of houses.

When I moved to dash to the next form of cover, a car in a driveway, Drav put his hand on my shoulder and stopped me. I glanced at him, and my eyes widened in surprise at the sight of his tearing eyes. For a moment, I thought he was crying.

"No," he said softly.

He blinked profusely, the light making his eyes water as he looked around. Before I could ask why he'd said no, he grabbed the side of my shirt and tugged me back the way we'd come.

The sudden and rapid *pop, pop, pop* not far away made me jump. Drav didn't mess around with more tugging. He flipped me over his shoulder and took off running. When he lurched upward and the distance between my head and the ground tripled, I almost screamed.

A second later, we landed on the inside of a fence. He didn't stop moving. Something cracked and we were suddenly inside someone's kitchen. He set me on my feet and turned to push the door shut. It didn't latch since he'd busted the bolt right through the jamb. I reached around him to use the security chain.

Outside the pops continued, a sign of people nearby. People with guns, who could possibly help me get home. Humans.

I started moving toward the living room at the front of the house, but Drav snagged me again and spun me around.

"No."

"But there's—"

"No," he said more forcefully.

I swallowed any further objection. When I stayed silent, he seemed to calm slightly and began to look around the room. I did, too. Items from pulled out drawers lay scattered everywhere. The people had either left in a hurry or their home had been looted.

I glanced down the hall at all the closed doors.

"Are we safe in here?" I whispered.

Drav nudged me toward the hall, and I hoped that meant yes. At the end of the hall, he turned and sat, blocking me in at the back.

"What are you doing?"

He laid his head back against the wall and closed his eyes.

"Uh..." I waited for him to do something more, but he didn't. He just stayed there.

The noises outside remained consistent, neither moving closer nor fading. My ticket home couldn't be more than a block or two away. I just needed to get past Drav, sneak out a broken door, hop a six-foot fence...shit. Front door then. I'd need to watch the front yard and street before even thinking about opening the door.

First, I'd have to cross over Drav. The hall wasn't wide so his bent knees created a barrier for what would have been an easy step. His wide shoulders and overall largeness didn't help either. I moved a little, making a slight noise to test him. His eyes remained closed. I lifted my foot and was halfway over him when his fingers closed around the ankle of my anchored foot. I yipped in surprise and almost fell on him before my other foot landed hard on the other side of him. He slowly tipped his head up at me and opened one eye.

"No."

The soft way he said the word made me shiver.

"I-I was just going to look for food. I'm h-hungry."

Drav tilted his head at me and released my ankle. He nudged me back as he stood up. He didn't move away, but stared down at me with very little space between us. When he leaned in and inhaled near my hair, I swallowed hard and hoped he wouldn't somehow detect the lie.

Finally, he stepped back and motioned that I could go. I retreated down the hall and went to the kitchen. The fridge still hummed, and I checked inside of it. Nothing remained but condiments. I checked the cupboards next. They'd been cleared out, too, except for some cans of peaches. I grabbed one then started looking for a can opener. The first drawer I opened had odds and ends and a pair of sunglasses.

"Look," I said, holding them up. He blinked at the pink and bedazzled frames. "They'll cover your eyes so the light doesn't hurt. Like this." I put them on then took them off and handed them to him. "If you wear them, we can go back outside. I can go home."

He looked them over then set them on the counter.

"No." He opened the next drawer. "Hungry."

With frustration, I searched the contents of that drawer, too. Finding the can opener, I opened the can and poured the peaches into a clean bowl. He closely observed everything I did. I stabbed a peach half with a fork and took a bite.

"Are you hungry?" I asked after I swallowed. Gathering my courage, and hoping like hell he didn't say "people," I asked, "What do you eat?"

He stole the fork from my hand and ate the rest of the peach.

"Uh...okay." Peaches were good. Much better than people.

Once I finished eating, though, he herded me back down the hall.

"You sure you don't want to try those sunglasses?"

"No." He sat in his same spot and closed his eyes.

This time, I sat as well. He hadn't left me much room. I wedged myself between him and the wall and sighed. My phone dug into my butt, a silent comfort. Temptation prodded me to check it, but I didn't want to bring it to Drav's attention. Instead, I closed my eyes and forced myself to relax. Hopefully, he'd been awake longer than I had before my nap. And, I hoped the little bit of sleep I'd gotten would be enough to keep me awake until he fell asleep. While I waited, I imagined the yards we'd crossed, the direction of the shots, and the cover I might find between here and there.

After a few minutes, my thoughts began drifting to what I would do once I reached home. What if my family had been infected? Where would I go? What was left in the world? Did we, the uninfected humans have any chance of surviving? How many hellhounds prowled out there? How many humans had already been infected? There was only one way to learn. I had to go explore. I had to find the people shooting and figure out what happened. I had to know my family was safe.

CHAPTER EIGHT

I WAITED A LONG TIME. THE SHOTS STARTED TO FADE. SEVERAL times, I caught myself on the verge of dozing off. The last time, I twitched and knew I had to try, now or never. I opened my eyes and observed Drav for several minutes. He had closed his eyes and leaned his head back against the wall. He seemed asleep.

Taking my time, I got to my feet. If he caught me again, I'd say I had to pee. However, this time, he didn't move.

Carefully, I made my way down the hallway and to the front door. I looked through the window, scanning the street, then slipped outside.

My nerves stretched tight as I sprinted to the first bit of cover. Alert for infected, hellhounds, and, possibly, a killer shadow man, I bolted for the next bit of cover. Sprint by sprint, I made my way south-west, further into the city. Tracking the shooters wasn't hard. They'd left a trail of dead infected bodies. However, the gun shots attracted more infected to the area, too.

A few times, I thought one spotted me. However, the infected never ran after me like they had on the road. The more I saw, the more I began seeing patterns. They shambled fairly directionless until they heard something. Then they ran toward the sound, but their speed only lasted for short bursts. So, if one heard me, I would need to quietly out distance it to avoid attracting more.

The gun fire grew louder around lunch, and I spotted the shooter. He stood by his truck, which idled at an intersection. The gun in his hands remained aimed down the road to the left. Knowing better than to call out, I waved my arms in the air to get his attention.

"There's a live one out there," I heard someone else call. "Ten o'clock."

Every infected between me and the shooter dropped, one right after another, gunned down before the man by the truck turned toward me. Movement near a chimney to the right drew my attention, and I looked up at a man dressed in brown and black. Blonde hair stuck out from his black beanie.

"I've got you," he called. "Get to the truck."

I didn't need to be told twice. I sprinted toward the truck, my shoes thumping against the blacktop. The shooter on the ground, dressed in the same black and brown clothing as the man on the roof, waved me past. A single shot rang out behind me.

I opened the back door of the huge pickup truck and climbed in. Behind the wheel sat a third man dressed similarly to the other two. I quickly shut the door as he scanned the area around the truck.

"Hey," I said, a little winded from the mad dash.

He continued to ignore me. I anxiously glanced out the window and tried to calm my racing heart.

No more pops sounded in the distance. Nervous, elated energy buzzed in my veins. Finding more humans, alive ones, was huge. They had guns and appeared military. I started to relax in my seat. I'd done it. I'd made it. I wanted to grin.

Static crackled from a hand radio before a voice came through.

"Jack's down from the roof. He said he spotted one of the big grey ones in the distance."

My grin faded. Images of the last time I rode in a truck flashed through my head. No, I thought. Not again. I frantically looked out the windows as the driver pulled the radio from the cup-holder.

"Got it," he said into the radio. "Girl is in the truck. Get your asses back here."

The door opened to my left, and I scooted over the bench as the man from the ground climbed in the back with me.

"Where did you come from?" he asked.

"Tulsa. I was at school."

His eyes swept over me as Jack, the blonde man from the roof, climbed into the front seat.

"Moving out," the driver called as he put the vehicle into gear. The engine revved as the truck started forward in a rush. Jack laughed, twisted around, and offered his hand over the seat.

"You surprised me," he said. "Very nice to meet you, ma'am."

I gave him a weak smile and shook his hand. After I released it, he turned forward and rolled his window down, his gun ready. The truck began picking up speed, but not enough. I knew how fast the shadow men could run. I looked out the back window, my gaze searching.

"What's your name, girl?" the man beside me asked. I met his tired brown gaze and noted the subtle wrinkles around his eyes.

"Mya."

"I'm Charles, that's Bill driving, and Jack up front."

"What were you saying about a big grey one?"

"Damn demons that control the hellhounds," Bill said from the front.

"What?" Hellhound-controlling demons? My stomach lurched.

"Wait until you see one. Then you'll know. Hell's rising, kid."

The image of Drav fighting off the hellhounds flashed through my mind. He certainly didn't control those hounds. They had attacked us. And he protected me from them. Did it really matter? I was finally in a moving vehicle in my home city.

I opened my mouth to ask more questions when a boom from Jack's gun filled the cab. I slammed my hands over my ears and turned in my seat to look out the window. Another infected started an all-out sprint toward us.

Jack fired again. I flinched as the bullet tore through the infected man's chest and knocked him backwards. Instead of going down, he still kept coming. Jack took another two shots, the last finally going through the infected's head. I cringed as he crumbled to the ground.

"First time seeing one die?" Charles asked quietly.

He held his gun steadily out the window, too. I had no experience with guns but still wished I had my own.

I slowly shook my head to answer his question. No matter how many I saw die, I doubted I'd ever forget the infected had once been a person.

"What happened here? My phone doesn't work," I said, pulling it from my back pocket.

"Don't bother," he said as I checked for new messages. "We've lost communications. First, the tremors, then communications, then the hounds. Most folks were in their houses for the night when the first wave of mutts came through the city. They didn't know what was happening out on the streets."

"What was happening?" I asked, even though I had a fairly good idea.

"Those hounds attacked anything that was out. Some people they killed. Some they bit then moved on. Alive or dead, didn't matter. The people bitten all got sick, and the sickness spread like wildfire throughout the night. Tinker started to mobilize an evacuation effort around two," Charles said, referring to the military base in Oklahoma City. "But, people didn't understand what was going on. As soon as they left their houses, they came into contact with neighbors, friends, and family that had been infected. One bite and they were done for."

Jack fired another shot, and a shudder ran through me. Would my family have tried to leave? Would I find them shambling around our neighborhood?

"What happened then?"

"We helped get as many uninfected civilians as we could back to base. They started flying out survivors to a fenced in location further north."

"Why are you guys still here?" I asked.

"This is home. We're not giving up on it. While we gather supplies and search for stragglers like you, we're clearing the infected. If we could manage to kill the hounds and their masters, we'd get our city back."

I remembered the way the hellhound had kept going even after being shot at the stadium.

"Have you killed any?"

"Hounds?"

I nodded.

"Not sure. They take off when we put a few rounds in them. I'm hoping that means they die somewhere."

"Those grey bastards are a different story," Jack said without taking his eyes from the passing houses.

"Why?"

"You don't see them," Charles said. "They are shadows that leave bodies behind. We only know they exist because we caught two on surveillance. Looked like a couple big men at first. The footage was blurry. We watched them take down seven armed soldiers. Shots were fired but never seemed to hit either one. We thought it was the shadows making their skin grey but learned the truth when one faced the direction of the camera. Its eyes weren't human."

No, Drav's eyes were far from human. And it terrified me that there were more of them out there.

"So it's just the three of you out looking for survivors?"

Jack laughed from up front.

"We're one of many units," he said, giving me hope. "After Tinker mobilized, we lost more than half. But we're still here."

The truck stayed quiet for a moment except for the dull roar of the engine and random bangs from the gun.

"Have you found anyone else?" I asked hopefully. "I'm looking for my family."

"You're the first we've run into. We have been out since dawn. But we were double-checking an area already evaced. Where did you live?"

The past-tense way he said it made my stomach cramp.

"Blueridge. North-west side," I said.

"We'll make sure someone goes out that way to check for signs of life today."

"What do you mean signs of life?"

"People hang sheets outside windows or doors. Some have painted help in their windows. Makes it easier for us to find them and, hopefully, get them to safety," Charles explained.

"Can't we check my neighborhood now?"

"We have orders to go further into the city for supplies," Charles said.

"Roll them up," Bill said from the front as he slowed for a turn.

"Did you really just use your blinker?" Jack asked, pulling his gun in and rolled up his window.

"Shut up."

Jack laughed, and I glanced at Charles who'd pulled his gun in, too, and frowned.

"Why are we rolling up the windows?"

"We're taking the highway," Jack said. "Splatter control."

As soon as we turned again, I saw the highway ahead. In the distance, infected shambled along the road.

"Why are there so many?"

"Failed attempt at a ground-evac."

"Here we go," Bill said, taking the ramp.

Bill's hands tightened on the wheel, and the engine roared to life as he pressed down on the gas. The roar announced our location to the infected. They came running at the truck. My stomach knotted. Bill aimed right for them. Half of one's body flew over the truck. More came at us like a swarm of gnats. Bill plowed through them all. I shut my eyes unable to erase the image of the blood that spattered the windshield.

The squeak of the window-wipers sounded then finally stopped.

"We clean up more of them every run," Charles said.

Slowly, I opened my eyes.

Jack leaned over in his seat and turned the volume nob up on the radio. Only static crackled out. He switched over to the tune nob, and twisted it around. A high-pitched screech emitted from a station that should have been playing rock. After Jack tried a couple more stations, Bill reached over and turned the radio button off.

"Has there been any news of what's happening anywhere else?" I asked.

"No. The last I heard, Europe had gone dark just after the local news stations reported sightings of those demonic hounds."

Yesterday afternoon. It had only been that long since the first tremor, since Germany fell with the same sickness. Yet it felt like I had lived a hundred years in those few hours.

I looked out the window at the quiet neighborhoods and occasional infected as we continued down the highway.

After taking an exit, the number of zombies thinned for a while. However, the closer we got to downtown, the more they came out. Jack and Charles shot out their open windows as Bill drove. The shots didn't deter any away from us. Instead, it did the opposite. More started to filter out, beckoned by the noise, and I began to rethink my itch to possess a gun of my own.

It wasn't much longer until we arrived at a shopping district.

"Bill, you keep the path between the truck and the store clear," Charles said. "The rest of us are going for the food and water. Take carts. Get everything you can."

"Me?" I didn't want to leave the safety of the truck.

"These supplies are going with you to the survivor camp. You want to eat, don't you?"

I nodded.

"We'll keep you safe. Just grab a cart and get as many canned and dry goods as you can. Use the radios. I want to be gone in fifteen."

Bill drove the truck around the back of a supermarket and killed the engine. The infected that had chased us slowed to a confused shamble in the quiet. We sat in the truck for twenty minutes, watching and waiting for the infected to slowly disperse.

Charles called all clear, and we went to the employee entrance, where Jack picked the lock.

"Quieter this way," he said softly when he caught me watching.

As soon as the door opened, Jack lifted his gun and stepped inside. Someone had left the lights on in the back room. Pallets of boxes sat just inside the large delivery doors to our right.

I pointed, but Charles shook his head.

"Too big."

Charles nodded toward the swinging door that led to the main shopping area. Jack checked the window then eased the door open. I slowly followed him through. Everything seemed quietly undisturbed. Charles motioned for us to stay. My stomach churned as I watched him walk away and disappear around the corner of an aisle.

A few minutes later, a couple of pops echoed through the store, and I jumped.

"Store cleared," Charles said softly over the radio.

Jack jerked his head to the left then started moving. I followed him to the front of the store. The instant scratch off machine had been pushed in front of the door. Bits of glass covered the floor around it.

"Hellhounds," Jack said softly.

"Here?" I asked, my panic going through the roof.

He shook his head. "Here and gone again. They move fast."

Exactly why I didn't want to be in a building with them.

"Get a cart," he said, holstering his gun. We each grabbed a cart and started for the shelves. Another few pops echoed, but from outside.

"Took out two infected. Keep your eyes open," Bill said over the radio.

Jack went ahead of me and started sweeping the nearest shelf of the nonperishable foods. We filled both carts and went to the water aisle next. Jack grabbed an abandoned cart and started loading the gallon jugs.

Another pop sounded from outside.

"Head back to the car now," Bill barked over the radio. Jack grabbed the food cart and hustled for the employee door.

"Grey one headed right for us. Get out, now."

"Shit." Jack spun around.

"What do we do?" I panted.

"Get out before it gets here. Leave the cart."

He grabbed my arm and started running toward the back. I struggled to keep up. Fear solidified in my stomach.

"Bill left the keys in the truck. Get it started. I'm almost there," Charles said through the radio.

We had nearly reached the employee entrance when a scream ripped through the air. I faltered, but Jack didn't pause in his running. He pulled me through the exit. I stumbled, blinded by the sudden sunlight.

Jack kept pulling me, and I squinted as I followed after him. The truck waited, only steps away.

Suddenly Jack's hand left my arm. I blinked, looking around in confusion.

When I turned a full circle, I saw Jack's body slumped against the truck, his neck bent unnaturally. Standing over him was a very pissed off Drav.

CHAPTER NINE

HIS SHOULDERS HEAVED WITH EACH ANGRY BREATH AS HE STALKED toward me. I shook with fear, unable to tear my gaze from the pink bedazzled sunglasses he wore. When he stood before me, he leaned down until his eyes were level with mine.

"Arm fall off."

The deep, quiet words turned my fear to confusion.

"W-what?"

He reached out and stroked one finger along my bruised elbow. The same arm Jack had just been tugging on.

"Get down!" Charles bellowed from somewhere behind me.

Drav roared in my face, put his shoulder to my stomach, and hoisted me into the air. An arm around my thighs anchored me. As he turned, I braced my arms on his back and lifted my head. Charles stood by the door, rifle poised and ready to fire. Our eyes met. His hopeless, sad expression ratcheted my panic higher, and I struggled in Drav's hold.

A large hand came down on my ass with a loud crack. I forgot to struggle as I choked on a pained squeal. Drav took off running.

"Sorry, kid," Charles said.

A moment later, a loud bang filled the air. Stunned, I stared at

Charles as he took aim again. He'd actually pulled the trigger. I cried out and tucked myself close to Drav's torso, wrapping my arms around his waist as he ran.

Another shot rang out. My heart wanted to pound its way out through my throat. Drav jerked but didn't slow. Blacktop, interspersed with flashes of green, continued to pass underneath me at an alarming rate. My hair whipped around my head. Even when the shots stopped, Drav didn't.

I loosened my hold on his waist and lifted my head. His arm tightened on the backs of my thighs and a hand settled on my sore butt cheek. That was all the warning I needed to resume my clinging position.

What I'd glimpsed had been enough. Infected trailed behind us, attracted by the sound of the shots and Drav's running. Although he outpaced them, I didn't want to know if one came close or if their numbers grew. If Drav wanted me to hold still so he could run, I would. And, I wouldn't think about what would happen when he stopped running or about the way he'd roared in my face. Nope. I'd cling to him like a second skin and think of how I would make it home and how we'd all go somewhere safe.

Charles had said they'd evacuated people to a location somewhere north of the city. I regretted not asking where and tried to focus on the positive bits of information I knew. An evacuation had occurred. People were safely flown away to a fenced in location. Fences had to be good. Especially if they were military. So, if my family was there—wherever there might be—they would be safe. I had to believe that. But, first, I needed to make sure they had actually been evacuated and weren't with the stragglers Charles had mentioned.

Drav jumped, startling me from my thoughts, and I looked down to see a fence pass under us. Another fenced in yard, proving my thought that fences were good. I heard the wood crack as he broke in through the back door. Finally, he set me on my feet.

For a moment, I wobbled unsteadily as the blood rushed from my head. Drav set his sunglasses on the counter then gently touched my shoulder. I fearfully met his gaze.

Before I could ponder what he would do to me, a whisper of noise came from our left. Drav spun toward the sound and crouched low in front of me. A man, his eyes lifelessly cloudy, rushed toward us.

I gasped and my fight or flight instinct surged. I would have run, but to where? A stupid fenced in backyard? I was a fish in a barrel.

Drav waited until the man came close, then lashed out, ripping the head clear from the body in one powerful swing. Dark, clotted blood spattered the wall behind the man. I gagged and closed my eyes.

"Mya."

The sound of my name made me wince.

"Mya. Eyes. Look me."

I opened my eyes and found him standing before me once more. The decapitated infected lay on the floor behind him. Would I be next? Was that why he'd come after me and killed the rest of Charles's group?

Nerves pushed too far, I trembled uncontrollably and numbly stared up at Drav. His gaze swept over my face as if he was checking for something. What, I had no idea. The heavy exhale he released made me jump. The way he reached around me to grab the back of my head made my heart hammer. I closed my eyes, waiting for the end. Instead, his forehead pressed against mine and his breath fanned my face.

Surprised, I opened my eyes. The up-close view of his eyes startled me less than the feel of his fingers gently massaging my scalp.

He stayed like that for a moment before slowly straightening. His gaze held mine as he lightly ran his fingers along my hair.

When his fingers reached the ends, he brought the long strands to his nose. With growing nervousness, I watched him inhale deeply. He killed a lot. People. Hellhounds. Infected. But not me. And, the potential reason why terrified me.

Releasing my hair, he turned to look at the fallen body. He grunted at it, as if annoyed, then reached down to pick it and the head up.

"Mya, no go back outside."

I nodded slightly.

He stepped around me, and I watched him carry the infected to the back of the fence then chuck both the body and the head over. The early morning sun caught on the face as the head tumbled down. Was this my life? Death and hiding and fear?

Drav turned, and his watery gaze never left mine as he stalked back across the yard. I stepped aside, hoping he would pass me, but he shadowed my move, crowding into my space.

"I'm sorry, Mya."

Was he just repeating Charles' words or was he really sorry for stealing me?

He glanced at the dark hallway then nudged me in that direction. This time, the doors weren't closed. The sight of the first clean, cozy bed reminded me how very little sleep I had gotten. Until now, adrenaline had kept my exhaustion away. However, that was fading fast.

When I saw a bathroom, I stopped.

"Mya." Drav's tone held a note of warning.

"I want to pee," I said. I didn't. Not really. I wanted to climb my ass out that big window and see if I could run my way back to Charles or some other humans.

He grunted and nudged me toward the bathroom. When I stepped in and tried to close the door, he blocked it.

"No."

"I'm not peeing with you watching me."

He turned and looked at the mirror.

"Not helpful. Leave," I said.

"No. Mya leave." He looked at the window, and I swallowed hard.

"Out the window?" I said, feigning disbelief. "I would never fit."

"You would fit," he said.

Not sure what to say to that, I went to the sink and turned on the water, unwilling to make it obvious that he'd correctly busted me. Before I bent to drink, I glanced at myself in the mirror. A smear of dirt decorated the bridge of my nose and one cheek. Crusted bits of blood clung to the skin under my nose.

Changing my mind about the drink, I opened the bathroom closet, grabbed a washcloth, and washed my face. Afterwards, I quenched my thirst and turned off the water.

When I turned toward Drav, I noticed a wet spot on his shirt.

"I think you got a little bit of blood on you," I said, pointing.

He looked down at the spot on his side and then lifted his shirt. A gash split his skin just over his lower ribs.

A bullet had grazed him. I glanced at his shoulder and realized it had been the side on which he'd carried me. My head would have been about right where that bullet had gotten him. My eyes widened as I realized Charles had been aiming for me, not Drav.

"Holy shit," I said softly.

I met Drav's gaze as the implications settled in my mind. Whatever Charles had seen on that video had been enough for him to think I would be better off dead by his hand than Drav's. The questions I'd tried to avoid thinking forced their way in. Why was I still alive? What did Drav plan to do with me?

"D-do you want to clean it?" I asked, instead.

I didn't wait for an answer but grabbed a new washcloth and wet it. He still had his shirt up when I turned back to him, so I held out the washcloth.

"No. You clean it."

He stared at me unblinkingly, unnerving me further. With a shaking hand, I bent forward and began to gently clean the blood away. Drav's free hand went to my hair, his fingers trailing through the strands. I didn't understand his fascination with me, but it had kept me alive so far.

When I finished, I moved away from his inquisitive fingers and grabbed the first aid kit I'd noticed on the shelf. He held still as I put butterfly bandages on the gash. Finished, I straightened away from him and he lowered his shirt.

He waited while I washed my hands then nudged me down the hall again. Instead of sitting on the floor, he steered me toward a small bedroom with closed curtains. In the dim light, the pink and white frilly decor did nothing to cheer me.

"I don't want to sleep on a bed. We can sit in the hallway."

"No. You sleep on the bed," he said, closing the door.

He nudged me toward the bed in question, and my mind raced. Would I now find out why Charles wanted to shoot me? Is this why Drav came back for me?

When I didn't immediately jump onto the bed once we reached it, he picked me up and set me on the soft mattress.

"I don't want to sit here." My voice shook like crazy. So did my hands.

He placed a palm on my chest, just above my thundering heart, and steadily pushed me down until I lay flat on the bed. With wide-eyed panic, I stared up at him. He lowered himself beside me, pulled me into his arms, and buried his nose in my hair. My heart beat so painfully hard and fast that I struggled to breathe.

It took several moments to realize he hadn't moved. I held still and tried to quiet my booming heart so I could hear his slow and steady breathing. Was he really sleeping?

I lifted my head slightly.

"No, Mya. Sleep," he said.

He reached up and gently ran his fingers over my face. When

he found my eyes, he swiped over them again and again until I kept them closed.

He grunted and wrapped his arm around me. Despite everything, his hold began to feel safe, not confining. I exhaled heavily.

It didn't take long for my body to agree with him, and I slept.

I OPENED my eyes to a darker version of the room. Comfortable on my side, I could have easily gone back to sleep for another hour, but the very warm hand cupping my left breast posed a problem. Behind me, Drav lay close, with the offending arm curled over my side. We were far too cozy.

Laying still, I listened to his even breathing then carefully pushed at his forearm to remove his hand. His fingers clutched a little tighter around his prize, and he moved closer, his breath tickling the back of my neck. A roller coaster started in my stomach and freaked me out.

"Drav, stop."

He grunted, let go, and sat up. I quickly sat up, too. He was right there, in front of me in the dark, not giving me any room to leave.

"Mya, hungry?"

"Yes." Anything to get out of bed.

"Yeeessss," he drew out the word and something about his tone made me think he was smiling.

"Yes, Mya. Yes, hungry. Yes, home. Yes." He stepped back, giving me some room.

"Uh...okay." I stood and let him guide me to the kitchen. The back yard light shone through the window and illuminated the space well enough to see.

This time he searched for the cans while I checked the fridge. I found a pizza box containing four slices.

"You can stop looking. We can eat this," I said.

I took a slice and set the box on the counter. He watched me take a bite then grabbed a slice and brought it to his mouth. He bit into the pizza, chewed, then spit it onto the floor.

I laughed before I caught myself.

"What's wrong?" I asked. "It's cold, but it's not bad. Don't you like it?"

"No." He went back to searching cupboards and produced a can of spaghetti sauce.

"You sure you want to eat that?" I asked, when he started looking through the drawers. He paused and stared at me.

"It's spaghetti sauce. It's close to the red stuff on the pizza you just spit out."

He grunted, set the can opener on the counter, and went back to the cupboards. Each can he found, he held up to me until I identified it. When he'd emptied the cupboards, he said my name and pointed to the cans.

"You want me to pick?"

"Yes."

I lifted the can of chicken and the can of fruit cocktail. "If you like meat, eat this one. If you like fruit, like we had last time, eat this one."

He took both from me, and I watched him pick up the can opener and open the cans without hesitation. Using his fingers, he picked out some chicken and some fruit and popped both into his mouth at once. He seemed to enjoy it. I took another bite of my pizza and watched as he ate it all and drank the juice left in the fruit can.

I took a glass from the cupboard and filled it with water, drinking three glasses before setting it down. My stomach felt tight, but I didn't know when I'd get food or water next. Drav picked up my glass and proceeded to turn the tap on and off without filling anything.

"While you're doing that, I'm going to use the bathroom."

He looked at me without blinking.

"Pee?" I said.

"Don't leave, Mya."

The progression of his speech and understanding continued to unnerve me.

"I won't leave. Please don't watch me. It's weird."

He didn't try to follow, and I hesitated at the bathroom door. He still watched me.

"I'm going to close the door," I said.

"No." He took a step toward me.

"Fine. I'll leave it open if you promise to stay right there."

He stopped moving. Taking that as an agreement, I turned and quickly stepped into the bathroom. Although the window tempted me, the darkness beyond did not. I decided I would wait and try to find a way to slip from Drav once the sun rose.

Finished using the bathroom, I stepped back into the hall and found Drav in the same spot by the kitchen sink. As soon as he saw me, he turned his attention back to the faucet. Had he really stared at the hallway, listening the whole time? My cheeks grew hot. Too busy getting a drink for himself, he thankfully didn't notice.

CHAPTER TEN

AFTER HE DRAINED THE GLASS AND SET IT ASIDE, HE LOOKED ME over. Not in a creepy way like when we'd first met, but more of a "are you ready?" kind of way. He confirmed that guess by heading toward the front door.

"Mya and Drav go outside," he said quietly.

I watched him wrap his hand around the knob and knew what would happen if he tore the door open. The noise would attract any nearby infected.

"Wait. I can open it," I said, hurrying to him.

He let go of the knob but didn't step aside. I pretended not to notice the way he leaned in to smell my hair as he watched me unlock the bolt then turn the knob.

"Yes," he said, carefully moving me out of the way again so he could open the door and leave first.

He didn't go far. His back blocked the opening as he scanned right to left.

After a moment, he reached back for me. It terrified me to have to step out into the night, knowing what waited in the dark. But, thoughts of my family gave me courage enough to lead the way as Drav and I sprinted for the first bit of cover.

The sound of his soft footfalls behind me eased some of the terror. As much as I worried about what he wanted with me, I also realized how relieved I felt that I wasn't trying to make my way home alone. Bit by bit we moved through one neighborhood to the next, making progress.

I dashed across a quiet street and ducked behind a car in someone's front yard to wait for Drav. A sound had me looking up as a woman came around the side of the house. Fear lanced through me at the sight of her. I could see bite marks through the tears in her bloody shirt. Infected. A small sound escaped me.

Her head jerked in my direction, her mouth opening and closing. She lunged at me, and a solid wall of grey-muscled Drav stepped in front of me. He growled low and caught her by the head.

This time, I shut my eyes. Even without the visual, the wet sounds and the soft thump made bile rise to my throat.

A gentle pressure on my forehead had me opening my eyes. Drav's forehead rested against mine.

"I promise Mya stay safe," he said.

His steady gaze held me, and looking into his odd eyes, I realized what he meant by those words. Drav would keep me safe from the infected. But who would keep me safe from him?

"Thank you," I whispered.

"Yes."

He moved back a little but stayed crouched beside me as I watched the houses and decided the next stop. Avoiding the infected who shambled along the roads posed little issue with a bit of stealth and patience. However, as the woman had just proven, they didn't all stick to open areas.

It took hours before I found myself in an area I actually recognized. During that time, we were discovered by an infected on six different occasions. Drav kept each one away from me. He also removed every head.

"We're not even halfway across town," I said quietly as we stood in the darkness between two houses.

Drav didn't say anything in return, just watched the street and yards before us. I wasn't sure how far he'd run with me, but I felt sure he'd covered more distance with me on his shoulder than we had by doing this duck and cover thing. Only the knowledge that he'd have no idea which direction to go kept me from telling him to carry me again. That meant we would need to keep traveling as we were, and it would be well after dawn before I reached my neighborhood.

Unwilling to give up, I selected the next target and sprinted toward it, Drav right beside me.

Near dawn, he tugged my shirt while we watched the street from behind a parked car.

"Mya, don't go outside," he said softly.

Since I already crouched outside, I had no idea what he meant. I began to understand, though, when he looked at a house with a fenced in yard further down the block. No sheets or paint indicated anyone needing help. Unlike some of the other houses, the front door and garage were closed. It would be a perfect place to rest for the day. If I wanted to rest. Which I didn't. I wanted to go home.

I turned to tell him we should keep going, but he tossed me over his shoulder before I could argue. Seething, I kept quiet as he sprinted toward the house. Behind us, the sky was just barely starting to lighten. In the daylight, I could maybe manage on my own.

The sudden jump he executed made my stomach drop. When he landed, I patted his back.

"Put me down."

He stopped moving and set me on my feet.

"This time you go inside first and check for infected."

He blinked at me, grunted, then went to the entrance. I

watched him put his shoulder to the door. As soon as it gave way, he went inside.

I moved quickly to the fence and prepared to jump and catch the top. A whisper of movement on the other side stopped me. Leaning closer, I peeked through the tiny gap in the board and almost screamed at the sight of an infected looking straight at me. Slowly, I backed away and edged closer to the door and Drav.

Drav came out several moments later with a body and a head. I almost yipped at his sudden appearance.

"Inside, Mya," he said, after he dumped them over the fence.

I willingly turned from the fence—and what lurked beyond— and walked into the house with Drav right behind me. He went to the kitchen to start searching cupboards, and I noted the thick blood that spattered his shirt in several places. Tearing off heads was messy business.

"I need to pee," I said, watching him.

He grunted and moved toward the hall. I followed him. As soon as I found a bathroom, I stepped in, closed the curtains, and turned on the light.

"Door open," he said over his shoulder as he headed back to the kitchen.

Seeing the infected on the other side of the fence had killed any urge to leave. Still, I kept the door open as I quickly used the bathroom and washed my hands. By the time I returned to the kitchen, Drav already had several cans of food open. I ate some chili and green beans. He consumed three cans of tuna and tried a bite of peas, which he swallowed but obviously didn't like, given the way he shoved the can aside.

"Not good?" I asked, trying not to laugh.

"Not good," he said, agreeing.

Once we finished, I wandered off in search of a bedroom before he could start his nudging. In the first one I found, I went to the closet to look for a shirt that might fit him.

"Mya, no," he said, snagging me around the waist and turning me toward the bed.

"Drav, stop. Wait." He let me go, and I turned to point at the blood on his clothes.

"You can't sleep in that shirt. It has infected blood all over it, and it's gross." But more importantly...what if it got into his gash and he turned into one of them? I wouldn't stand a chance.

He grunted and had his shirt untied and off in two blinks. My brain malfunctioned slightly at the sight of all that chiseled, muscled flesh.

"Ohhh-kay. Ah, I'll just see if I can find you a new one."

He blocked my step toward the closet then slowly moved toward me. I retreated, until I realized he was backing me toward the bed. Thoughts of how he'd pressed against me yesterday while I slept and his current exposed state had me scrambling for a way to distract him. The red spotting his white bandage caught my eye.

"Wait. I, uh, should check that cut on your side." I gestured at it. "We should clean and change that."

"Yes," he said, stepping back.

Relieved, I hurried from the room to the bathroom, where I dug out what I could find for first aid supplies. There wasn't much. With a tube of ointment and several knee-sized band-aids on the counter, I faced Drav, who waited in the doorway.

He didn't make a sound as I eased the old bandage away. One part stuck and I had to carefully wet the cloth before removing it. After reapplying ointment, I put several new band-aids on. He waited in the hall while I threw away the wrappers and washed my hands.

"I'll get you a clean shirt," I said as I joined him.

"No clean shirt."

Crap. I didn't resist his nudge toward the bedroom as I struggled to think of another solution to my half-naked demon problem.

"There's another bedroom if you'd rather have a bed to yourself," I said.

"No. You go outside."

Damn. Unable to think of anything else to prevent snuggle time without making him angry, I reluctantly entered the room. Before I reached the bed, he tugged at the bottom of my shirt.

"Gross, Mya."

I turned to face him, understanding what he was saying. Up to this point he had been relatively respectful when I asked him to give me a sliver of privacy, so I shook my head and took a step backwards.

Drav pulled at my shirt again.

"It has infected blood all over it," he said, using my words.

Glancing down, I saw flecks of spattered dark brown blood mixed in with the grunge from falling, sweating, and other mishaps on the road. Yeah, my shirt looked pretty gross, but I wasn't about to part with it, not with his fascination with my boobs.

"No, my shirt stays on."

"No shirt."

"Yes shirt."

Dear lord, now I was arguing like him. Before he could say anything, a jaw-cracking yawn took me by surprise. Drav stared at my wide-open mouth. The yawn ended with his finger lifting my upper lip.

"What the hell, Drav?" I said as he bent down to take a closer look.

Drav's lips parted as he slid his tongue down one of his long, sharp canines.

"Yeah, we have different size teeth," I said, pulling back. He dropped his inquisitive fingers and glanced at my top again.

"I will sleep easier with my shirt on."

I climbed into the bed, and Drav grunted, which I took to mean he would allow me to keep my shirt.

Once I settled in on my side with my back to him—the safest position, in my mind—he lay down behind me and wrapped an arm around my waist. His hand drifted dangerously close to the prize he'd held this morning. I frowned as I realized it hadn't been this morning because the sun was just rising. Traveling at night and sleeping during the day was messing with my head. How long had it been since the first attack? Two nights ago?

His hand crept closer, his fingers brushing my underwire, and I quickly grasped his wrist. The feel of something under my palm had me looking down. A leather bracelet wrapped around his wrist. I tried lifting his hand, but he didn't budge.

"No, Mya." Drav whispered, his breath warm against the back of my neck.

"I'm not leaving. I just want to look at your bracelet."

His tight hold on my waist loosened, and this time, he let me lift his arm. A beautifully crafted bracelet, leather bound with rough crystal with markings engraved on the top, circled his wrist. I touched the crystal, my finger tracing the marking.

Drav hummed and snuggled closer. Carefully, I set his arm back down where it had been. His chest expanded against my back as he drew in a deep breath.

"Sleep, Mya."

After running through Oklahoma City the whole night, my body felt like lead. Hoping I wasn't making a mistake, I closed my eyes.

I was blissfully warm and well-rested when I woke, too cozy to want to open my eyes. That changed the moment a warm hand stroked the bare skin of my back.

My eyes popped open, and I stared at the expanse of grey-honed skin before me. At some point in the night, I had turned in my sleep and now lay chest to chest with Drav. I looked up to find him watching me. His hand didn't still on my back as our gazes locked. Uncertain if a roving hand on my back was any safer than an over the shirt boob grab, I tried to scoot backwards, but he held me tight.

"No, Mya."

"I wish I hadn't taught you that word."

My stomach growled, which caught Drav's attention. He glanced down between us with a concerned frown.

"Just hungry," I said.

"Hungry, Mya."

I nodded, and he rolled away from me, sitting up. With some breathing room, I glanced at the windows and noticed the weak light peeking around the curtains. Another day gone and another night waited filled with running from things that wanted to kill me.

"Did you want to put your shirt back on?" I asked when I finally looked his way.

"No. Gross."

He held out his hand, but I ignored it and slipped out of bed on my own.

After I made a pit-stop at the bathroom, where Drav again insisted I keep the door open, we ate a quick meal of canned food. Drav watched me carefully through our "breakfast," and I avoided looking at him. His bare chest was intimidating.

Once we finished eating, we made our way back outside where the sun had dipped below the horizon.

Without any warning, he threw me over his shoulder and jumped the fence, giving me no chance to warn him about the infected I'd seen that morning. A second later, Drav landed and set me on my feet. I looked around with wide eyes. Thankfully, the infected person no longer waited on this side. I was so ready to be done with this trip home.

CHAPTER ELEVEN

GATHERING MY COURAGE, I TURNED TOWARD THE SIDE YARD AND made my way to the front. The streets were quiet as I slipped behind a camper parked in a driveway.

We took care moving from yard to yard, neighborhood to neighborhood. The quarter moon rose, and Drav moved confidently in its weak light, obviously having an easier time seeing now than he did in the daylight.

The roads became familiar as we moved closer to my neighborhood, and a quiet settling warmth filled me. *Home.* Yet, it would not be the home I remembered. The white bedsheets that flapped in the night breeze of a couple of homes we passed made that point clear. I hoped there were still people inside and that there would be a similar sign at my house.

I readied myself to make the next sprint when Drav halted me with a hand on my shoulder. Like last night, he'd kept me from running into any of the infected. He watched everything carefully, and if he spotted something I didn't, he nudged me in a different direction.

Now, I glanced at him while he alertly searched the streets.

"Drav?"

"Mya, stay."

He walked off, but didn't go too far before he stopped. It wasn't until I heard the quiet rustle of fabric and a spatter of liquid that I gathered he was relieving himself. I turned away, my cheeks still hot as I tried to give him as much privacy as possible. Had he been relieving himself outside all along? How had I not noticed?

Drav returned to my side, and I moved to the next area of cover, refusing to acknowledge that he'd just gone to the bathroom in the open street.

My anxiety grew the closer we got to my neighborhood because I had noticed a few houses that were lit up. A living person wouldn't want to draw attention to themselves; they would have turned off the lights. We crossed the road where my elementary best friend, Amber, lived. I didn't have the heart to glance at her house to see if there were any signs of life.

We crossed between two more houses with fences, where Drav lifted me over his shoulder and jumped, before we reached my street. Halfway down, the familiar sight of my house greeted me. Instead of rushing forward to the next tree, I hesitated. I couldn't shake the worry that once I got to my house, the lights would be on and there would be slow, unnatural movement in the windows or the windows would be dark with no signs of life, and Drav and I would go inside and he would rip off the heads of my family. I shuddered at the thought.

Drav put a hand on my shoulder again when I would have moved. I stayed by the tree while Drav disappeared for a moment. Instead of relieving himself, I heard the distinct snap and squelch I'd come to associate with his head ripping. I tried not to freak out. He didn't just kill a member of my family, did he? No, I had to stay positive that they were safe. Ryan's last text warned me about the hounds. That meant he'd known what was happening. The thought of his last text had me touching my back pocket to reassure myself my phone was still there.

Drav rejoined me, and I sprinted across the street, ducking behind a large SUV that belonged to our neighbors only two houses away. From my angle, I could see my house. The blinds were drawn, and the lights were off. Excitement, fear, and emotional exhaustion had my hands shaking.

I ran from my hiding spot, heading straight for my house. Before I could reach for the doorknob, my hand met unrelenting flesh. I looked up in surprise and found Drav frowning down at me.

"No, Mya."

"This is my home. My family is in there."

"No. Drav go."

"You can't," I said in panic. If he went in there, he might kill my family.

"No. They're fine, safe. I need to go in." I tried to step around him, but he blocked me.

"No."

"Yes, Drav."

In my desperation to get inside I forgot who I was dealing with and pushed on his chest to emphasize my point. I swallowed hard and backed up fearful of how he would react. He didn't do much more than scowl at me, but he made his stance clear. He wouldn't let me in.

"What if we go in together?" I asked, attempting to compromise. "But you can't hurt anyone. Please."

He didn't look happy about it, but he could tell I wasn't going to budge.

"Yes?" I prompted.

"Yes."

He moved aside, and I set my hand on the knob. For a moment, I couldn't bring myself to turn it. I sucked in a breath and twisted. The door caught, locked of course.

"Drav, I need you to open the door, but just open it."

I moved out of his way. He grabbed hold of the doorknob, gave it a sharp turn, and put his shoulder to the door. The frame cracked, and the door swung inwards revealing an inky darkness.

Drav touched the edge of my shirt and coiled it in his hold. We entered together. I didn't hear anything, and I worried what that meant.

Fear bubbled up my chest. I couldn't hold it in anymore.

"Mom? Dad? Ryan?"

My brother's name came out as a hoarse cry, which Drav smothered with his hand. His low growl rose around us.

A sick dread twisted in my stomach as I held still and listened.

Please not my family, I thought.

A soft feline growl reached me, and a sob of relief escaped. I pushed Drav's hand from my mouth.

"Pots," I said softly. "Come here, kitty kitty."

The cat hissed in the darkness before us, and Drav growled in response.

"It's okay, Drav. It's our cat. A pet."

I tried to step forward but Drav blocked me. Instead of arguing, I stepped back, used the dead bolt to latch the door, and felt for the wall switch.

"I'm turning on the lights," I warned a moment before I did.

Drav grunted, and I squinted as I looked around the entry and dining room.

"No infected. Let's keep checking," I said with relief.

This time when I stepped forward, he moved with me.

Pots shot down the hall when we turned the corner and walked into the kitchen. I barely paid Drav's growl at my cat any attention because a note on the fridge had caught my eye.

I crossed the room and snatched the paper from the magnet.

Mya,
We love you so much. We've seen the dogs and what they do. We're

heading to the cabin and hope you're already there and never read this. But, if you do come home first, stay strong. Stay safe. Get out of town, and try to get to the cabin. We'll be waiting for you there. If you're not there in two days, we'll come find you.
Love, Mom and Dad

I sniffled past the tears and focused on the note Ryan had scribbled below my parents' message.

The dogs hate light. Travel during the day, and hide somewhere bright at night. Left you a present in my closet. Get your ass to the cabin. Love, Ryan.

They hadn't been infected. At least, not here. I wiped my eyes, folded the paper, and tucked it in my back pocket. My fingers brushed my phone and I pulled it out, checking it again. The low battery and no signal didn't give me any hope.

"Mya," Drav said from behind me. I turned and found his watery gaze on mine.

He, like the dogs, didn't like the light. And, since he didn't seem inclined to leave me that meant I'd be traveling in the dark. With the hounds. And the infected. And, according to Jack and Charles, the other shadow men.

"My family isn't here. They headed north." I glanced at a clock. We still had hours of night left. Plenty of time.

"I'm going to grab some things and then we can get moving again."

"No lights," he said, pointing toward the ceiling light.

"I can't see in the dark like you. And the infected aren't attracted to lights. They're attracted to noise. And the hounds are afraid of lights. I'm turning every light on in the house. Here," I said moving to the fridge. I plucked a pair of my Dad's sunglasses off the top. "Put these on and don't touch the lights or...or I'll throw

M.J. HAAG & BECCA VINCENZA

the cat at you."

He frowned at me but took the glasses. I didn't wait to see if he'd use them.

Heading down the hall, I started thinking of what it would take to make it to the cabin. There wouldn't be as many houses to raid for supplies once we left city limits. So I'd need basic things. A water bottle. Simple food. Warmer clothes.

In Ryan's room, I checked the closet and found one of my dad's burns-your-retinas-like-the-sun flashlights on the shelf. Ryan's foresight had me grinning. If any family had a chance at surviving this mess, it would be ours because of Ryan. I reached under his bed hoping for his hiking bag, but found the space empty. Having the bag would have made my life easier but there were other options.

I turned around and almost face-planted into Drav's chest. The smooth skin of his pec brushed my nose before I backed up a step.

He looked down at me. Despite the tinted lenses of the sunglasses, I could still see his eyes watering a little bit.

"Can you see better? With the glasses on?"

"Yes. No."

"So, just a little better?"

"Yes. Mya go outside."

"Not yet. I need to grab some more stuff."

Going to my parents' room, I looked for the next thing that would make my life easier...something for Drav to wear now and several spares for later. His head ripping, while it kept me safe, was disgusting and messy.

Dad's robust figure meant the shirts had a decent amount of girth, but he didn't even come close to Drav's height. As I studied the selection I had to choose from, I wondered if any of them would even reach Drav's navel.

I tossed a few dark options on my parents' bed.

"Try those on. I'm going to grab some clean clothes for myself."

In my room, I stuffed an old backpack with two clean changes of clothes, the flashlight, and a sweatshirt. I shouldered the bag and turned to find Drav, still shirtless, standing in my room. His continued shirtlessness didn't surprise me. My reflection in the mirror just behind him did.

Dark spatters and splotches covered my face and shirt. Stepping closer to the mirror, I cringed at the dot that stuck to my skin dangerously close to my mouth. Infected blood. My stomach churned and a hint of panicked paranoia burrowed into my mind. What did it take to become infected? A bite from a hound, yes, but were there other ways? Obviously so, because it was spreading like crazy. Bites from the infected. Charles had said that, hadn't he? Bites were a form of fluid exchange...like ingesting a drop of blood. How close had I come to being infected without even knowing it?

A chill chased through me. I didn't want to touch the blood but I wanted it off. Now.

"Are we safe in here?" I asked.

"Yes."

"For how long?"

"Long."

"Ok. I'm going to clean up. This blood is giving me a mental twitch."

Without waiting for a response, I paced down the hall to the bathroom I shared with Ryan. I started closing the door and groaned when Drav stopped it with the flat of his hand.

"Mya, no."

"Drav, I'm not running away again. I promise. I'm cleaning the blood off me and changing my clothes. You don't need to see that. I'll be out when I'm done."

"Infected outside. Hounds outside."

"Yeah, I know. That's why I'm inside with all the lights on."

He studied me from behind his lenses before grunting and

releasing his hold on the door. He even backed up a step. But he didn't walk away. I closed the door in his face and locked it.

"Mya," I heard through the door.

"Drav, stay out."

I pulled off my clothes, started the shower, and stepped in. I didn't care that the water still ran cold. I needed the blood off me.

Before I'd wet more than my shins, the door splintered and a bang filled the room. A startled scream escaped me, followed by another when the curtain and rod were completely ripped from the wall.

CHAPTER TWELVE

Drav and I stared at each other. For a moment, I'd thought an infected had broken in, and relief swelled at the sight of him before anger overwhelmed it. What the hell had he barged in for? His gaze remained locked on my very exposed breasts then moved lower. Fear of Drav began to worm its way back into my mind.

I slapped one arm across my chest and used the other to shield my lady bits. It didn't stop him from staring.

"Drav, leave."

"No."

He tilted his head, continuing his perusal, and frowned. My panic started to rise.

"Boobs," he said, pointing at my chest. Then he pointed at his own. "No boobs." Next, he grabbed at his happy stick with one hand and reached for my crotch with the other.

I pressed back against the tile and swatted his hand away.

"Yeah. Congratulations. You've noticed I have no penis. Most girls don't. Now stop staring and give me back the shower curtain so I can finish washing."

He bent down and reached for the fallen curtain and rod, but his gaze zeroed in on my crotch once more. He forgot about the curtain and leaned forward.

"Back off Drav or I'm going to kick you in the damn face. This isn't anatomy class." Fear shuddered through me.

"No penis. See better?"

"Hell no!"

He grunted and straightened. Then he focused on the now steaming water and the shower head. He raised his hand and put his fingers in the water. He sniffed them and grunted again.

My heart thundered in my chest as I watched him reach for the string holding his pants up.

"Stop." The word came out breathless in my growing panic.

He froze and blinked at me, an action I began to suspect he did when he didn't understand something. Figuring I had little to lose by stating the truth, I started talking.

"I'm terrified. Of the infected. Of the hounds. Of you. Of why you didn't kill me. I can't keep going like this. I just wanted to go home to know my family was safe. But my family isn't here. I want my family. I want to be safe."

He tilted his head at me.

"I didn't kill you. Boobs. No penis."

"You didn't kill me because I'm a girl?"

"Yes."

I swallowed hard and blinked against the sudden sting in my eyes. Would he now start doing more than looking and groping?

"What are you going to do?" My voice warbled.

He blinked back at me. "Keep you safe. Take you home."

Too afraid to hope and too afraid to be anything but more afraid, I sniffled.

"Mya, clean."

"I can't with you watching me," I said, desperate for him to leave and let me just think for a minute.

"Why?" he asked.

"Because it makes me uncomfortable."

He bent down and picked up the shower curtain and rod and handed it to me. Sacrificing my cover, I reached for it. He pulled back a little bit, his gaze inspecting my bits again.

"Please just let me have the shower curtain."

He grunted and gave it over. I quickly put the tension rod back in place, knowing Drav wasn't leaving.

"No touching the curtain," I said, staring at the white material blocking me from his view.

"Clean, Mya." He said it like an order.

"Fine." I exhaled shakily and stepped into the spray.

Paranoia still held me in its grip. I felt certain I would somehow become infected. So I kept my eyes and mouth closed as I soaped and rinsed. Then I began to worry that Drav might try to watch me while my eyes were closed. Because of that, I took the fastest shower of my life.

When I turned off the water, Drav spoke up from the other side of the curtain.

"Mya, no. Let me shower."

His increasing spurts of sensible speech continued to surprise me. Who learned that fast?

"I'll turn the shower back on for you. But, you need to leave now so I can get a towel and dry off."

I waited behind the curtain, listening. The door opened followed by a soft sound that I thought might be it closing. It was hard to tell since I didn't know in what condition he'd left the door. I hadn't even thought to look at the damage after he'd ripped away the shower curtain.

I hesitated a few moments, then hearing nothing, I peeked out.

Drav stood by the bathroom closet with a hand towel in one hand and a folded bath towel in the other. When he heard the curtain, he turned toward me and held both up.

The pieces of material in his hands barely registered as I stared at his now very naked bottom half.

"Towel?" he asked.

I couldn't help but look. Yes, he'd waved his goods around when we'd first met, but I'd been scared beyond imagination. I still felt jumpy and freaked out, but I also started to believe him. He acted like he'd never seen a girl before. He'd killed any infected or hound that came near me for the past two days, and he'd admitted he wanted to keep me safe. On top of all of that, he did help me get home.

His eyes still seemed weird to me. Also, the ease in which he killed really worried me. And, his semi-erection didn't ease my fears about what might yet happen if I continued in his company. But, for now, it seemed like I'd gotten my wish. I was safe.

"Yeah, those are towels. We use the bigger ones to dry our bodies. The smaller one is for drying our hands when we wash them in the sink."

He grunted and brought the bigger towel to me. Keeping the curtain between us, I reached for it. This time, he didn't tease me by keeping it out of my reach.

With the towel in hand, I ducked back behind the curtain and quickly dried off. The big towel adequately covered my torso so I could step out without exposing myself.

Drav hadn't moved, which made my exit a little cozy. He took the opportunity to lean in to sniff me.

"Why do you do that? Smell me, I mean. Do I smell bad? Good? Please don't say you think of chicken when you smell me."

"You smell good. Not Drav." He didn't lean back to speak, so his words, close to my ear, made me shiver.

"I smell different than you?" I asked, trying to ignore how very uncomfortable he was making me.

"Yes."

"It's probably the soap," I said.

I turned my back to him, pulled open the curtain, and reached for one of the bottles on the shower caddy. Drav's hand slid up along my leg.

"Hey," I said, quickly spinning around holding the bottle. "No touching."

"Why no touching?"

"Because it makes me uncomfortable."

"What not makes Mya uncomfortable?"

"At this point in my life, everything is making me uncomfortable," I said, giving him a flat look.

"Towel uncomfortable?" The sly way he said it, and the slight upward curve on his mouth, made me snort.

"Nice try, buddy. The towel is staying on, and you're keeping your hands to yourself. Now, do you want me to explain how to use this stuff or not."

"Explain."

I quickly went over turning the water on and off and how to wash and rinse—along with a caution not to let soap get in his eyes —and suggested he remove his bandages.

"Mya clean it."

"Nope, not this time. The shower will clean it."

He grunted then tore off the bandages without a wince. The wound already appeared well on its way to being healed.

Lacking any hint of modesty, he lifted his leg high and stepped into the shower. Swallowing hard at the well-endowed sight of him, I turned away to grab my bag and leave the bathroom. The sound of the curtain closing and the shower starting assured me that he now believed I wouldn't run. And, I wouldn't. A considerable number of zombie infested miles still separated me from the cabin. I had the smarts to know that sticking with Drav increased my chances of seeing my family alive.

Holding the towel tightly around my body, I made my way down the hall to my room. Even with all the lights on, the house felt eerie in its silence. Usually, Ryan had music playing or a TV show on, and the washer or drier would be running non-stop. I couldn't help but smile a little at the memory. It always amazed Mom how much laundry four people could produce.

In my room, I hurried to dig through my drawers for fresh clothes. Although Drav had set aside his curiosity about our physical differences just now, I knew it would resurface if he finished his shower before I managed to dress. Dropping the towel, I put on fresh underwear and a clean bra. It almost made me feel human again.

I tugged on a pair of jeans and a tank-top before digging in my closet for an old hoodie. Walking here had been chilly, and it would only grow more so as the days passed. The hoodie I found had enough substance to it to keep me warm. I put it on, glad to get the mass of wet hair off my back.

After towel drying my hair, I searched the top of my dresser for a hair-tie. I scraped my fingers through the wet strands and wrapped my long, thick hair into a tight bun on the back of my head.

Glancing around the room, I tried to decide what more I needed in my bag. The thought of the blood splatter so close to my lips made me shudder. Soaps and washcloths were a must.

"Mya," Drav bellowed.

I poked my head into the hallway. Drav stood just outside the bathroom door, dripping wet from his shower. His long black hair, the only thing covering him, hung loosely over his chest almost to his bellybutton.

When he saw me, rage lit his eyes. He stormed toward me while stringing together a bunch of words and noises I couldn't understand.

"Whoa, what? Drav, what's wrong?"

He clutched his hair, then touched my head. I frowned, confused and just a bit afraid.

"You don't like my hair up? You had yours up."

"Where hair, Mya?"

He was having a fit over my hair?

"I tied it back."

His hand gripped my shoulder, and he spun me around. I felt a tug on my bun. A moment later, my wet hair came tumbling down. He combed his fingers through the strands and pulled them away from my neck. A glance back confirmed he was once again smelling my hair. A contented rumble sounded from his chest.

Okay, time to stop whatever was happening.

"Please let go of my hair and go put some pants on. You're making me uncomfortable."

Drav let out a quiet growl, clearly agitated that I stopped him mid-sniff, but he released my hair and left the room. I exhaled slowly, releasing any lingering anxiety. The things that set him off would probably never make sense to me.

Focusing on my bag, I considered what we would need. It all depended on how long we'd be gone and how we'd be traveling. The cabin was a little over an hour away, roughly, by car. However, taking a vehicle seemed out of the question, given what Drav had done to the truck. Plus, the noise of the engine would draw too much attention from the infected. That left walking, which would take forever, especially since Drav would only allow us to walk at night. I tried doing the math in my head, using a five mile an hour estimate, and guessed it would take at least three nights of walking, minimum. More if we ran into trouble. So, I needed to pack light. I couldn't be weighed down if I needed to run.

I added three more pair of underwear and socks to what I already had packed, then left my bag on my bed while I went to my parents' room to see what would fit Drav. He joined me a moment later. This time with pants on.

"Go ahead and try those shirts on," I said, pointing to the shirts

I'd laid out on the bed. I turned back to the closet to start searching for more options.

Behind me I heard the sound of fabric rustling, and I glanced at Drav in the mirror.

Drav tried to pull the first t-shirt over his head, but the material got stuck by his ears. I hurried to him and helped tug the shirt the rest of the way down. It circled his neck snuggly, but he didn't seem to notice. Instead, he continued to attempt squeezing into what I'd given him. A stitch ripped.

"Hold up. You can ditch that one."

I started to help yank the tight fabric over his head, but he wrapped his hands around the neckline and ripped the top down the middle. I stared at the two pieces. He'd just ripped the shirt I had given my dad after I finished my freshman year at OU.

"Oooh-kay, try this one." I handed him an oversized flannel shirt.

Drav manage to tug the shirt on, but the sleeves were tight around the biceps. One good flex and he'd be sleeveless.

"Hang on. Let me go grab some of my brother's stuff." Ryan took after our dad but often bought a size too big to use when working out.

I rifled through Ryan's things, looking for his workout clothes. The athletic shorts would probably work if Drav needed something beside his sturdy pants. I tugged out a couple of longer navy t-shirts and a pair of loose black shorts.

With my new finds bundled in my arms, I went to my room for scissors so I could cut into the neckline. Drav walked in before I finished.

"Got more shirts for you to try."

I held up one of the t-shirts. He pulled it over his head. While the neckline was looser, thanks to the cut I'd made, the rest of the shirt molded to him like a second skin once he got his arms through the sleeves.

"A bit snug but it will do. Let's find a bag and we can head out."

"Head out?"

"We have to go to my grandfather's cabin. North of here."

I tucked his extra clothes into the bag with my stuff then went to the bathroom for the washcloth and soap. I was very tempted to take the toilet paper, just in case, but knew I didn't have much room left. Two travel packs of tissues were the next best thing.

Drav watched me from the doorway as I set everything on the bathroom counter and opened a vanity drawer. Before looking in my bedroom mirror, I hadn't realized how disgusting I'd gotten. Now that I knew what to expect while traveling with Drav, I pulled three bands from my stash of hair ties.

I raked my fingers through my hair to throw it up in a messy bun. Drav grabbed my wrist gently and stopped the movements.

"Come." He nudged me out of the bathroom back to my room where he tried steering me to the bed.

"No, Drav. We still have plenty of night left. We have to go, not sleep." Finding my family already gone had been a huge disappointment. The longer we stayed, the longer it would take us to find them, and the less chance I had of finding them healthy.

When I turned to go back to the bathroom, he picked me up and sat me down on the bed. I glared up at him.

"Stay. Mya hair." He tugged at his strands then gently did the same to mine.

"Are you telling me I can't go outside with a wet head? Because, that's dumb."

"No. Mya hair. Stay."

He sat beside me and combed his fingers through my hair.

"We don't have time for this," I said, growing frustrated with his apparent hair fetish.

I moved to stand, but his hand caught my thigh and I sat back down with an "oof."

"Hair," he said, sharply.

He leaned in to smell it again, but before I could complain some more, his fingers delved into my hair. With quick, sure movements, he created three sections, gently parting the strands. I sighed and resigned myself to allowing him to play with my hair for a few minutes, hoping it would be enough time to get it out of his system.

A couple of times, he found knots, which he slowly worked through. I focused on the mirror on the other side of the room and watched as he fashioned three French braids, two on the sides and one on the top of my head. When he finished, I had three braids tied together in the back. I looked stunningly badass, and his skill at braiding amazed me. The hair style would keep my hair much cleaner.

I twisted on the bed and patted his knee.

"Thank you."

I left before he could respond.

In the bathroom, I grabbed the items I had planned to take. From there, I went to the kitchen and filled two reusable water bottles. I was checking the cabinets for light-weight portable food when Drav joined me. He'd braided his hair much like mine.

"Are you hungry?" I asked.

"Are you?"

"I suppose we should eat before we head out."

I pulled out a can of pineapple chunks, popped the top open, and set it in front of Drav before turning back to the cupboards. We had a ton of canned food, but that would be too heavy.

"Mya."

"Hmm."

Drav captured me by the shoulders and led me back to the table.

"Mya, hungry. Eat."

He didn't give me much of a choice. Sitting, I stuffed a chunk of pineapple in my mouth then attempted to stand again. He pushed me back into my seat and tried to feed me another piece. He didn't relent and started to growl in frustration when I kept trying to get up and pack. I eventually gave in and ate the food he offered.

Once we finished with our small meal, he helped me pack some granola bars and trail mix. I lifted my bag, judging the weight of it. Manageable. Sliding it onto my back, I looked around the kitchen one last time.

The waning moon, still high in the sky, confirmed we had plenty of night remaining. But, leaving proved harder than I'd thought. A quiet part of my mind, because I had refused to acknowledge it, reared its ugly head.

What if this was the last time I saw home?

I shook my head. My family was my home, not the house or objects inside of it. None of that stuff mattered. Well, besides our cat. However, considering his reaction to Drav, he couldn't come with us. I placed his bag of food out on the floor with the top open. He would have to self-feed, but I knew he would be okay until we could come back and get him.

Drav went outside first and beckoned me forward. I set the direction, heading northwest toward my family's cabin.

CHAPTER THIRTEEN

Once we left the last of the city lights and infected behind us, Drav walked beside me. We didn't talk. Noise carried too far in the dark. Even the soft brush of our passing through the dried grass worried me. However, Drav didn't seem as tense now that we'd abandoned the city. He walked with fluid ease, taking slower steps so I didn't have to jog to keep up as we traveled the countryside.

Before the hellhounds invaded, we would have seen headlights on the roads we crossed or heard the distant hum of engines on the highway we passed. Instead, there was silence. Not even the chirp of crickets or chatter of small animals could be heard. The silence was the one unsettling, continuous reminder of just how much the world had changed. So, I focused on the slight sound of our passing until something distracted me.

In the trees to our right, I saw a dot of light. White, not red. It disappeared, but I kept my eye on the spot and saw the light again a few feet later. A distant yard light to a house nestled in the trees. I wondered if the people who lived there had escaped the notice of the hounds and the infected. I hoped so. If they could survive this close to the city, my family had an even better chance at our cabin.

Drav grabbed my arm without warning, jerking me to a stop. The aggressive way he angled himself in front of me and growled had my pulse spiking. I froze and peered ahead, trying to see what had provoked him. However, beyond the shadowy shapes of trees, shrubs, and grass, I couldn't see a damn thing. I moved closer to Drav and wished for my flashlight. I should have walked with it in my hand instead of stuffing it in my bag.

Drav growled again. From the darkness came a faint, answering growl. Something was definitely out there.

Slowly, Drav straightened and said something. It wasn't English, just a bunch of garbled nonsense to me. However, the same sounds came back from the dark. Another shadow man.

"Crap."

Drav loosened his hold on my arm and looked at me. Gently, he ran his fingers over the area he'd grabbed.

"I'm sorry, Mya. Arm fall off?" he questioned quietly.

I almost told him it wouldn't but reconsidered as I thought of the easy strength he'd used to pull the heads from all the infected bodies.

"Not yet. Who's out there?" I asked, looking into the darkness again.

A distance ahead of us, a shadow moved, steadily growing bigger. Big like Drav, confirming my suspicion.

"Is he going to want to kill me?" I asked, unable to stop myself.

"No."

Drav looked away from me and spoke to the approaching figure. I heard my name thrown in with the gibberish. When Drav quieted, the shadow answered in a growly voice. Drav listened then looked down at me.

"Ghua good. Ghua family."

Ghua? Based on the tone of their conversation, I didn't feel reassured.

The new shadow man had finally walked close enough that I

could see the subtle differences between the two men. While the dark loose shirt and pants seemed similar in style and color to what Drav had worn when I'd first met him, this shadow man's skin shone even darker than Drav's, almost black. The same reptilian like eyes blinked at me. However, Ghua's seemed more yellow than green and much creepier because of the coloring. His long black hair hung in a single braid that didn't quite match Drav's in length but still extended well past his shoulders.

Ghua said something more then started to crouch. Drav laughed, a first. The deep, soft sound unnerved me.

"What's going on?" I asked quietly.

"Mya, stay," Drav said, taking my shoulder and guiding me back a step. He let go and turned back to Ghua, whose white teeth flashed in the dark as he grinned. Drav crouched low and tensed. My stomach dipped and twisted sickeningly as I grasped what was about to happen.

They flew at each other. The impact made a deep thud in the dark. A growl escaped one of them as they grappled. Seeing the way Drav's muscles bulged in effort made me swallow hard. In all the head ripping he'd done, he'd never exerted himself the way he did now. Just how strong was he?

I had my answer when he laughed and flipped Ghua over his back. Ghua landed with a thump. Drav reached out with one hand and picked him up by the neck. Ghua punched Drav in the ribs, drawing a pained grunt from him. Drav didn't let go, though. With his other hand, Drav gripped the top of Ghua's head in a familiar move.

"Drav, no," I said, far too loudly for my own comfort.

Drav paused, and Ghua stopped trying to hit Drav to look at me.

"I thought he was your family. Family don't kill each other."

Drav grunted, let go of Ghua, and said something I didn't understand. Ghua laughed in return.

Drav started talking again, and Ghua stared at me the entire time, his gaze shifting from my face to my hair then back to my face. His barely discernable brows started to sink lower on his forehead the longer Drav spoke. I didn't like not knowing what they were saying, but I wasn't kept wondering for long. Drav said a familiar word, and Ghua's gaze dropped to my chest.

Ghua made a noise of disbelief and tore his gaze from me to stare at Drav. When Ghua spoke, the tone seemed rough and demanding.

Drav began speaking once more and gestured with his hands near his chest. When he said "boobs," I cringed but kept quiet. My difference had kept Drav from killing me. If being an oddity kept me safer with Ghua, too, then Drav could explain away.

Ghua said something and they stopped talking. Both turned to look at me.

"Ghua want Mya to show boobs."

I crossed my arms over my chest.

"I am not showing my boobs to anyone, Drav. I told you, it makes me uncomfortable."

"Yes," Drav said before speaking to Ghua.

Ghua listened quietly until Drav gestured between his legs. Ghua made a choked sound, grabbed at his package, and spoke a few syllables. Drav grunted acknowledgment, and my cheeks turned red when Ghua's attention whipped to me. His gaze swept my face, then my chest, and finally he ducked his head a little as he tried his best to see through my pants.

Even clothed with jeans and a hoodie, I felt completely naked and exposed to his inquisitive gaze.

"Yep. No penis," I said.

Ghua started talking fast to Drav, who started talking just as fast back. Both fell completely silent again. Then, Ghua moved toward me.

"Ah...what's he doing?" I stepped behind Drav and kept him

between me and Ghua when Ghua tried to follow.

"Mya, Ghua smell you."

"I don't want to be smelled. You've smelled me enough for both of you."

Drav caught me in his arms and pulled me to his chest. I struggled to push away from him, but he held firm.

"Drav, let me go." My words were muffled but still clear. He didn't release me, though.

Something brushed against my back. My face pressed into Dad's old shirt, I listened to Ghua get a good whiff of my hair. Anger boiled inside me. Drav held me still so his friend, who'd just wanted to see my boobs, could smell me. Hell no. I opened my mouth and bit Drav's chest. He grunted and abruptly released me. I surged back and solidly collided with Ghua. His arms came around me, and his hands landed just above my boobs.

Eyes wide, my mouth dropped open as his hands drifted lower and he thoroughly groped me.

Before I could yell, Drav stopped rubbing where I'd bitten him and growled. For a heartbeat, I thought he meant the growl for me. But when Ghua immediately let go, and Drav silently opened his arms for me without looking away from Ghua, I launched myself at Drav. He caught me, and his hand gently settled on the back of my head as he held me close.

He spoke to Ghua briefly in their language. When they quieted, I lifted my head enough to look up at Drav. He stared down at me in his unblinking way.

"Don't ever do that again. I'm not a toy. You don't get to share me."

"I won't share you. Ever," he said.

Not quite the reassurance I'd wanted. The way his hold had tightened on me just a smidge when he'd spoken didn't reassure me either. I eased myself from his arms and put some distance between us. He looked me over before focusing on Ghua, who watched us closely.

I studied the darkness around us while they started yet another quiet conversation. Not only were we wasting precious travel time, we weren't being quiet.

"Is it smart to be out in the open talking like this?" I asked, interrupting them. "How well do your hellhounds hear? I really don't want to get bitten by one."

Drav grunted and Ghua spoke briefly, gesturing back the way he'd come. Drav turned to me.

"Ghua go home with me and you. Keep Mya safe."

I didn't want Ghua traveling with us. He was still trying to see through my hoodie and my pants. But, standing in one place served no purpose.

"Fine. But no touching me."

"Yes," Drav said. Ghua answered with a clear, "yes" as well before he turned and headed back the way he'd just come.

Drav nudged me to follow.

"How are you learning my language so quickly?" I asked, walking.

Drav tapped his pointed ear.

"Just by listening?" I said.

"Yes."

"That's crazy."

Since Ghua was leading us, I moved closer to Drav.

"Do we have to stay with him? He's giving me the creeps with all his staring."

Ahead of us, Ghua grunted, which made me worry.

"Does he understand me?" I whispered to Drav.

"Yes."

After that, I kept quiet.

We didn't walk very far before Ghua veered into the trees. I kept close to Drav and tried to walk and breathe as quietly as possible while what little light the quarter moon provided faded even further under the barren branches.

When we stepped into a clearing with a house, Ghua headed straight for it. I tugged on Drav's arm.

"I don't want to go in there."

"Mya not stay outside."

The familiar phrase he used to get me inside for the day worried me.

"We're done walking for the night?"

"Yes."

"But why? We have hours of dark left yet."

"Drav listen to Ghua for the night."

I frowned trying to understand what he meant by that.

"He's your boss for tonight or you want to talk to him tonight?"

"I want to talk to Ghua tonight. We're walking"—he said something I didn't know—"night."

"Tonight we're going to talk with Ghua and tomorrow night we're walking again?" I guessed, hopefully.

"Yes."

"Without Ghua tomorrow night?"

"Yes."

"Fine. But no killing anyone in that house unless they're infected."

Drav grunted and spoke to Ghua who waited several yards away. Ghua answered then started toward the already broken in front door, and I realized whoever had been in there was probably already dead.

Following Drav into the house, I stepped into a neat and cozy living room. Drav closed the door behind me and started talking to Ghua. Unwilling to stand there and listen to a meaningless exchange, I went to the couch, turned on the lamp next to it, and sank into the comfy cushions with a sigh. Having a moment to just relax seemed surreal, and I soaked it up. Who knew what would happen from one moment to the next in this new world. I needed to start taking what I could get.

When the conversation stopped, I glanced at the pair and found them watching me.

"What? Am I not supposed to sit? We're staying the rest of the night, right?"

"Yes," Drav said, walking toward me. He looked at the couch then sat beside me. He studied the cushions a moment before running a hand over them.

"Comfy, isn't it?" I said.

"Yes."

Ghua went to a chair and sat as well.

Staying here with Ghua made me anxious. He still seemed too interested in the fact that I had boobs and no penis. Ignoring Ghua's stare, I turned to Drav.

"So what is he to you? Your brother? Cousin? Uncle?"

"No."

"Dad? Grandpa?" Ghua didn't look old enough to be either. "Nephew?"

"No."

"Oh, come on. I don't think I missed any...unless he's some kind of in-law."

"No."

"You're annoying me," I said, with a flat stare.

"Ghua is family, but not family."

"He's a friend?"

"Yes," Drav said happily.

I made a sound of disbelief. But, I didn't say anything more. Soon the two of them started talking, mixing English with their words. The more Drav said, the more Ghua started to say.

"Hold up," I said, interrupting them. "Do you really only need to hear a word once to understand it?"

"Yes," Drav said.

"Holy shit."

CHAPTER FOURTEEN

I TRIED TO WRAP MY HEAD AROUND THE CONCEPT OF INSTANT learning while the two of them continued their conversation. It made sense why Drav spoke such limited and broken English since I was the only one talking to him. Fear of being discovered by something that seemed to want to kill all humans had kept me from saying a lot.

Quietly, I considered the implications of their ability. That Drav could understand when I explained something could work in my favor.

Since their conversation contained only a few words of English, I lost interest in it and decided to go search for food. They stopped talking as soon as I walked into the hallway. Knowing Drav's concern, I peeked my head back into the room.

"Just going to the kitchen to find food."

Ghua's yellow eyes watched me intently, making my skin crawl. Drav grunted, pulling my attention to him. He stood and came toward me, which didn't bother me until Ghua stood as well.

"You can stay in there and talk."

"No, go to kitchen with Mya," Drav said, slipping past me to head down the hallway. I followed, not wanting to be left alone with Ghua.

The kitchen looked as if the world hadn't been upturned. Cozy and clean, it seemed like a place where someone's grandma had baked countless cookies.

Drav opened a cupboard door, and Ghua watched him while I continued to look around. My eyes caught on a dirty plate beside the sink. I stepped closer and saw one side of the double sink half filled with water. Clean dishes occupied the drying rack on the other side of the sink. A towel draped over one plate like it had just been set down. I couldn't look away from it.

"Were there people here?" I asked without looking at Ghua.

He spoke in his language, and Drav answered.

"There were infected outside."

I sighed and rubbed my face. It didn't mean anything that the people here hadn't escaped infection. They were close to the city. In the more rural locations, like our cabin, there would be less risk. My family would be fine.

Determined not to worry about what I couldn't control, I went to the pantry door as Drav searched in the cupboards. The closet was much bigger than I expected, and I tugged the string for the light in order to see.

There were cans of fruits on one shelf, boxed food on another, jugs of water and vinegar and jars of homemade jelly and pickles on another. The selection made my mouth water. Since Drav enjoyed the peaches and pineapples we had before, I grabbed those then stared longingly at a box of mac and cheese. It hadn't been that long ago since I had a hot meal, but it felt like years. If we were staying the night, I didn't see why I couldn't eat more than canned fruit. I snagged the box and came out.

Ghua stood with his back against the fridge, arms crossed. He and Drav were speaking again but more quietly this time.

"Do you guys want to try some mac and cheese?"

They stopped their talking and glanced at me.

"Never mind." I'd make it and if they wanted some, I'd share.

Setting the fruit and the box on the table, I turned toward the fridge.

"Excuse me. I need to get in there," I said, pointing at it.

Ghua moved to the side, and I stepped forward and pulled the door open. The homeowners might have had a stocked pantry, but the items in the fridge were on the light side. The half-gallon container of milk and the half sticks of butter made me think again of someone's grandma alone during that first night the hellhounds had appeared. Anger welled up inside of me. Why had this happened? I glanced at Drav, wanting to ask questions. Could I trust him to be honest? I just didn't know. Yes, he'd kept me safe. But, he admitted he'd only spared me because of my gender. What if my questions made him mad? Would his consideration for my gender go out the window?

"Mya?" Drav asked.

I realized I was just standing in front of an open fridge, staring at nothing, so I grabbed the milk and butter then turned around.

"You guys might as well sit," I said with a gesture at the table. "This will take a while."

While I searched for a pot, the guys took seats around the table. They continued to speak softly and I tried to listen to see if I could learn anything more about why they were here. However, I really couldn't understand much of what they said.

Filling the pot with water distracted me with a more pressing need. I had to pee. Ignoring it, I brought the pot to the stove and switched on the burner. However, the urge didn't go away. But, I didn't want the two of them hovering outside the bathroom door.

In an attempt to sneak out of the kitchen, I roamed the room until I reached the opening to the hallway.

"Mya, no."

Of course Drav had noticed.

"Just going to the bathroom. Can you keep an eye on the stove?"

Drav didn't say anything else so I swiftly retreated.

I found a half-bath tucked under the stairs leading to the second floor and quickly stepped in and shut the door. Unbuttoning my pants, I sat on the toilet placed under the sloped part of the ceiling.

I was finishing up when the doorknob twisted.

"Drav, I'm still in here."

It didn't stop him. The door swung open before I had my pants all the way up. Instead of Drav, Ghua stood in the doorway, watching with rapt interest as I finished yanking up my jeans. My cheeks flushed with embarrassment and anger.

Where the hell was Drav?

"Ghua." Drav's voice came from the hall as if my thoughts had brought him.

Ghua flinched as Drav's lighter gray hand landed heavily on his shoulder with a loud clap. Ghua was pulled backward out of the doorway and replaced by Drav. His gaze swept over me from my head to my toes, and I hurriedly buttoned my jeans, grateful that my underwear had at least been up before Ghua had barged in.

Drav reached out and touched my cheek where I could feel the heated stain of embarrassment the strongest. His gaze held mine as his fingers smoothed over the spot. Abruptly, he turned and left me staring at an empty doorway.

Shakily exhaling, I went to wash my hands, but a thump of flesh meeting flesh in the hall interrupted me. Wiping my clean hands on my jeans, I cautiously peeked out the door.

Drav and Ghua stood near the base of the stairs. Ghua reached up and touched the blood dripping from his nose. He looked at his wet fingers then at Drav, who threw another punch. Ghua grinned, his smile bloody and his eyes sparkling with delight.

Drav drew back for another punch that Ghua didn't even try to block. Ghua's head snapped back, but he still didn't retaliate. He just stood there happily letting blood drip onto the floor while Drav beat him.

What was wrong with these two?

Drav took a step back just then.

"Friend," Ghua said.

Drav nodded and stuck his arm out. Ghua clasped Drav's forearm tightly, pulled him in for a quick hug, and released him with a shove.

Seriously? We had to stop walking for this?

Ignoring the pair, I stalked back to the kitchen and poured the noodles into the now boiling water. I felt a stab of betrayal that Drav had already forgiven Ghua for coming into the bathroom to sneak a peek. How ridiculous. Drav had done the same thing to me when we'd met. In fact, he had been much more forward than Ghua. I shook my head and stirred the noodles.

A chair scraped against the floor behind me, and I glanced over my shoulder to see the two of them in the kitchen. Ghua sat at the table, and Drav moved near me.

Ghua's eyes met mine, and his lips peeled back into a sharp toothed grin. I wished he would just go away. Glancing at the clock, I noted the time and turned back to the pot. I watched the pasta boil and let my mind wander as the two conversed in their language.

For the next eight minutes, I considered what was happening to the world outside this old house. What had caused the hellhounds and shadow men to appear? The obvious answer was the earthquakes. But why and how had the earthquakes brought them? The mysteries of our world were still being solved every day.

But usually only small discoveries. How had we missed an entire species of intelligent beings? I glanced at Drav and considered the possibility that he was an alien.

The water started to boil over, distracting me from my thoughts. I turned down the heat and spooned a noodle out to test it, carefully blowing on the steamy shell before lifting it to my lips. It was still a little too firm when I bit down.

Ghua's chair clattered to the tiled floor as he stood with a growl. I jumped, startled, and turned to stare at him with wide eyes. He spoke sharply to Drav, gesturing at me, then left the room. I glanced at Drav. He stared at the empty hallway. While I didn't mind Ghua leaving, how he left made me nervous.

"Is something wrong?" I asked.

Drav studied me for a moment.

"No. You stay."

He left the kitchen, presumably to talk to Ghua, and I dug out a strainer for the noodles. By the time I finished up the mac and cheese, both men had returned to the kitchen. I set out three plates and spooned equal portions to each plate.

After opening a can of mandarin oranges, I drained the juice and found a bowl to put them in. Both men watched me set the bowl in the middle of the table, but neither reached for the food even after I sat.

I glanced at Ghua, who looked annoyed. Did they think I'd poisoned it or something? Picking up my spoon, I scooped up some noodles. Drav watched with interest but made no move to eat. Ghua watched Drav, his eyes narrowing a fraction. I shoved the hot noodles in my mouth and wanted to sigh happily. It was, by far, not the most elegant meal, but it reminded me of home. Of happier times, eating and sharing with Ryan. Or rather, fighting with Ryan to get the last bit.

"Eat," I said, feeling uncomfortable with their hesitation.

Drav gripped the spoon, scooped some up, and carefully lifted the bite to his lips. I watched as he chewed slowly then with more enthusiasm. After he swallowed, he went for another bite. I followed suit.

Ghua ignored the spoon and scooped his cheesy noodles up with his fingers. He didn't look bothered by the heat and ate with gusto. Whatever had upset Ghua seemed to no longer be a problem. Eventually, Drav gave up on the spoon, too, eating faster without it.

When they cleared their plates, both looked at me expectantly.

"It's all gone. Sorry, guys. Try the oranges."

We finished our meal, and they started talking, mostly in their language. I set the plates on top of the other dirty plate beside the sink and considered washing them. The world was going to shit, and the owner would never return. Who cared about clean dishes? Yet, as I looked at the neatly folded towel, I couldn't walk away. I emptied the sink of the cold water and quickly cleaned up the mess we'd made. When everything was back to the way we'd found it, I left the kitchen for the living room.

The couch called to me, and I cuddled up. The murmur of their voices lulled me, and full from the warm meal, it didn't take long for me to sleep.

A jostle to my arm woke me. I groaned and opened my eyes to find Drav bent over me like he was getting ready to pick me up.

"I can walk," I said.

He didn't move away.

"Back off, I can't get up."

He grunted and took a step back. Once I stood, he led me through the house to one of the bedrooms with a neatly made queen-sized bed. It looked very inviting. Tired and ready to go right back to sleep, I headed for the bed, but Drav stopped me with a tug at my shirt.

It took a moment to understand why. When I did, I pulled my shirt out of his hand.

"Nope. It's staying on. It's not dirty."

Drav huffed but let me climb into bed with my shirt on. He took his off, however, and snatched me around the waist when he joined me.

I fell back to sleep within seconds.

CHAPTER FIFTEEN

SWEAT COATED MY NECK AND CHEST. NOT A PLEASANT SENSATION TO wake to. Drav held me closely, one hand under my shirt, fingers spread so his thumb rested just under my bra line and the tip of his pinky touched the waist of my low riding jeans. The position felt entirely too comfortable despite the sweat.

I grabbed his hand and untangled it from under my clothes. He pressed closer to me, his breath tickling my ear.

"Mya, no," he said, trying to put his hand back.

"Drav, no. You don't get to touch me whenever you want. It's rude. I thought we talked about that."

He sighed and rolled away. Cool air brushed over me as he got out of bed, and I breathed in relief.

"Are you hungry?" he asked.

"Not yet," I said, sitting up.

Bare chested, he stood by the bed, watching me with green eyes that were becoming less unsettling. His gaze moved over my face. Now that I'd met another of his kind and had someone for comparison, I realized Drav didn't look at me the same way as Ghua. Ghua watched me with open curiosity, like a visitor at the zoo. Drav studied me with an expression that said I meant something more. The idea made my stomach dip and dance.

"I'm going to use the bathroom. Without an audience," I said, needing to escape his scrutiny.

He didn't try to follow me when I left the room. I closed myself in the bathroom and looked in the mirror. My cheeks were flushed and my stomach was still twisting and dipping at the way he'd held me. Why had Drav taken an interest in me? Every person he'd encountered since we'd met, he'd killed. He said he hadn't killed me because I was a girl, but what about all the infected females? He'd never hesitated to behead them.

I splashed water on my face to settle my confused thoughts. It didn't really help much. After using the toilet and washing my hands, I hesitated to leave. Had I been smart enough to grab my bag when I'd left the room, I could have brushed my teeth and taken a few more minutes for myself. Instead, I did a quick swish and rinse with water then opened the door.

Drav stood in the hallway. He wore his too small shirt again.

"You might want to look in the closets for something that fits better. That looks weird on you."

He didn't do as I suggested. Instead, he followed me to the kitchen. The window near the sink gave a view of the dusky sky. Another day almost gone. What day was it? Did it even matter? There weren't any schedules to cling to anymore. Just the drive to keep moving. To get to the cabin and ensure my family was safe. The sooner we ate, the sooner we could leave.

I took the eggs out of the fridge and dug some sausage out of the freezer for a big breakfast. Well, dinner, since the sun was close to setting. While the sausage fried, I grabbed my bag and brushed my teeth. Ghua had taken a seat at the table by the time I returned to the kitchen. Ignoring him and his scrutiny, I scrambled some eggs and grabbed three clean plates.

Neither said anything as I set the food before them. Drav again watched me pick up the fork and waited until I'd taken the first bite before trying his own food, which seemed to annoy Ghua. I couldn't wait to leave him. The company of one shadow man was enough for me.

When I finished eating, I took my plate to the sink, washed it, and filled up the water bottle that I'd kept in my bag.

"We ready to go?" I asked Drav.

He glanced at the now dark window.

"Yes, Mya go outside."

"Good." I moved toward the door and, with disappointment, watched Ghua follow Drav.

Outside the house, Ghua gave Drav a clap on his back and then walked away, heading in the direction of Oklahoma City. Drav motioned for me to start through the trees, continuing our way north.

"Everything came from the south, didn't it?"

"Yes."

"Then why is he going back that way?"

"You talk and I learn."

"What the heck does that mean?"

"No word for why he is going back that way."

"Ah." We really needed to up his vocabulary. Just not while we were walking in the zombie infested dark where hellhounds might also roam.

We traveled in silence for an hour before we came to our next major highway. Most roads came and went, barely discernable in the weak moonlight. This highway differed not because of the divided lanes but because of the distant light. Drav didn't try to stop me as I continued toward the far-off beacon. It wasn't until we'd moved much closer that I saw floodlights illuminated the on and off ramps and the over pass. A generator rattled loudly, somewhere near the center of the bridge, the noise blending with the hum of electricity. Excitement bloomed in my chest. Humans had put this here.

Movement to our left caught Drav's attention. He stepped in front of me and stopped our progress.

Frustrated, I leaned to look around him. Before I could ask what he was doing, an infected came sprinting into the light near the on ramp. Its awkward gait and the loose way its arms swung at its sides gave me the shivers. A gun shot rang out. The infected jerked backwards, as if hit in the head, and fell. On the bridge, a person stood and walked to where it had gone down.

"There's people, Drav," I said.

"Mya, no," he said quietly, turning to look down at me with a scowl.

"You seem to like me well-enough. You might like more people if you just try," I said. It wasn't just my desire to be with my own kind that prodded me forward but the need to see who guarded the bridge on the route my parents and Ryan would have taken to the cabin.

"Mya, no."

"What if we stand by those trees and just watch for a while? Maybe you'll change your mind," I said, hopefully.

His gaze swept over my face.

"We go by the trees," he said, nudging me toward their safety.

Grateful not to hear another "Mya, no," I willingly complied. Once hidden in the shadows of the barren branches, I watched the lit area for signs of the shooter again.

It took a few minutes before I spotted movement. A single figure walked the length of the overpass from the edge of the light to the right to the edge of the light to the left. As I watched something to our right caught my attention. A glint of grey moved against the black, and it made my stomach dip in fear.

"Can you see what's over there?" I asked Drav, pointing.

"A human."

Relief flooded me that it wasn't another shadow man. I didn't want to have to go through the whole boobs and no penis thing again.

"How many humans are out there?"

"No words," he said, and I quickly counted up to twenty.

"Seven humans."

Goosebumps broke out on my skin from my head to my toes. Seven seemed like such a little number. But seven survivors in one place...seven who had set up lights as if they knew it would keep them safer from the hellhounds and from—I glanced at Drav and felt a tinge of guilt that I seemed safe with him while others were not.

However, the number showed me a possibility of surviving without Drav and gave me hope.

"Drav, my parents would have driven this way. I want to ask these people how long they've been here and if they saw a red car with two men and a woman."

"It's not safe."

"Why? They won't shoot me. You stay here. I'll come back when I'm done talking to them." I only managed a step before he blocked my way.

"Stop. Wait."

Drav turned and pointed toward a light coming from the south. A car.

"We got a live one," a man yelled. The phrase echoed what Charles and his group had said when they saw me. It boomed in the dark from somewhere near the bridge. Were these people military, too? Part of the Tinker evacuation?

I looked toward the bridge and saw the man on the overpass move to the center of the lit area. He held his arms up, waving the car to a stop. When the car approached, it slowed.

The man waited until the vehicle stopped then walked to the driver's side. He leaned toward the window and stayed there. It remained hard to see more detail from our distance and impossible to hear anything.

"Can you hear what they're saying?" I asked quietly.

"No."

Disappointed, I watched and waited. After a moment, the person on the bridge straightened and pointed to the north. Another moment passed before he backed away from the car and the driver's door opened.

"I really wish I could hear what's going on," I said. "The car made it here okay. There doesn't seem to be any hellhounds around. Let's just move closer. I'll be safe in the light when I talk to them."

"Wait," Drav said again, not taking his eyes from the bridge.

"You're really starting to annoy me, Drav." I almost said he couldn't stop me from doing what I wanted, but it'd be a lie. He'd stopped me before, and if he wanted to, he'd keep stopping me.

Frustrated, I crossed my arms and continued to watch the driver get out of the car. As soon as he left the car, another man, this one held a gun, stepped from the shadows to the north.

"Is he pointing the gun at the driver?"

Drav remained quiet as we watched the original person on the bridge step forward and open the back door. Several times he went to the back and took a few steps away, as if unloading something. The enraged driver stepped forward and talked with his arms. His voice rose, and I caught some of what he was saying.

"Bullshit...supplies for everyone...it'll come..."

Several scenarios ran through my head but the one that made the most sense was that the men on the bridge were military and collecting supplies for the evacuated survivors. But if that was the case, why take from a single person? There were plenty of supplies in the city from what I'd seen. That is, if they were brave enough to face the infected to get the supplies.

Maybe the person in the car had come from the survivor camp.

Maybe he was delivering supplies to these guys? I mean, they had light and a generator, but with no houses nearby they had no convenient food source. Of course they would need supplies, too. But he said supplies for everyone. I wasn't sure what to think.

As soon as the back door closed, the driver got into the car and squealed north, blaring his horn. The man with the gun pointed the rifle at the vehicle. Fear seemed to solidify into a heavy ball in my stomach. Who were these men? The original man called out for him to lower his weapon.

"He just brought the infected to us," the man with the gun called.

"All the more reason to save the bullets. Back to your post."

His words reassured me slightly. Still, I second-guessed my need to approach them. I would find out if my family went this way when I got to the cabin. But, what would we do next? How long would my family and I be safe at the cabin? Charles mentioned a safe zone but not its location. I needed to know where.

"We go, Mya," Drav said.

"No. I think they're with the military. They can tell us where the survivors are, so when I find my family, we'll know where it's safe for us to go."

Drav turned to look at me. Something in his gaze made me feel really guilty for saying what I had. Did he really think I'd want to stay with him after I reached my family?

"Drav, I—"

A branch snapped behind me. Drav's head jerked toward the sound.

CHAPTER SIXTEEN

"I KNOW YOU'RE OUT THERE," A VOICE SAID SOFTLY. "I HEARD YOU talking."

Drav's lips pulled back to show his teeth.

"Drav," I whispered, reaching out to grab his hand. "Please don't kill him. Please let me talk to him. Then we can go."

He looked down at me.

"Not safe."

"It will be. I promise."

He grunted and then vanished.

"I'm over here," I said, nervously. I worried Drav would change his mind.

A rustle of movement came from further within the trees. A moment later, a man dressed in dark clothes stepped out. He carried some kind of rifle loosely in the crook of his arm and looked me over carefully before speaking.

"Where'd you come from?"

"Oklahoma City. I'm looking for my family. How long have you guys been watching the bridge? They would have passed through this way the night the hellhounds attacked."

He made an odd sound between a laugh and a snort.

"Hellhounds. That about sums them up. And they strike every night, sweetheart. How'd you manage to get this far?"

"I avoid the roads," I said, not knowing what other excuse he'd buy. I certainly wasn't going to admit Drav had helped me. Based on what Charles had said and all the killing that Drav had done, this guy wouldn't have believed me.

"Who were you talking to?"

"Myself. I know noise attracts those things, but sometimes the quiet's worse, you know?"

He didn't say anything. His eyes just slowly traveled the length of me once more, then he tilted his head, considering me.

"They would have been in a red car. Two men and a woman." He still didn't say anything. His silence and Drav's warning were making me nervous.

"Never mind. I'll just keep going."

"Can you pay the price?" he asked, finally.

"What are you talking about?"

"Supplies for passage, little lady. But, in your case, information. Although, I might be willing to trade for something else."

My heart leapt to my throat as I realized I'd misunderstood everything.

"You're not with Tinker."

A harsh smile twisted his lips.

"Fuck no. Like we wanted to be herded into some over-crowded fence like a bunch of animals. We'll take our chances out here. There are plenty of opportunities out in the woods. I mean, look at you."

His eyes slid over me in a skin-crawling way.

Drav had been right. It wasn't safe. I should have believed him.

"I'm okay without the information," I said, starting to back up. "I'll just—"

I stepped wrong, twisting my ankle, and crying out as I fell.

"Shut up," the man said as I landed hard on my ass.

Wincing at the pain in my tailbone, I looked up at the man. He stood over me, his rifle turned so the butt end was aimed at my head.

"How are you still alive?" He drew the rifle back. My heart jumped to my throat.

Behind him, a familiar shadow moved. Drav's eyes glittered with anger as he stalked forward. Relief calmed me enough to have a measure of concern for the asshole with the gun as Drav reached us. My fellow human obviously wasn't nice, but did that mean he should die for it?

"No head ripping," I said.

Drav fisted one hand and raised it high. Unaware, the man looked at me with angry confusion.

"What the hell are you—"

Drav brought his fist down, hitting the man squarely on the top of his head. The man fell forward, almost landing on top of me. I stared at the fallen body for a second. The leaves by his mouth moved slightly. He was knocked out but still alive. Good.

Drav squatted down beside me. Tearing my gaze from the fallen man, I looked up at Drav. He still looked angry enough to rip off someone's head.

"I'm sorry I didn't listen," I said with sincerity.

The tension in his expression melted away, and he exhaled heavily before cupping the back of my head and touching his forehead against mine.

"You are safe with me."

And I realized that I really was. Safe. Safer with him than my own kind, it seemed. I gently touched his upper arm and leaned against him. His fingers twitched slightly in my hair.

"We go," he said.

Was it my imagination or did it sound like those two words were filled with regret?

He pulled away and offered me his hand. In a hurry to leave the man before he woke, I clasped it and stood. My ankle ached, and I took a minute to brush the dirt and leaves from my pants to give it time to settle down. But it didn't. With each step, my ankle hurt worse.

"Drav," I said, stopping. "I think I did something to my ankle. It hurts to walk."

He glanced down then made the familiar move to hoist me over his shoulder.

"Wait, wait, wait," I said, holding out my hands. "I appreciate the gesture, but it doesn't feel so good when you carry me like that."

He considered me a moment then removed my bag and put it over his shoulder.

"Thanks. Losing the extra weight might help—"

Before I could finish that thought, Drav scooped me up into his arms. He didn't move right away, but stared down at me, as if waiting for my opinion on the new arrangement.

"Ah, this works, I guess." I tentatively wrapped my arm around his shoulder.

He breathed deeply, briefly set his forehead against mine again —I was beginning to think the gesture some kind of hug or something—and then took off running. His speed amazed me. The scenery blurred, and the wind made my eyes tear. I turned my head into his shoulder, which made it difficult to give directions. Drav had to slow every so often so I could lift my head long enough to see where we were. He didn't seem inconvenienced by the interruptions or carrying me. In fact, given the way his fingers occasionally brushed my side, I'd say he rather liked the arrangement.

Although being carried helped my ankle, the backs of my knees soon became sore from the press of his forearm. I tried to ignore it until my calf started to cramp.

"Drav, we need to stop," I said against his shirt. "I'm getting a cramp."

He slowed near a group of trees, not far from the next road we needed to cross, and eased me to my feet. A dull ache throbbed in my ankle, but there were no shooting pains once I put my weight on it. Taking care, I stretched one leg then the other, determined not to let my discomfort slow our progress more than necessary.

Drav watched me closely, his gaze tracking each move I made. His scrutiny didn't bother me as much as it probably should have, and I couldn't help but wonder what would happen after I found my parents.

"I'm fine now. Could I have the bag?" I asked, thirstily.

He shrugged it off his shoulders and handed it to me. I sat with the bag in my lap and dug out the water bottle. When I looked up, his attention was no longer on me but on the woods to our right. I followed his gaze and saw the dark shape of a house through the trees.

"Stay," he said softly before disappearing into the thicket without further explanation.

The night immediately became more menacing without his presence. I listened for any whisper of noise, my need for a drink no longer important. The breeze rattled some branches, and I jumped at the sound. I wanted to call out to Drav, but not knowing why he'd left, I didn't think it safe to make any noise.

Something rattled to my right where there were no trees. A sick feeling settled in my stomach. Swallowing hard, I slowly turned my head and scanned the shadowy grasses. A shape moved, low to the ground, not far from me, and the rattle reached my ears again. Metallic. I squinted and watched the shape creep closer on four legs. Eyes reflected at me in the weak moonlight. Panic seized my lungs, robbing me of the air I needed to yell for Drav. I opened my mouth anyway. No sound emerged. At least not from me.

A low whine preceded a loud rattle as the thing launched itself at me. I barely had time to register what was happening. One minute I was facing certain death and the next I lay on my back, getting my face bathed by the happiest yellow lab on the planet.

I turned my head and wrapped my arms around its neck in relieved gratitude.

"What a good dog," I crooned, running my hands over its fur while it continued to attack me with affection.

Suddenly, it moved back and began growling. I sat up and saw Drav stood over us, his expression fierce. He growled in return and stepped toward the dog.

"It wasn't hurting me," I said quickly. "It's a dog. A pet. It's friendly." However, the dog looked anything but friendly with its lips pulled back in a silent snarl.

I put my bottle aside and got to my knees.

"Hey," I said softly. "It's okay. Drav's nice." I patted my leg and the dog moved closer, pressing against me. I pet its head, trying to sooth it, but it continued to growl at Drav.

"Mya. We go. Infected."

My heart dropped. I quickly grabbed the dog's collar, removed it, and tossed it aside. With one last pat for the dog, I stood.

"I'm sorry," I said softly. The infected wouldn't hear the dog now when it ran, but if it stayed...I swallowed and went to Drav.

The dog whined when Drav scooped me up in his arms. Branches broke to our left, and Drav took off running. I looked back at the dog. It growled once at the person emerging from the trees then took off after us. More figures appeared behind the first.

The dog tried to keep up but eventually fell behind, though it still remained well ahead of the infected. I laid my head against Drav's shoulder and tried not to think of that poor dog's desperation. What was happening in the world? Where were all the animals? What would tomorrow bring?

A few times, I felt Drav switch directions only to correct his course a few minutes later. I didn't raise my head to find out why.

His pace remained consistent through the remainder of the night. The sky gradually brightened with rosy hues and streaks of orange so I could see. The area looked familiar, and the ache in my chest tightened with the fear and anticipation that grew the closer we drew to the cabin.

The sun crested the horizon when we emerged from the trees into the back yard of our family retreat. Sunlight streamed between the naked branches and illuminated the rear of the small cabin. Despite the bright rays, the still air had a bitter chill to it.

"You can put me down."

Drav squinted against the light as he glowered at the back of the quaint little building. I wiggled but his hold on me tightened.

"Seriously, Drav. Put me down. I'm sore from being carried like this, too." He relented and set me on my feet.

"Stay here." I took one step toward the back door, eager to get into the house.

Drav moved in front of me, halting my progress. His lips were a thin line in his displeasure.

"Mya, no. Infected," he said.

"It's okay. My family is in there."

I stepped around him, and he set his hand on my shoulder to stop me. Batting his hand away, I spun to face him with a scowl. After being separated from my family and worrying about their safety for so long, I didn't want to play nice anymore.

"I get that you're worried about infected, but I'm not letting you go first. Think about it, Drav. You and your hounds show up—"

"Not my hounds."

"—and the whole world goes to shit. They're afraid. I'm afraid. Infected people are everywhere, your kind goes around ripping off heads, and nothing feels safe anymore. I won't let you scare my family more by walking into the house first."

Drav grunted, which I took as his agreement. He stayed only a couple of steps behind me when I started forward, but it was better than him taking the lead.

Tension coiled in my stomach as I clasped the doorknob. I took a steadying breath and opened the back door. It led into the laundry room, which led to the kitchen. Inside, everything was dark and quiet. Too quiet.

I stepped into the room and turned on the first light before moving forward. Fear and anticipation had me opening my mouth.

"Mom! Dad! Ryan!" My hopeful calls echoed through the house.

Drav stepped in front of me, a growl deep in his chest. I held still behind him, listening. Nothing moved, and no one answered. A lead weight settled in my stomach.

No. They had to be here. They were.

I stepped around him and moved into the kitchen. Even with the sun streaking through the windows, I flipped the switch on. The kitchen looked neat. Unused. My knees went weak. They hadn't made it. Stumbling forward, I called down the hall.

In the answering silence, my sweeping glance caught on the white piece of paper stuck to the fridge. A small sound escaped me. Drav, who stood off to the side by the pantry, watched me stumble toward the note.

Carefully, I unclipped the letter from the refrigerator. My hands shook and the paper crinkled as I leaned against the counter for support.

Mya,
If you're reading this, we made it here safely, but the military started evacuating the area just after we arrived. We wanted to stay and wait for you, but they're telling us it's not safe here. The infected from Fairview are moving south and those hounds are still in the area. I hope we find you at the Tinker Base before they fly us out. Please stay safe, sweetie.

All our love
Mom, Dad, and Ryan.
PS Hurry up slowpoke.

The last bit appeared to be written in Ryan's messy scrawl. A laugh-snort escaped me. More burst out until I was gasping for air, trying to breathe through my hysteria. I kept missing them. But the cause of my hysteria stemmed from more than that. My entire world no longer existed.

Dreams of finishing college, dating, stupid parties, or watching Ryan graduate high school vanished. I slid down the cabinets. The handle poked me in the shoulder, but I could barely feel it. Infected were everywhere. How could the world possibly come back from this? It couldn't. Humanity was done, and I doubted anyone had any idea how it had happened.

Quaking laughter turned into wracking sobs as I spiraled out of control. I'd only made it this far because of pure, dumb luck. Because of my boobs. The thought sparked another bout of hysterical laughter.

Warm, strong hands lifted me. Arms cradled me. Drav's forehead pressed against mine before I turned my head and wrapped my arms around his neck. He held me while my tears soaked his shirt.

The gentle strokes of his fingers over my head slowly soothed me. Sobs turned to hitched breaths between quieter sniffles. It took a while to realize I sat in his lap, draped against him like a rung-out rag. I was still too shattered to care, though.

We stayed like that as the living room lightened. His stomach growled. Guilt had me lifting my head.

"I'll get us some food," I said without looking at him.

His arms around me didn't loosen.

"No, Mya."

His fingers brushed under my chin, nudging me until I looked up and met his green gaze.

"Mya, shower."

I groaned.

"Drav, I really don't want to do this right now—"

"No. Mya shower. I find food."

Guilt hit me harder. He'd remained quiet the entire time he'd held me, putting aside his need for food to comfort me. I could feel tears threatening again so I quickly hugged him and whispered my thanks before getting off his lap and escaping to the bathroom.

Robotically, I kicked off the shoes I'd forgotten to remove at the door. My reflection distracted me from thoughts of what my mom would have said about shoes in the house.

The tears had made my eyes puffy and red, and a riotous halo of kinked hair sprang from my head, a side effect of Drav removing my braids while he'd held me. I sniffled loudly and cringed at the ache in my head but didn't move to blow my nose. Mud smeared my face. Probably from the dog. No wonder Drav had suggested a shower. I exhaled heavily and opened the bathroom door.

In the room I shared with Ryan, I dug through the drawers until I found a pair of Ryan's old gym shorts and an old t-shirt of mine. I grabbed clean underwear from the dresser and took it all to the bathroom.

While the shower water warmed, I brushed my teeth with the spare toothbrushes Mom had always kept on hand. Thoughts ricocheted around in my mind too quickly to sink in. Nothing seemed real outside the bathroom. I let the world shrink to the current moment and the current goal. Shower. Bathed in the heat of the steam-filled room, I stripped and stepped into the spray. The water soothed my headache as I worked in shampoo then conditioner. The floral scent wrapped around me, a small sliver of normality. It didn't fool me.

I took my time toweling off and lingered after I finished

dressing and brushing my hair. The door to the bathroom had stayed shut the entire time, thank goodness. I would need to deal with what had happened and what I would need to do next. But not yet. First, I'd eat. Then, I'd sleep. I couldn't deal with anything more than that. Anything else would have to be put on hold until after.

Drav waited for me in the kitchen. Several cans were open on the table. I didn't have an appetite but sat and picked up my fork. I only managed a few bites before I pushed the rest of the can toward Drav. He didn't try to make me eat more.

As soon as he finished, I stood and went to my bedroom.

Even though heavy clouds filled the sky and muted the light of the sun, I closed the open blinds before laying on my bed. Ryan's bed rested only feet from mine, but Drav didn't even glance at it. He joined me and carefully tucked me close to his side.

I didn't fight the closeness. I needed it too much.

CHAPTER SEVENTEEN

CRACK.

I jolted upright in bed, my breathing labored. The room shouldn't have been so dark, even with the blinds closed. It took a moment for the noises around me to register. Rain drummed against the window. I shivered as lightning flashed and cast an eerie blue glow around the room for a split second. Thunder followed, rumbling through the skies and house.

Another bolt lit the room, and Drav's fingers wrapped around my arm with bruising force. The quiet rumble of his growl echoed in my ear. He acted like this was the first storm he had ever experienced. His grip tightened around my waist, tugging me back down to bed. I glanced at the clock on the nightstand behind him. Four in the afternoon. Too early to be up on our new sleep schedule. I rested my head on his shoulder and tried to calm my racing heart.

"It's okay. It's just a storm," I said, for his benefit as much as mine. He didn't move.

"Drav, ease up. You're hurting me." He continued staring out the window, his lips back in a silent snarl.

"Drav!" I set my hand on his cheek and forced his attention back to me.

"It's okay. It's only a storm."

My touch calmed him down a bit. But, there was no way we could travel in this kind of weather. Even with Drav's quickness, I'd probably get sick from the wet and cold.

"The storm will pass, but until it does, we will stay here." He just growled softly. "I think we've slept enough," I added when he didn't loosen his hold. Finally, he let me move.

The chilly air outside of the blankets gave me goosebumps. I nudged the thermostat up and listened to the heat kick in. Drav followed me through the house as I turned on all the lights. It made me feel safer.

Uncertain how to entertain ourselves until the storm blew over, I prowled the cabin for ideas. To keep the focus on family time, my parents had decided to limit the technology here. That meant no TV. I doubted there would be anything airing other than the EAS warning, anyway, but it would have been nice to check. A movie would have been a good way to pass time, too. And, it would have helped Drav learn some new words since we were back to 'Mya, no' a lot while I walked through the house. He didn't like me getting too close to any of the windows or doors while the lightning still streaked across the sky and thunder boomed outside.

In the living room, we had an old buffet filled with various board games. Ryan and I passed a lot of time playing them when we weren't outside. I trailed my hand over the different boxes. Monopoly would last us forever, which wasn't a bad thing, but it might be a bit complicated for someone who was still learning the English language, even if he just needed to hear a word to understand it. Twister brought an unbridled image to mind of Drav's body twisted around me as we tried to maneuver through the game. Nope, absolutely not. However, Yahtzee sat right next to the Twister box.

I removed that box, figuring it would be easy enough. Drav followed me to the living room table and sat beside me as I arranged the game pieces. He picked up one of the dice and inspected it closer. I started explaining the purpose of the dice, cup, score cards, and game.

Two hours later, he was still kicking my ass. For a game of chance, he played annoyingly well.

"Let's take a break," I said.

As I stood, another crack of thunder vibrated the cabin. Fortunately, the storm had calmed down a bit, and Drav's agitation had lessened. I thought the game had helped calm him, too. I, unfortunately, wanted to do something else. Besides, my rumbling stomach had been demanding food for the past fifteen minutes.

We walked down the hall to the kitchen where Drav and I made a simple meal of ramen noodles. Afterward, Drav went straight back to our game, but if I had to hear him yell out Yahtzee one more time, I would need to strangle him.

I looked around the room for something else, and my gaze landed on Mom's old iPod. An idea bloomed in my mind.

"Drav," I said, heading for the little device. "I think you're really going to like this."

I opened the Audible app and scrolled through Mom's book selection until I found one marginally appropriate. A non-fiction book about beekeeping, one of many hobbies Mom always wanted to try. There would be plenty of new words for Drav to learn, and maybe it would keep him busy for a bit.

He watched me closely as I unwound the earbuds and held still as I placed the right one in his ear and the left one in mine.

"You'll be able to listen to someone talking and learn new words with this," I said.

As soon as I started the book, he blinked at me and his mouth opened slightly in shock. I grinned.

"Thought you'd like that." I took the earbud from my ear and held it out to him. "You can put this in your other ear so you don't hear the thunder." He took the bud but didn't put it in.

I showed him how to adjust the volume then handed him the device. He was so enthralled he didn't notice me walk away.

Messing with the iPod had reminded me that I should charge my phone. We kept extra chargers at the cabin because it never failed that somebody would forget to pack one. In the bathroom, I dug my phone out of my jeans, which still lay on the floor. The phone turned on but still had no signal. I walked back to the kitchen to get a charger out of the drawer.

After that, I hesitated, unsure what to do next. Sleeping all day and staying awake all night had messed with my internal clock. I wasn't sure if I should be eating, watching TV, or going to class...in my old world. I felt completely lost in the new one. So I wandered through the house, looking at the pictures on the walls, until I got to my parent's room. I sat on their bed and picked up Dad's pillow. A hint of his aftershave drifted to my nose. My eyes watered as I looked around the room and hugged the pillow.

Just before fall semester started, we'd come to the cabin as a family. I'd been working all summer, saving what I could for tuition. Ryan had been working and hanging out with friends, too. Mom had called family time and had insisted on a family retreat. She had packed the coolers. Dad had packed the truck. Those three days had been amazing in so many small ways. The time with my mom, cooking in the kitchen. Canoeing with Dad on the nearby river. Playing volleyball outside.

We weren't the kind of family who didn't like each other. I never recalled a time I'd tried to avoid spending time with my parents or Ryan. Sure, I did stuff with friends, but not for the sole purpose of avoiding family time. Why would I want to? We had fun together. We laughed. We talked. We cared.

I hugged the pillow tighter and swallowed hard. I was afraid. Terrified, really. What if those three days were it? What if I never saw my family again? What if all the good people, like Jack and Charles, were dead and only jackasses like the guys by the bridge were left? Was I really all alone?

No. I wasn't alone. I had Drav. He might not be human or understand much, but he wasn't bad. At least, not with me. And, that was far better than being alone.

I set the pillow back on the bed and went to the living room. Drav hadn't moved from his spot. He looked away from the iPod, which he now held, and watched me cross the room. He still only had one earbud in, probably to listen for me.

"I'm fine," I said. "Thank you. For bringing me here. For keeping me safe. For not ripping my head off like you've done with everyone else."

"I wouldn't do that to you, Mya. Ever."

Wow. A full sentence?

"Uh, thanks. That audio book seems to be helping."

"Yes."

"Well, I'll leave you to it then."

His gaze stayed on me as I went to the cabin's one storage closet.

Mom kept everything from blankets to spare mud boots in the modest space. I dug for ponchos. I'd give the rain until tomorrow night. If it didn't stop by then, we'd be leaving, no matter what.

It proved easy to find something that would fit me, but the largest poncho would be a snug fit for Drav, just like his shirt. That thought had me heading back to my parents' room. The odd clothes, stuff that was new but maybe the wrong size, always found its way to the cabin as spares for guests. When I started going through drawers, I found a big and tall shirt for Drav but also a small photo album. I opened it up and thumbed through pictures of Ryan and me playing in the yard at home and here. We were laughing or smiling in each image. Happy instigators. I missed Ryan. I missed them all so much.

I removed one picture of all of us and tucked the folded memory into my bra before I replaced the album. Carrying everything back to the living room, I set the ponchos on a chair.

"If it's still raining tomorrow, we can wear these," I said, gaining Drav's attention. "And this shirt will fit you better than the one you have on." I tossed the shirt to him, and he caught it in his free hand.

"I'm going to check the freezer and see if there's anything we can make for dinner."

Nothing waited in the freezer but ice cube trays, which unsurprisingly were empty. The fridge had the normal condiments that lasted well and a box of baking soda. With a sigh, I went to the cupboards and found a shake bottle of pancake mix. It was better than another can of fruit.

I had a stack of pancakes ready to eat when I went to check on Drav. He sat in the same spot, still listening to the iPod.

"I made some pancakes if you're hungry."

He didn't seem to hear me. I mentally shrugged, went to the game cabinet, and grabbed a deck of cards.

In the kitchen, I played solitaire while I ate pancakes and applesauce. I grew bored with the cards after a while and busied myself with cleaning up. Standing by the sink, I took my time washing the dishes.

Outside, the rain continued to lash at the windows. Dim outlines of the trees swayed in the wind. If Dad were here, he would probably put on his poncho and his mud boots and go out to check the gas in the generator just in case the storm knocked out the power. He would come in, soaking wet, and Mom would be waiting with a towel at the door. I smiled slightly at the mental image and rinsed my plate.

Lightning flashed, and something moved outside the window. The shape looked heart-stoppingly familiar. I covered my mouth with my hand and watched our neighbor, Doug, shamble along the tree line. When the thunder cracked loudly, he sprinted for several yards then went back to a shamble.

Dad's note about the military evacuating them meant we couldn't stay here long. Going out in the rain might serve as a layer of protection even if I wouldn't be able to see or hear as well. It seemed that Doug couldn't hear well, either.

I finished up with the dishes. The leftover pancakes and applesauce I wrapped up and put in the fridge. The lights flickered when I went back into the living room. Drav watched me cross the room to look out the window. Doug had circled the house.

"There's an infected out there," I said. "Do you think he'll try to get in?"

When I glanced back, Drav no longer sat in his spot. The iPod lay on the cushion, though. I looked out the window. Doug had stopped shambling and faced the side of the house. A moment later, Drav appeared from around the corner. Doug started running toward him. Drav caught him up by the head.

I turned away from the window before I witnessed another beheading, and distracted myself by going to get Drav a towel. However, as soon as he stepped inside, he shook himself like a dog before I could hand it to him.

"Um, this is to dry off if you want it," I said, holding the towel out to him.

"Thank you," he said, taking it.

"Good thing you left the iPod inside. They don't work well when they get wet. Do you want me to back up the book and show you how to pause it? Just in case you need to leave again?"

"No," he said quickly. "I understand."

"Oh. Okay. Good."

He moved past me, tugged off his wet shirt, then picked up the iPod to set the towel on the chair. Without a glance my way, he sat and had the ear bud back in his ear a moment later.

I could appreciate his draw to the device. Being able to

understand what I said could be pretty useful to him. Yet a tiny voice in the back of my mind questioned his eagerness. What if his enthusiasm wasn't just to understand me? Would he use the knowledge of our language to hurt uninfected people? I thought of the incident at the bridge and doubted it. I'd asked him not to kill the man and he hadn't.

Giving him one last glance, I went back to the kitchen and played solitaire until four in the morning. A full day—or night—of idle time left me yawning much sooner than expected. I stood with a stretch and glanced at the window. The rain hadn't yet let up. In the living room, Drav still listened to the iPod. The book must have been longer than I'd thought.

"I think I'm going to go to bed," I said.

He turned his head and looked at me. For a moment, I thought he would say something. Instead, he gave a slow nod before focusing on the iPod again. I didn't know beekeeping could be such an interesting topic.

After seeing our infected neighbor in the yard, I felt a little nervous going to bed by myself, but I didn't want to ask Drav to come with me, either. So, after staring at him for another few seconds, I slowly made my way to the bedroom and left the door open. I made sure the blinds were still closed.

Fully dressed, I got into bed and curled under the covers. When I woke, rain or shine, we'd keep going.

CHAPTER EIGHTEEN

A SHIVER SHOOK ME FROM MY DREAMS, AND I CURLED TIGHTER under my covers. It took a moment to realize why I shouldn't be so cold. Drav wasn't with me. My eyes popped open.

I sat up and looked around frantically. Something on the floor beside the bed moved. I looked down and met Drav's gaze as he turned to glance at me. He sat next to the bed, an earbud still in his ear. A relieved breath escaped me. He was fine. Why had I assumed he wouldn't be? Not much out there seemed to match his strength.

I rubbed my forehead.

"Did you get any sleep, or have you been listening to that all night?"

"I've been listening all night."

If I wasn't mistaken, a small smile tugged his mouth. I stared for a moment. It was the first smile I could remember seeing.

"Hopefully, you weren't too bored," I said.

His smile changed slightly.

"I wasn't bored at all."

I glanced over at the clock on the night stand but it flashed twelve, leaving me with no idea of how long I'd slept or what time it might be. The subtle, muted light filtering through the blinds didn't help. I could pull them back to check, but a small part of me feared I would see an infected shambling around outside. Of course, last night I hadn't even had to tell Drav before he'd left to dispose of our old neighbor.

Regardless of the hour, I didn't want to spend more time here than necessary, not without knowing what had happened to my family. The note they'd left ran through my head. *Before they fly us out.* Where would they be taken? So far, I had missed them every step of the way. If I didn't get to Tinker in time, I feared I might lose them altogether.

"It sounds like it stopped raining," I said, looking at Drav, who watched me steadily. "Are you ready to travel or do you need some sleep?"

"I don't need any sleep before we travel."

That was good. But, first, we needed to get some food in us and check the weather.

I climbed out of the bed and went to the window. With Drav still nearby on the floor, I bravely nudged the curtain back. Heavy grey clouds blotted out the sun's midday rays, providing enough light for me to see. Remembering the way Drav's eyes had watered, I tugged the curtain open a little more and glanced back at him. He watched me closely as his pupils adjusted to the slight change in light. However, his eyes didn't water.

"You're watching me closely. What is it that you are trying to figure out?"

Wow. Those books really helped.

"I was seeing if the overcast light affected you the same way the sun did."

"You could have asked."

"Uh, sorry." The full conversation we were having seemed too weird after only days of broken ones.

Drav stood. He had changed his shirt. The new one still looked a bit snug.

"You can probably put that away for a while," I said, motioning to the device in his hands. He made no move to remove the earbud still tucked inside of his ear.

"I have much more to learn and would like to bring it with us. Let's get some breakfast. We can head out when we're finished."

More to learn? He sounded just fine to me. Hopefully he'd be willing to listen to me for a bit because, now that he could talk, I desperately wanted to ask him questions.

Drav followed me into the kitchen where I grabbed another bottle of pancake mix.

"Is it all right if I ask you some questions now?" I asked as I added water and started to shake the container.

His steady gaze held me for several long moments.

"Ask me anything, Mya."

"Where did you come from? Why are you here? Not in this house, but here, on earth, destroying things?"

"I'm from a place called Ernisi. I'm not sure what happened. But something broke the barrier and a hole opened to the surface. The hounds and two of my kind escaped first. We followed to see where they'd gone and found this..." He looked around at the cabin. "and you..." His gaze landed on me again.

I pulled out a pan and started warming some oil.

"Ernisi," I said, testing the name. "That's where you lived?"

"Yes."

"And it's underground?" It had to be if a hole opened from above.

"Yes, it would seem so."

"What do you mean, seem so?" I asked as I poured some batter into the pan.

"It has always just been Ernisi. I never thought there might be something above or below our dark sky."

149

I turned the pancakes and thought about what he'd said.

"That had to be a shock then, having your roof open up."

"It was."

But it hadn't been the only shock. I thought back to when he'd first seen me.

"I have another question, but I don't want to make things weird by asking."

"Nothing will be weird."

I stacked the first batch of pancakes for breakfast—or whatever meal this was. I set the plate on the table and watched him as I asked my next question.

"Why did it shock you that I'm a girl?" I asked.

"Ernisi has no girls."

"No gir—" I closed my mouth abruptly as several thoughts collided in my mind. He had a penis and testicles. He'd shown me both during our first meeting. What the hell were they for if they didn't have girls? That wasn't a question I wanted to ask.

Instead, I finished making the pancakes and sat down to eat in silence.

After we were both fed, I started to wash the dishes.

"I'm going to take a quick shower," Drav said.

He set my mom's iPod down and went to the bathroom. As I listened for the water to crank on, I heard a tiny voice. I glanced at the device and saw what had kept him so occupied all night.

Ice Planet Barbarians by Ruby Dixon. The cover was a sultry image of a blue skinned male holding a very human female.

My mouth dropped open, and I slowly reached for the earbud and placed it in my ear.

"*I don't know if she's humming or saying another one of her strange human words. I lick her breast to distract her, and she moans. Then she reaches down and grips my cock in her hand and strokes me through the leather of my leggings.*"

My breath choked in my throat. *Oh shit.*

I immediately stopped the book and gazed down the hallway in shock. He'd gotten into my mom's romance novels. I tugged the earbud out and scrolled through the last books he had listened to. Ruby Dixon. All the covers with bare-chested men. He'd only listened to three percent of the damn bee book.

I coiled the earbuds around the iPod and set it back on the table. Thankfully, Drav still lingered in the shower. My cheeks flamed hot at the thought of the things he'd been learning, and I was twice as glad I hadn't asked anything more about why there were no girls.

Determined to pretend I didn't know anything about what he'd been listening to, I went to the front closet where Mom liked to store everything. Although my bag had the clothes I needed, I wanted to be prepared for anything and knew Dad kept an extra pocket knife around somewhere, as well as a lighter and first aid kit. I hoped to find both in the clutter.

Leaning deep inside the closet in my search, I heard Drav's footsteps and tried not to cringe.

"Mya?"

"Here, in the closet."

I was pulling down a small tote from the shelf when he crowded behind me. He plucked the tote from my hands, and I turned around ready to thank him. The words died when I saw he wore his pants but no shirt. Why wasn't he wearing his shirt? I thought of the men on the romance covers, mentally cringed, and met his gaze.

"Did you want me to braid your hair before we leave?" He spoke the words with such ease in his deep, gravelly voice

"No, I'm fine." No way would I allow him to touch me after what he'd been reading. "Go ahead and finish getting dressed then we can go. I'm almost done in here."

Drav nodded and walked back down the hall.

I refocused on finding the spare pocket knife and any other

supplies we could use. I found my old, sturdy hiking boots. My parents and Ryan had gotten me a new pair for my birthday the year before. I'd left these up here in case I ever forgot to bring my new ones. Given the rain, boots might not be a bad idea. I considered the room left in my bag and decided the shoes I'd worn here would fit.

I closed the door to the bedroom, changed clothes, and braided my hair. Once I finished and packed my new finds into the bag, I came out to the living room where Drav sat on the couch waiting. He stood when he saw me. He had rebraided his hair to look much like it had the first time we'd crossed paths. Had it only been a week ago?

Glancing around the cabin sadly, I kept reminding myself that it was only a place as I prepared to leave. My family was what I missed, and because of the storm, we were already days behind them. We had to get to Tinker.

"Ready?" I asked, hiking the bag up on my shoulder.

"Yes."

He held out the iPod. Now that I knew what he listened to, I hesitated to take it.

"It's probably low on battery. We should leave it here."

"Is there a charger?"

Seriously? How did he know that?

Reluctantly, I nodded and went to grab the iPod charger along with the one for my phone. I'd already tucked my phone into my back pocket, safe and sound. When I had everything, I checked the lock on the front door then led Drav to the back, the way we had come in. It might only be a place but it still held memories, and I didn't want anyone coming in and destroying anything. My thoughts roamed to the men on the overpass. Though our paths had crossed briefly, I now knew what type of people they were. No doubt there were more like them out there.

After locking the back door, Drav and I started off through the trees at a brisk pace. He didn't seem remotely tired from staying up all day. I looked at the late afternoon sky, trying to find just how low the sun might be behind the thick clouds. The consistent grey didn't give me a clue.

From the corner of my eye, I caught Drav watching me. I glanced toward him, but he immediately focused on our surroundings. I frowned but said nothing. Twice more I caught him watching me only to have him quickly look away. He was weirding me out. Or maybe, my imagination was weirding me out.

The cold, damp smell of late fall tickled my nose, and I tried to pay more attention to where we were going than to Drav. The ground, still wet from all the rain, squished under my feet. Although my boots kept my feet dry, they were heavier than my running shoes, and it wasn't long before my steps started to lag. Drav didn't say anything about the pace. He stayed beside me no matter how slowly I walked. Night descended as we continued south.

Twice, he had me stop while he disappeared to take care of a nearby infected. I used each break to lean against a tree or building where I sipped water from my bottle. Each time he returned, I offered it to him as well.

Despite the breaks, I was getting tired. It was a couple of hours later when my feet went out from under me. I yipped and swung my arm out to grab something as I fell. Drav's hand gripped my flailing arm, steadying me. Before I could thank him, his steely arms slipped behind my back and under my legs, and he lifted me up. With me cradled in his arms, he continued to walk as if he hadn't decided to randomly pick me up.

"Um, Drav? You don't have to carry me."

"I don't want you to strain your ankle."

"My ankle is fine now. Seriously, you don't need to carry me."

"I don't mind."

He might not, but I did.

"I'd rather walk."

"And risk injuring yourself if you slip? Are you no longer in a hurry to find your family?"

I shut my mouth. Stupid iPod.

Drav carried me like that a couple hours longer, going about the same speed I had while walking. I couldn't imagine how tired he must be. A light sprinkling of rain gave me the perfect excuse to ask to be set down.

I pulled out the ponchos I had grabbed from the cabin and gave Drav his. Like I'd thought, it fit him snugly but did the job. I tugged mine over my head then slung the bag across my body again, determined to walk some more. Drav didn't argue.

Where the ground had been squishy before, mud now slicked the surface. He started slipping, too, and our progress slowed to a crawl. The poncho kept me from freezing in the cold rain, although not by much, and Drav caught me each time I slid, preventing me from landing face first or ass deep in the slippery earth.

The rain eventually let up, but we didn't stop to remove the ponchos. We kept walking, one foot in front of another. Sleep tugged at me, but with the sky still dark, I refused to quit before the sun rose.

My arms and legs felt like lead. My blinks became longer until I realized I was taking steps with my eyes closed.

Drav touched my arm gently, and I knew I was busted.

"You need to rest. Come, there is a house nearby."

"No, I'm fine. We gotta keep going."

Drav scooped me into his arms again, putting an end to my resistance.

"No, Mya. We won't make it there before sunrise. We need to stop for the night. There's a house ahead," he said, steering us toward what I couldn't see in the dark night.

Giving into my exhaustion, I relaxed in his arms until he

slipped and tightened his hold on me. I clung to him the rest of the way to the old farmhouse.

No lights were on when Drav set me down on the porch, with a stern "Stay here." I watched him break the lock and slip inside. Cold wrapped around me, and I tucked my chilled fingers under my arms, trying to warm them.

When Drav reappeared, his gaze dipped briefly to my poncho-covered chest before he met my gaze.

"Is it safe?" I asked.

"It is. Come." He held out his hand for me to take.

I easily slipped my much smaller one into his grasp and let him lead me into the house. The heat was on, and I shivered at the warmth. Drav closed the door behind us, and we both struggled out of our wet ponchos. He took mine from me and hung it on one of the many hooks near the door. I moved further into the house, turning on lights downstairs as I looked around. Another nice place. This one thankfully empty.

Tiredly, I followed Drav upstairs, where he led me to a room with a queen-sized bed.

"Go ahead and change your clothes. I will go downstairs to find some food."

I nodded absently, tugged my bag off, and rotated my shoulders to relieve some of the stiffness. Taking out the sleep clothes I had used at the cabin, I quickly changed.

I didn't go downstairs for food but crawled under the covers and fell fast asleep.

CHAPTER NINETEEN

I SNUGGLED CLOSER TO THE HEAT BEHIND ME AND TUCKED MY HAND under my cheek. The bed was so comfortable and warm. I never wanted to leave it.

Then reality pressed ever so slightly against my backside, and my eyes popped open. That wasn't...it couldn't be his...

Drav's fingers smoothed over my hair, moving the few strands that had escaped from my braid off my face. His warm breath caressed my neck.

I bolted. One minute I lay in bed, the next I was all flying elbows and legs as I fought my way out from under the covers. I didn't stop until a solid bathroom door separated me and the horny demon who'd been snuggling my backside. A soft growl answered the sound of the lock snapping into place.

"Don't you dare break that door," I said, taking a cautious step backward.

"Then unlock it."

"No way in hell."

A moment of silence passed as I stared at the door with wide eyes, waiting for it to explode inward. But it didn't. Instead, he spoke again.

"Why did you run?"

I frantically looked around the space for a reason that did not involve the raging boner he just had pressed against my butt.

"I needed to pee, Drav. Why else?"

"Then why aren't you peeing?"

"Because you're listening. Go away."

Something thumped on the other side of the door.

"I think you're hiding from me," he said softly. "And I don't like it."

I watched the door nervously, but nothing happened. This new, more communicative Drav confused me in a whole different way, now.

"What are you going to do?"

"Wait for you to come out."

I closed my eyes and mentally groaned. There was no way I would walk out of the bathroom just so he could nudge me back to the bedroom for more snuggle time. I wasn't stupid. Demon or human, if it had a penis, there was a purpose for it. I'd been safe because Drav hadn't known or understood, it seemed. However, those damn romance novels had spelled out the reason for him.

"Fine. You want the truth? You scared me just now, almost as much as you'd scared me the first time we met." Not really, but I didn't want to admit that, not even to myself.

"How?"

"Remember how grabby you were? Remember all the times I told you to stop because it made me uncomfortable? You were doing it again this morning."

"My hands weren't on your breasts. They were on your hair."

I covered my face.

"I can't talk about this with you."

"Then we won't talk. Just open the door."

"No." What if he was standing out there, naked, waiting to pounce? "Now that you can understand, we need some rules."

"Rules?"

"Yeah. You understand that word, right?"

"Yes."

"Good. Rule one. No more touching me whenever you want." I paused, trying to think of another rule that the first one wouldn't already cover.

"And the next rule?" Drav asked when I remained silent.

"No more iPod."

"Fine. Now, open the door."

I stood there for a moment, hesitating. I couldn't stay in the bathroom forever. My family was in Tinker, and I needed his help to get there. So what if he'd sprung some wood while snuggling. Like he'd pointed out, he hadn't been groping me. Just snuggle-business as usual. Taking a fortifying breath, I reached for the knob and opened the door.

Drav slowly looked up from where he'd had his forehead pressed against the door—the thump I'd heard. His tormented green eyes pinned me with guilt. I looked away from the emotion there and wished I hadn't when I saw the bare expanse of his smooth, darkly-chiseled chest. He'd slept with no shirt again.

Don't look lower. Don't look lower.

I did and to my relief, he wore pants and was no longer in pounce mode.

"You are the only thing I like about this world," he said.

My gaze flew to his as my stomach gave an odd flip at his words.

"Please don't ever run from me."

He held out his hand, not touching me, but silently asking to be touched. It surprised me how much I wanted to take it.

"What's going to happen when we reach the city again?" I asked, not taking his peace offering. "When we find my family, are you going to let me go?"

He slowly lowered his hand.

"I will."

"Honestly, I'm not sure I believe you."

He studied me for a long moment.

"I will let you go because I know you won't go far. We both know you won't be safe for long without me."

He said what I'd been trying not to think since before we'd reached the cabin. Once I did find my family, I had no idea how we'd survive this new world. Our only hope lay in whatever location the military had secured for the survivors. A location that wouldn't welcome Drav.

"And if I am safe without you? Will you let me go?"

"Yes. I will let you go."

I nodded, trying to ignore the tightness in my chest, and reached for the door.

"Now I really do have to pee. Please don't stand out in the hallway. It's weird."

"All right. I'll be in the kitchen."

I closed the door and took my time washing up. When I reemerged, the hall was empty. I crept back to the room, changed clothes, then reclaimed the bathroom to brush my teeth and rebraid my hair.

With nothing else to delay me, I went to the kitchen. Drav sat at the table, a can of peaches before him and another can near the chair beside him.

"Will you eat with me?"

I nodded and sat beside him. My mouth was already full of peach when he spoke.

"My life was lonely before I came here, but I didn't know loneliness then because all I knew was my day to day life. I understand now, and I don't want to go back to it. When we find your family and it comes time for me to let you go, I will. Until then, I ask for your company."

I choked on my guilt as I swallowed down the peach.

"If my being near you upsets you, I am sorry. I never stopped to think that while your presence was giving me comfort, mine caused you distress. I never intended for that to happen. I will be more considerate in the future."

Aw, hell.

"Drav, you have been considerate. You've kept me safe. And I am forever grateful for that. I didn't mean for it to sound like I don't enjoy being near you. You're different and, sometimes, a little frightening to me."

The vertical slit of his eyes narrowed slightly, and I realized my fear of him as a shadow man or demon, or whatever his species, had faded. My only fear remained of him as a man.

"You're not scary to me anymore." I reached out across the table and set my hand on his, where it rested beside his untouched fork.

He turned his hand and wrapped his fingers around mine.

"Thank you, Mya."

I gave his hand a light squeeze then let go and quickly ate my breakfast. After I finished eating, Drav went to the bathroom. I waited for him at the table until he was ready to leave.

Dusk muted the clear sky as we stepped outside. Near the garage, an infected heard the backdoor click and ran toward the house.

Drav growled and stepped in front of me protectively. I smiled slightly and stayed in place as he charged the man and tore off his head. The fact that I no longer flinched at that level of violence worried me. My world seemed so scarily different now. Hellhounds. Infected. Corrupt survivors. And, hopefully, decent survivors, too.

I thought of the men at the bridge and how they clung to their light and weapons for safety. Not me. I walked around at night unarmed and without fear because of Drav.

He turned back to me as the body fell to the ground.

"It's safe now, Mya."

I nodded and stepped forward.

The ground felt less muddy and slippery than the night before, and I walked on my own two feet without trouble. As the moon rose, we made good progress, but not good enough. Miles passed and I still didn't see the major highway we would need to cross. The one that signaled we were halfway home.

Stopping, I looked at Drav, whose questioning gaze met mine. His talk in the kitchen hadn't been a ploy to win his way back into my good graces. He really did care about me.

"We'll get there faster if you carry me, won't we?" I asked.

"Yes. But I would need to touch you."

Obviously. I was moved that he remembered my earlier concerns.

"That's okay."

I'd barely gotten the words out before he had me in his arms. He held me firmly against his chest and looked down at me. The slit of his pupils widened the longer he stared.

"Am I too heavy?" I asked, just to motivate him to start walking.

"No, Mya. You are perfect in my arms."

The way he said it reminded me how perfect he'd found me in his arms when I'd woken up.

"Maybe this isn't a good idea. Maybe we should find a car, instead."

"A car is too loud."

Then he ran. Without much choice, I tucked my face into his shirt to avoid the brisk wind.

After a little less than an hour, he slowed to a jog. I lifted my head and saw a dome of light shining in the distance.

"The same bridge?" I asked in a whisper.

"It is."

"Can we see if they are still there without going too close?"

"We could, but why risk you like that again?"

His concern warmed me.

"There aren't many of us uninfected left. Even though they are douchecanoes, I want to know they are still uninfected."

He grunted and continued walking. When we were close enough to see the bridge, he hesitated for a minute then continued moving, creating more distance. I didn't speak, just looked over his shoulder and watched the bridge growing smaller.

"There are twelve now," he said when the light disappeared behind some trees. "Three men are in the trees where we'd stood the first time."

I felt torn by the news. I didn't like that more had joined the untrustworthy group, but I was glad I wasn't the last uncontaminated human on earth.

"If it's safe, can you put me down so I can walk a bit and stretch my legs?"

"Of course."

His touch lingered a bit as he put me down, but I pretended not to notice.

We walked in silence, and I watched the horizon for the soft glow of city lights.

"You know what really bugs me?" I asked.

"Touching."

I rolled my eyes.

"No. I want to know why we lost communications but not power. If I could use my phone, it would be easy to know where my family is right now. To know they are still alive."

"Phone?"

I dug in my bag and produced the phone I'd turned off after recharging it at the cabin to conserve the battery.

"My brother and I used to text a lot. His last message said to watch out for the dogs and to stay safe. If this were working, I could send him a message asking where he is." I tossed the phone back in my bag. "Instead, we have to run all over trying to find them."

"I don't mind. It means more time with you."

I hooked my arm around his and leaned into him just a bit, guilt and pity welling up inside of me.

"I know. And I don't mind more time with you, either. But, I do worry that the longer it takes to find my family, the less likely it will be for me to find them uninfected."

He frowned but didn't say anything.

"I think I'm ready for you to carry me again if that's okay."

"It is. Thank you."

CHAPTER TWENTY

HE PICKED ME UP ONCE MORE AND STARTED RUNNING SOUTH. I DIDN'T turn my face into his shirt this time. I couldn't stop thinking about what reaching the city would mean for him.

"What will you do after we reach Tinker, and I find my family?" I asked, looking up at him.

He stared straight ahead, a muscle in his jaw twitching.

"Tell me about your family," he said, instead of answering.

"I love them, and they're fun to be around. My mom is a hobby jumper. She'll try anything. Sometimes the hobbies stick. Sometimes she loses interest. There was one summer we tried noodling—that's where you fish with just your hand. Ryan was really into it. He loved it. I wasn't as into touching the fish as he was."

"What hobby do you enjoy?"

I smiled at the memory the question brought up.

"When Ryan turned thirteen, my mom decided we were both old enough to try Fire Poi. It's kinda like dancing with fire on strings. It's beautiful to watch and makes you feel so graceful. That was my favorite. I kept it up until I went to college."

We were quiet for a few more roads as I remembered the time before the world went to hell.

"And your father? What did he think of your mother's hobbies?"

"He has stars in his eyes when it comes to her."

"How did his eyes not burn out if he had stars in them? Are stars not balls of gas in the sky?"

"I didn't mean it literally. It's just a saying. It means to him, she couldn't really do any wrong. He loves her exactly how she is."

He remained quiet, and I gave into the lash of the wind and turned my head into his shirt.

It wasn't long before Drav slowed, and I looked up. Spread before us were the sprawling lots signaling the outskirts of the city.

"You can set me down," I said quietly. He seemed more willing to listen this time and set me on my feet.

Together, we started the hide and sprint method of working our way into the city. With each block, the number of infected wandering around increased. Although I wanted to avoid the densely infected areas, the fastest way to Tinker was to cut straight through them. I wasn't willing to lose another day. I'd been too late too many times.

Without speaking, I signaled the destination for the next mad dash to Drav. He shook his head and nodded down the road. I waited, watching the houses. A small group of infected suddenly ran from around the side of a house almost a block down. A chill raced down my spine as they slowed as a group and continued down the street toward us.

Drav laid a hand on my back, the only thing that kept me from freaking out completely.

Why were they moving as a group? They hadn't done that before.

In silence, we crouched in the shadows of a truck as the herd shambled past. We didn't move until they suddenly sprinted across the yard two houses down. When they disappeared, I looked at Drav.

He slowly shook his head. No talking. Got it. Then, he lifted me into his arms.

After that, we began a different game of run and sprint. The infected's hearing had grown more acute in just a few days. Most now moved in herds, about four to six in size. A few shambled individually, which I took as a sign of being newly infected. I spotted a single infected person dressed in military fatigues further away and swallowed past a lump of fear.

Empty houses lined the streets. Sheets no longer hung out the windows but lay on lawns or bundled up on the curbs. A few cars still sat in driveways or on the side of the road, but the sight of cars grew a lot less frequent. That meant there'd been human movement since we'd left. That had to be a good sign. However, the continued presence of the herds dampened my hope.

Oklahoma City was a shell of the city it once was. Dead.

Halfway through the city, the herds of infected we encountered grew larger, making progress more difficult. Even with me in his arms, Drav made no sound as he moved. I gratefully clung to him, letting him navigate through the danger.

We entered a neighborhood that must have been scheduled for garbage pickup on the day everything went to hell. Bins lay tipped over in driveways and on lawns. Litter cluttered the sides of the road and against the houses.

Drav unexpectedly sprinted toward a car and put me down. Without needing to be told, I squatted beside him and watched the end of the street where he was staring.

A herd of at least twenty infected shuffled into view on a cross road. Men and women. Even a child. They all moved the same...as if coordinated. They turned onto our road, and I tried to control my breathing and remain calm. It proved difficult, though. Only

Drav's presence next to me kept me from complete panic as they drew closer with every shuffling step.

The car's trunk obstructed my view of their progress, which was probably for the best. Each scrape of their approach made me flinch. Drav's hand settled on my shoulder.

One of the shamblers kicked a discarded bottle which rolled under the car and stopped by my foot. The shuffling stopped. My gaze locked with Drav's. My eyes widened while my breath remained caught in my throat. I started to reach for him, ready for him to take off with me but the shuffling resumed down the road.

I released a quiet breath and offered Drav a relieved smile. Tension lingered around his eyes as he gave me a tight smile in return. Neither of us moved.

My need to find my family, to make sure they were safe, was putting both of us at risk. I wasn't stupid enough to think I could make it to Tinker without Drav's help. But, I was smart enough to know he wouldn't be able to take me right to the front door.

The other healthy humans at Tinker probably wouldn't take too kindly to a shadow man. Especially if Charles had made it back. A shiver ran down my spine. The last time I saw Charles, he had shot at me. Yeah, in his own morbid way he had been trying to save me because he thought death favorable over being taken by a demon. That mindset just reinforced why I couldn't take Drav with me to Tinker. I didn't want to see him hurt. Yet, as I looked at him, I knew he would resist leaving my side when the time came.

Once the herd of infected disappeared, I jerked my chin toward the fenced in, lit house across the street. After that close call, I needed a few minutes to calm down and let the shaking stop. Drav nodded and picked me up. In seconds, we stood by the back door. The lock had already been broken. Drav eased it open and moved inside. I waited until he came back and motioned for me to enter.

"I need to use the bathroom," I said softly after he closed the door.

He followed me around the corner and stayed in the hall while I shut the door. With all the stealth we'd been using, the sound of me peeing made me cringe, and I hoped the house was well-insulated. I didn't want to be trapped inside, surrounded by a pack of infected.

Not daring to flush, I washed my hands and opened the door.

"Are you hungry?" Drav asked quietly.

"No. I just want to get to Tinker. We don't have much time until the sun comes up."

I would feel better if he could at least get me to the edge of the compound, but I also didn't want to leave him stranded in the sunlight.

"Hang on a sec."

I went to the kitchen and rummaged through the drawers in the buffet to see if they had any sunglasses stashed there. I found a pair of reflective aviators...a much better fit than the sparkly, glammed up glasses I'd found him the first time in the city. I turned and discovered him right behind me.

"Found you a new pair of sunglasses." I offered them up.

Drav leaned down, and I placed the glasses on his face. My fingertips brushed against his cheeks. I swallowed. My reflection looked back at me. Wayward strands of my hair stuck out at odd ends.

"They look good on you," I said with a smile.

He didn't comment, just held his hand out for me.

Taking Drav's hand, I followed him to the door while an anxious excitement prickled over my skin. It felt strange not holing up somewhere for the approaching day. But we were so close. Even if my new night-time was slowly approaching, the stress and exhaustion that had pulled at me, melted away. Soon I'd be with my parents and Ryan. I wasn't sure I would ever let them out of my sight again.

The moment we stepped outside, Drav released my hand and

caught me up in his arms. He looked down at me, his expression subdued, and some of my excitement faded as his words came back to me. He'd said he had been lonely but that he hadn't known it until he'd met me. Yet, he would willingly let me go and return to that loneliness because I'd asked him to. My heart hurt for him.

He leaned toward me. The gentle curve of his lips held my attention. A rush of hot and cold zipped through me the closer he came. The world narrowed to the feel of his warm breath caressing my skin. My heart beat wildly in anticipation, any fear or doubt completely forgotten. At the last moment, he tilted his head and briefly set his forehead on mine. Regret consumed me. Then, I gently cupped his cheek and returned his version of a hug.

He exhaled heavily, lifted his head, then took a running start to jump the fence. He didn't set me on my feet. Safe in his arms, we left the subdivision and made our way through the rest of the city, clearing the last of the houses well before sunrise.

Beside the road that led to Tinker, he stopped and let me walk. The infected out here were scarce, and we reached the golf course near the military base without incident. As we stood in the shadows of the trees, a small, pessimistic part of my brain wondered if we would find the military base under attack by the infected. But that wasn't the case.

Tinker lay quietly before us, the area lit by so many utility lights that Drav squinted behind his sunglasses.

The infected weren't around but neither, it seemed, were the humans.

"It looks empty," I said softly.

"It does."

Empty meant safe for me to go the rest of the way on my own. I studied his profile as he continued to watch the airstrip and the buildings beyond.

"I would have never made it to the cabin or back to here without you," I said, with an aching heart. "Thank you for looking out for me. I hope you find your friends." I hugged him spontaneously. His arms immediately wrapped around me in return. How had a creature so alien and frightening become so comforting?

When I moved to pull back, he was a little slower to release me.

"I don't want to wait anymore, Drav." Dragging out leaving would only make it harder for him. For both of us.

"It's time for me to go."

CHAPTER TWENTY-ONE

"No, Mya. You will not go in there alone." Drav reached up and gently smoothed back some of my escaping hair.

"Drav, humans with guns will shoot at you if you go with me. What if you get shot again?"

"Then I will remove the head from the one who shot me."

Yeah, that's what I figured he'd do.

"You're a giant pain in my butt, you know that?"

He tilted his head, a look of concern pulling at his features, and I rolled my eyes.

"No, you are not literally causing me pain, you're just annoying me." I sighed. "I don't want to see you hurt."

"Then you understand why I can't leave you yet."

I shook my head at him. He was making this hard on both of us.

"Please, Drav."

"I would do anything for you, but not this. I'll leave you when you find your family. Not before."

I knew arguing would be useless and would only draw unwanted attention from humans and infected alike. So, I sighed and threaded my fingers through his.

"Will you at least hang back a little and let me go first?"

"No. We go together."

I glanced at the main gate again. My frustration built. As much as I wanted to see a living human to know that the base wasn't as abandoned as it looked, I really hoped there wouldn't be one popping up as soon as we approached.

"You're so stubborn. Fine. Let's go."

I released his hand, in case he needed to run, and started forward. We walked silently over the dead greens and across the pavement toward the gate. No one stepped from the guard house or from behind the thick lane dividers as we approached. Nothing moved but the light breeze and a piece of paper taped to the window.

I stepped closer to read the rain-smudged ink.

"Proceed to the air strip," I read softly for Drav's benefit.

Looking away from the note, I met his gaze.

"Are you sure you won't stay here?"

"I'm not leaving you, Mya."

I looked beyond the gate. Although I had high school friends who'd joined the Air Force, I'd never been on the base before and wasn't sure where to go. A large, empty parking lot stretched from the road to another building. I started walking toward the structure until I could read the sign. The Commissary. Someone had painted "Cleared of supplies" across the front of the building.

Uncomfortable in the open, I picked up my pace and jogged toward the building then turned right and followed the store fronts. Drav kept up with me as we passed each business. All had the same message painted on their doors and windows as the Commissary, and I knew everything had been cleared and taken to the secured location Charles had mentioned.

However, seeing inside the empty restaurants only fed my fears. The whole place felt too quiet. No men with guns to guard survivors waiting to be flown out. I thought of all the infected roaming the streets, the one I'd spotted dressed in fatigues, and the lack of houses with rescue needed signs, and picked up my pace as I jogged across an expanse of dried grass. We passed another fast food place, tagged with the word "clear," then ran along another road parallel to more stores.

Ahead, I spotted the airstrip.

"Almost there," I panted.

I didn't slow until we reached the edge of the field-like expanse of lawn. To our left, a sea of empty blacktop. To our right, the long airstrip. Straight ahead, a long length of chain-link fence. The dirt mounded around the posts indicated it was a new addition.

The fence didn't protect anything. Its straight line ran less than fifteen feet long and parallel to the air strip. Papers littered the surface of the fence and fluttered in the wind.

With a sinking feeling in my stomach, I went to the fence and looked at the papers. Notes and letters to loved ones left behind. Pictures of people who were missing. All of it left behind by the survivors evacuated from the base.

I pulled out the picture of my family that I had moved to my pocket.

"Help me look for them. Or a picture of me," I said, handing Drav the photo.

He didn't tell me the effort would be a waste of precious time or that the sun was less than an hour from rising. He took the photo, looked at my family, and then started looking at each photo on the fence. I went to the other end and did the same. I didn't just look at the photos but examined the letters too. Minutes passed as I searched and read. So many families ripped apart. So many lost. Some of the notes were goodbyes to family already known to be infected. An ache grew in my chest with each foot of fence I inspected without anything from my family.

"Mya," Drav said, softly.

I looked up as he pulled a photo from a place on the fence

before him.

"This is you," he said.

I rushed to his side and stared at the high school picture of me. Four years had changed me a lot. Yet, Drav had recognized the girl with the shoulder-length haircut and heavy makeup job. Hope washed through me, and I looked at the fence. They'd made it here. How long ago? Had they actually gotten on a plane?

"Where did you pull it from?" I asked.

"Here." He pointed to the empty space I'd been staring at. A space surrounded by images of other people. Letters to other families. Nothing from mine.

I swallowed in an attempt to ease the tightness growing in my throat and took the photo from Drav. It was something. At least one of them had been here.

"There is a mark on the back," he said.

I turned the photo over, and my eyes started to water.

We haven't lost hope. We will see you soon.

"We. They're still alive, Drav." I sniffled and wiped at my eyes and nose before looking at the fence again then the buildings beyond. I needed to know where they'd gone.

"How am I always just behind them?" I said, more to myself than Drav. He seemed to understand because he didn't answer.

I went back to reading the letters on the fence. Near the center, I found one with useful information.

"Drav, look at this," I said with quiet excitement.

"What is it?"

"A notice. The city's been evacuated, but any survivors should wait here. It says they will do a noon fly over and pick up anyone they've missed."

"They want you to wait in the open, without protection?"

"Well, once the sun is up—"

"The infected are not bothered by the sun. It isn't safe."

"What other choice do I have?"

He didn't say anything as he continued to look at me from behind his sunglasses.

"It'll be okay," I said. "I'll be with my family soon. You should go."

He looked away, the muscle in his jaw twitching again.

Before he could say anything, a phone started to ring. Loudly. Another joined it. Then another. I turned a slow circle, hearing ringing coming from everywhere, and realized what it meant.

"Communications are back. Drav, we need to get to the nearest phone," I said.

He picked me up without question but didn't start running.

"I don't like this. The infected will come."

"No, listen. The phones are ringing everywhere, not just here. They won't know where to run."

"They'll know to run toward the noise."

"Please, Drav. Just go!" I pointed toward the large buildings north of us, and he took off running.

It wasn't hard for him to break into the empty hangers. He set me on my feet and closed the door behind us. I ran for the nearest phone, getting it by the seventh ring. I pressed the receiver to my ear, trying to hear something besides my racing heart.

"State of emergency has been declared for Oklahoma City. Uninfected residents have been cleared. Any remaining survivors should clear city limits within the hour." The message just kept repeating after that.

I slowly hung up the phone. Thoughts whirled in my mind as I turned to look at Drav, who watched the door. As if sensing my regard, he glanced at me.

"What was that?" he asked.

"A message. A state of emergency has been declared for the city. It said we need to clear city limits within the hour." But, why clear the city limits? And who declared the emergency? There was no one here.

"This doesn't make sense," I said, looking at the empty hanger. "Why declare a state of emergency now? Everything is already gone? All that's left are infected. And that automatic message probably just pissed off all of them." I frowned, thinking again. "Why are the phones suddenly working now?"

Drav gave a very human looking shrug.

"What do you want to do? Leave or wait for the plane?" he asked.

"I don't know. The infected were acting weird, right? Maybe the call is to warn survivors to leave the suburbs because of that." Yet, that didn't feel right. Again, why call now? Why hadn't an automated call gone through during the hellhound wave to warn people to stay inside? Instead, phone service had just vanished.

The phone started ringing again. I picked it up and listened to the same words before quickly hanging up. Dread settled heavily in my stomach.

"We need to leave," Drav said, echoing what I'd been thinking.

"Agreed." He peered through the window then picked me up.

Outside, he didn't head back toward the airstrip but stuck close to the buildings. His slow, stealthy movements and the constant distant ringing crawled under my skin until tension coiled tightly around my heart and lungs.

"I don't want to leave again," I said. "But, this place feels all wrong and is weirding me out."

Drav slowed to look down at me.

"I think maybe we should leave city limits like the message said. Just for today. We don't need to go far, just somewhere we can keep an eye on things and figure out what's going on."

"Mya, slow your breathing." He leaned his forehead against mine, the cool rims of his glasses biting into my skin. But I didn't mind. It was real, and it helped me realize I'd been starting to panic.

I closed my eyes and took a deep, slow breath before opening them again. As soon as I did, he pulled back to look at me.

"Better?" he asked.

"A little."

The phones stopped, the sudden silence as unnerving as the collective ringing. Drav turned his head, looking at the open expanse of parking lot and further to the dead grass beyond. His arms tightened around me slightly, which scared me.

As I focused on the area, shadows moved just beyond.

"Infected?" I whispered.

"No. Ghua and others."

A cold sweat broke out over my skin as I counted shape after shape emerging from the far tree line in the predawn light. Six shadow men ran together toward us.

"Drav, I think we should go."

"You are safe with me, Mya."

"From infected and hellhounds, but you let Ghua sniff me."

He grunted but still didn't move.

"At least put me down."

"You will stay?"

He really thought I'd try to outrun six demon men?

"Yes. I'll stay." Like I'd go anywhere alone with all the phones ringing.

Even with my promise to Drav, it was hard not to turn and run at the sight of six large shadow men sprinting toward us. And they weren't even going their full speed. Ghua's familiar face stuck out from the others.

"Drav!" he said, as he made it to us first.

His sharp, eerie yellow eyes swept over me. His gaze had lost some of its curiosity since I had last seen him but those of his approaching companions worried me. I shivered and moved closer to Drav. He better not let them sniff me.

Drav stepped in front of me and partially blocked me from their view. I reached up and laid my hand on his back, in thanks.

However, Drav's gesture proved pointless when the others arrived and crowded around us.

Drav tensed under my touch as one of the shadow men walked around the half circle they had created to get a better look at me. He stood shorter than Drav but seemed more heavily muscled. His skin was even darker than Ghua's, and his eyes were more of a mustard yellow. His gaze swept over me, lingering here and there.

"What are you all doing here?" Drav asked in English.

Ghua said something, drawing my attention back to him and the others. It was unfair they could understand me but I couldn't understand them.

"No," Drav said, turning to look at the man who had stepped around us. Drav's fingers brushed against my hip, and he tugged me to his side.

"What's going on? Why are they here?"

"Ghua told them about you. They have come to see some women for themselves and crossed our trail."

Worry twisted around my heart like a vise. Drav had said they didn't have women in their world. And although it concerned me that I'd sparked their interest, I still felt a small measure of safety. Not only did I trust Drav, but I also knew Drav hadn't seemed to grasp the point of a girl until the stupid audiobooks, which I refused to think about further.

"Did they find any?"

Ghua spoke briefly before Drav translated.

"The ones with guns took the healthy, leaving only infected females. After they removed the head of one, they looked—"

"Okay. That's enough. I really don't want to hear any more."

Mustard eyes stepped closer, claiming my attention, his focused intensity so like Ghua's the first time we'd met. It worried me. When the new shadow man spoke, I couldn't understand a single thing he said. But the way Drav growled and stepped in front of me let me know it wasn't good.

CHAPTER TWENTY-TWO

"No," Drav said.

"Drav? What's going on?"

"Phusty wasn't there to see the infected female. He doesn't believe you have no penis and wants to see your breasts and pussy."

I choked, hearing that last word. Drav was never getting that iPod back.

"Yes," the one who I assumed was Phusty said. "Show no penis."

"No, she doesn't want to," Drav said, answering for me. "We are not here to look at women. We are here to search and learn."

Phusty scowled. With a low, angry voice, he spoke to Drav in their language.

"I lost their trail on one of the many roads that crosses this land. I was searching when I found Mya, and I continued searching while learning about this place," Drav answered in English.

I wasn't sure what was going on, but some of my worries about Drav learning our language started to resurface. What had he been searching for?

Phusty snorted, said several more incomprehensible words, then gestured in Drav's direction.

Drav began to speak in his language, and a pang of hurt stabbed at me along with my doubt. He knew English and knew I wouldn't understand that language, just as I knew they could easily understand mine. Drav was purposely hiding something from me.

Before I could ask what they were talking about, Drav said Ghua's name then mine. Ghua stepped forward in a flash and wrapped his arms around me. Pissed didn't begin to cover how I felt about this betrayal.

"We are not doing this again. Dammit, Drav!"

Since my arms were pinned to my sides because of Ghua's hold, I kicked out with both legs at the man who'd slowly won my trust. Drav, however, missed my awesome display of vengeful fury. The shithead was too busy snarling at Phusty.

"Let me go!"

Ghua's steely grip didn't waver as I kicked and thrashed. It wasn't like before when he'd groped me. This time, his hands stayed clear of my breasts. It didn't matter.

"I swear to God I will bite off your precious man-stick if you don't let me go now, Ghua."

Ghua made a disturbed noise.

"Stay, Mya. Ghua good. Drav friend."

His attempt to communicate penetrated my anger, and I stopped struggling long enough to blow some loose hair out of my face. With a cooler head and a clearer view, I saw why Ghua still held me. Two of the shadow men faced off in the center of their loose circle. Phusty crouched before Drav, his lips peeled back over his canines in a fierce snarl. Drav didn't react but remained tense and ready. What were they doing?

Dread filled me as Phusty lunged toward Drav. Like when Ghua had faced Drav, their movements were almost too fast to track. But,

I saw enough to know this was no friendship match like back at the house.

Phusty slammed his fist into Drav's side. The thud made me wince, but it didn't slow Drav. He snaked an arm around Phusty's neck before he could pull back and held him in a chokehold. No one moved to interfere. The only sounds came from the two struggling.

A red hue crept into Phusty's face as Drav exerted a scary amount of force around his neck. The man didn't give up, though. He landed several rapid, brutal blows to Drav's ribs. Drav grunted and stumbled backwards, releasing his hold. Free, Phusty sprang back and crouched low, ready to attack again even while he coughed and sucked in several breaths.

I tapped Ghua's forearm, and he loosened his hold but didn't let go. I didn't mind so much anymore. Gaze fixed on the pair, I watched like the rest of the group.

Phusty stopped coughing, grinned, and said something that caused a low, warning growl to rumble through Drav's chest. Before the sound stopped, Phusty rushed forward again. Drav twisted out of the way at the last second, and Phusty stumbled without a target. As the man flew past, Drav brought his fist down with a meaty thunk onto Phusty's back. The demon spun around quickly and clocked Drav in the face.

The sound of his teeth clacking together had me wincing again, and I almost missed him catch Phusty's arm. Drav gave the appendage a sharp twist, wrenching it behind the other man's back. Phusty's angry gaze met mine, and his lips upturned into a mean smile. In a flash, he flung his head backward, connecting with Drav's face.

I hissed in an empathizing breath and saw Drav's nose start to bleed and his eyes water. The watering could be from the hit to the face or the rising sun.

Phusty tried and failed to pull out of Drav's hold.

"How long are they going to do this?" I asked, Ghua.

"Drav not share Mya. I don't know...talk."

"You don't know the words to tell me?"

"Yes."

I frowned.

Drav drove his knee into the back of the other man's. Phusty buckled, landing hard on his knees before Drav. He yelled something in his language as Drav heaved back on his arm.

One minute I watched Phusty's face contort in pain, the next I was staring at a spatter of blood and gore as Drav pulled Phusty's head clear off.

Bile rose in my throat. I gagged, and Ghua released me. None of the others seemed even mildly upset by what they'd just witnessed. They watched dispassionately as the body fell forward onto the ground. Drav dropped the head near the body, his gaze on me.

My throat felt tight as I tried to wheeze in a breath.

I didn't like Phusty. Hell, from the moment he arrived, he'd freaked me out. Why, then, couldn't I breathe? Why did I feel sick? Why was I shaking? Shock. I'd just watched a fight to the death. It could have been Drav.

Drav moved toward me, covered in Phusty's blood. I reached for him, grabbing his bicep with shaking fingers. His hand cupped the back of my head, and he leaned down and pulled me forward to press his forehead against mine. Blood slicked my skin at the contact. It didn't matter. His comforting green gaze held mine, and slowly the panic began to ebb. He was here. He was alive. I was alive. We were okay. I took one breath then another. My grip on his forearms tightened as I exhaled shakily.

"Mya."

His lips formed my name quietly as if reassuring himself that I was still here. Safe.

"It will be okay. He will not try to claim you again."

"No kidding. You killed him."

"Yes. But, when he awakens he will not try again," he said calmly. He gave my forehead one last press then took a step back, breaking the spell around us.

The others stood near Phusty's body. Ghua nudged it with his foot.

"What are you doing?"

Ghua stopped and looked at me.

"He's dead. Leave him be."

The men around Phusty stopped what they were doing and looked back at me. Drav stepped into their line of view.

"What did you say?"

"He's dead."

Drav's gaze flicked to Phusty then back to me.

"Dead?"

Drav hadn't questioned words before. I didn't understand why he seemed confused by the word now.

"Drav?"

He didn't say anything. Instead he left me to go to the others, who had been listening to our conversation. They started to speak in their language again. Based on the rise in their voices and their gesturing, they were arguing about something.

Oranges and pinks painted the sky with the rising sun. I shook my head at them and picked up the bag that Drav had dropped at my feet, a reminder of why we were even at the base.

"Do you really have time for this?" I asked, rather loudly.

They didn't seem to hear me. I shouldered the bag and started walking toward the airstrip. I wasn't going to miss another chance to find out if my family was still alive.

"Mya."

I stopped and turned back to see Drav coming toward me. Worry pinched his features. Behind him, the others were picking up Phusty's body and head.

"What's going on?"

"Ghua and the others have decided to take Phusty back," he said, joining me.

I guess it made sense that they would want to bury him or something.

"Okay. You should go with them, Drav."

He reached for my hand and threaded his fingers through mine.

"I'm not leaving you, Mya."

He tugged on my hand lightly and started leading me toward the airstrip. His words and company warmed me, but I knew he couldn't stay. I waited until we were beside the fence with all the pictures.

"I would never have made it this far without you. Thank you," I said. I rose to my toes and pressed a kiss to his clean cheek then wrapped my arms around his shoulders. He hesitated a moment before hugging me in return. My chest felt tight, and I struggled not to cry. This world was scary because of the shadow men, but it would be scarier without Drav, too.

He held me close until I leaned back.

"Now, hurry up. I don't want you having to return home all alone." And that was the truth. I didn't want him to feel lonely again.

"I will wait until the plane arrives."

"Drav, you can't. I won't risk your life because you're stubborn."

"I promised to get you to your family."

He had promised to bring me home. And that had changed along the way. I knew he wanted me safe before he left me. But that meant staying until the plane arrived, something that would put him in too much danger. I couldn't allow that.

"You *have* gotten me to them."

"No. We found your picture, not them. I need to know they are not infected, too, before I leave you."

The note had given me hope they'd made it to safety,

uninfected. But I had no way to prove it. That thought set off a tiny explosion in my mind. The phones. With the phones ringing, maybe that meant my cell would work now, too.

"Here. Let me check my phone," I said, quickly digging in my bag. "If I can get a message to them and they answer, will you leave then?"

Drav didn't comment but watched me power on the phone. My heart beat hard in my chest, and my hands shook as I sent a quick message to Ryan's number.

At Tinker base waiting for pickup.

Hope tormented me with a new kind of agony as I stared at the display, waiting.

The sun broke over the horizon, and I looked up at Drav, who squinted painfully. He needed to find shelter now.

I opened my mouth to say so, but the blare of sirens cut me off. Clapping my hands over my ears, I looked up the pole at the nearby speaker that emanated the deafening sound. My eyes widen as I glanced around the empty army base. Why were the sirens going off with no one here?

Drav shoved the bag into my arms, picked me up, and sprinted away from the base and the noise. When he stopped, the alarms still blared in my ears, but the sound was bearable.

"What is that noise?" he asked.

"Sirens. I don't understand why they're going off though. There's no one here but—"

Oh my god.

The phone calls...the evacuation. They wouldn't. Would they?

I lifted the phone that I still clutched and saw Ryan's name. My gaze dropped to the single word he had texted.

Run.

My head snapped up, and I met Drav's unwavering gaze. Above us, something moved in the sky. Several planes. He must have seen the panic and fear in me.

"We need to get out. Now!"

He lifted me in his arms and took off running, heading south. His speed robbed me of air. I looked over his shoulder and watched the base and the city fall behind us.

In the distance, I saw the first bomb fall.

A single word remained burned in my mind.

Run.

The deafening boom and shockwave from the bomb slammed into us, knocking Drav forward. My ears rang, disorienting me further as he stumbled. Heart hammering, I forced myself to look over his shoulder and saw an old tree slowly topple behind us. Beyond it, a giant, misshaped smoke plume rose like a mushroom in the sky. A second bomb erupted not far from that cloud. High over the city, a plane zipped in, and I watched another silent explosion mushroom upward.

My family was still alive and safe somewhere to the north. But a war zone now lay between us, adding to the obstacles I would need to face in order to reach them.

How was I ever going to find them?

DEMON FLAMES

CHAPTER ONE

IT WAS ALL SO SURREAL. THE CONTINUAL RINGING IN MY EARS ADDED to the despair of realizing the world around us was being bombed to hell. Drav's fingers bit into my side with each jarring stride as he sprinted to put more distance between us and the Army base. But, I barely noticed the ache.

Staring at the clouds of dust and smoke that rose into the air caused a numbness to spread through me. I'd survived so much in the last week. Zombies. Hellhounds. Now this.

In the distance, the second shockwave flattened debris with a devastating force that raced toward us. I ducked my head down and hung onto Drav with the same desperation he held me. His arms tightened, and he seemed to run faster. The force of the impact jostled him, but he didn't stumble this time.

I glanced up at him. Tears caused by the brightness of the sun streamed down his cheeks, dripping from his tense, stubborn jaw. That stubbornness had saved me. If he'd left like I'd wanted, I would have died.

I caught the sun's reflection off the large body of water to our right while I listened to the north side of Oklahoma City fall to its knees.

When the shockwaves no longer touched us, I peeked over his shoulder again. Trees blocked most of the view, but I still saw the smoke and dust-clouded horizon. My breath lodged painfully in my throat. My city, my home, was gone.

My family.

"Drav, stop. Put me down."

He immediately halted and placed me on my feet. Before I could look at the phone I still clutched, he clasped my face between his large hands. His squinted, worried gaze swept over me.

"Are you all right? Were you hurt?" he asked.

The panic in his voice warmed me. Even with everything I knew gone, I wasn't alone. I gripped his wrist with my free hand.

"I'm fine. Are you okay? That first aftershock hit us hard."

He nodded and, with a shaky exhale, set his forehead against mine. I appreciated the sentiment. My insides still felt like Jell-O. Leaning into his embrace, I released his wrist and placed my hand on his chest. Our breaths mingled while we stood in the relative safety of the trees, the distant continuing blasts emphasizing the fate we'd escaped.

"Drav, I need to call my family. I need to let them know I'm safe."

His hands slid from my cheeks to the back of my head.

"I need to know you're safe, too." The look in his eyes made my heart stutter for a moment, as did the way he gently trailed his fingers down the side of my neck. Emotions that I didn't have the time or luxury to examine raged inside of me. My breath caught at the feel of his fingers toying with the ends of my hair. Everything felt confusing when it came to him.

"I am safe," I managed to whisper.

He nodded and pulled back a bit.

Exhaling slowly, I tore my gaze from his and lifted my phone. I still had a signal. I half laughed and half cried as I fumbled to dial

Ryan's number. Drav stood close, watching me, his thick fingers still playing with my hair.

Ryan picked up on the first ring.

"Mya!" His voice echoed like he had me on speaker phone. Hearing him cracked the hold I had on my frayed emotions. He really was alive.

"Mya, baby, are you okay?" Mom asked.

"I'm fine. We barely got out. I can't believe I'm talking to you." Silent tears choked my words. Drav's fingers immediately traced down my hair.

Mom began to cry, and Ryan's voice shook when he next spoke.

"Oh my God, Mya. I wanted to call you as soon as they turned the phones back on, but I was scared you had your ringer on and the infected would hear."

"It's okay. I'm okay. I'm safe. I promise," I said. "Where's Dad?"

"When we saw your text saying where you were, he went to try to stop the bombing," Ryan said.

I laughed through my tears. That sounded like Dad.

"You'll probably need to bail him out from somewhere. Where are you? I've been at least a day behind you. At the house. The cabin. The base."

"They're not telling us where we are."

"What? Why not?"

"Because they're afraid." His voice lowered. "There are some rumors that it's not just the hounds and the infected out there. I've heard something else showed up with the quakes. Something smart. Something the military's afraid of."

I met Drav's steady gaze.

"I don't understand what that has to do with them not telling you where you are."

"Whatever these things are, they can understand us. Communications went down to stop them from getting any potential information they might be able to use against us."

"Then why turn the phones back on?"

"They weren't going to. People here rioted when we heard the military was going to bomb the cities. Everyone is missing someone and hoping they're still alive."

"Cities?"

"Yeah." Yelling erupted in the background on Ryan's end and grew louder.

"Head north," Ryan said quickly. "There's more than one safe zone for survivors. Stay away from the cities."

The line went dead. Pulling the phone from my ear, I checked the connection and immediately tried calling back. No one answered. A moment later, I lost my signal.

Without warning, I found myself once again holding my bag and cradled in Drav's arms. He took off running. The wind battered my face, but I didn't protectively duck into his chest again.

"Wait," I said, trying to breathe. "Where are you going?" I looked around at the blurring trees and the sky, trying to get my bearings. We needed to head north. Where in the heck was the sun?

"We must keep moving," he said without slowing.

The trees gave way to a few houses in the rural outskirts of the city as well as a hazy view of the sun before we ran under their cover once more.

"But we're going the wrong way. The sun needs to be on our right side."

"Listen," he said, maintaining his focus on running. "Do you not hear it?"

Ducking out of the wind, I concentrated on the sounds around us. The absence of bird song and animal chatter still creeped me out. That left the faintly discernible whoosh of our passage under the noise of the explosions going off—getting louder, actually— and the hum of the planes in the sky.

"What should I be hearing? The bombings or the planes?"

"Both. And they are in the direction you want to go. You have many cities, and they plan to destroy them all. You are not safe here. If I take you north, you will get hurt."

My stomach sank as I realized he was right. He couldn't take me north. Ryan had made humanity's fear of Drav's people clear. If Drav tried helping me reach a safe zone, he'd be the one hurt. I couldn't risk that. I had to reach my family on my own. Yet, the idea of leaving him upset me. This new world scared me less with him at my side. And, he certainly wouldn't like the idea of me going off on my own, either. However, the bombings would give me the cover I needed to use a different mode of travel.

"We need to find a road or a car," I said.

He veered out of the trees without question and found a quiet stretch of country road within minutes. He ran beside the worn blacktop, passing the occasional house. Nothing moved and there were no cars. I needed to figure out where we were.

"Stop," I said when I spotted a road sign.

Drav did as I asked, but he didn't set me down.

We were running alongside 60th Avenue. Perfect. Kind of. We weren't as far south as I'd thought.

From his arms, I eyed the quiet expanse of road. A few abandoned cars dotted the blacktopped length further south, near Highway 9. In the distance, heading north in our direction, I saw a few infected. They were sprinting toward the sounds of bombs and their eventual ends.

"This will work," I said. "If we find a car with keys, I can drive north. The infected won't bother me much. With all the bombing, they won't hear me unless they're really close. And in a car, the people bombing will know I'm not infected, and I'll be safe."

I looked up at Drav. The tears hadn't stopped streaming, and I wished Phutsy hadn't head-butted Drav and broken his sunglasses.

"It's not safe even with a car," he said.

"Look around, Drav. Nothing's safe anymore. Driving a car to where I need to be is the safest option."

He studied me for a long, quiet moment before moving toward the first car. The broken driver's side window gave a clear view of an infected woman strapped into the front seat. She didn't lurch forward or move anything but her head. Only her eyes tracked our approach, almost as if she was aware she couldn't reach us...that we needed to come to her.

"Skip this one. It's probably out of gas," I said, not wanting to get any closer.

Drav jogged to the next car. The driver's door hung open, the inside empty.

"Let me down so I can see if there are keys."

He set me on my feet and took the bag from my arms. I quickly found the keys in the ignition. The excitement at finding them died when the engine failed to turn over. Dead battery. However, after checking the visor, glovebox, and center console, I found another pair of sunglasses for Drav.

The dark lenses provided him a measure of relief and stopped the watering so we could continue our search.

We hit the jackpot with the fifth vehicle parked in the driveway of one of the homes on the road. The truck started on the first try and had a full tank. I looked up with a smile, expecting to see Drav standing by the driver's door. However, the space was empty. Across from me, the passenger door opened, and he got in.

"Uh..."

"Close your door, Mya."

"Drav, you can't come with me. Where I'm going—"

"You need me to get there safely. Now, close the door."

I frowned but did as he wanted. The sounds of the blasts were growing louder and the infected drawing closer. We didn't have time to argue out all the reasons he needed to let me head north by myself.

Shifting the truck into reverse, I backed out of the driveway and started south. I would take him as far as possible. When I found a place to turn west so I could circle around the city, I'd drop him off.

"Can you open the glove box? It's that compartment tucked into the dash right in front of you."

I swerved, trying to avoid one of the infected running at us but ended up hitting it anyway. Blood spattered the windshield, and I fumbled to figure out how to clean it off.

"What do you need from in here?" Drav asked, drawing my attention from the mess.

"A map, if there is one."

"There is," he said, pulling out an old map of Oklahoma as I crossed over a deserted highway nine.

"Good. Because the only roads I know heading north are the ones that cut through the city they're blowing up. See if you can find us a way around."

Paper crinkled beside me. I pressed the wipers again and removed the rest of the blood in time to hit the next infected. I'd run out of washer fluid at this rate.

"I can't read this," Drav said.

"What do you mean? I thought you just needed to see a word to know it."

"No. Once I hear a word, I know it. Writing is different."

"Why?"

"I'm not sure. Maybe because we don't use writing."

"Really? Okay." With the road before us clear, I slowed down, not bothering to ease off onto the shoulder. There was no point without traffic.

"Let me see the map," I said, once I stopped.

"Wouldn't it be easier if I drove and you told me where to turn?"

"You can drive?"

"I think so. The pedal on the right makes the vehicle go. The

M.J. HAAG & BECCA VINCENZA

pedal on the left makes it stop. The wheel gives it direction. The handle beside the wheel cleans the glass."

"There's a bit more to it than that. Just hand me the map."

Drav passed me the map. As I studied the map, he began to run his finger lightly up the length of my arm. I shivered and peeked up at him. All of his focus remained on gently stroking me. I swallowed then slowly leaned away and focused on the map.

After a few moments, I figured out the route I would take to drive around the city so I could head back north.

Something thumped into my door, making me jump and squeak. A boy around my age, stared at me with cloudy eyes. He swayed side to side on his feet, his mouth gaping open and close. Behind him, I saw another infected sprinting our way, attracted to the sound of our engine instead of the distant blasts.

Sliding the shifter back into drive, I took off, continuing south.

"Is it just me or are they getting creepier?"

"You've always found them creepy," Drav said, watching the road in front of us.

"And you haven't?"

"No. Not creepy. Unpleasant and numerous."

I couldn't argue with that. The two infected fell behind, and I paid attention to the road ahead. Because of the river, I ended up driving all the way down to Lexington and through Purcell before heading north-west on I-35, more than an hour after the bombing had begun.

The attempt to stop and drop off Drav failed completely. He refused to get out. I couldn't say I experienced any disappointment over his unrelenting refusal to leave me, yet I did worry about what would happen to him when we reached our destination. I didn't want him to get hurt.

As we drove, a solid, light grey filled the sky to the east. Not just above Oklahoma City, but off in the direction of Tulsa, too. The bombers were destroying everything. I understood why. Getting to the military base had been hard. The infected far outnumbered the survivors. Bombing had been an easy way to kill them and the hounds. But what about the shadow men like Drav? I glanced at him. They were different, overly clueless about girls, and prone to acts of violence. Yet, they weren't all bad. Especially not Drav. I hoped his people wouldn't die because of the explosions.

Despite the destructive activity to our right, we continued north at a reasonably steady pace. Some people must have tried evacuating on the highway earlier, because the further north I drove, the more cars we saw crowding the road. A heavier degree of dust had settled on them, as well.

A jaw-popping yawn made my eyes water as I navigated through the abandoned vehicles. I leaned forward, trying to see through my yawns and the silt covering the windshield.

"You're tired," Drav said. "Stop and rest or let me drive."

I was exhausted, and Ryan's crappy "head north" directions likely meant we had a lot of driving in our future. It would be easier if I taught Drav how to use the truck now.

"Fine," I said, slowing. I slid the gear shift into park. "The letter P stands for park, R for reverse, and D for drive." I pointed to each one as I spoke then moved to open my door.

"No," he said, grabbing my arm.

I glanced out my window, expecting an infected. Drav's hold vanished, and his fingers gently traced over the sleeve of my hoodie. I looked at him.

"I didn't mean to hurt you," he said softly.

"You didn't."

He brushed his fingers along my cheek and smiled slightly.

"I'll get out. You slide over. It's safer if you stay in here."

He opened his door and missed my blush. Trying to control the summersaults in my stomach, I once again realized how thankful I was that Drav had refused to leave me.

A second later, he climbed into the driver's seat and glanced at me, as if making sure I had truly remained safe for those few moments he'd left. Apparently satisfied with what he saw, he buckled his seatbelt and focused on the truck. I watched him move the shifter into drive while keeping his foot on the brake.

"Good," I said, impressed. "Now ease off the brake and gently give it some gas with the right pedal." The truck lurched forward then smoothed out into a steady acceleration.

"Go slow until you get a feel for steering and stopping," I said, feeling a little nervous.

He wove through the vehicles and even stopped to move one out of the way. My mouth popped open when I saw him lift the back end of the sedan. He swung it off the road with ease then got back in and took off without a hiccup.

"Rest, Mya. I'm comfortable driving."

"You're not tired?" I asked. "I don't want to crash because you fall asleep at the wheel."

"No. I'm not tired yet. I'll wake you when it's your turn to drive."

I willingly closed my eyes. The steady sound of the tires on the road and Drav's presence lulled me into a restful sleep.

CHAPTER TWO

THE TRUCK SLOWED, ROUSING ME SLIGHTLY. THE SOUND OF THE DOOR opening and closing finished the job, and I groggily opened my eyes. The bright light of the sun blinded me. It took a few blinks to focus and understand why we'd stopped.

Two abandoned cars sat crossways in the road, blocking our way. I frowned at the odd sight. No way they'd been left like that accidentally. The thought had barely formed before Drav lifted the back of one and took a step toward the shoulder to clear a path for us.

In the space of a heartbeat, four infected emerged from the new gap between the cars and ran at Drav. My mouth fell open in shock. Drav dropped the car and ripped off the head of the first one. The spray of blood bathed the remaining three as Drav tossed the head away. The infected didn't seem to notice the loss of their companion as they circled Drav.

One lunged at Drav from behind, its teeth snapping at Drav's sizable biceps. Drav turned swiftly, barely avoiding being bitten. However, the other two used the distraction to charge forward. My heart jumped, and I shouted a warning.

With a burst of speed, Drav pivoted and moved behind the

snapping infected. While he ripped off its head with a quick jerk, one of the remaining two gave up on him and sprinted toward the truck. Toward me.

I slammed the locks down. It didn't matter that the infected couldn't open my door. Going from a nice, peaceful nap to a zombie attack had freaked me out, as had the idea that the cars had been positioned in the road on purpose. But, by what?

Breathing hard, I looked up and came face to face with an infected. The woman's stringy brown hair hung over her pallid face, but not enough to stop her milky white eyes from tracking my movement inside the truck as I eased away from the window. Drool spilled from her gaping mouth.

One moment her dead eyes stared at me, and the next, Drav stood in her place, his green eyes full of life and anger. He chucked her severed head over his shoulder and stalked around the front of the truck. It took a moment for me to see he'd already moved both cars.

I unlocked the door, and he slid into the driver's seat, his leg pressing against me. Even with the way clear, he didn't immediately start driving. He gripped the steering wheel tightly and stared straight ahead.

"Drav?" Hesitantly, I reached over and touched his arm. The hard muscle twitched under my fingers.

"Are you okay?"

"Do you see how dangerous it is for you?" he asked, not looking at me.

"Yes, I do." I patted his arm soothingly. "But you don't need to worry. I'll be safe with my family. Where they are is safe."

He turned and met my gaze. The intensity in his eyes, behind his sunglasses, made my stomach flutter.

"I will protect you, Mya."

I wasn't sure if he said it for my sake or his own. Giving his arm a gentle squeeze, I scooted back to my side of the bench seat and buckled up.

Drav put the truck into drive and focused on maneuvering us through the scattered vehicles. After the past week of being in the dark, it felt odd being awake while the sun still sat high in the sky. As more miles passed quietly, I relaxed and closed my eyes, lulled by the motion of the truck.

Blood spattered dreams, showcasing my family with milky white eyes, plagued me until the truck slowed.

My door clicked open, jolting me, and the cool air brushed against my skin. I blinked my eyes, trying to focus.

"I have you, Mya." Drav's gravelly voice brushed against my ear.

I turned my head toward the sound and found him leaning over me to unhook my seatbelt. Once freed, he scooped me against his chest. I looped my arms around his neck, snuggling close with a sigh. Something brushed my temple. It took a moment for the sensation to have meaning. A kiss. The gesture warmed me.

"I can walk," I said, making no effort to pull away.

"This is safer." He started moving, and the steady motion comforted me more than it should have. Traveling in Drav's arms sure did feel safer. I relaxed and started to drift sleepily, but my stomach growled loudly and brought a measure of reality back. I was hungry because we'd been running since sunrise.

I lifted my head and glanced around. The sun hung lazily on the horizon.

"Why did we stop?"

"The truck stopped making noise."

I bit back a groan of frustration.

"We probably ran out of gas."

I studied our surroundings. We were stuck in the middle of nowhere, and there wasn't another vehicle in sight. A vehicle had been ideal while near the cities, but as those four infected on the road had proven, we were hitting quieter areas. And with the sun rapidly dropping, the noise of a vehicle would not only attract the infected but also the hounds.

"It's probably for the best. Are you tired yet? Should we find somewhere to rest?"

"No. You need to eat."

Instead of arguing that he'd gone days with little sleep, I tugged the bag from his shoulder and cradled it on my stomach so he could run without making any noise. He picked up his speed, and I turned my face into his chest. The wind whipped past, whistling in my ears for several minutes before he slowed.

Glancing up, I saw an old farmhouse. He placed me on the screened-in wraparound porch and told me to stay while he checked inside. The world remained eerily quiet while I waited. However, the sound of all those explosions continued to haunt me. Were the planes still out there destroying cities? I wrapped my arms around myself and hoped the bombings had stopped. It would be one less problem I needed to worry about. I still had to figure out how to find one of the safe areas without Drav getting hurt in the process.

As if my thoughts had summoned him, he returned. In the fading light, his gaze swept over me. I could see the tender concern in his eyes.

"Come," he said softly. He held out his hand, and I threaded my fingers through his.

He led me into the little house's foyer where stairs led up to the second floor. Passing by those, I followed him through the house to the kitchen in the back. I spotted a switch and turned on the lights.

A small breakfast table was tucked next to the big picture window. He told me to sit while he searched the cabinets. I glanced out the window at the lowering sun, and my stomach tightened both with hunger and nerves.

My family waited for me out there somewhere. How would we ever find them? We had so much working against us.

The thump of Drav setting a couple of cans of food on the table interrupted my thoughts.

As I looked down at the fruit, tuna, and Spam, I finally noticed the infected blood speckling Drav's hands. Hands that I'd just held. I quickly looked at my own. Although the blood didn't appear to affect Drav, it still posed a threat to me.

"Wait, we need to wash up."

I stood and went to the sink, scrubbing my hands with soap. After I finished, I turned and found Drav just behind me. I squeaked and looked up at him.

Infected blood splattered his forehead and cheeks, several little dots close to his eyes and mouth.

"Wow. You really got them good. Or, I should say, they got you good. Just a sec."

I searched the drawers near the sink for a towel. Finding one, I wet it with a bit of soap then faced Drav. He hadn't moved. Midway to handing him the towel, I changed my mind. Without a mirror, he'd never get it all.

"Let's move to the table after you wash your hands."

He quickly scrubbed his hands free of infected blood. His shirt remained spattered. I considered digging in my bag for a clean one then changed my mind on that, too. If he didn't plan to spend the night here, he'd probably just get dirty again, anyway.

As soon as he sat at the table, I stepped between his open legs and began to wipe away a small spatter of blood closest to his eyes.

He exhaled slowly. A tug on my sweater caused me to look down. Drav's fingers curled around the hem and held tight. I knew it wasn't fear. He just liked hanging on to me. I might have smiled a little when something started to swirl in my belly at that thought.

Moving to the other side, I continued to clean away the blood spatter. When I finished, I took a new cloth and wet it to rinse away any soap residue. His fingers once again toyed with the bottom of my shirt.

I hated knowing that he would be in even more danger now because of me. Any human who spotted us together would think Drav had taken me and was dangerous, just like Charles had. Drav would not only need to work at keeping me safe from hellhounds and infected, but he would need to keep himself safe from humans, as well. We had so much stacked against us.

When I finished, I pressed my forehead to his. He closed his eyes at the contact.

"Thank you," I said.

"For what?"

"For everything."

I went to place a kiss on his cheek, but he turned his head at the same time so my lips landed on the corner of his mouth instead. His hands suddenly gripped my sides. Not painfully, but possessively. I pulled back quickly. His gaze held mine for a moment while my face heated. Then, he slowly released me.

Escaping, I returned the towel to the sink before washing my hands once more. I took my time, letting the warmth in my face cool and the butterflies in my stomach calm. When I felt more in control, I turned off the water.

Drav watched me closely as I walked to the table and sat down again. I didn't know what to say or do, and his intense look and lack of response made me even more on edge.

A rumble from my empty stomach gave us both something else on which to focus. Drav pushed a can of food toward me.

"Eat, Mya."

I wrinkled my nose at the Spam and pushed it away, choosing mandarin oranges instead. All the cans had pull tabs, and I immediately opened mine. Drav watched me fish out an orange wedge and pop it into my mouth before he grabbed the tin of Spam that I'd scooted away.

He popped a hunk of gelatinous meat into his mouth and chewed. I watched his reaction, waiting to see what he thought.

Based on his expression, he liked it. When he caught me looking, he offered me some. I declined, and he ate the rest while I finished the oranges and then some tuna.

Drav pushed another can toward me.

"I'm full," I said. More than that, I couldn't waste any more time on food or whatever had just happened between us. I had to find my family.

Before I'd been chasing after hope, but hearing from Ryan and Mom had changed hope to reality. Even though I knew they were protected by a fence and men with guns, I also knew all the dangers that waited out there. I doubted there was anywhere truly safe anymore.

"Are you okay to keep going?" I asked. "We could probably find another car to use until the sun goes down."

"I'm okay, Mya. But, don't you want to sleep a little more?"

"No. We need to get moving."

The longer we stayed, the more my stomach knotted. With the bombs and the weird infected behavior on the road, I worried that we wouldn't be able to travel at night as swiftly as we had been. It felt safer to keep moving while we had a bit of daylight remaining.

We left the farmhouse after I stuffed some cans of food into my bag, which Drav shouldered. Once outside, he didn't ask if I wanted to be carried. Instead, he picked me up and began running before I could even protest. Not that I would have. He could get us there faster—where ever "there" was—if I wasn't slowing us down on foot.

With a sinking feeling, I realized he'd left the map in the truck.

"Drav, we have to go back and get a map."

"We don't need it. I will keep running in the trees alongside the road."

I reluctantly agreed. Although, I would have felt better with the map, I didn't care for the idea of backtracking and wasting precious time. We could check cars along the way.

The sun dropped closer to the horizon as Drav ran. A pretty sunset peeked through the trees, and the soft, warm reds and oranges slowly began to darken. Although breathtaking, something about it felt wrong. Ominous. Unable to figure out what, I tucked my face into Drav's chest to avoid the wind until he suddenly slowed.

"What's wrong?" I asked, looking up at him.

His attention snapped to the right, toward the remnants of twilight. In the distance, a howl echoed, followed by another. A shiver chased through my body.

Hellhounds.

"Hold on tight," Drav said.

He took off faster than before. I squeaked and put my head into the crook of his neck to protect my face. The air whipped past us, lashing at me with icy fingers.

A howl sounded closer, and Drav quickly changed directions. Snapping branches and a sharp snarl jerked me from my protective cocoon. I peeked over Drav's shoulder and caught a flash of glowing red eyes. The dark shape wove through the trees, slowly closing the distance between us. Behind it, another set of red eyes flashed.

He tightened his hold on me. Fear swam in my stomach. Would we be able to outrun them? I had no idea who was faster. Drav or a hound? He and I hadn't seen any since the night we'd met. Sure, Drav had dealt with that pair, but I would prefer he not stop to fight these two.

The trees blurred with Drav's speed, but the hounds were still too close. Drav took a sharp turn and dodged around some trees.

Ahead, something flickered through the barren treetops. A second then a third appeared. Houses. Maybe if we—

In the dim light before us, more shadows moved. My hope that we could make it to a house, or somewhere safer, died. They had us surrounded.

Drav didn't slow, though. He ran straight toward the oncoming numbers, shadows that moved...familiarly. I squinted into the wind, trying to see better, and finally grasped that the shapes were much too large to be hounds. Demons. Shadow men. Drav's kind.

The first one blurred past us. A snarl, followed by a grunt, sounded in our wake. Three more men sprinted by us. I glanced back and watched them work together to face the oncoming hounds. The first beast yipped in pain when one of the men tore its jaw away. Trees blocked my view from seeing anything further. Still, I listened for signs of anything coming after us, until Drav slowed.

I faced forward again to see the trees giving way to the end of a house-lined road. Street lights illuminated the two shadow men waiting for us.

"Drav," one said.

"Kerr. This is Mya. She is a female."

Kerr's mouth dropped open, and the man next to him grunted in disbelief. I realized, with that one word, we'd just bypassed the whole no-penis talk.

"Hi," I said, politely.

"Asking to see her breasts or pussy makes her uncomfortable—"

"Geez, Drav!"

"And she does not like to be smelled or touched without permission."

Kerr's mouth snapped shut, and he stared at me. I glared up at Drav.

"I can't believe you just said that."

"You want them to smell you?" Drav asked, frowning down at me.

"Of course not."

"I don't understand."

"Just...never mind. Is it safe to put me down? Are your friends killing the hellhounds?"

The man with Kerr said something in their language, stealing Drav's attention. Drav answered in kind.

"I don't like when you do that," I said. "They understand what you say when you say it in English. But I can't understand you when you speak your language."

Drav glanced down at me but kept talking, throwing in a few words like Ghua, Phusty, no penis, smell, and dead to clue me into his conversation. I waited for outrage, accusations, or anger. But, there was none. The two men listened impassively.

I peeked back at the trees and saw the blood-spattered men who'd run to help us, standing behind Drav. They listened intently to Drav's explanation of what had happened with Phusty. Each one of them watched me, but none had the aggression that Phusty had immediately shown.

When Drav stopped speaking, they remained quiet. I glanced up at Drav after a moment. I didn't have much experience with his kind. Sure, Drav was great and Ghua had been okay. However, the whole fighting thing with Phusty, because he wanted to see my bits, still had me slightly unsure.

"Does this mean they are going to be okay with me?"

Drav's gaze held mine, and he nodded.

"No fighting?" I asked.

"No fighting."

I glanced at the men again, knowing they understood everything we'd just said. Their expressions remained mildly curious, without any hint of aggression, and they continued to stare.

"Then, can you put me down? My legs are starting to hurt."

He grunted and gently set me on my feet. I kept an eye on the others while I casually stretched my legs.

"Come. We'll walk for a while," Drav said. He seemed to sense my hesitation around our new companions because he set his hand on my lower back and led me forward. The others fell in step around us.

Drav's abbreviated and slightly crude introduction seemed to have done the trick. No one made any move to sniff, touch, or get close to me. They stared, though. A lot. Since they'd never seen a girl before, I could understand the gawking. Maybe being around so many of Drav's kind should have made me nervous, but I felt more relief than anything else. They'd just proven how useful traveling in numbers could be.

We walked down the center of the quiet street. A few cars sat in driveways, making me wonder if it wouldn't be wiser to travel by vehicle. This area seemed quiet, but how far were we from the next big city? I looked at the cars again, thinking about at least looking for a map before I realized it wouldn't do me any good. I had no idea where we even were. At the corner, I glanced at the street sign, which only showed a numbered avenue. No help there.

Three infected came running at our group from behind the corner house. Drav lifted me into his arms as two of the group dashed to meet the infected before they got closer. In seconds, three heads went flying and the headless bodies fell to the pavement.

"You are safe, Mya," Drav said.

I looked up at him, slightly amused by how quickly he'd snatched me up and reassured me. He didn't look amused. Worry creased his brow as he set his forehead to mine. I reached up and smoothed a hand over the back of his head.

"I know I am," I said softly. "Thank you. Can I keep walking for a little longer, though?"

Reluctantly, he let me down.

A pretty, birdhouse-style mailbox caught my eye on the side of the far street, and a brilliant idea struck.

"Can we go look at that?" I asked. After the hellhounds and the infected, I wasn't foolish enough to move more than three feet from Drav's side.

He walked with me as I veered toward the mailbox. I opened it and wasn't surprised to see an empty cavity. The hellhounds had attacked Oklahoma late at night. It was unlikely that the mail had been delivered after the attack. But there had to be at least one person in this neighborhood who'd forgotten to take in their mail.

I kept checking mailboxes while we progressed down the street, until I found one with a letter. I grinned and pulled it out. My grin slowly faded. I didn't know the town, but I knew the state. Texas. The ominous foreboding I'd felt when staring at the sunset clicked into place. The sunset had been to our right, not our left.

Drav had admitted he couldn't read the map, yet I'd closed my eyes as soon as he'd offered to drive so I could rest. What had I really thought would happen? I'd been dictating our direction since the moment we'd met.

"Drav," I said, looking up at him. "We somehow got turned around. We've been heading south instead of north."

CHAPTER THREE

DRAV GLANCED AT KERR AND THE REST OF THE MEN BEFORE MEETING my gaze.

"Yes, I know," he said.

Was this some kind of man thing where he couldn't admit he'd gotten us lost? Or had Kerr already told him where we were? I needed a crash course in their language.

"What do you mean, you know?"

"It is not safe to talk here," he said. A noise further down the street confirmed his words.

"Come." He opened his arms to me.

I frowned but quickly went to him. Held safely against his chest, I only freaked out a little when a group of six infected appeared between two houses. They ran toward us, a united mass of movement...except for one. Its right arm flapped uselessly, barely attached by a bit of gore. The mangled mess of meat had me cringing more than their numbers.

The rest of the shadow men moved forward with almost military precision to meet the attack while Drav hung back, cradling me in his arms. With quick efficiency, Drav's friends proved his head ripping tendencies a common trait among his kind. Finished dealing with the infected, they once again surrounded us and kept pace with Drav as he sprinted through one neighborhood after another.

I watched the passing scenery over Drav's shoulder and began to notice trees leaning heavily to the side. Leaning turned to uprooted trees laying in yards, broken windows, and one partially collapsed house. My stomach dipped with worry. Earthquake damage. How close to Irving were we?

"I don't think we want to go any further south," I whispered against Drav's neck. "Are we almost there?"

"Almost," he said.

Any signs of houses, yards, streetlights or even trees, abruptly stopped. Moonlight cast long shadows on piles of wood, shingles, and twisted siding where houses once stood. Pot holes and chunks of blacktop replaced the smooth surface of the road.

My throat tightened as the destruction grew to the point where I could no longer identify what had been house or road or yard in the weak moonlight. Hints of smoke and burnt rubber or plastic tainted the air, and I buried my face in Drav's shirt. I didn't want to see more anyway. Bombings had wiped everything out and left ruin in its wake. If they did this to every city, what would be left of our world?

I thought of my parents and Ryan and wished the phones still worked. Did the military understand what the bombings were leaving behind? Ryan probably did. But what good was one teen against terrified adults with heavy artillery. I realized it could have been worse. At least whatever they were using to destroy the cities wasn't nuclear. I frowned. I hoped it wasn't nuclear...

"We really need to get out of here," I said against Drav. "It might be dangerous to breathe this air."

"We're getting closer," he said.

I lifted my head for a quick peek and immediately ducked back down out of the wind.

"Closer to what? There's nothing left but rubble," I said. I started to wonder how the shadow men could possibly run through it all. As though he was reading my thoughts, Drav jumped over something, and my stomach dipped like it did when I drove over a hill too fast.

"Somewhere safe where we can talk," he answered.

He ran tirelessly, weaving, clambering, and jumping over debris to get to wherever his friends were leading us. Suddenly, he stopped.

"Mya, I can't carry you like this. I need you to hold onto my back."

Drav set me down and tossed my bag to Kerr. I studied the dark area, puzzled.

In the dim light of the moon, our six companions surrounded us, watching me closely. Beyond them, several other shadow men stood encircling a large area of shadowed ground, facing outward as if guarding the space from the darkness beyond. If they were guards, they weren't very good at it because they kept casting occasional glances our way. To be fair, though, we were the only living things as far as I could see. Beyond us, there was nothing but dirt and stone.

"Your arms got tired?" I asked, looking at Drav.

"No, Mya. I could carry you forever."

The tender way he said the words made my cheeks heat.

"I don't understand, then," I said, glancing around once more. That's when I noticed one of the guards looking down and to his left. I followed his gaze and realized the dark area I'd assumed to be shadowed ground was actually a pit. A very, very large pit about the size of an Olympic swimming pool.

I tore my gaze from the darkness and looked up at Drav.

"What's going on?"

"It's not safe up here, Mya. You could die," he said softly.

Disbelief and understanding slammed into me.

"You brought me here on purpose? You turned us around on purpose? I trusted you!" I slammed my hands against his chest, trying to push and hurt him at the same time. The blow didn't move him.

A frown creased his brow, and he caught my wrists and tugged me toward him. I stomped on his foot, then hit him again when he released me.

"Asshole! Fucking asshole!" Tears of frustration and anger welled in my eyes. "My family is waiting for me. They are alive, Drav. Finding them was the whole point of everything we've done since the moment I met you."

"I know, Mya. I'm sorry. It's too dangerous to try to reach them. Your people are willing to kill you to destroy the infected."

"They didn't know I was there," I yelled.

His impassive expression remained unchanged with my words. Seeing my anger had no effect, I stopped pushing him and moved closer to set my shaking hands on his chest. I licked my lips, took a calming breath, and looked up at him.

"Drav, please. You helped me get home and to the cabin and back to the base. You've kept me safe. I know we can reach the safe zone. Please." I didn't care that I was begging. My family thought I was on my way. I knew they were worrying as much as I worried about them.

His fingers brushed the tears from my cheeks, and my hope surged.

"No, Mya. We're not going back. We're going to my home now."

"Fuck that." I pushed away from him, wiped my eyes, and glared. His betrayal hurt. A lot. And I refused to literally disappear from the face of the planet just because he couldn't get over his worry that something would happen to me up here. The idea of walking away from him terrified me. But, was he really leaving me with any other option?

"I'm not going with you."

He exhaled heavily and reached out to gently smooth back my hair.

"I am not leaving you, Mya."

I swallowed hard in relief.

"Good. Let's go." I turned away from his touch and made it about three steps before he stood in front of me. He stooped low in a familiar move and tossed me over his shoulder. Anger and disbelief coursed through me. He wouldn't...

He turned and moved back toward the pit, answering my doubt. Furious, I twisted and kicked and tried to escape his hold. The other shadow men watched, their gazes curious, but made no move to help either of us.

"Put me down," I yelled, not caring if I attracted an infected's attention.

Fisting my hands, I hit his back. His large palm came down with a crack on my ass cheek. The pain robbed me of breath and stilled my struggles.

"Give me the rope," Drav said in very clear English.

"I swear to God," I choked out, "if you tie me up, I'm going to kill you."

His hand smoothed over my sore butt.

"I won't tie you, Mya. Hold on."

With that, he turned, and I found myself staring down into a black abyss. My stomach did a nosedive to my toes. I grabbed Drav's shirt just before he hooked an arm around my legs and stepped back into nothing.

As we dropped into the darkness, my scream echoed around us, followed by a gruff laugh from above. It took a moment to understand we weren't falling. Drav's muscles rolled beneath my hands, and his hold on my legs tightened and relaxed rhythmically. He was climbing down. Very hesitantly, I lifted my head.

"Don't move, Mya. We'll fall."

The warning was enough for me to plaster myself against him.

Drav continued to climb steadily downwards, his shoulder rotating under my stomach, creating a bruising ache. How far were we descending?

"I'm never going to forgive you for this," I said into the darkness.

His movements hesitated for the briefest of moments before resuming.

"I understand."

"Since you've never dealt with a girl before, I really doubt you do."

I blinked several times and tilted my head to look down again. My eyes seemed to be playing tricks on me because I thought I saw something.

My stomach jolted when we dropped suddenly. Drav's shoulder jammed into my stomach as his feet hit solid ground. I grunted and tried to free myself. He held tight.

"Put me down."

"I'll carry you."

"Put me down, or I swear I'm going to start biting." My voice shook with anger and unshed tears.

"You will not be able to climb up the rope. The others are coming down."

I slapped his back, annoyed that he had easily guessed my intentions. It didn't matter that rope climbing wasn't my strong suit or that Drav would have stopped me before I'd made it more than three feet or that I was almost blind. At this point, I just wanted to put some space between Drav and myself.

"Your shoulder is hurting me. Put me down."

Instead of doing as I asked, he flipped me over and cradled me in his arms.

"You will not be able to see. It'll be safer if I carry you."

He walked forward down what felt like a steep slope. While the blood rushed back out of my head, I looked around, straining to see, and realized it hadn't been my imagination that I could see again.

A subtle glow from the crystal on Drav's wrist illuminated the area. I looked over his shoulder and saw several more glows behind us and a brighter one still several feet above. One for each of our six companions.

In the weak, slightly blue-tinted light, I could see the dark rock walls of the tunnel.

"It's light enough for me to see, Drav. Put me down now."

His shoulders lifted with a heavy sigh. But, instead of fighting me, he put me on my feet then steadied me by placing a hand on my arm. I shrugged off his hold and stepped away.

"Kerr, walk ahead of Mya."

Kerr slipped past us, his bracelet lighting enough of the dark that I saw the different shades of color in the walls. I also saw my pack on Kerr's shoulder.

"Can I have my bag back, Kerr?"

"It would be better if he carried it. The path is steep," Drav said.

"Kerr?" I said, ignoring Drav.

"Mya, it—"

"I'm not talking to you," I snapped.

Kerr said something, but of course, I didn't understand a word.

"I hope that was a yes," I said.

Neither man spoke.

"My flashlight is in the bag."

"It's not safe to use it yet," Drav said quietly.

Semi-blind, I angrily followed Kerr. My foot slipped and loose stones tumbled down the rocky slope. And, they kept tumbling, the sound growing quieter but never really ending. Just fading away.

"I'm going to die down here," I said to myself, jerking away from the hand Drav had used to steady me.

It took effort to maintain my footing on the slow-going hike downward. Between that and the increasing temperature, sweat plastered my hair to the back of my neck in no time. My head began to ache and my clothes felt like I had sweated out all the moisture in my body.

Just when it started to feel like a never-ending march, the slope bottomed out. Two steps onto the even surface, a tingling sensation rushed over my skin and my ears popped painfully. I blinked back my tears and kept shuffling forward, wondering at the sudden drop in temperature. On the third blink, I froze and looked around in stunned awe.

The area before us stretched further than I could see. And I *could* see.

Ethereal blues and greens lit different type of rock formations rising up from the cavern floor. I realized the unique designs, with their crude edges and unsymmetrical patterns, could only have been made by nature.

Weird strings dangled from the ceiling further into the cavern, lighting the way and giving this area its breathtaking, subtle light. Underneath the strings to our right, a still pool of water reflected the beautiful glow.

It all seemed so surreal. Why did that surprise me? I had been taken into this pit in the Earth on the shoulder of a demon man, while hellhounds, infected, and humans destroyed the world up top. Unreal no longer seemed to have the same meaning it used to.

One of those demons walked past me and quickly scooped some water into his hand from the still pond, jolting me from my thoughts. He moved to the side while he drank. I'd forgotten about the others in my surprise.

I twisted to look behind me. Rock, shaped like a series of frozen waterfalls, bordered a gaping blackness where the light didn't reach. The rest of the shadow men were magically emerging from the hole's gloom.

"What the hell?" I half-whispered.

Drav stood near me, watching but saying nothing. The final man gradually appeared. A leg then torso and head emerged as if he'd stepped through a curtain of invisibility. It let me know that something insubstantial had kept me from seeing Drav's world until I stood in it.

I took a step toward the dark, wanting a closer look, but Drav blocked me.

"You're not leaving, Mya."

"You're a tool, Drav," I said, turning away.

Kerr stood behind us with my bag. He handed it over with a nod then moved to where the others crowded around a small cave in the waterfall rock formation. They sifted through the group of weapons piled there. Knives, long walking stick things, and bows.

Drav watched them for a moment then turned toward me.

"Stay. I will be right back."

He turned away from me before I could flip him off. Pissed, I looked at the magical darkness that led the way home.

CHAPTER FOUR

WHERE THE HELL WOULD I GO? I THOUGHT ANGRILY.

Sure, that black abyss promised a way back to the top. But, it also led to a place where I wouldn't be able to see and to a rope I wouldn't be able to climb. Even if I could somehow manage to reach the surface, I would be facing infected-central alone and without the vehicle I'd counted on to get me to a safe zone. In what world would I have any hope of making it out of the city and further north without help? Definitely not the world I currently lived in. I was at Drav's mercy, and it pissed me off.

Bending down, I dug through my bag until I found my water bottle. Nothing swished inside when I shook it, and I berated myself for forgetting to refill it at the farmhouse.

Glancing at the pool, I wondered how safe the water would be to drink. Sure, the shadow man had done it, but he came from here. However, since I knew finding a nearby faucet wasn't going to happen, I didn't see that I had much choice but to do the same.

Kneeling beside the pool, I dipped my hand into the cool water and brought it to the back of my neck to bathe away the sweat. The second handful, I lifted to my mouth and bravely took a drink. It tasted a little like lake water, but it wasn't too bad. I let it settle in my stomach for a moment, debating the chance of it making me sick. The world was falling apart, and I was in my own underground hell. Why not throw in some dysentery? I scooped both hands into the water to take a bigger sip, partially quenching my thirst.

Not knowing when I'd get another chance for a refill, I dipped my bottle into the water. Ripples raced out over the previously calm dark surface, making the reflection of the green glowing lights from above dance prettily.

Mesmerized, I leaned over the edge of the pool, wondering how deep it descended. Something moved in its depths. Before I could see what, the water erupted.

Time slowed as a fish with knitting needle like teeth rose toward my face. In frozen fear, I stared at its bulbous eyes.

A sharp tug pulled me off my knees just before the thing reached my face. As I fell backwards, Drav stepped in front of me, his wide shoulders partially blocking my view. He drew back his arm, spear in hand, and skewered the fish through its gaping mouth before I landed hard on my butt.

My pulse pounded in my ears while I stared at the writhing creature.

Drav tossed it and the spear to the cave floor then turned to me. The thing gave a final flop, then stilled. My shaky breaths echoed in the sudden silence, and I looked up at Drav.

His wild, rage-filled eyes swept over me before he squatted next to me and cupped the back of my head. I readily leaned toward him, pressing my forehead to his, needing the feel of safety that only he could provide.

"Those waters are not safe, Mya." He threaded his fingers through my hair and rubbed his forehead lightly against mine.

I exhaled shakily.

"Yeah, I see that."

"You must be careful." The chiding way he said it rekindled my anger. I wouldn't have needed to be careful if he hadn't dragged me down here.

I pulled away from him and got back to my feet. The others watched us like we were some daytime soap opera.

Kerr made a comment in their language. Ignoring them, I capped the half-full bottle I still clutched in my hand.

Drav moved away from me, picked up my bag, and lifted the strap over his head to settle it on his shoulder.

"You can walk for a bit, but we need to move fast, and I will need to carry you."

I didn't bother saying anything. He wouldn't give me a choice anyway.

Kerr led the group out, and Drav nudged me so that I would follow right after Kerr. The other men spread out around us. They carried spears in their hands now, gathered from their supply pocket back in the cavern. The three before us had bows strapped to their backs and a quiver of arrows attached to their waists. Drav carried a spear in his hands. The sudden need for weapons now made me nervous since it just hit me that Drav hadn't used any up top. And, the way he had used the spear on the fish with such precision showed he was no novice.

A few of the men drifted closer as we walked through the massive rock formations. As we threaded our way between the structures, I couldn't help but notice the difference in shapes. Some looked like pillars reaching up to the weird lights on the cavern ceiling. Others looked like clusters of misshaped, upside down ice cream cones. Bits of glowing moss clung to the tips, making me think of distant snowy mountains.

While we walked, I tried to come up with some reason that might persuade Drav to bring me back to the surface. The need to find my family motivated me but held no meaning for him. All he seemed to care about was keeping me safe.

"I don't understand," I said angrily. "You thought you could keep me safe before. Why change your mind now?"

"Your people are bombing the cities."

"So what? We could have driven around the stupid cities!"

"No, Mya. You have many, many cities. No more talking. It is too dangerous."

"If it's so dangerous, why'd you bring me down here?" I whispered harshly.

Kerr said something softly and Drav grunted but didn't answer either of us.

I fumed and marched on.

At times the pillars and other formations crowded so closely, it felt like we were in a large tunnel, rather than a cavern. The confining space in some places meant we walked close together, making it hard to ignore the not so subtle sounds of sniffing around me.

The further we walked, the better I began to see. Not that it helped.

The shadow men moved expertly through the tunnels. Drav reached out constantly, steadying me each time I tripped over rocky areas. I barely stopped myself from smacking his help away each time. Yes, I was angry, but was it smart to piss Drav off when I wanted him to take me back to my world? Probably not.

The tunnel opened wider ahead of us, and a brighter glow came from that space. I glanced at the men, but neither Drav nor any of the others were squinting.

Suddenly, Kerr rushed forward, two others following after him. They reached the opening and waved us forward.

"Yeah, yeah. I'm hurrying," I grumbled, looking down to watch my feet once more. If I tripped again and Drav grabbed me, I'd deck him. Screw the consequences.

A warmer breeze brushed my hair back, and I looked up just as we reached the opening. For the second time since dropping into hell, I forgot to be angry and stood in awe.

The crowded cones and pillars in the first cavern had nothing on this new one. Its massive roof rose three times as high, making it at least six stories overhead. Imbedded in the ceiling, jagged glowing crystals illuminated the area in a soft blue light. Four giant columns rose up near the far end of the space, the only large rock formations. Fernlike vegetation, interspersed with white, stunted skeletal trees, filled the rest of the cavern. From those skeletal trees, small brown globes hung from thin branches, like an eerily beautiful orchard.

"What is this place?"

The sound of my voice startled something in the blue-green fronds a few yards in. Kerr whipped his bow up and let an arrow fly. The bolt shot forward and disappeared into the growth. The rustling didn't stop but zipped away from us toward the trees.

Kerr gave me a disgruntled look and stalked forward to retrieve his empty arrow. I didn't understand why he was upset. The thing —whatever it had been—had run away from us, not toward us.

"I don't know the word for this place," Drav said from beside me, nudging me forward. "It's an old place where we grew epella."

I'd forgotten I'd asked something, and it took a moment for the last word he said to sound familiar.

"Apples? This really is an orchard?" I studied the brownish spheres doubtfully. A sheen of blue light reflected off the almost opalescent dark skin.

"Yes. An orchard. A very old one that still produces a good harvest."

Drav picked a globe and offered it to me. I glanced at the fruit then him. Did he think a kind gesture would remove the sting of his betrayal? I walked passed him, trying to ignore the squeeze of my heart.

Skirting around the trees, we moved through the ferns. Their feathery tips brushed my fingers. I would have reached out to feel them, but the way the men remained alert made me nervous. Kerr had his bow ready with an arrow notched.

"What was that thing running through the ferns, anyway?"

"Food," Drav said.

No wonder Kerr had looked annoyed. I'd scared away dinner.

"So there are a lot of animals down here? Are they all like the hellhounds?"

"Yes, there are many animals but not like the hellhounds. The hellhounds are not food. The other animals are."

"Oh." That was good. No...not really. It was a little concerning that he didn't consider the other animals like the hellhounds after that fish had tried to eat my face. I glanced at his killer fish spear.

"If you all had weapons, why did you leave them down here when you went up top?"

"We didn't go up top to hunt."

Kerr said something, sounding impatient. Whatever Drav said back held a warning tone that shut him up.

"What did Kerr say?" I asked.

"He said he thought you weren't talking to me."

"Kerr can bite me."

Drav growled low at my words and stepped defensively in front of me. I rolled my eyes and looked around him to Kerr, who had stopped walking and was rattling off a string of unintelligible words at Drav.

"Kerr will not fight you," Drav said angrily. "Not without a life crystal."

"Fight? I said bite me. You know...like kiss my ass."

Drav's head swung around to me, his expression one of shock. I groaned in frustration.

"You are way too literal. It's a saying." I looked at Kerr. "Bite me isn't a challenge to actually bite me. It means shut up and mind your own damn business."

Kerr grunted and turned away to resume walking.

Drav straightened, still studying me. I decided to address Kerr's not talking comment to set Drav straight.

"Just so we're clear, I haven't forgiven you, and I don't trust you anymore. While I know there's a very good chance you'll lie to me again, no one else knows enough English to answer my questions. So, yeah, I'll talk to you, but I'm still mad enough to hate you."

I sidestepped, planning to go around him, but he shadowed my move, blocking me. I glared up at him.

"I will take your anger gladly," he said, his gaze holding mine as he reached up to caress my face. I jerked my head away from his touch.

"We'll see."

I stomped my way through the ferns, following after Kerr and trying to ignore the rest of the men. Something small ran right in front of me. I squealed and backpedaled at the flash of fur, red eyes, and horns.

Drav was right there, putting a comforting hand on my shoulder. In no mood for comfort, I swatted him away and soldiered on, mumbling the entire time about grey skinned assholes who thought they knew everything, face-eating fish, and jackalopes.

"Fucking jackalopes aren't supposed to be real. Obviously, this place didn't get that damn memo."

Something bumped into the backs of my legs. I flung my arms out as I fell backwards...into Drav's arms.

"You make too much noise," he said, softly. "Not all the hellhounds found the way out."

"I wouldn't be making any noise down here at all if we'd stayed up top like I'd wanted. We can still turn around." Although I'd said it quietly, I'd still managed to convey a satisfying amount of anger. I wasn't going to just give in to the abduction.

He exhaled heavily and leaned forward. I turned my head

away, rejecting his version of a hug, and crossed my arms, refusing to make this any more pleasant for him than it was for me. He had the nerve to nudge my neck with his nose and inhale deeply. A shiver chased through me, and his hold tightened before he straightened and started walking. My reaction gave me an uncomfortable idea that I immediately rejected. I would not stoop to using my body to negotiate my way back home. Nope. Not happening.

"I'll carry you until we reach the source," Drav said, softly.

"What's the source?" I asked before I could stop myself.

"The place we recharge our life crystals."

"Life crystals?"

"Shh," he said a moment before the light began to fade.

I looked around and saw we'd stepped behind the giant columns. There were no trees in their shadows, only a sparse growth of stunted ferns that dwindled with each step that Drav took toward the dark void ahead.

A cool draft of air brushed my face. I uncrossed my arms to hold onto Drav more securely. He shifted me higher, and I looked over his shoulder at the light we were leaving behind. Too late, I remembered the flashlight in my bag. The threat of hellhounds was enough for me to swallow any request for it. If they weren't already in the dark, I didn't want to call them.

Drav moved forward steadily, a soft glow coming from his wrist as well as the wrists of the other men around us. Being so close together created a small bubble of visibility, allowing me to see. The cavern we were now entering had craggy rock formations, but they were broken up by occasional pools of still, dark water. I leaned into Drav, grateful he carried me. I did not want to fall into one of those pools while stumbling around in the dark.

Thankfully, the dark was short lived, and the creepy cavern merged into one that had numerous, small green-tinted crystals poking from the ceiling. Once again, I noticed a change in temperature when we crossed from dark to semi-light and wondered what it meant.

The group picked up its pace until Drav was sprinting. Each cavern we passed through appeared slightly different than the last, and I always felt some subtle change in temperature or moisture. The caves didn't stretch in a linear grouping but in a webbed network of interconnecting spaces.

Finally, Kerr stopped in a cavern with a small waterfall. The water churned near the fall but smoothed out into a sizable pool further away. The dim blue light from the crystals above reflected prettily on the surface, which I was not going near.

"We'll rest here," Drav said, setting me on my feet.

"By the water?"

"No, over here."

He attempted to thread his fingers through mine, but I pulled away.

"I can follow without being tugged or nudged."

He frowned but led the way to an area of ferns and rocks. I followed hesitantly, remembering the jackalope. When nothing jumped out and the ferns remained quiet, I took the last few steps to where he stood on a mossy patch of level ground.

He stomped on a bunch of surrounding ferns, tamping them down to create a Drav-sized area in which he lowered himself and stretched out.

"You mean we're sleeping here?" I said, eyeing the ferns once more.

"Yes, Mya. We both need sleep."

I'd managed a nap in the truck—how long ago had that been? —but he hadn't slept since the first night in our cabin.

With an expectant look, he motioned for me to join him.

"Not happening."

"Mya, it's safer sleeping with me."

"Pft. Snuggling up next to you was fine when we were on the surface and you were actually helping me."

He frowned at me, but I ignored him and checked out what everyone else was doing. A few men stood in nearby positions, creating a loose outward-looking circle around us. The rest had done the same thing Drav had and were already laying down in their own little nests. I moved a yard away from Drav, stomped down my own spot, and settled in.

The blue crystals scattered above almost looked like stars. Big ones. Instead of closing my eyes to sleep, I stared at them and wondered about my family. Were they worrying? Had Dad convinced someone to help him look for me by now? Were they still safe? I sighed and tried to think of nothing... especially not creepy horned rabbits hiding in the tall grass.

Eventually, I slept.

CHAPTER FIVE

MALE LAUGHTER AND DRAV'S VOICE NEAR MY HEAD WOKE ME. I LAY on my side, comfortably warm with Drav curled around me. His arm draped over my waist and a hand rested on the skin of my stomach under my shirt. For a sleepy moment, all was right in my world. I was warm and safe because of the man holding me close. Then, reality came crashing back. He'd taken me from the surface. From my family. Against my will. And now, the jerk had cozied up to me while I slept.

I elbowed him hard and rolled away. He grunted and frowned up at me while I glared at him.

"There was a reason I laid down here. I didn't want to be by you."

Another smattering of laughter came from the others, and I gave the sources a dead stare.

"Laugh again, and I'm feeding you to the face-eating fishes."

My threat didn't wipe the grins from the men's faces, but it did stop the laughter.

I stood up and cringed when I realized what I'd need to do next. In a large cave filled with ferns, a waterfall, and an unsafe-for-humans swimming pool, there wasn't one place a girl could relieve herself that was private and safe.

Drav got up with a sigh.

"Are you hungry?"

"No." I really was.

"Are you thirsty?"

"No." I could drink a little.

He gave me an indecipherable look then moved toward the water's edge where he relieved himself. One of the other men got up from his spot and did the same. There was no way in hell I would dangle my ass over the water after what happened yesterday. I'd hold it.

I sat down in my fern nest and tried not to think about how hungry or thirsty I was. Thinking about either made all my physical discomforts harder to ignore.

The two men finished their business. Then, to my relief, they went to the waterfall to get a drink. I noticed another man sitting by a nearly flat boulder. On his way back from the water, Drav picked up something from the surface of that rock and popped it into his mouth. He caught me watching and said something in his language to one of the other men. The man grunted, took something from the stone and came toward me, holding out his hand.

"Mya, food," he said, squatting beside me.

I looked at the shiny clear bit of jelly looking stuff in his palm.

"What is it?" I asked.

"Food."

This language barrier thing sucked.

"Am I going to die or get sick eating it?"

"No."

"Is it gross? It looks gross."

"No."

I sighed and picked up the clear glob that felt much firmer in texture than it appeared. I sniffed it. It didn't smell like much. A little fishy. I popped it in my mouth and almost gagged. With everyone watching me, I choked it down with a shudder.

"Was that raw fish?"

"Yes," he said.

"Yeah, I'm not a fan. Thanks, though."

He stood and moved back to the others who were eating more clear bits from the rock. That explained why Drav liked the canned tuna fish. The thought had me jolting to my feet.

"Where's my bag?"

"Mya," Kerr called, holding it up from where he had laid it in the ferns.

I waded through the fronds to collect my bag then sat down not far from him. He leaned on one elbow and watched me dig through my supplies until I produced a can of peaches. I had my finger on the pull tab, ready to open it, when reality stopped me. There were four cans of food in my bag. Four. The piece of fish, while disgusting, had eased some of my hunger for now. If I had a drink, I'd be fine. It would be smarter to save the canned food for when I really needed it. After all, I had no idea how long Drav would make me stay down here.

Half-growling at the reminder of how much control Drav had over my fate, I stuffed the can back into my bag. When I stood and placed the strap over my shoulder, my need to go to the bathroom could no longer be ignored.

I glanced at the seven sets of eyes trained on me.

"I have to pee. Since I don't have a dangler like the rest of you, I'm not peeing in the water. I'm going to go over there," I said, pointing to a taller group of ferns, "and all of you are going to stare at the waterfall until I'm done. Agreed?"

"No," Drav said, standing up.

I saw red, picked up the nearest loose rock, and threw it at him with an angry yell. The jagged stone clipped the side of his head, making him jerk.

"It's not enough you took me from my family?" I seethed. "Now you're going to take my dignity?"

Without taking his gaze from mine, he stalked toward me. I held my ground, glaring and wishing for another rock.

When he reached me, blood dripped freely from his head.

"I'll watch the opening behind you," he said, his words calm and quiet.

Not waiting for any reply, he moved toward the tunnel entrance beyond the tall growth of ferns and stood there with his back to the rest of us. Kerr rose, then gave me a censuring look before joining the other shadow men.

A sharp pain stabbed at me. Though I tried to swallow it, I couldn't. Even down here, with me telling him how much I hate him, Drav still protected me.

Guilt and shame curled inside me. Drav hadn't taken my dignity, but I'd lost it all the same. Trudging to the ferns, I set my bag to the side then dropped my pants. I cried and peed. Both, fairly quietly.

I hated that I'd thrown the rock at Drav when he'd only been trying to, yet again, keep me safe. What I'd done was wrong. Just like making me come down here against my will was wrong of him. I couldn't take back my actions, but he could take back his. He, however, refused. With that thought, some of my anger returned.

Finished, I pulled up my pants with a cringe. I hoped wherever we were going had a shower. Wiping my eyes, I took a calming breath before picking up my bag.

"I'm done," I announced.

The others, who talked quietly near the falls, left their positions and gathered up their weapons. Kerr picked up a bow and spear then nodded toward me. I glanced back at Drav. Blood dripped from his earlobe to his shoulder, and he wore a wary look on his face.

"I need to carry you again," he said.

I felt guilty I'd hurt him but not sorry. Too much anger still boiled inside for me to feel remorse. I hated where we were and what it had done to us. I wanted to hug him and bring the closeness back. I wanted to trust him again. But I couldn't. He hadn't just taken me from my family, he'd robbed me of what I'd thought we'd had together.

"I shouldn't have thrown the rock," I said. It was as close to an apology as he would get from me.

"We should stop the bleeding or you'll end up fainting and falling over on me." I knelt beside my bag. The first aid kit wasn't elaborate, but it had gauze and some tape. I grabbed what remained of my water and stood.

"You might want to take your shirt off. I'll need to clean the blood away to see what I'm doing." I shook the bottle for emphasis. Not that it was needed. He had his shirt off in a heartbeat.

He sat where he had been standing and looked up at me. The others waited near the tunnel where Drav had stood guard. Kerr gave me an impatient look. I rolled my eyes at him and went to Drav's side.

Using the last of my water, I began to rinse away the blood.

"I know you are still angry with me," he said softly. "Do you want to throw another rock?"

"I already said I shouldn't have done that."

"Yes." He set a hand on the back of my calf. "But you did what you felt you must do at the time. Just like I did what I felt I must to keep you safe."

His hand slid down the back of my calf. The gentle stroke made my pulse leap. It also made my temper flare.

"Keep it up and I'm kneeing you in the face," I said softly, not pausing my work.

He removed his hand from my leg, but his gaze remained locked on my face. Ignoring him, I set the water aside and took a bit of gauze to press to the wound. I'd gotten him good, and it would take a while for it to stop bleeding.

"I thought beauty meant the way the crystals lit the water in the caverns or the way the inuchu flower blooms in the dark," he said, drawing my attention. "But I was wrong. Beauty is seeing the soft look of concentration on your face as you touch me. It is seeing your peaceful face and parted lips as you sleep beside me. It is the look in your eyes when you search for me as soon as you wake."

Heat rose to my cheeks that had nothing to do with anger. With those simple, earnest words, he'd reminded me just how much I meant to him and it tore at me.

He truly didn't see what he'd done as something wrong. He'd only been protecting the one thing that mattered to him most. Me. Unable to stop myself, I set my hand on his cheek before quickly stepping away.

Bandaged and cleaned up, Drav put his shirt back on and lifted me in his arms before I had a chance to join the others. He looked down at me, his gaze intense. Then he leaned closer. My heart hammered hard in my chest as he glanced at my lips.

Kerr said something, halting Drav's advance. When I looked at the man, I found him half-smirking. Heat burned my cheeks. I couldn't believe I'd almost let Drav kiss me after a few pretty words. Swallowing hard, I focused on reigning in my emotions.

"What did he say?" I asked.

Before Drav could answer, Kerr's expression changed. He spoke a smattering of loud words. From somewhere behind us, an answer filtered its way back.

Drav turned and I saw Ghua, jogging toward us through the ferns.

"Drav," he said. "Mya."

Behind him, his companions carried Phutsy's body. I'd forgotten about them and their need to return home.

"Ghua, I'm glad you made it," Drav said.

The men carrying Phusty's body followed the edge of the pool, circling toward the shadows on the far side of the water.

"Any signs of them?" Drav asked.

Ghua answered in his language while glancing at me.

"Tell Molev we're coming. We must go to the source first."

Ghua nodded, said something with my name mixed in, then turned and jogged toward the party disappearing into the darkness.

"What did he just say? And let me just add, I'm glad we're not going that way." I was tired of dark caves.

Drav moved toward Kerr while he spoke.

"He is going to our city to tell Molev, our strongest fighter, what happened between Phutsy and me. He is also going to tell Molev about you."

Great. Good ole Ghua was running ahead to tell an all-male city that the first female ever was on her way. Fear re-ignited my anger.

"You shouldn't have brought me down here. It's not too late to turn around and take me back."

Drav picked up his pace and said nothing.

With no sun, I couldn't tell how much time we spent traveling through the subterranean maze. We took several breaks, mostly so I could stretch my legs. Drav always stayed close while the other men watched me with open curiosity from a distance. Both actions frustrated me.

During one of the breaks, Kerr got lucky with his arrow and shot a jackalope. Hungry, and no stranger to wild game, my mouth watered at the thought of cooked rabbit. Kerr, however, didn't light a fire once he skinned the critter. He butchered it and started handing out raw chunks of meat that the men immediately began to eat. I quickly shook my head when he offered me my share.

"Mya, you need food," Drav said from behind me.

"Not that." I wasn't nearly starved enough to consider munching on some raw jackalope.

ONE OF THE oddest things about Drav's world was the lack of normal sounds. No wind rustled the leaves. Nothing chirped or sang. I found the silence eerie, but that changed the first time something did make a sound.

As we approached the next large pillar, something rustled the grass then became still. A noise rose that started out like an infant's cry then morphed into the creaking sound of a rusted door, slowly opening. Goosebumps broke out on my arms. Creepy and mournful didn't begin to describe the noise.

The rest of the group made a rapid halt while Kerr jogged forward with his bow. A thump almost immediately followed the thwang of his arrow. Drav and the others quickly moved forward.

Beyond the column, I could see Kerr going to the deer he'd killed. The thing looked completely normal. Brownish fur. Antlers. Brown eyes.

Having had venison before, I couldn't say I was sad to see Kerr hit his target.

"If you cook that, I'll definitely eat," I said.

All the men turned to look at me with serious expressions.

"No, Mya. That is not food," Drav said, turning and moving away from the men.

I arched my neck to look closer at the deer as the rest began working together to skin it. The creature had hooves, no claws or anything. Its teeth weren't jagged or threatening. I wondered why they didn't eat it.

"You said everything down here but the hellhounds was food," I reminded him. "If it isn't food, why did you kill it?"

"For the skin. We use it to make clothes."

"And you waste the meat? Seriously, I'll eat some of it. Give me a fire and a stick, and I'll hot dog that thing."

Drav stopped walking and considered me for several long moments.

"I can't. Not even for you." He set me on my feet. "Stay close. When they are finished, we'll move again."

It frustrated me that the one thing that looked edible was off the menu. Not that I would argue. They lived down here, and I didn't. If Drav said something wasn't food, I wasn't going to put it in my watering mouth.

Sighing, I walked circles in the soft grass until I noticed the light fading. I blinked up at the crystals, wondering if something was wrong with my eyes. Kerr called out, holding up the skin. As he rolled it up, a baying howl echoed in the air around us. Further away, the grass rustled as jackalopes sprinted in the other direction, running from the threat of the hound.

Drav had me up in his arms before I could panic.

"It smells the blood," he said.

He continued in the direction we'd been headed. At least, I thought it was the same direction. The rest of the group hurriedly fell into place around us.

More baying joined the first, and the sounds kept getting closer.

I looped my arm around Drav's shoulder, and the wound on his head caught my gaze. Red dotted the white. I glanced behind us. Four of the six men ran in our wake. Beyond them, fifteen red eyes blazed in the sea of darkness. No...sixteen. I was pretty sure one of those fuckers had just winked because that pack of hellhounds had skipped the deer for better prey.

My act of pissiness was going to get us killed.

"WE'RE ALMOST THERE," Drav said.

I looked forward and saw a bright light in the distance.

"They won't enter the source."

"Neither will we if you can't run faster," I said.

He did. I alternated between watching the distance between us and the light filled opening versus us and the salivating hellhounds.

Halfway to the source, Kerr and his friend, who were running in front of us, stopped. Drav raced past them without hesitation. The others stopped as well. The six men faced the oncoming pack. Eight to six wasn't bad odds, I hoped. After all, Drav had taken on two hellhounds, and we'd survived.

The two groups clashed with yells and growls. The hounds jumped and circled the men but didn't pursue us. I watched as Kerr, using Drav's spear, stabbed one in the side. The beast didn't fall.

Distance and the lack of light blurred the details of the battle, until the men and hounds disappeared from view. I looked toward the spot of light that I thought was the source and watched it grow larger until we stepped into a different cavern. The bright light after so much darkness made my eyes hurt.

Drav lowered me to my feet and hugged me hard, almost suffocating me. I pushed away, needing to breathe and still angry.

"Enough, Drav," I said, pulling my head back to glare at him. "What is your deal?"

He released me and spun me around so I faced the source of light. This cavern was smaller, about the size of three football fields. Ferns, grass, trees, and other strange vegetation grew in a dense tangle around an odd formation of crystals in the center of the space.

The massive cluster of crystals extended down from the ceiling and up from the floor, creating an hour-glass shape. A white-blue crystal connecting the two, pulsated with life and power. My stomach churned uneasily, looking at it.

"Go, Mya. Touch the source."

"Uhh...why? What's going to happen?"

He stepped in front of me and earnestly met my gaze.

"Nothing bad. The source keeps us alive. Safe. I need you to be safe, too."

I narrowed my eyes at him.

"I don't trust you."

He frowned slightly, stepped aside, and pointed.

"Follow the path."

A thin trail led through the growth to the crystal in the middle. Fear shivered over my skin at the sight of the glowing source.

"No."

He tossed me over his shoulder, turned around, and started for the crystal.

"Drav! Dammit!" I hit his back. "You can't do this every time I disagree with you," I yelled.

He didn't stop until he stood right before the glowing mass.

"Touch it," he demanded.

"I don't want to. I'll probably explode."

"You won't explode. It feels pleasant when you touch it."

"Yeah, right." I went to cross my arms, but he grabbed my hand. I guessed, whether I wanted to or not, I was going to touch it.

He gripped my hand and stretched it forward. A sickening feeling rolled through me a moment before the pad of my finger pressed against the pulsing light.

My breath left me, and everything around me changed.

CHAPTER SIX

A GROUP OF WOMEN AND MEN, ALL MOVING WITH SILENT GRACE, WALKS *between the colossal trunks of towering trees. The simple muted colors of their clothing blends well with the forest. If not for the pale perfection of their faces, they barely appear visible. Intricate braids adorn their long, silken hair and allow a view of elegantly pointed ears.*

"Here," one of the women says, stopping and looking up at the nearest tree. "It weakens."

"We will give it strength," another says.

Each individual steps forward and sets their hands on the ancient bark. A soft glow lights their palms and spreads into the bark. One of the women faints after only a few seconds. The rest remove their hands and sit heavily upon the earth.

"The forest is dying," a man says. "The more it weakens, so too do we. It is time to send scouts to search for a new home."

The woman on the ground rouses enough to speak.

"Yes, it is time."

I INHALED...

. . .

TEN MEN RUN TOGETHER through the trees. Nothing stirs at their quiet passage, despite their impressive speed. Ahead, a light appears a moment before the trees give way to a sunlit body of water. Ten large boats wait upon the shoreline, along with other fey.

A woman, regal and beautiful beyond compare, stands apart from the rest, watching as farewells are made and each boat fills with ten men.

"Be blessed on your journey." She steps forward and touches the first boat. The vessel moves away from her as if she's pushed it out to sea. She does the same for the remaining boats then stands on the shore until they fade from sight.

I EXHALED...

THE BOAT SCRAPES against the rocky shore. The first man nimbly jumps from the vessel and touches the soil as the rest gather up the supplies.

"There is strength here, but muted," the man says to the others.

A fey from the boat throws out a travel bag and looks at the shoreline.

"The trees are so small," he says.

"New, perhaps," the one on shore says.

"Perhaps," he agrees.

The group of ten set out from the boat, exploring the trees together. A deer startles not long after they enter the forest.

"A good sign," one says as they move on.

The trees and wildlife are abundant the further they move inland. They stop often to touch the earth and the vegetation, sensing a strength in this new place, a strength different from their home. After several hours, they spot something that makes them stop.

A primitive woman in furs and leathers gathers berries from a nearby bush. Her skin, the color of wet sand, is darker than theirs.

"She is pretty," one of the men says softly. "And, another good sign."

The rest agree and quietly move away to continue their exploration of the new land.

On the second day, something subtly changes. The strength they sense when they touch the earth now touches them in return. With growing excitement, they trace the source to a cave entrance.

"This is unusual," one says. "The power feels so similar to the heart tree." He thinks of the largest and oldest tree in his ancestral home—a single tree that provides shelter to a third of his people. Meanwhile, the rest of the group debates exploring the caves.

"We are not hill dwellers to live underground," one says.

"We are not. However, it is wise to understand the strengths of this new land in every form."

They agree that exploration is needed, not just of the cave, but the land, too. The group splits. Five to explore the caves and five to continue exploring the land. An agreement is made to meet at the cave entrance in three days.

After those exploring the land leave, the others step into the darkness, taking turns to use their power to light the way, until the first one shudders and disappears from view. He reappears a moment later.

"There is a barrier here. Magic like none I've felt before. Come see for yourself what it hides."

One by one, the men step forward and disappear from the darkness and appear in a cave lit from above by beautiful glowing crystals. Wonder fills them at the sight of vegetation and a few animals.

"This is no hill dweller home," one says softly. He thinks of the short men and women who search the earth for metals and stones. His people trade with the hill dwellers often for the metals they find, and he knows their rustic dirt-filled dwellings.

"No," another agrees. "Let us explore further."

They wander the cave system, feeling the barrier occasionally when passing from one cavern to the next.

"I think this place is larger than it seems."

"And not pleasant everywhere," another comments when they step

into the first of several caverns, all dark lifeless places with still pools of water.

Finally, in a cavern filled with crystal light and apple trees, they decide to rest.

"It is odd to sense it is night, but not to see the stars or moon."

"That is why we will never live in these caves. We are people of the earth and sky. There is no sky here."

One man lays down and looks up. "No sky or moon, but the crystals glow like stars."

"They do seem to flicker," another says, staring up. After a moment, he glances at a nearby pillar. Near the top, a cluster of crystals peeks from the stone ceiling.

He starts for the column.

"What are you doing?" one asks, setting aside his hard-biscuit dinner.

"I want a closer look." The man agilely climbs the pillar and clings to the surface at the top as he reaches out to touch the crystal.

A room fills his mind. Bright and bursting with light, it beckons. He releases the crystal and joins the rest.

"There is a cavern here filled with these crystals. I believe the crystals are the source of the power we're feeling. Not just here, but throughout the land. To connect to the power of the land...to survive...we will need to connect with the crystals."

"How do you know?"

"When I touched the crystal, it showed me."

"We will look for the cavern after we rest," another says, picking up his own hard-biscuit.

"We should have hunted before entering the cave."

"We can hunt here. Perhaps one of those horned hares."

Two of the group split off to hunt while the other three rest. The hunters trace their way back to a vast cavern filled with unusual trees. There they startle a doe, which they quickly bring down with an arrow. They thank the doe for giving her life then clean her and carry her body back to the others, along with branches from a nearby tree.

Working together, they start a fire and begin butchering the small deer.

"Look up," one says. "The crystals no longer glow. They stopped as soon as we lit the fire."

"We'll cook quickly and put it out again," one says, seeming troubled.

The fire crackles, and the smell of roasted meat fills the space. The men hungrily take their portions and put out the fire. There is a brief darkness before the crystals come to life again.

Near the group, the deer, once a carcass, suddenly jumps to its feet, whole and healthy and very much alive. After a moment, it takes off running. The stunned men stare. One sets down his skewer of meat.

"This place is unnatural."

"Unusual, but beautiful and with endless bounty, it would seem."

"We should leave this place," one of the men says. Another nods in agreement. They both decline to eat the meat, choosing the dry bread.

The others exchange looks before taking up their skewers and biting into their portions.

I INHALED...

THE GROUP of five steps out of the cave into the blinding light of day. The other group, who had explored the lands, is already there waiting.

"Brothers!"

The men embrace each other.

"The lands are plentiful of game and harvest. But full of humans," one of those who had remained above ground says.

"Humans?"

"Like the one we saw gathering. They hunt and gather but do not farm or harvest. They live together in caves. Tell us what you found."

"The caves are the source of the power we sense in this land. And full of hidden secrets. Come, we will show you."

Together, the large group explores, reaching further into the cavern's depths. Each cave is different. Some are filled with greenery and crystals and trees while others are dark and filled with pools of water or empty of everything but stone. Some caverns are so vast the men need to rest before continuing. Through it all, the newcomers are in awe of the things they see, and find themselves brushing their fingers over the odd fruits and greenery.

One man, with familiar-feeling bright blue-green eyes, steps up to a small tree, plentiful with fruit. He plucks a small brown globe from the thin branch and brings it to his nose. The sweet smell fills his nose and makes his mouth water. But he does not eat the fruit. He puts it in his sack and joins the others who are nearby. One of his brethren brings a finger to his lips for silence.

Ahead, three of the fey stalk a deer. The buck lifts its mighty head, ears flickering between its massive antlers. The men move with agility and swiftly take the buck down.

The hunters reverently thank the buck for its sacrifice as the others join them.

"We will need much wood to cook and dry the meat for such a large kill."

"No. That is part of the magic here. Watch."

The men work quickly, taking only the choicest pieces of meat while leaving the body otherwise untouched. The meat is set aside, and the men step away from the buck.

"We do not waste like this," one of the newcomers says.

"Watch," another says, motioning the others back.

High above, the crystals pulse with power. Energy surges from the ceiling down the walls and into the ground. The men feel the recoil of it as they watch the buck twitch. The skin knits back together, muscling filling in the void beneath where it has been removed.

It doesn't take long for the buck to recover. The others stand in awe as it jumps to its feet and bolts away. The two, who had declined the meat, share a look of apprehension. The others are in awe.

"It's alive."

"And whole."

"This place provides endless meat but no sun," one of the two objectors says.

All the men look up to the forever night sky.

"We have much to learn about this place," the one who'd collected the apple says quietly. "Were you able to connect with the plants?"

"We did not yet try."

"And we did not hunt outside to know if all deer are reborn. Let us separate again. Four of us will return outside the caves to hunt. The rest should continue to learn more about these caverns. We will meet at the entrance in two days."

Two from the original party in the caves choose to return to hunt outside. The six who remain inside travel slowly and continue to learn what they can of the magic of the place. However, what they learn is limited. When they touch the trees and plants, they feel the power coursing through the stems and trunks, but they cannot direct it to encourage growth and health.

Touching the crystals themselves always shows the men the same vision of a light-filled room. The men set out to find the main source of the crystals and unravel the mysteries of the underground world.

A small group of three walks into a cavern illuminated brightly with white-blue light. Crystals descend downward from the ceiling and upward from the floor to form a pillar in the center of the room. In the middle of the pillar, a solid, huge crystal connects the top and bottom.

Magic pulses from the crystal source so strongly, the men feel it in the air. The fey who'd plucked the fruit steps forward to the cluster of crystals and touches the center stone. Power surges through his veins. He places his other hand on the crystal and gently presses his forehead against the cool, calming surface.

A flash of light blinds the room for a moment. When it fades, the fey steps back from the crystal. Cradled between his hands is a small crystal glowing softly. A symbol is etched onto its surface.

"What happened when you touched it?" another asks.

"It welcomed me to its home and gave me this gift. I can do more than feel the energy now," he says.

He opens his pack and removes a seed. He bends down and places his hand with the crystal on the stone floor over the seed. The soft glow brightens in pulsing waves for a moment. When the man removes his hand, a small mound of soil cradles a tiny sprout.

"With the crystal, I have a connection to the source."

The next man moves forward and presses his forehead to the source crystal. The same light flashes, and he too steps away with a crystal, making room for the next to receive his.

The six each spend time working with the energy in the room until each has coaxed a plant to grow for them.

"We should go back to the entrance and tell the others," the first says.

They agree and return to the beginning with their crystals.

The men emerge from the caverns, and their eyes water at the harsh light of the midafternoon sun. It takes a moment for them to see the others standing around two fallen deer a distance from the opening.

One of the hunters spots them and waves them over.

"We hunted this one in the caves and brought it out. This one is from the woods. Neither has revived."

"Perhaps we need to wait longer out here where the power isn't as strong," one of the new arrivals says.

"Or perhaps we try to use the crystals," another says.

"Crystals?"

The six with the crystals explain what happened in the source cave, and one of the skeptical fey speaks up.

"You should have left the unnatural magic down there."

"The crystals are of the earth as are we. Thus, the magic is not unnatural, just different. Do not fear something because it is new and unknown. We were sent out with a purpose. To find our people a new home. This land is full of life and energy. We must learn what we can then let our people decide."

No one objects after that, and the six step forward with their crystals. They wait for the familiar rush of power to revive the deer, but nothing comes. They try for hours, which turn into a day.

The deer do not come back to life.

I EXHALED and an involuntary shudder ran through me...

TEN FAMILIAR MEN stand on a shoreline and face a group of older fey, just disembarking from a ship. Thousands of ships dot the waters on the horizon.

"Welcome," one of the men says.

"Greetings. What have you found here?"

"These lands are different than our homeland, new and not yet grown. Yet, there is so much power in this thriving place. Can you feel it? Even here on the sands?"

The older ones nod.

"There are caves further inland, the source of this land's power. The animals there revive. We will never have to worry about starvation. Plant life grows in abundance."

"You say the animals come back to life?" one of the Elders questions with a hint of eagerness.

"Yes."

"Tell us more of this new land."

While the ships moor, each of the ten imparts to the elders some of what they have seen or learned. The two objectors share their concerns about nurturing a magic that would so cruelly bring back to life an animal only to see it slain and eaten again and again. The elders listen with care to everything then dismiss the explorers so they may discuss what they've learned.

The rumors of the wonders of the caverns spread throughout the fey.

More men come to the original explorers to listen to them speak about the land and what it has to offer. Many inspect the crystals.

Almost a month's time passes as the elders consider the new land. During that time, the elders visit the caves with the original explorers and learn more of its magic, creatures, and terrain. The main body of settlers stays near the shore and makes temporary homes in the trees. Not in the branches, but on the forest floor. They begin to farm, planting the seeds they brought with them from their dying homeland.

Under the elders' watchful presence, the explorers use their crystals to encourage growth, but their connection with the power above ground is weak. The elders grant the original ten explorers permission to use seeds in the caverns. The men work tirelessly. What grows is different from what they knew in the homeland but not bad.

The elders make note of their bountiful results and require the explorers with crystals to surrender their connection with the source while they continue to deliberate. Everyone waits, wondering if this new land will become their home.

When a meeting is called, the people gather among the trees and listen. The ten explorers have places near the front of the crowd.

Four of the elders stand before the gathering.

"We have made our decision. We will remain in this land, but we will not live in the caves. The power goes against the laws of nature. The laws we live by," the eldest woman on the council says.

One of the explorers steps forward.

"The power in our home is dying. With its death, we lose our connection with the earth and plants. We will become just like the human cave dwellers and will have no power to nurture nature. We have proven we can bond with the power in the caverns and influence the nature there. The power is neither good nor bad, only the intent of the user. With this new source, our people and way of life will not die out."

"No. We will live above ground and connect with the power of the earth here."

"The power here is not of the earth, like our old home, but of the crystal. Truly, you must all feel the difference in power. There is no malice in it," the one who had been gifted the first crystal says. "To survive, we will need to connect with the crystals."

"Enough. The decision has been made."

"You have decided on behalf of the people. I ask to be allowed to decide for myself. I wish to live in the caverns."

"Then you are not of the people. The cavern lands are forbidden."

Denial rises from some of the men in the crowd. During their time waiting, they had heard of the energy that the crystals offered.

The first to receive his crystal turns from the elders and makes his way through the crowd. Others follow, until just over three hundred men split from the main tribe and begin their journey to their new home.

I EXHALED...

"WE CANNOT ALLOW them to return to our lands," an elder says to another.

"What do you propose we do?"

"Seal them inside, taking their memories of their lives with us. To help them understand the fault in their thinking, we will curse the deer within the caverns. Each time their flesh is consumed, they will return a shadow of their former selves."

The others on the council agree.

"We will need many of our people and the power of the six crystals for this banishment."

The elders chip away at the small cluster of crystals and take pieces of the broken crystal to give to the people.

Over one hundred of the oldest fey squat to the Earth, pressing their hands against the soil. They sing to the trees and Earth and bend the power of the land to their will. The Earth rumbles and shakes. The singing grows louder, weaving a web of power over the minds of the men now in the caverns.

The Earth closes over the entrance to the cavern, blocking out any way into the underground realm. With the unnatural magic locked in along with those who chose to use the magic they should not bear.

The Elders remain in place as they finish the curse upon the men who have gone against their laws.

"MYA..."

I inhaled painfully...

THE LIGHT FEY move from the place they had temporarily called home to escape the memory of brothers, cousins, and friends, who no longer live with them but remain trapped under the soil and a constant sour reminder of the sacrifices made. The elders weaken as the power of their homeland fades.

The fey begin to mingle with the humans, who are much more than what the fey first believe. They are beings born without any type of magic. Beings who survive the lands, respecting it as the fey do. The fey learn from them and soon find themselves living in villages with the humans and taking human spouses.

The powers from the fey's homeland fades, and only their half-fey children survive the loss.

Underground, the dark fey thrive with the source's magic. Memories of the sun and life above ground have disappeared.

The men set out on a large hunt for meat. They plan to use the skins for clothing and bedding, for they have nothing. The deer they slay and consume morphs into something dark and rises again. But this time when it stands, it howls.

CHAPTER SEVEN

THE POWER IN THE CRYSTAL PUSHED MY FINGER AWAY, RELEASING ME from the vision. My stomach clenched nauseatingly, and I swallowed down the bile that wanted to rise.

I looked at Drav in disoriented shock. His features, though darker, were the same as the man who'd picked the fruit. The same as the man who'd first touched the crystal. All the pieces fit together in my head, and the resentment over his callous disregard of my freedom of choice seemed insignificant in comparison to what had been taken from him.

He didn't understand the situation like I now understood it. He'd brought me underground because he truly believed this was a place of safety. Instead, it was a prison. His people had put him here because he and his friends had differing opinions. That wasn't even the worst part. They'd taken his memories. Everything. He'd stolen me to save me. But, his people had stolen from him because he saw the world differently.

"Mya?" Drav said softly.

His concerned gaze traced my face.

"I'm so sorry," I said a moment before I flew at him.

He caught me in his arms and held me tight. His cheek pressed against the top of my head, and he breathed in deeply, running his hands down the curve of my spine.

"You have no reason for sorrow. I told you, I accept and understand your anger."

I pulled back and looked up into his odd eyes. Eyes that had once been blue like the sky. Eyes that had changed as he'd adapted to his life underground.

"I'm not sorry for being mad at you. What you did is wrong. And I still want you to take me back to the surface. But Drav, I saw you and your people when I touched the crystal. I saw what you don't remember."

He frowned.

"What do you mean?"

"Before you came here, you lived in a forest. The trees were bigger than any building I'd ever seen. There was magic in that place, but it was dying. That's why you came here. At least, I think it was here, to the states. It was so long ago it's hard to tell, and the magic in these caves seems to warp distance or something. It would explain the hellhounds in Germany. Oh, the hellhounds! Drav, those were once deer."

"Yes. That is why we cannot eat the deer." The look in his eyes softened, and his hand brushed over the length of my spine. "I'm sorry I could not give you that."

I struggled not to shiver and to stay on topic.

"No way. Don't be sorry. Had I seen that thing pop back up with glowing red eyes and an attitude that I was prey, I would have been mad you hadn't warned me."

"What else did you see?" he asked, tenderly trailing his knuckles over my cheek.

"When you first came to the caves, you had pale skin and eyes lighter than a blue daytime sky." I reached up and ran my fingers over one of his braids. "You all wore your hair in braids like this. And your clothes blended with nature." With his caresses distracting me too well, I let my hands smooth over the material covering his shoulders. His muscles twitched under my touch and a hint of desire flared to life inside me.

I stepped back from him, putting some much-needed space between us so we focused on more important things than how good it felt to be touched by him.

"Drav, your people trapped you down here. They disagreed with your use of the crystals, but that didn't stop them from combining their power with that of the crystals they'd stolen. They used that power to curse the deer here, take your memories, and cause a cave-in. A very long time ago, you had a life before these caves. As much as what they did was a dick move, it also saved you."

The words struck a chord in me. I'd had a life before these caves, too. Drav taking me down here was a dick move. But, what if he really had saved me by doing so? I immediately rejected the similarities between what his people had done to him and what he'd done to me.

"When the magic of their world died, so did they. Well, the original ones died. The kids they had with us humans continued to live on the surface just fine."

He remained silent for a moment.

"Do you understand what that means? You aren't meant to be down here, just like me. We're meant to go back, Drav. To the surface."

Before he could answer, someone spoke from behind him. I peeked around his side and saw the rest of the men standing on the path, bathed in the crystal's light, their clothes bloodier than before. Despite the gore clinging to them, they all seemed unharmed.

"How long was I touching the crystal?" I asked Drav.

"Not long." He turned to look at the other dark fey.

"The source did not give her a life crystal."

They seemed troubled by the news.

"I don't understand why that's so important to you, Drav."

"When we wear our crystal, we are safe. You need one."

I didn't see how he thought the crystals kept him safe. Maybe because of the weak light that those things cast? They sure hadn't seemed to provide any extra protection from the hellhounds just now. I didn't point any of that out, though.

"Maybe the source didn't give me a life crystal because I'm not meant to connect with its power the way you guys do. You possessed magic to start with. Even though I'm some kind of descendant, I never have. So, maybe it wouldn't have worked on me, anyway. Like I said, the magic of the world died out a long time ago. Well, everywhere but here."

Kerr said something while Drav continued to study me. Finally, he grunted in agreement.

"We need to go to the city, Mya. We only have a short time before the hellhounds return."

Because of the vision, I now had an idea of what that meant. Apparently, dead things didn't like staying dead down here. A shiver of fear travelled my spine. Drav must have seen it. He cupped the back of my neck and drew me forward, pressing his forehead against mine.

"I will keep you safe."

"But, why go to the city now? I just told you that you came from the surface, which happens to be the very same place I belong. The place you took me from against my will."

I pulled back, but he didn't look the least bit affected by my attempt at guilting him.

"We need to share what we've learned. Here and above," he said.

"And after that?"

"We will decide together."

The answer sounded reasonable, but I knew a covert "no"

when I heard one. I didn't throw a fit, though. I'd learned my lesson from the last one. Instead, I decided to play nice for the moment. Fighting didn't work with Drav. I needed to figure out a way to convince him the surface was the best place for both of us. And fast.

"Ok. Thank you."

He moved to pick me up, and I stopped him.

"I feel bad that you have to carry me all the time. Would it be easier if I hung onto your back or maybe if the others took turns carrying me?"

Several of the men said, "I carry Mya," at the same time, which started a new thought. Maybe I could convince one of—

Drav growled and turned to face the rest of the men.

"No one carries Mya but me."

I cocked my head at him, trying not to be annoyed.

"Drav, I only suggested it so you wouldn't get tired. I'm not a bone to fight over."

He turned back to me, a fierce light in his eyes.

"I swore to you I would not share you again. Ever."

He had me there. I sighed and gave in, wrapping my arms around his neck when he bent to lift me. The other men made comments in their language, but Drav ignored them as he started forward.

"What are they saying?" I asked.

"They want to know if you have friends."

I laughed. Species didn't change some things. My humor quickly died as I thought of Kristin and wondered if she'd made it to Irving. I hoped not. It had been a wasteland.

"Why are you sad?" Drav asked, studying my face.

"I used to have friends. I don't know if I still do. I need to find out, Drav. How long will it take to get me back home?" A desperate note crept into my voice despite my intention to play it cool.

"We will see what Molev has to say."

He looked forward, following the three men who led the way from the cave.

I settled in his arms, idly brushing my fingers against the back of his neck as I considered what waited for me at the city. Drav turned his head to look down at me, and the fingers of his hand supporting my lower half started to tease the skin of my thigh. I quickly stilled my movements and looked back at the three men traveling behind us. Each of their gazes flicked to me before returning to their study of our surroundings. I no longer resented their interest or curiosity. I couldn't begin to imagine what their lives had been like here.

AFTER HOURS OF RUNNING, we took a small break. Half the men left to fish at a nearby spring while another one took my water bottle to refill. I'd only surrendered it after he promised to fill it upstream from everyone. I didn't want to drink toilet water.

While the remaining two men and Drav lounged in the grass and conversed, I wandered through the protected grove. Even though I had Drav's assurance we were safe because of the light from the glowing crystals above, I didn't go far. I didn't need or want to. I only wanted a little space so I could think about everything the source crystal had shown me. A world of colossal trees and magic. A world of fey and dwarves and who knew what else. Despite experiencing the hellhounds and seeing people become zombies with my own eyes, the idea of there being even more to this new, upside-down world dumbfounded me. How had we forgotten so much of our history?

More importantly, why hadn't Drav seemed upset when I'd said his people had trapped him down here? I had no doubt he understood my words. However, I was beginning to doubt he understood the deeper meaning behind what I'd said.

His people had condemned all those who wanted to learn about the crystals to an eternity trapped in these dark caverns. For a people of earth and sky, that was essentially condemning them to living in hell. A hell that Drav was condemning me to, as well.

Yet, Drav and his friends had adapted. Maybe removing the memory of their time before the caverns had been a mercy, but anger still boiled inside of me on Drav's behalf. What if he'd had a family? The thought made my chest ache. I didn't want to disappear from mine like he had.

I glanced at him and found his watchful gaze on me. He stood and came my way, leaving one of his friends shaking his head.

"What's wrong?" he asked.

"Nothing."

"Why did you look so sad just now?"

"I was thinking about what happened to you. Why aren't you upset by the fact you were trapped down here?"

"Because I didn't feel trapped."

"Ever?"

He looked out at the trees for a moment.

"Ever. My oldest memories are of walking these caverns, learning to navigate them. It's a place of beauty. My home. I never wanted anything more until I met you."

His words made my heart jump and my guilt rise.

"Don't," he said, moving closer. He reached up and set his palm along my face, burying his fingers in my hair.

"Don't what?"

"Look at me with sorrow."

"You're right. I should be looking at you with annoyance. I haven't forgotten how you slapped my butt. I think I still have a handprint there."

He didn't say anything to that, only brushed his thumb over the skin of my cheek. I could see his regard for me in his gaze, and I struggled with what I felt in return. Before he'd brought me down here against my will, I would have said that what I felt crossed the line of mild interest. Okay, fine, what I felt leapt over the mild interest line. But now, I didn't know if it should.

Taking a breath, I decided to be honest. After all, Drav had no experience dealing with the opposite sex and likely no idea why what he'd done was wrong.

"I get that you forced me down here because you care and you want to keep me safe," I said, holding his gaze. "But knowing that you tricked me, that you took the choice to return to my family from me, hurt. It's like a lie, Drav. I need you to try to understand what you did. How would you feel if you were in my place? If I was your family and someone took me away and you didn't know if I was alive or dead?"

His thumb stilled.

"You are my family, Mya. And no one is taking you away from me."

The implied threat and his tone sent a shiver through me. He saw it and cupped my head in his hands, setting his forehead to mine. I rested my hands on his arms, taking comfort in his touch.

"You are safe here, with me. I will not allow anything to happen to you."

"That's a big promise in a world going to shit."

He tipped his head and lightly brushed the tip of his nose against mine. His breath warmed my lips, and a tingle of awareness ran through me. My heart tripped. I swallowed hard and pulled back to meet his gaze, the move bringing our mouths closer. His fingers twitched in my hair, and his biceps tensed under my palms.

He wanted more. We both knew he did. And, the idea of using his affection to get my way again teased my mind. It would be so easy to tilt my head up just a bit further. What would it feel like to kiss him?

My lips parted. I wanted to try. And, not just to get my way. I tightened my grip on his arms. His breathing quickened as I started closing the gap.

Someone said something behind him, stopping me cold with the reminder that we had an audience.

Drav growled menacingly.

"You gotta stop growling in my face. I almost peed myself the last time you did."

He exhaled heavily, searched my gaze, then turned away from me to say something harshly in his language. I peeked around him and saw the others had returned. One caught my gaze and held out a leaf stacked with gelatinous globs of fish.

"Oh, thank you, but I'm more thirsty than hungry right now."

Drav turned on me.

"You need to eat."

"Maybe next year."

He frowned at me.

"Mya—"

"Drav, you spanked me and made me follow you into your scary-ass version of wonderland with rabid once-upon-a-time deer and face eating fish. If you make me eat when I'm telling you no, I'll make you wish you'd never been born. Got it?"

I felt bad about what had happened to him, but not bad enough to let him bully me.

He leaned close, intimidating me with his unblinking stare.

"Here we take threats as challenges. You will eat the next time we stop."

He turned away and took his portion of the fish before laying back down in the grass. Making a face at his closed eyes, I went to the man who was holding my water bottle and thanked him for filling it. I drained over half of it in an effort to drown the gnawing hunger in my belly. It wouldn't be too much longer before the raw fish started looking good. I put the water bottle away, and ignoring the knowing grins from the rest, I went and settled in next to Drav.

Wrapping his arms around me, he pulled me close. I shut my eyes.

A HOWL SPLIT THE AIR, and I jolted upright. Drav squatted beside me, putting a calming hand on my shoulder. He lifted a finger to my lips, an unnecessary warning to be quiet, then scooped me up into his arms. Exhaling shakily, I clung to him and watched the other men move silently, gathering their supplies and my bag.

Together, we ran through the grass, away from the howls.

"They won't come in here," Drav said against my ear as he ran. "Not until after the crystals dim."

"They dim?" My stomach dropped.

"Yes. Like your sun and moon, there is a night and day in most of the caverns. The crystals here will not dim for a while yet. We will have a lead."

A lead? That meant the hellhounds would follow us. I shuddered at the idea of being chased from one cavern to the next.

"How long until we get to the city?"

"Two more resting periods."

That didn't help me. I had no idea how long resting periods were or the time we spent running in between them. A watch would have been helpful. Briefly, I thought of my phone, but I didn't want to waste the battery. Without anything else to do, I settled into Drav's secure hold and listened to the slowly fading baying.

The dark fey moved swiftly, and Drav's steady pace carried us into the next, dimmer cavern. Knowing the hounds liked the dark and running into a space with less light after just hearing them didn't sit well with me. The men seemed to have the same thought because they increased their already fast pace.

"After we leave this area, we will rest again."

The greenery around us thinned and the ground slowly changed to dry, hard silt. Each of the men's steps kicked up dust in the semi-desolate area, leaving prints behind. Theirs weren't the only tracks I noted.

Huge paw prints covered the area. As I stared, the dull light seemed to fade even more. Maybe it was the dimming that Drav had spoken of earlier. I didn't really start to worry until it grew too dark for me to see ahead of us. The barely audible sound of the men's feet hitting the ground kept time with my racing heart.

How much of a lead did we have?

A distant howl echoed behind us, and I jerked my head to look over Drav's shoulder.

"Mya," he said, chiding me. "You are safe."

Kerr, who ran ahead of the group, picked up his pace and the others followed suit. Not comforting. Drav held me tighter and kept up.

"We are approaching our next resting spot," Drav said.

How could he even think of resting with the hounds somewhere behind us? And why didn't he even sound winded? My worry about him carrying me for too long seemed crazy, now. With the shadow men's ability to run, I wondered if they ever really needed to worry about the hellhounds. Even as I thought it, my mind flashed to our first encounter with the beasts, and I wondered what would have happened if one of them had caught us.

The thought sent a shiver down my spine.

"Are you cold, Mya?" Drav asked.

"I'm fine."

A lie I would keep telling myself until I believed it.

CHAPTER EIGHT

DRAV'S VERSION OF NOT LONG AND MINE WERE TWO VERY DIFFERENT things. The back of my knees and shoulders ached by the time the men started to slow.

The next cavern proved to be well-lit and lush with thick trees and wildlife. A bird took flight as we startled it from its perch. Distracted by the noise, I wasn't prepared when Drav suddenly leaned forward.

Startled, I gripped the back of his neck tightly and clung to him.

"We will stop soon, but I thought you would like to walk," he said, turning his head to look at me.

The realization that he'd been attempting to put me down barely registered. Our faces were only inches apart. Drav's exhale teased my mouth while his gaze held mine with an intensity and an awareness that robbed me of breath. Thoughts of home and caves fled with the slow heat that ignited in my stomach.

He inhaled slowly and whispered my name. His hands, set on my sides to steady me, smoothed up over my ribs, stilling just where his thumbs brushed the underside of my breasts. Nothing mattered more in that moment than discovering the feel of his lips against mine.

Unable to resist any longer, I set my hand against his jaw, my thumb stroking the tensed muscle there. He turned his head just enough to nip the pad of my thumb. The flickering fire in my belly grew.

Tilting my head up, I inched closer until our lips were barely an inch apart.

"Take me home, Drav," I breathed before moving to close the distance.

Someone spoke from behind me before our lips met. Drav growled in annoyance. I wanted to do the same.

"It's okay," I said. "You're right. I could use a break."

With reluctance, Drav released his grip on me.

Bargain then kiss, I berated myself as I stepped away, stretching my legs.

It felt good to move around. Drav stayed close to my side, and the men once again spread out around us. This time, I determined the pace as we moved forward.

My bag, slung across Kerr's back, caught my attention. My stomach, which had been emitting increasingly louder growls, needed something in it. Although I desperately wanted to get my hands on my bag and my water bottle, I didn't want to call attention to my growling stomach.

Kerr turned slightly, a notched arrow poised to fly. I followed his watchful gaze, half-expecting to see a hellhound, despite the light.

"If you only use your weapons for hunting, then why use them now?" I asked Drav.

"We must find food," he said, giving me a pointed look.

So much for hiding my hunger. He'd probably heard each growl.

"My hunger wouldn't be a problem on the surface," I said softly, not wanting to startle away whatever critters Kerr hoped to shoot.

"We need to reach my city first, Mya."

My gaze again sought out my bag where the four precious cans hid. So little food. If I knew how long it would take for us to get to the city and back to the surface, I'd consider sacrificing a can now. Without knowing, though, I needed to try to hold out. My stomach clenched in rebellion.

Kerr lifted a hand, and Drav clasped my arm, stopping me. A few of the men ahead of us dropped to a crouched position, their hands brushing against their quivers, readying arrows. One of the others, who had a spear, lifted the deadly tip.

Before I could ask what was happening, Kerr's arrow flew. It whistled through the air and landed with a meaty thump. The men in front of us relaxed as they stood again.

Kerr motioned to the closest man, who took off in the direction the arrow had flown. Instead of trailing after him, the group started forward, veering in a different direction. Drav nudged me to follow.

We hadn't gone too far when the fey who had run off returned with a jackalope hanging from his belt. Without stopping, he handed Kerr the cleaned arrow and joined the group.

The men remained alert. I didn't hear anything, but a couple of times the men startled me with a sudden change in direction. The next time an arrow flew without warning, I squeaked and jumped, bumping into Drav. He wrapped a protective arm around me and pressed me to his side as the hunter ran off to fetch his kill.

"It's okay," I said against Drav's chest. "I was just startled by the sudden movement."

He nodded, releasing me. We continued to walk with the others.

"Is it always this difficult to find food?"

"No, but we are still on the outskirts. This hellhound territory, and the other animals tend to stay away."

"Is that why there are fewer and smaller trees in these caves? Because we aren't closer to the source crystal?"

"No. The source crystal doesn't control all the growth. Each cave's crystals control that. The trees grow best in the light of strong crystals." The tone he'd used to answer me seemed abrupt.

"Are you annoyed?"

Drav grunted, and a few of the men shot me looks.

"Because my talking is scaring away potential food?"

Drav gave me a matching look.

"I'll take that as a yes."

"Mya, you need to eat. We need to hunt for that to happen. You must stay quiet," Drav said, not scolding, but I could see the worry in his eyes because I wasn't eating.

At the thought of food, my stomach growled loudly and my head throbbed. My gaze found its way back to my bag and the water that remained.

"One last question...will we be resting soon?"

"I will carry you," Drav said, misunderstanding the reason behind my question.

A couple of eager, 'I will carry, Mya' comments followed.

I shook my head, both at the willing men and Drav's offer.

"I'm good."

We walked through the knee-high, dusky purple grass growing between the pale blossoming trees. Grasping the passage of time or distance in this place proved too hard, and I gave up trying. Instead, I focused on the abundant plants and the way the grass squished underneath my feet.

While Drav remained beside me, the other men moved more swiftly through the trees, often disappearing from my sight for a minute before emerging. They seemed so at ease here that, although I felt bad for all they had lost, I could tell they had found the home they had searched for. Even as cruel as their home could be.

When the men finally slowed a few minutes later, I saw dead jackalopes hanging from most of their belts. One even had a bird. The men walked over a patch of grass, flattening it down, then unhooked their kills and set them in the middle.

"We will make camp here," Drav said, tamping down an area of tall grass for a sleep nest just off the main circle.

The fey brought out small skinning knives and started to work on their kills. My empty stomach turned at the sight, and I frowned. Under normal circumstances, I didn't think myself a squeamish person when it came to food prep. Hunger was messing with me. How long had we been down here already? Almost two days? And only a raw piece of fish to eat during that time.

I plopped down in the space Drav had created. He sat beside me and brushed the backs of his fingers along my arm. The touch comforted me, his need for constant contact not bothering me in the least.

Kerr came over, handed me my bag and Drav a jackalope. I immediately opened the bag, ignoring Drav's work, and dug inside for the water, which I sipped carefully. That action only added to a new urgent need, and I pressed my legs together.

"Drav..."

Hands full of jackalope innards, he paused to glance at me.

"Is it safe around here?"

"I will protect you."

"I know, but if someone had to take a quick walk, would it be safe?"

Drav stared at me, obviously confused. I leaned close, my lips just about to brush his ear.

"I have to pee," I whispered.

"I will take you," he said gently.

I wanted to groan because I didn't need company, just the assurance something wouldn't attack me with my pants down.

Drav handed his jackalope to the closest man, who took it with a nod. The others continued their work as we walked away.

After relieving myself, my stomach cramped painfully with the need for food.

The subconscious hope I held for something resembling fried chicken died when we returned and I saw raw meat laying on a large frond in the center of their circle. It didn't escape my notice that the men hadn't yet touched the meat they had so carefully cut into strips. There could only be one reason for that. That shit tasted as bad as it looked.

Drav sat smoothly and waited for me to join him. Reluctantly sitting, I glanced at the meat. Drav picked up a few pieces and tried to hand them to me.

"You're not going to cook that?"

"The kill is fresh, and the meat still warm."

My brain gagged on that thought, and I picked up my water bottle, shaking it at him.

"I'm good."

"No, you must eat."

"I'm really okay. Seriously. You guys eat up."

"I warned you, Mya. You will eat."

I glanced at the bloody meat that Drav was offering. If I ate raw meat from a demon-eyed rabbit, I'd be lucky if the only thing I got was a tapeworm. With the world up top going to hell, I couldn't take the chance.

"Don't try bullying me. I'm not the one running around carrying another person or fighting hellhounds. You guys have to keep your strength up. I will be fine."

Drav let out a slow breath, and I realized I'd really annoyed him. Good. I owed him.

"If you will not eat this," he said, "you will eat your food." He glanced meaningfully at my bag.

I followed his gaze, beyond tempted. Yet, worry still niggled the back of my mind. My stomach growled loudly.

"Your stomach agrees that you need food."

"It's a liar."

"Mya."

The warning tone of his voice didn't allow for argument. Not that I had any. Or willpower. I dug into the bag and pulled out a can of green beans. Thankful for the pull tab, I took the top off and tucked the metal circle back inside my pack. Drav and the others watched in fascination as I poured out the brine and fished out a piece.

I lifted the green bean to my lips. He shadowed my move with the piece of meat he held, the message clear. He wouldn't eat until I did. Rolling my eyes, I popped the bean into my mouth and chewed. He nodded and bit into the meat. The rest dug into their portions.

The quick, quiet meal of beans settled my angry stomach. Content, I scooted back a few steps and curled on my side. Drav settled in next to me.

Sleep tugged at me but not before I felt his lips brush against my forehead then my cheek.

Too bad we were surrounded by other people.

THE UNEXPECTED FEELING of my body leaving the ground penetrated my peaceful slumber. Before I fully woke, though, the press of Drav's forehead to mine and the firm hold of his arms reassured me. I became aware that we were moving again, but I didn't open my eyes. Cradled in his arms, I couldn't resist the temptation of sleep.

I roused again when Drav's arms tightened around me, his muscles rolled with his impressive pace. I'd just opened my eyes to see what had him moving so quickly when the desolate call of a hellhound echoed around us. Dread coated my mind.

"We are close to the next crystal source," Drav said, noticing I had woken up.

Looking around, I saw no welcoming glow of light.

The rhythmic sound of thumping feet grew louder behind us. When I peeked over Drav's shoulder, I saw the three dim blue lights from the feys' bracelets. Further back, I saw two sets of red eyes rushing toward us.

"Shit."

The men running behind us fell back to meet the attack. I watched the dim blue glow of their lights as they clashed with the hounds. The thwang of arrows and the thump of them hitting their marks echoed around us. After a grunt and a yip, one of the hounds fell behind, its eyes still glowing and moving slightly. Whatever the fey had done had stopped it, but not killed it. Just like on the surface, nothing seemed to kill the hounds.

The other set of red eyes neared one of the men, and I saw the lunging hellhound clamp down on his arm. Teeth dug into flesh. The fey grabbed the hound's snout with his free hand and pulled back almost as Drav had all those nights ago. The other two fey hovered close. As soon as the first fey pulled free of the beast's teeth, one of the men jumped on the hound, slitting its throat with a small blade.

The hound fell to the ground, not dead, but struggling to breathe and to get up again. The men left it and caught up with the group. Drav shifted my weight in his arms and ran faster.

The injured hound's noise began to fade with distance.

"Shouldn't we bandage him?" I asked, looking pointedly at the one with the injured arm.

"No. We must leave this area before the hounds heal."

My gaze returned to the wounded fey. He ran with the rest, seemingly unbothered by the blood coating his arm. If the hound's bite affected them as it did humans, the others would have been more upset. Right?

Just like before, the terrain changed slowly with the approach of another lit cavern. The barren ground gave way to short, sparse grass then wispy ferns.

A shiver shook me when we crossed from cool, dry air to humid warmth. The crystals' soft glow from above pulsed. Drav moved quickly and the sights flew by. Glimpses of trees with thick, broad drooping leaves and of vines twining up the rocky pillars teased me. A few times, I thought I saw a flower or colorful piece of fruit.

The group stopped after several minutes, and Drav slowly set me on my feet.

"We will rest for a bit, but we must leave before the crystals dim."

Drav's words about the crystals dimming during their version of night came back to worry me. The hellhounds would follow the scent of the wounded fey's blood.

I glanced at the man, who stood not far away, wiping at his wound with a huge leaf. Blood still smeared his arm. I moved toward Kerr.

"Can I have my bag, please?"

Kerr looked over my shoulder, where Drav hovered, before handing it to me. I took my bag and went to the wounded fey. With interest, he watched me approach.

"What's your name?" I asked.

The man glanced behind me before answering.

"Shax."

"May I look at your arm?"

Shax looked over my shoulder once more. This time I turned to glance at Drav, too. Drav met my gaze then nodded at Shax.

"Seriously? What do you think I'm going to do?" I said with an arched a brow. Drav didn't comment.

Turning back to Shax, I examined the arm he held out for my inspection. The blood ran darkly over the jagged bite. When I looked up to check Shax's eyes for any hint of cloudiness, he stared at me with unblinking focus.

"Let me know if you start craving human brains, okay?"

Not expecting an answer, I dug into my bag and pulled out my half-empty water bottle. Damn. Not cool, but I knew the wound needed to be cleaned. Wetting a large white bandage from my first aid kit, I gently washed away the clotting blood. The wound looked less horrifying once cleaned.

The others crowded around us, watching as I pulled out another bandage to wrap around his arm. Drav stopped me.

"He will be fine," he said.

"It should be covered so it doesn't get dirty."

"Save the wrap. He will be fine."

Drav gave Shax a look, and Shax nodded once before walking away without the bandage. I watched him pluck a new leaf and wrap it around his wound.

"He could have had the bandage," I said, turning to look at Drav. "There are more of them."

"He does not need it, but you may."

A frustrated groan escaped me.

"If you really think that, then why am I down here? Wasn't the point because it's supposed to be safer? Just take me home, Drav. Let the rest go to the city."

"We go together.

Frustrated, I turned away from him and started to put my things away. Immediately, I noticed my water bottle missing. I checked the nearby plants in case the empty bottle had rolled. However, I didn't find it. Panic began to grow. Without the water bottle, how would I drink? Stuff in the water wanted to eat my face.

Drav said nothing as he watched my increasingly frantic search.

One of the other men approached and said my name, interrupting my efforts. Glancing up with impatience, I saw my filled water bottle in his hand. Relief coursed through me.

"Thank you." I stood and accepted the cold container.

"Upstream," he said with a smile.

I grinned in return and put the bottle away. Kerr came for my bag, and I noticed the crystals certainly had dimmed during our short break.

"Did you need to go pee?" Drav asked.

"I'm good."

"I will only be gone for a moment. The others will watch over you."

After he relieved himself in the trees, we were on the move again. As we passed from cavern to cavern, I caught glimpses of beauty in this underground world. Different trees that spiraled versus growing straight and plant life that grew as tall and strong as the trees.

We emerged from a fertile cavern into a vast space which easily stretched for miles and had a ceiling so high the crystals twinkled like distant stars. In the distance, a larger crystal shown like a full moon on a clear night.

The men moved swiftly, their leather clad feet barely making a noise against the hard surface of this cavern's floor.

Awe filled me as I studied everything I could see. That awe turned to stunned disbelieve when I caught sight of a stone wall stretching beyond sight in both directions.

The closer we drew, details became clearer. The soft light played on veins of white running through the gray and black stone that seamlessly rose out of the cave's floor. Carved out of existing stone, or made from magic, the wall was a part of the cave.

"What is this place?" I asked.

"Our city," Drav answered.

CHAPTER NINE

KERR PULLED AHEAD, OUTDISTANCING THE REST OF US.

"Where's he going?"

"To tell the others to open the door," Drav said.

"Door?"

Kerr's faint shout reached us, and I watched a figure appear near the top of the stone wall. A moment later, the figure waved an arm and disappeared again. A grating, low rumble filled the air and a crack emerged in the smooth expanse of rock just as Kerr reached the wall.

We joined him not long afterward, and I stared at the massive stone entrance before me.

The wicked, long furrows in the heavy slabs that comprised the entry to the city momentarily distracted me from what lay inside. When I did finally focus, shock filled me. The uninhabited, wild areas outside the wall had misled me into believing Drav's "city" would be nothing more than hovels grouped together in more of the same wild. I should have known better.

A dirt trail, bordered by thick flowering vegetation, wound its way toward a vast grove of trees towering high in the distance. In the immense space between the gate and the grove, neatly planted fields spread out to the right and left, illuminated by countless crystal lanterns suspended at the top of long poles. Soft, glittering lights gave the land a surreal feel.

"It looks like fairy lights," I said softly.

Drav jogged through the opening and deposited me on my feet. I felt him leave my side as I continued to look around.

They were farmers. Even with what the crystal had shown me, my mind struggled to process the concept of cave farming. Actual dirt lay beneath my feet, not stone. How?

I already knew the answer. The source had shown me that the magic to influence nature ran in their blood. The proof of what their powers, combined with that of the crystals, could accomplish stunned me. Not only had they created a wall, they'd created arable earth.

The grinding rumble of the gate drew my attention, and I turned around to watch Drav and another man strain to push the stone slab closed. Their muscles rolled and flexed with each laborious step.

"I wouldn't want that job. How many times a day do they need to open the gate?"

The gate closed with a rasping thud. Drav moved back to my side as two men slid an enormous log into place to brace the stone slab.

"The gate is almost never used," Drav said. He pointed to a pair of tall ladders that leaned against the wall just inside the door. "We use the ladders. There is less chance of the hounds slipping in that way."

"Wow."

A group of new men stared at me from where they stood near the gate.

"Hello," I said before Drav could speak. "I'm Mya. I'm not a male like you, but a female from the surface."

Their eyes widened with sudden understanding, and they

looked at me with even more interest while the men in our group sniggered and said a few words under their breaths.

"No, I'm not willing to show you my physical differences. No, you can't touch me. I'd prefer you not smell me, either. It makes me nervous and uncomfortable. I don't understand your language, but know you can understand me. I don't have a crystal or magic like you all do. Thank you for opening the gate and letting me in."

Speech given, I glanced at Drav and found him considering me.

"What?" I asked.

"They will all want to touch you and smell you no matter what you say."

"Then we're going to have problems, aren't we?"

He sighed and nodded as if it were a foregone conclusion, which I found unacceptable. I needed a deterrent. How did one discourage a city full of demon men who ripped off heads for fun?

"Would it hurt if I kicked you guys in the balls?" I asked.

He tilted his head and gave me a puzzled look. So did the rest. Slang didn't translate well.

"Your soft bits that hang between your legs. The two balls."

Understanding lit their gazes. Several of the men in our immediate group grunted and moved a little further away from me. Kerr chuckled and said something to Drav, who frowned.

"We don't kick there. Ever," Drav said, quite seriously.

"Well, I will if I'm touched or sniffed without permission." I glanced at the men. "You've been warned." I hoped I'd put some fear in them because that empty threat summed up the whole of my weak defense. Bigger, stronger, faster...they could overpower me at any time. I knew that. Deep down they probably did too.

"Are you ready?" I asked, changing the subject.

"Yes. It is safe for you to walk here. But, I would like to carry you so we can reach the city faster."

"Go ahead. I'm all for faster."

The words had barely left my mouth before Drav scooped me

up. The men by the wall called out a word as the rest of our group started running down the path.

Drav didn't immediately move to follow as I expected, and I looked up to see why.

The expression he wore heated my cheeks.

"I've wanted this a very long time."

"What?"

"You here. Safe. Letting me hold you."

"But just to deliver the information and go, right?"

Our gazes locked, and his fingers brushed my ribs near my breast.

"Maybe you should focus on running instead of me."

"I'm always focused on you, Mya. Especially when I'm running with you in my arms. I like the way you jiggle."

My mouth dropped open.

"I do not jiggle," I said indignantly.

He took off, sprinting down the trail, and his gaze dipped to my chest. I followed the direction of his focus and rolled my eyes at the sight of my ever so slightly bouncing boobs.

"That is barely a jiggle. You made me sound like a bowl of Jell-O."

"I think I might enjoy Jell-O."

I snorted. "Probably."

Now that he'd pointed out his fascination, I paid more attention to him instead of the landscape. His eyes did indeed repeatedly return to my chest.

"You really do have a thing for boobs, don't you?"

"Yes. They look interesting when you are undressed, and they feel so soft. I like when you sleep and let me hold them."

"Wait a minute. Sleeping isn't permission to hold them. It just means I'm not conscious to object."

"Yes. I like that."

His ignorance kept him safe from me slugging him.

"How would you like it if I waited until you slept and grabbed your balls really, really hard?"

He frowned for a moment, and I realized he was considering it.

"Seriously, Drav? The point is that you wouldn't like me doing stuff to you while you slept, so you shouldn't do it to me."

"I might like it. Your hands are soft and gentle. You're not as strong. It might not hurt so much."

I groaned and looked away from him for a moment, trying to think of a way to help him understand.

"Do you understand the concept of stealing?" I asked, looking up at him.

"Yes. Stealing is forbidden here."

"It's forbidden where I'm from, too. When you touch me without my agreement, it's like stealing from me. I need to give my approval for the touches to mean something. It's supposed to be special, Drav."

"It is special," he said, looking troubled.

"If I haven't agreed to it, it's only special to you, not me. Do you understand?"

"Yes." He stared ahead for a long while.

I checked the path and could barely see his friends further ahead.

"When will you give me your permission?" Drav asked, drawing my attention again.

Not will you, but when will you. His confidence amazed me.

"If you don't take me back to the surface, I might not ever give it," I said with an arched brow.

He grunted and focused on the path for a long while. I smothered a grin at the tightness in his jaw and turned away to watch the grove.

Even though the view of the forest grew larger, the distance to reach it never seemed to change. With each field we passed, I began to wonder just how big the towering trees would be. I had to admit more than a mild curiosity filled me when I began to see tiny specks of light within the inky tops.

Given the size of the cavern, I could understand the need for the field lanterns and the ones in the trees. The wall stretched out so far, I lost sight of it. Not only was the area hard to light, but how could they possibly guard the whole thing?

"Have they ever gotten in? The hellhounds?"

"A few times. But we return them back to where they belong."

"How do you know when they get in? This place is huge."

"The outlying villages guard the walls. If any hounds do manage to climb over, the light of the crystals in the fields hurt them, and they make plenty of noise to let us know where they are."

When I turned back to the grove, I could finally make out the shapes of the outer most trees, which seemed small in comparison to the central ones. Drav's reason for wanting to carry me became clear. What I'd thought a distant, normal grove of trees was turning out to be a forest of the largest trees I'd ever seen.

"Just how tall are those trees?" I asked.

"I do not know. Very tall."

Details became clearer, and I realized just how giant the massive trees were. They towered high above, their inky leaves almost touching the vast cavern's soaring top and kissing the crystals inlaid there.

Entering the shadows of the trees, I saw what Drav's people had done. Without even knowing it, they'd recreated the home of their ancestors. The home they'd been sent to find. My eyes watered, and Drav noticed. He slowed to a walk.

"Why are you crying? Are you afraid? I will keep you safe."

I leaned my head against his chest and put my hand over his heart.

"I know you'll keep me safe. And, I'm not crying exactly. Just emotional. Girls do that sometimes."

He grunted and held me a little closer, leaning his head in to smell my hair and nuzzle my neck. A tingle of awareness shivered through me.

"Is it all right if I walk for a while?" I asked.

"Yes." He set me on my feet and held out his hand. I threaded my fingers through his and walked by his side, marveling at our surroundings.

"You brought seeds with you into the caves," I said, sharing what the source crystal had shown me. "I think these are seeds from the trees of your homeland. Trees that were dying. I think that your people's magic was connected to the forest's magic somehow. When the magic faded from the surface, so did theirs. But not here. Maybe because the crystal helped feed the magic of the trees. Your magic."

We came to one tree that had vines twisting up its ancient bark. Large, white, bell-shaped flowers drooped from thin shoots. The fragrant air tickled my nose, and I gave in and inhaled deeply. The intoxicating smell wrapped around me, seeming to sooth away all my travel aches.

I inhaled again, appreciatively.

"It's like a fairytale in here," I said. "So pretty."

"Careful. The scent of that plant can be very relaxing."

"Really?"

"Yes. We use it for healing and celebrating."

The image of a bunch of men standing around and smelling flowers filled my head and I giggled. I could picture Drav with one in his hair and Kerr asking to sniff it. I snorted hard, and a laughing fit had me bending over in near tears.

Suddenly, the world spun, and Drav was carrying me again at a run.

"Too much fieayla flower for you."

It took a few minutes for my head to stop spinning and for the laughter to settle down.

"That stuff is strong." I leaned my head against his shoulder and looked around at the trees. "I hope that's not growing in the city."

"No. We keep it to the outer trees."

A glimmer of lights in the treetops caught my attention. I squinted, trying to determine if I was seeing through the canopy or if someone had placed crystal lanterns in the trees.

"Are there lanterns up there?" I asked.

"Yes. To mark every home."

"Home?"

Drav stopped running and looked up at the tree.

"Welcome to Ernisi, our city."

I blinked, feeling quite Drav-like, and looked around at the empty forest floor then at the towering canopy. There was nothing here. When he'd said city, I'd kept imagining a bustling underground metropolis. That's not what I saw. I saw a quiet forest.

On my second sweeping glance, I glimpsed a set of stairs cleverly created out of curled pieces of massive bark.

"Holy shit," I said for the second time.

Drav smiled slightly and started for the nearest tree. He took the steps at an easy-for-him run. My stomach plummeted at how quickly we ascended and at how very tall the tree rose and at how no railing existed on the not too wide stairs.

I squeezed my eyes shut and focused on my breathing.

Several minutes later, Drav slowed.

"You can look, Mya."

I opened my eyes and saw we stood on a massively wide branch. The abnormally flat surface created a roadway that stretched out far from the trunk of the tree. Smaller branches, wider than an RV, protruded from the main branch, along with enormous burls.

Nearby, men stood gathered before a hut carved out of the first burl on the main trunk. A lone man stood on a raised part of the burl, giving him height and making it easy for him to see out over the crowd and for the crowd to see him. His gaze locked on us.

"Who is that?" I said softly.

Drav eased me to my feet.

"That is Molev."

Even without the help of the burl, the dark fey stood a bit taller than Drav. He, like all the other men, wore his black hair in tight, masculine braids that gave him a Viking look. His face seemed vaguely familiar. One of the original ten.

Molev stared at me with the same curiosity as the others had. The crowd of men noticed his regard and turned to look at us. The numerous gazes pinned me, and the urge to repeat my speech from earlier arose.

Molev spoke, reclaiming the men's attention.

"Who is he to your people?" I whispered.

"Our leader."

Molev continued to speak to the men in Drav's language.

"What is he saying?"

"He is telling the group what happened to Phusty."

"Oh."

I glanced at Drav and saw the hopelessness in his expression. A sweeping urge to offer him some sort of comfort had me clasping his hand and giving it a gentle squeeze.

"I'm really sorry."

The guy hadn't been nice, but according to the crystal, Drav had known him a very, very long time.

Drav gave a minute nod, and the longer he listened to Molev, the more his lips tightened. A figure broke away from the group and came toward us. Ghua's frown matched Drav's. When he reached us, they spoke in quiet tones. The more Ghua said, the more Drav looked pained.

"What's wrong?" I asked.

"Phusty has not come back."

"They lost his body?"

"No. He did not return to the waters," he said.

I opened my mouth to ask what he meant, but Molev spoke loudly, recapturing my attention. Whatever he said had the men dispersing. As each passed us to descend the stairs, they gave me a good once over. No one stopped to speak with Drav, though. I glanced at Molev and found him watching me. His gaze shifted to Drav, and he tilted his head to indicate the burl.

Drav touched the small of my back, and Drav, Ghua, and I joined Molev inside. Several small lanterns filled with crystals lit the interior of the burl. The soft glow danced on the smoothly carved walls curved to allow for seats and a built-in bed around the perimeter. Stepping closer, I studied the swirls in the woodgrain of the stunning walls and ran a finger along a curve. With that one touch, I understood that no carving tool had created this place. Magic had.

Molev spoke a stream of words while looking at Drav. Hearing Phusty's name mentioned a couple of times, my worry grew not only for Drav but for myself.

"Phusty had his crystal on him," Drav said when the man quieted.

Molev spoke some more and Drav responded.

"He challenged me for the right to study Mya. We fought. I won. He did not return. Ghua and the others brought him here, thinking that might change."

Molev turned his attention to Ghua and seemed to ask him a question.

"The waters did not mehornan. He had his crystal on him," Ghua said.

The mix of their language and English didn't help me understand anything.

"What's the big deal with his crystal?" I asked, trying to piece together their conversation.

"The life crystal we wear protects us from death," Drav said.

"Yeah, you mentioned it keeps you safe."

"Not just safe. I don't know the right word, but when we wear the crystal, we don't have a real death."

All the little things Drav had been trying to explain finally clicked into place. They didn't have death because the crystals brought them back to life. Like the deer in the vision.

"That's why you wanted to get me a crystal," I said slowly.

Drav stepped up to me and pressed his forehead against mine. The caring of this man made my heart race.

"It wasn't just protection. You didn't want me to die."

"You are safe here. Even without the crystal."

"Safe, but not staying, right?"

His thumbs brushed across my cheekbones, and I wrapped my fingers around his wrists, holding him in return.

"Safe," he repeated.

Drav took a step back, and I released my hold on his wrists. Ghua and Molev were watching us closely. I cleared my throat, feeling awkward under their curious gazes.

"Drav, Ghua," Molev said. The string of words that followed had the two nodding as they listened.

My thoughts drifted to Phusty's death and the men's reactions. When Drav ripped off his head, none of them had batted an eye. After a few minutes, though, they'd nudged the fallen man with their feet and had argued. It all made sense, now. They'd expected Phusty to get back up. The idea of it boggled me. Sure, I'd seen it in a vision, but the deer had come from the caves and...I recalled the way the men in the vision had brought the deer outside, and my stomach sank. They couldn't resurrect outside this place.

"There haven't been any traces of them yet," Drav said, interrupting my thoughts.

Molev glanced at Ghua, who shook his head. I frowned as I listened. Molev paced, speaking again.

"It is possible that they were attacked by the hounds on the surface," Drav said.

Molev nodded but waved his hands angrily as he spoke a clipped smattering of words.

"Good that they stay on surface," Ghua interjected.

"Who?" I asked.

Molev spoke over my question and Drav answered him, ignoring me.

"We've had guards on the entrances. Someone would have seen if they had returned."

Molev calmed at that and stared into space. He directed his next words at Ghua, who nodded and left the room.

"What's happening?" When Drav didn't immediately answer, I poked him. "What the hell is going on?"

"We didn't only go to the surface for exploration. Long ago, two of our people did something unthinkable. They killed another after taking his crystal. Without his crystal, he did not return. It is an unforgivable act. The men were exiled and forced to live outside the city walls."

I glanced at Molev then focused on Drav.

"Are you going to be exiled?" I asked.

"No. I did not know what would happen on the surface. Phusty wore his crystal. He should have returned."

"So what's the big deal about the two who were exiled? Why's he so upset?" I glanced at Molev who listened patiently.

"When the hole opened, we believe they fled with the hounds. They went to the surface."

CHAPTER TEN

PIECES OF THEIR CONVERSATION MADE SCARY SENSE NOW. GHUA wanted the criminals to stay on the surface because the fey could die a real death up there. However, he was only thinking of this world's safety, not mine. What chance did humanity have against two powerful fey who didn't care if people came back or not?

"You can't leave them up there. We have to go back, now, to find them and to find my parents."

"No, Mya. It is too dangerous."

"It's too dangerous for every uninfected human if those two stay up there."

"Mya."

"No," I said, stepping away from him. "We came to your city and shared the information like you said. Now, you keep your promise. You said we would decide together. Telling me it's too dangerous sounds a hell of a lot like you're trying to decide for me, not with me."

"Mya..." He stalked me, backing me to a wall.

My gaze snapped to his, and I saw the worry there.

"Molev has commanded everyone to return below. Ghua is heading out now to share the news."

"What? Why didn't you say that sooner? He could have taken me with him." I looked at the door, wondering if I could catch Ghua.

"I said I would not share," Drav said with a growl.

"Going with Ghua isn't sharing. He could have taken me back home. Like I want. Like I've been begging you to do since the moment you tossed me over your back, you ass."

"No."

"What do you mean no? You don't get to decide, Drav. I'm not one of you. Molev can't keep me here, and neither can you."

I slapped my hands to his chest, trying to push him away. Instead, he caught my hands and leaned in, his expression fierce.

"Don't forget, Mya. Your people are destroying the surface to kill the infected. To kill anything that is not human. They do not care if they kill healthy humans while doing so."

I scowled at him, hating he was right about that.

"Fine, my people are assholes. But so are yours. Just because your people can die on the surface, your leader is leaving the criminals and having the rest return without cleaning up the mess that you all created." A sudden thought stopped me cold, and I stared up at Drav in shock.

"Did you know that would happen? That once Molev found out you guys could die up there, he would command everyone to stay underground? Is it one of the reasons you brought me here? To trap me?"

"No. I said I would keep you safe. With the bombs up there, it is safer to wait down here. If the source would have given you a crystal and Phusty would have returned..." He sighed. "Please stay until it is safe for you to go home."

Like I had a choice without his help. We'd nearly died twice trying to reach the city.

A grunt sounded from behind Drav, a reminder we weren't

alone. Drav released me and stepped to the side to face Molev. Molev studied me and spoke. Drav translated.

"He wishes to learn more of your words," Drav said. "You could give him the device you allowed me to use to learn your words."

I tightened my hold on my bag, which hung over my shoulder.

"Oh, that's not a good idea. Definitely no."

"Mya."

"No."

"He only wishes to be able to communicate with you in your language."

"I'm good with using you as a translator."

"It would be much easier for him to learn with the device."

There was no way I was going to give them the iPod with my mom's more scandalous reads on it. Perhaps I could delete them off. I would have to check later to see if that function existed. Until then, though...

"No," I repeated, more firmly.

Molev chimed in again, the look on his face thoughtful. Drav listened and nodded.

"We will discuss this later. Since we have travelled so far, Molev suggests we rest. Afterwards, there will be a feast so he can share the news about the surface."

Molev left the burl mid-explanation. Resting sounded amazing, but I couldn't stop thinking about Molev's decision.

"You mean about abandoning the surface?" I said as Drav led me out. "Drav, my family is still out there. I need to find them."

Drav remained quiet for a moment before halting me.

"I promise, Mya, when it is safe, we will return for them."

His words didn't reassure me. Who would determine when it became safe? I doubted the bombs would kill every infected or hellhound, and with them still present, Drav would want to keep me down here forever.

"When, Drav? Up top may never be safe again," I said. "And

that's exactly why I need to go back. My family needs me, and you, if they're going to have any hope of surviving. I'm willing to compromise and give the bombing a few more days to settle down, but that's it. With or without you, I'll leave." Or at least I would try to. I really hoped it didn't come to that.

"Agreed." He said the word quickly and firmly, leaving me no doubt that he meant it. A few days was more than I wanted to give, but Ryan said they were in a safe zone, and they'd survived the first week. They would survive a few more days. They had to.

When Drav threaded his fingers through mine and gently tugged me in the direction of the massive tree trunk, I begrudgingly followed.

"Are we going back down?"

"No. Up. We'll find an open home to rest."

"Open home? Don't you live here?"

"My home is in one of the outer villages. I only come to the city when called."

"You know, when you said city, I thought you meant something...more."

He glanced at me.

"What do you mean?"

"Are there any shops here? Or anything else besides homes?"

"No. We don't need anything more than somewhere to sleep."

"So all you do is farm and sleep?"

"No. We hunt and train, too."

When we reached the steps, he stopped.

"Do you want me to carry you up?"

I didn't bother to look up or down, just nodded.

Safely in his arms, I closed my eyes and concentrated on the wind on my face until he stopped again.

"It's quieter up here and not often used," he said.

I opened my eyes and found we stood on another wide branch. Wide by surface standards, but not as broad as the one Molev called home. Thankfully, no wind disturbed the branch or caused any swaying when Drav eased me to my feet.

"You may choose for us," he said, gesturing to the line of four burls.

"The one closest to the tree might be best." I moved toward the entrance, glad I didn't catch a view over the edge of the branch. I never had a fear of heights. To be fair, though, I'd never needed to be up so high without guardrails before.

The inside of the burl looked the same as Molev's. A natural bench curved from the wall and widened near the back. A depression near the door looked like a large empty basin, but other than that, the place was bare.

"There's not much here. Do you really do nothing else but sleep here?" I set my bag on the part of the bench near the door.

"Just sleep."

"The bed doesn't look very comfy."

He glanced at the wooden platform at the back and frowned.

"Your beds are softer," he agreed.

"Yeah. By a lot."

"You can sleep on me."

I glanced at him and saw he looked entirely serious. Warmth started in my face and spread in tingling waves throughout my body. We were alone and safe for the first time in days. My gaze drifted to his lips, and I couldn't deny I was tempted by his offer. Too tempted. If I gave in, he'd never want to take me home.

"Sleeping on you might not be a good idea."

"Why?"

Crap.

"If all you do is sleep in this room," I said, changing the subject, "where do you eat, bathe, go to the bathroom, and all the other stuff?"

"We do all of that on the ground. Why don't you want to sleep on me, Mya?"

"You're annoyingly persistent sometimes."

"I only want to understand." He stepped closer to me, crowding into my space. Lifting a hand, he trailed his fingers down my cheek.

"I want to understand why touching you like this makes me hurt right here." He captured my hand and laid it on his chest. At the contact, he closed his eyes. "I want to know if you like being touched by me as much as I like being touched by you." He opened his eyes to look at me. "I want to understand why it is not special to you when it means everything to me."

I swallowed with difficultly, trying hard to stifle the wave of heat that washed through me.

"It is special, now, when I'm awake. I only meant you shouldn't do stuff when I'm asleep."

"I won't touch your breasts or pussy. I will just hold you."

What the hell was I supposed to say to that?

"Uh, thanks. I'll think about it."

"Good." His fingers brushed over my skin once more then stilled as he continued to stare down at me. Several long moments passed.

"I didn't mean I'm going to think about it right now. I need some time to decide."

Disappointment clouded his expression before he exhaled heavily. He really wanted me sleeping on top of him. The idea of just how badly he wanted that had my insides dancing.

"Maybe you can show me around on the ground so I know where everything is. That feast Molev mentioned sounds interesting. Will there be something other than raw meat?"

"Yes. Are you hungry?"

"Maybe. It all depends on the food."

"Come. I will carry you below."

A few minutes later, I had my feet firmly planted on solid terrain, and we walked side by side under the giant trees. Rich dark soil covered the paths that wove through the random vegetation.

Unlike the fields, everything in the forest felt naturally placed, like seeds in the wind. However, the longer we walked, the more I noticed subtle patterns.

"These weren't randomly planted, were they?"

"No. Plants for healing are grouped together. Plants for weaving are spread throughout, so the harvest doesn't empty one place. Plants to sweeten the air are used around bathroom areas as are the soft plants for cleansing. And, plants for washing are closer to the water."

"Wow. I guess you'll need to teach me a lot of plants. Especially the soft ones for cleansing. I don't want to mess that up with something else...you know, just in the few days we're going to be here."

He nodded and began to point out the different types. Their unique leaf patterns and the way the plants grew made them easily distinguishable from their neighbors, once I knew what to look for.

Before long, we stood at the edge of a large clearing. Stumps, like campfire seats, were scattered in an almost haphazard way around a huge central piece at least ten feet in diameter. About half the number of men from the earlier meeting walked about in the clearing. Some of them conversed in small groups, and some set down leaves covered with bits of something onto the communal table.

My stomach growled, and Drav nudged me forward. The murmur of male voices quieted as we approached, and it felt like every man present stared at me.

"Hello," I said, clearly. "My name is Mya. I'm not a male, like you, but a female from the surface. I don't like to be grabbed or touched or smelled. It makes me uncomfortable."

A low murmur spread throughout the gathered crowd. A few of the men approached us right away. They spoke to Drav but stared at me the entire time.

Drav repeated the story of finding me in a truck, accidently grabbing me, and discovering I had different parts. While I listened, I glanced around, mostly trying to see what kinds of food the newcomers were adding to what already waited on their table. The can of beans was just a distant memory, and my stomach made sure to let me know that with a steady stream of cramps and growls.

One man carried something past that looked like a stuffed cabbage roll. My mouth watered, and my feet decided we needed to follow. Drav didn't say anything when I stepped away. I could feel him watch me, though. However, everyone seemed to respect my little don't-touch-me message.

The man set his leaf on the table then walked away after giving me a once over. Stepping closer, I looked over the food already waiting. Most of it looked like raw meat, but a few things appeared to be some kind of fruit or vegetable. I even saw one of those flowers that had made me laugh. The best-looking dish, in my opinion, remained that cabbage roll looking thing.

My brain took a backseat as my stomach made the decision we needed to eat right then. Snatching up a roll, I had half of it in my mouth before anyone could stop me. The mouthwatering flavors burst upon my tongue as I chewed. The outside of the roll was some kind of leaf, and the inside seemed stuffed with a blend of meat and soft grain. Although probably uncooked, it still tasted like heaven.

Yelling exploded somewhere behind me, but I kept eating, not bothering to turn and look. Not even when I heard my name. My thoughts remained focused on the next roll I grabbed. The second roll caused more people to yell. I knew I should have felt bad that I'd started eating before the feast officially began, but I couldn't manage it. Instead, I chewed and groaned in bliss.

The arguing quieted, and it took a moment for it to click that everyone stared at me again. I swallowed and lifted the half-eaten roll.

"This is so good. I was starving."

Drav stepped away from the three men glaring at him and came to me. His tender expression swept over my face. When he reached me, he cupped the back of my head and touched his forehead to mine.

My stomach did a tiny flip that had nothing to do with food and everything to do with the man smoothing his thumb over the skin near the corner of my mouth.

"Eat as much as you want," he said softly.

Grumbles and angry shouts erupted after that statement. Drav pulled away to face the crowd.

"Enough," he roared. The men quieted, some glaring at him. Some glaring at me. Most just watching everything.

"Mya's world is not like ours. They do not have the same customs. She is hungry, and I want her to eat."

I picked up another roll and took a bite to show I agreed. One of the glarers took offense and said something to Drav in angry tones.

"She does not have a life crystal. She isn't one of us to be challenged."

Whoa...what?

"What's going on?" I asked after swallowing my mouthful.

"Groi, Vair, and Limar are angry you ate before them. They believe they have the right to challenge you. However, it is not our way to challenge someone without a life crystal." He looked at the men when he spoke his next words. "I will accept challenges on Mya's behalf."

That didn't sound good. Worried, I glanced at the angry men, hunger forgotten. Two of them said something, continuing to look fierce. The third waved his hand and stepped back.

"Is anyone else offended?" Drav asked. No one came forward. "Good. We will go now."

The two men nodded and strode through the crowd in the

direction opposite from where we'd arrived. Drav nudged me to follow.

"What exactly does a challenge mean?" I asked, nervously.

Drav threaded his fingers through mine as we walked the path out of the clearing.

"It means that I will fight Grio and Limar. May I carry you? We will get there faster."

"Yeah, sure, but—"

I was up in his arms then robbed of air as the sudden wind hit my face. Instead of trying to finish my thought, I turned my head into Drav's shoulder.

What the hell had happened? I'd eaten three dumb rolls out of a ton of food set out for everyone. It shouldn't have been a big deal, but apparently here, it was. I'd managed to offend them by eating first. I hadn't even considered it might be something more than just rude. I'd been so hungry I hadn't thought of anything else.

Drav stopped and put me down. Before looking around, I apologized.

"I should have asked. I wasn't thinking. I was just hungry."

Drav tenderly stroked my cheek.

"You did nothing wrong."

"Apparently I did, or we wouldn't be here."

Here turned out to be a large area of packed, barren ground at the edge of the forest. A faint rumble caught my attention, and I turned my head to see water cascading from the craggy face of the far cavern's wall. A subterranean waterfall. Droplets of mist rose in the air, sparkling dimly from the few scattered crystals near the water's source.

"That's amazing," I said quietly.

"We will go there when I'm done with these two."

That drew my attention to the two men standing in the center of the clearing. Both waited, shirtless and facing us.

"You're fighting both of them?"

"Yes."

"Like how you and Ghua fought, right?"

"No, Mya."

My stomach dropped as I remembered Drav's fight with Phusty. The intense struggle between the two of them would have upset me more had I known someone would end up without a head.

The idea of Drav fighting like that now terrified me. Yes, I understood that Drav thought the crystal would keep him safe, but I'd seen what had happened to the deer they'd taken outside in the vision. It hadn't come back. What if, when he'd gone up to the surface, he'd weakened whatever connection he had with his crystal? What if going to the surface had broken it?

I couldn't think like that. Drav had overcome Phusty. He would win this challenge, too. No problem. I glanced over his shoulder at his opponents. Both men looked fierce and strong, and they each closely matched Drav in size.

"You're facing them one at a time, right?"

"No."

Panic bubbled up inside me.

"That's not fair."

"It is how we settle arguments." He pulled off his shirt and tossed it to one of the men behind us.

Two fey wanted to fight him at the same time because of a dumb cabbage roll? How could he be so casual about this?

"Kerr, stay with Mya."

With that, Drav started to walk away.

"Wait." I grabbed his hand, and he turned back to me.

Standing on my toes, I wrapped my arms around his neck. He leaned in and set his forehead against mine. His steady green gaze swept over my features as I shook with fear for him. I couldn't survive in this new world alone. I needed him. He needed to win this.

His arms circled around me, giving me comfort and adding to my desperation.

"Come back safe. Please."

Before I could second guess myself, I pressed my lips to his.

He jerked slightly, then growled softly. One hand slid down to my butt, gripping me and lifting me while the other cradled the back of my head. My breasts flattened against the bare expanse of his chest. The contact sent a shiver through me, and I made a small sound.

With another growl, he licked my parted lips. I gasped, giving him the entrance he sought. His hot tongue swept over mine without hesitation. He wanted, and he took. Heart thundering, I slid my fingers into his hair and lost myself to the sensation of his lips against mine.

Someone nearby yelled something. Drav pulled back. While I gasped for breath and struggled to think clearly, he set me down and put his forehead to mine.

"Thank you, Mya." He released me and walked toward the waiting men.

I blinked at his chiseled back. My lips felt swollen and tingly. The brief, passionate kiss hadn't lasted nearly long enough.

CHAPTER ELEVEN

KERR TOUCHED MY ELBOW TO GAIN MY ATTENTION, AND MY MENTAL fog parted enough to let reality settle in.

"Come, Mya," he said.

He directed me forward, closer to the center of the area where the men would fight. Other fey filtered into the area, too, forming a circle. The majority of them had witnessed what had happened at the feast. Thinking of the angry stares I'd received while horking down those two rolls, I moved closer to Kerr.

The two challenging fey joined Drav on the packed dirt. Their darker skin stood out in comparison to Drav's, and their rage-filled eyes glowed with brighter yellow tints.

Most of the crowd's attention stayed focused on Drav and the two men as they faced off. Some cast glances at me, though, and I could see the burning resentment there. I cringed, wishing I could take back my actions.

A fey stepped up next to me, blocking out most of the irritated glances.

"Mya," Shax said in greeting.

"Hey, Shax. How's the arm?"

He lifted it to show me an almost healed bite.

"Looks good."

The smack of flesh against flesh drew my attention back to the challenge in time to see Drav hop away from Grio. The man stumbled backwards, clutching his bloody, broken nose. Limar snarled and lunged at Drav. Drav swung but missed, enabling Limar to knock him off his feet. As they fell, Drav twisted so they landed on their sides, instead of allowing Limar on top. A plume of black dust rose around them.

While that kind of impact would have knocked the wind from me, neither man seemed to notice. They rolled on the ground, both fighting for control over the other. Meanwhile, Grio shook his head and blew the blood from his nose. With an angry shout, he rushed the pair at the same moment Limar managed to muscle his way to the top.

Drav roared, flexed his arms and kicked up with his legs, using leverage and Limar's weight against him. He flipped the man up and over his head and shoulders. Limar flew into Grio and both men fell hard. Limar's back hit the ground first with a slap, and I flinched as more dust was kicked up.

Limar leapt to his feet and charged Drav. Grio gained his feet, too, but was slower to rejoin the fight. He stood back, studying the pair, and I caught the brief moment Limar's eyes met Grio's.

Drav ducked under Limar's next swing, and Limar jumped back a step, circling Drav. I saw right away what they were doing. Limar was positioning Drav so he wouldn't see Grio coming. I opened my mouth to call out a warning, but Grio moved too fast.

He rushed forward and had Drav's head in his hands.

"Drav!" I shouted in panic.

I took a step forward. Kerr moved in front of me, protecting me from myself, but also blocking the fight from my view.

"I'm good. I promise," I said hurriedly.

Shaking, I leaned around him, dreading what I'd see.

Grio sat on the ground, holding his nose once more. Limar

threw his arms out to catch Drav around the waist, but Drav ducked and landed a strong fist into the man's gut. Limar grunted and backed away, doubled over.

Heart in my throat, I watched in relief, knowing Drav had narrowly avoided a very dangerous situation. Drav spared me a glance before his attention returned to the two men he fought.

"Why is this necessary? All because I ate before someone?"

Kerr grunted, but it was Shax who answered. Most of it I couldn't understand, but I caught Phusty's name intermingled with the other words. I had no idea what that might signify. The men were more upset about what had happened to Phusty?

A loud roar echoed around us as Drav trapped Limar in a headlock. Grio jumped to his feet and pounded on Drav's back and softer sides. The brutal thuds reverberated around the otherwise silent circle. Pain flickered on Drav's face, but the muscles in his arm tightened around the neck in his grasp.

My lungs emptied of air, and my attempt to inhale caught in my throat.

Drav wrapped his hand in Limar's hair and, with a mighty cry, pulled back. His muscles bulged as he tore Limar's head from his shoulders.

Blood splattered on the ground. Even though I should have been prepared since I'd witnessed Drav do it before, this time was so different. This time, the fight really had been my fault. All because of two stupid cabbage rolls. I sniffled slightly. Shax glanced at me, but I didn't turn away from the scene of death before me.

The coppery tang of blood filled the air, and my stomach churned. Drav, Ghua, and the others had made such a big deal out of Phusty's death. And, two criminals had been exiled for the death of another fey. If death upset them so much, why were the challenges centered around killing each other?

Drav tossed Limar's head aside, and no one in the surrounding group even blinked an eye. I seemed to be the only one upset by the ordeal. Grio didn't seem particularly angry that his partner was gone.

Covered in Limar's blood, Drav faced off with Grio.

As much as I needed Drav to win, my focus didn't stray from Limar's remains. The blood stopped gushing from the stump of his neck, and his arms and legs twitched. I waited for a sign that he would heal like the animals in the vision, that his head would grow back or reattach or something. Instead, the body vanished, leaving behind a flat pair of pants.

My mouth dropped open.

"Wh-what?"

I glanced at Drav, who circled Grio. Blood dripped from Drav's nose now, too, and his breaths were labored. Grio was in much worse shape with a fat lip and a cut above his eye. He breathed even harder than Drav.

It didn't matter. Seeing Drav hurt and bleeding spiked my anger. This whole challenge was ridiculous. No one should die over the fact that I took a bite of food first. Or because Phusty had attacked Drav first, to get to me. Drav was only trying to protect me.

I stepped forward ready to try to stop this from going any further, but Kerr grabbed my arm. His grasp, not unlike Drav's when we first met, bit into my skin. I cried out in surprise. Kerr obviously didn't realize his strength.

A familiar roar reached my ears, and I looked over to find Drav glaring at Kerr. The rage painting his features worried me, and I swatted Kerr's hand to get him to release me. He did, but not soon enough based on Drav's murderous gaze.

Grio took the distraction as an opportunity to attack Drav again and lunged forward, grabbing the back of Drav's head. He fisted Drav's hair around his hand and yanked backwards.

The move only pissed off Drav more. He reached back and

grabbed the hand tangled in his hair. Snarling, he bent forward, throwing Grio over his shoulder.

Grio landed hard in front of Drav, his head slamming against the ground. None of the men jeered or heckled the fallen man. They remained quiet, watching the fight with rapt attention as Drav kneeled on Grio's chest and pummeled his face. Blood spurted from Grio's nose, splattering Drav's already blood soaked chest.

"Drav!"

His face twisted in rage as he continued to pound on Grio. I called his name one more time before he finally stopped. Grio's face was a bloody mess, and the man didn't move. I wasn't even sure he still breathed.

Certain that Drav would get up now, I wasn't prepared when he reached down, grabbed the sides of Grio's head, and tore it away with a gag-inducing sound.

I stepped back as Drav threw the head away and it rolled to the other side of the circle. The fey, who had gathered to watch, nodded in Drav's direction and began to disburse.

Drav turned toward us. His tangled braids were shiny with blood, and it looked like a darkening bruise colored his chest. Blood dripped down his face and from his knuckles. I wasn't sure how badly he was hurt and hesitated to step forward to find out.

Drav still looked ready to kill someone. But he wasn't looking at me.

Kerr stepped back, looking ashamed. Shax stayed by my side as Drav made his way over.

"Thank you, Shax," Drav said. Shax nodded then left with the rest.

Drav bypassed me and stepped up to Kerr, speaking in their language, his voice harsh. My name was thrown in there, and I stepped forward with the intention of halting Drav from whatever he might do. Yet again, I was too slow. Drav drew back and landed a punch to Kerr's right eye. Kerr didn't seem upset about the attack as he faced me.

"Ego veniam," Kerr said, bending at the waist in a sweeping bow.

Confused and annoyed by the whole shit storm I'd just witnessed, I shook my head and glared at Drav.

"What the hell is going on?"

"Kerr apologized."

Kerr took that as his cue to leave and stepped around us.

"You didn't have to punch him. He didn't mean to hurt me."

"But he did hurt you."

I rubbed my face, trying to stay calm.

"He stopped me from interfering, Drav. A mild grip on my arm. Nothing compared to what you just did. You killed those men!"

"Yes, to protect you. They will not bother you any longer."

"Yeah, no kidding. Dead people usually don't bother anyone. And what the hell happened to their bodies?"

"The crystals protected them."

"No, I'm pretty sure they didn't. You ripped off their heads, just like you did to everyone who annoyed you on the surface. I very much doubt their crystals can heal that."

Drav looked frustrated, and threaded his bloody fingers through mine. He tugged me forward in the direction of the waterfall. I tried to pull away, unsure that I wanted to go anywhere with him just then. I was relieved that he was safe, but I needed a minute to process what the hell had just happened.

"Come." Drav pulled me more insistently. I glanced at his gory chest and knew I needed to keep up or risk being carried.

The sounds from the river, the quiet babble of water and the occasional random splash, grew louder as we neared.

"Drav..."

"I will show you, Mya."

At the river, some of the men from the challenge gathered near an inlet. They stared at the still waters pooled there. I looked, too. Two completely bare-assed men were emerging from the depths. I quickly spun around.

"Mya, look," Drav said, gently tugging my fingers.

Did he seriously want me to eye up two naked men?

"What is the point of this, Drav?" I asked, feeling the heat in my cheeks.

"Do you not recognize them?"

"What are you talking about?"

"Turn around and look."

Huffing a breath, I did as he asked but kept my eyes trained on the men's faces. They met my gaze. Both nodded respectfully at me and repeated the same words Kerr had used before leaving us. Why were these guys apologizing to me?

It took another moment for me to recognize them. Grio and Limar stood in the thigh deep waters, both completely bald. No hair on their heads, eyebrows or...

I quickly shifted my gaze to Drav.

"Why are they bald now?"

"We come back hairless."

"Come back. How...how is that possible?" In the vision, everything they had killed had healed, not disappeared.

"The crystal protects us."

Not just protection, and far more than resurrection. All those times he'd ripped off the heads on the surface had he thought his victims would come back like this? Was that why it had been so easy for him to kill?

I stared at Drav, unsure how to react.

"All the heads you took off up on the surface...did you think they would come back?"

"Yes."

My eyes started to burn with unshed tears. As much as I'd

started to like him, another part of me had held onto the fact he'd coldly killed so many. But that wasn't who he was.

Concern etched his features when he saw my tears, and he stepped closer. I stopped him before he could set his forehead to mine. He was still covered in blood. Some of which belonged to him.

"You need to clean up," I said. "And when you're done, you have my permission."

A wide grin split his lips.

"Yes." The drawn out, triumphant way he said it set my heart racing.

CHAPTER TWELVE

DRAV TOOK MY HAND AND LED ME FURTHER UP THE RIVER WHERE THE waterfall crashed down. Other men swam in the churning waters. I waited for Drav to dive in and join them, but he didn't. He turned to me with an intense look in his eyes.

The roar of the water filled my ears until he leaned in and said four little words that sent a bolt of panic and desire through me.

"Take your clothes off."

I jerked back and looked into his eyes to see if he was serious. Raw determination lit his gaze, and he reached down to tug at the tie holding up his pants. My gaze followed, and my mouth went dry when the material pooled around his ankles. Completely unashamed of his nudity, he stood still and let me stare at his massive erection. My face heated, but for the life of me, I couldn't bring myself to look away for several long seconds.

When I finally did, he kicked his pants aside with an indifference that didn't match the stark hunger in his eyes. He reached out, this time to tug at the hem of my shirt.

"Why?" I managed to croak.

He trailed his fingers along the side of my neck.

"So I can look at you and touch your softness."

I shivered and swallowed hard, wanting that too, more than I thought possible.

Someone moved in the water behind him, reminding me that we had an audience. I stepped back, and he shadowed me, denying me the distance I needed to think clearly.

"W-what about everyone else? I don't want them watching and getting ideas."

Drav turned his head, glancing on the few men washing in the water, then at the men who had followed us.

"Go. Mya wants to bathe in private."

"What?" I squeaked.

Drav's gaze pinned me as the men left the water. I tried again to put some space between us, but he followed me, step for step, until he reached out and gripped my waist and pulled flush to his torso. Anchored against him, I felt his desire. He lifted my hand and placed it around his neck. Heart beating rapidly, I held still as he lowered his head and tenderly kissed my bottom lip. Just that small contact made my knees weaken and reminded me of the kiss before the fight. I wanted that again. Badly.

Just enough sanity remained to discourage the idea. If I fully gave in to him, would he ever take me home? But he wasn't asking for everything. Just a kiss...

Drav's heat radiated from his bare skin, warming me. Enticing me to lift my lips more fully to his.

Someone called out a few words and laughed. I turned my head away and saw the retreating backs of several bare-assed men.

"Bathe with me, Mya," Drav said against my ear. "I will teach you what plants to use for washing."

I exhaled shakily.

"If it's all right with you, I'd rather just sit here and wait until you're done." My voice shook as I spoke, a sign of how much he tempted the hell out of me.

He pulled back and frowned slightly, but stepped away. The

corded muscles of his back and tight ass held my attention as he walked to the water's edge. I tore my gaze from his fluid dive into the pool and saw all the men had left us. No one even lingered at the distant tournament grounds. No witnesses if I really did want to bathe. No witnesses but Drav.

Indecision had me turning back to the water. As if anticipating my uncertainty, I found him watching me from where he swam in the middle of the pool.

"Last time I got near some water, a fish tried to eat my face," I said loud enough for him to hear.

"There are no fish in these waters. I will keep you safe."

I shook my head and sat on the edge. A few sure strokes brought him close to me.

"Are you afraid of the water?" he asked.

"No. I can swim and normal fish don't really bother me."

"Are you afraid of me?"

"No."

"Then why won't you bathe with me?"

He had me there.

"I don't know. I guess I am afraid. But I'm not sure what I'm afraid of," I said, not wanting to put into words my concern about him keeping me down here forever.

He nodded slightly then swam to the far edge to pluck a few leaves from one of the plants. While he rubbed them between his hands, I considered my hesitation. The thought of cleaning up did appeal to me. I hadn't showered since we'd left the cabin. Undoubtedly, I smelled. And, some of the blood that had coated Drav now clung to my clothes. So why not hop in? It wasn't like I was overly shy. I'd walked around the dorm halls in a t-shirt and underwear for Pete's sake. What was my problem?

I glanced across the pool at the big, grey guy soaping his broad, chiseled chest and knew my problem lay with how much I really didn't want to wear anything if I joined him.

"Screw it," I mumbled, toeing off my shoes. I peeled off my socks, and with a quick glance over my shoulder, I stripped down to my panties. Before he could notice, I jumped into the water.

The chilly temperature hit me like a fist, and I came up gasping and squealing. Drav's warm arms immediately wrapped around me, and I clung to the only source of heat.

"Did you hurt yourself?" he asked, concern clipping his words.

"Yes! This is f-fucking cold!" I attempted to wipe water from my face as I wrapped my legs around his waist. He held me close and rubbed my back as I shook.

"Why would anyone bathe in this?"

His lips skimmed my neck in a very pleasant way. Yet, as much as he'd interested me outside of the water, the temperature had helped cool that.

"I'm not trying to play hard to get or anything, but if I stay in this water too long, I might end up with hypothermia. Can you show me how to wash so we can get out?"

His immediate alarm assured me he understood. Keeping his hold on me, he swam to the other side then started crushing leaves again. His body heat made the water barely tolerable, so I continued to cling to him while he washed my hair for me. When it came time to rinse, I hesitated, not wanting to submerge again. However, it didn't feel as shocking the second time, which worried me.

Hating to give up my only source of warmth, I moved out of his arms enough to remove my underwear and finished washing in a hurry.

"Drav," a voice called.

I froze and stared at Drav with wide, panicked eyes. The water lapped at my collarbones, covering me. But I couldn't stay in the water much longer. With an arm looped around Drav's neck for support, I turned to look at the opposite bank.

Molev stood there with my shirt pressed to his nose.

"Oh, c-come on," I stuttered. However, I got over my annoyance rather quickly when I saw he held a clean shirt in his other hand.

"I'm d-done," I said to Drav.

He crossed the pool of water with me wrapped around him.

"Mya would like you to turn around. Looking at her without clothes makes her uncomfortable," Drav said before I could.

I pressed a quick kiss to his jaw in appreciation while Molev turned around without complaint. Drav lifted me out of the water and set me on the bank. The warmer air made the shivering worse and without Drav's hand, I wouldn't have been able to stand. His gaze swept over me, and I didn't miss the irony of what he'd just said to Molev. Drav's gaze no longer made me uncomfortable, though. Besides, I looked my fill, too. The water had done nothing to wither his desire for me.

Ignoring his heated expression, I gestured at the clean shirt in Molev's hand.

"Can I wear that?"

The man said something in their language.

"He brought it for you," Drav said.

"Thank you," I said, plucking the shirt from his fingers.

Molev began talking again, his tone conversational, unlike when I'd heard him at the tree.

"Can you tell me what he's saying?" I asked Drav just before I tugged the shirt on over my wet skin. The soft, dry material fell to my knees, giving me enough cover that I tossed my wet underwear to my pile of dirty clothes.

Drav made no move to dress or hide what the water hadn't cooled.

"He heard what happened at the meal and came to congratulate me," he said, translating. "He also wanted to see you without clothes."

"Not happening," I muttered, gathering up my things.

Molev turned around and waved at the dirty garments while speaking.

"Leave them," Drav said. "Grio and Limar will wash them."

I dropped the pile again. If someone else wanted to wash my stuff, fine by me. I just wanted to get warm.

"Please tell me you have blankets hidden around here somewhere."

"We do," Drav said. "May I carry you back?"

"Please."

He had me up in his arms, but thankfully didn't run. The wind on my wet hair would have made my chill worse. Molev fell into step beside Drav. While they walked, they talked. Mostly Molev asked questions that Drav answered with descriptions of the surface. However, when he said no animals existed above, I had to correct him.

"They exist. They just ran off when the earthquakes happened. I'm not sure where they went. Actually, we did see that normal dog, remember?" I said, looking up at Drav. "And it isn't just my world, it's our world. Yours and mine. The crystal showed me that you had all come from the surface, too. Your own people trapped you down here and took your memories. If you came up to the surface and let my people get to know you, I think you'd like it up there."

Molev grunted but said nothing. At the base of the tree, he waved us off and I closed my eyes. Tucking my face against Drav, I waited for the breeze to stop.

"We're here, Mya."

I opened my eyes and looked around in surprise. The burl had my bag but looked nothing like it had previously. Numerous crystal lanterns lay scattered about the room, giving everything a pretty, soft glow. And everything included a mound of cloth stacked on the bed.

"What is that?" I asked.

"The material we use to make our clothes. It's all we have that is close to blankets."

"You don't use blankets?"

"No."

Damn.

"Let me know who I need to thank for bringing them here."

"Probably Kerr. While we were traveling, he noticed you became cold easily."

I owed Kerr big time. Without waiting for an invitation, I walked over to the bed and burrowed in under half the pieces, using the bottom half as a cushion. Still shivering, I looked up at Drav and lifted the covers.

"You joining me?"

He smiled and climbed in next to me. His body heat, and his hands gently rubbing my arms, helped warm me. In the soft light, we stared at each other. I wanted him to kiss me again. A lot. And that troubled me.

"I thought you'd be all over me after I gave you permission," I said.

"I want to, but you look sad. I don't want you to take your permission away."

"I won't. I'm just...I don't know where this is going to go," I said. "Not right now, this moment, but in the long run. My people are afraid of you guys now. Of you, the hellhounds, and the infected. People in fear do stupid things. They don't think. And that scares me as much as it scares you. But not enough to hide away forever."

I sighed and snuggled in against his chest.

"I don't want to stay down here," I said, softly. "I want to go back to the surface with you. Both our kinds belong up there. But, what if my people see you and try hurting you again? I don't want you hurt. And I don't want you hurting any of them. We're not like you. When you rip off our heads, that's it. That's the end."

I pulled back and looked into his eyes as I said what was really on my mind.

"That ache you feel? I feel it, too. More each day. And I think that ache is going to cause us both problems."

"We will face any problems together," he said. "I will keep you safe."

He pressed his lips to mine, a gentle kiss, then tucked me more securely against his bare chest.

"Rest, Mya. We will talk more when you wake."

Snuggling close, I closed my eyes and let his warmth lull me. I wasn't quite asleep when he whispered, "Do I still have permission to touch you?"

"Yes," I said softly.

His hand crept under my shirt, and he lay his palm against my breast. It felt hot compared to my skin and oh so good.

"Thank you for asking."

"Thank you for saying yes."

I woke with a headache and groaned. The murmur of masculine voices nearby quieted.

"Are you hungry?" Drav asked.

When I lifted my head, I saw he'd dressed. He and Molev stood on the far side of the room next to my bag.

"No, I'm okay. What's going on?" I asked, feeling oddly exposed. I tugged the covers more securely around my waist as I sat up. It was weird knowing they'd been having a conversation in here while I still slept.

"Molev has suggested that we go to Lacus."

"What's Lacus, and why do we need to go?"

"It is like an ocean but not so big. We don't need to go. He thought you might enjoy seeing it."

"A lake?"

"Yes," Drav said with a smile.

"Where is it?"

"Outside of the city. Only one rest away if I carry you."

Outside of the city meant hellhound lands. But it also meant we would be that much closer to the surface tunnels. With the men being told to return, we might run into some who had news about up top. I hoped the bombings had stopped.

It wasn't only the thought of news that had me considering. A trip anywhere would mean more alone time with Drav. After giving him permission to touch me, I really wanted more time together.

"What would we be doing at this lake?"

"Noodling," Drav said with a smile, making my heart thump just a little harder because he'd remembered.

Molev glanced at Drav with confusion, and I snorted.

"Molev also said that by the time we return from the lake, the rest of the men should be back with information. If we went, you would not be bothered by the new men, and I can teach you how we fish."

I'd already decided it was a good idea, but knowing it would get me away from the sniffing, stares, and attempts to see what lay beneath my clothes sealed the deal.

"It would be just me and you?" I asked, just to be sure.

"Yes."

"Wouldn't that be too dangerous?"

"I will keep you safe, Mya. We will only travel the lit caverns."

I nodded.

"Okay. Well, I need my clothes." I looked at my bag sitting near their feet. Drav picked it up and handed it to me. However, neither of them seemed ready to leave once I had new clothes out. I looked at them expectantly and arched a brow.

Drav grunted.

"Do you wish for us to turn around?"

"Yes."

Molev did without hesitation, but Drav moved a little bit slower. Poor guy. I told him he had permission then made him turn away. I'd need to explain that permission only worked when we were alone.

After changing in record time, I told them it was okay to look again then shouldered my bag.

"Leave that, Mya," Drav said gently. "We need to travel light, and we will find food on the way."

"Oh." It made sense since Drav had to carry me. But, I hesitated to just leave the bag in his doorless hut. I didn't want anything to happen to it while we were away. It had my phone, my life line to contacting Ryan when we got back to the surface.

"Mya?"

"I'm being silly, but will my bag be safe here?" Drav had said stealing was forbidden, but I needed their word.

"Yes, it is safe. No one will use our room."

"Okay." Setting the bag on the bed, I went to him. "Let's go noodling."

CHAPTER THIRTEEN

Drav ran tirelessly through the lit cavern. Instead of focusing on my niggling headache, I studied him. The strong line of his jaw. His proud nose. The curve of his lower lip. I couldn't ignore the pulse of desire that shot through me at the thought of having him to myself for the next couple of days. Suppressing a grin, I began to play with the hair at the back of his neck.

He glanced down at me, then my boobs, then back up again. Having fun, I reached a little higher and trailed a finger along the edge of his opposite ear. His speed decreased.

"Don't slow down," I said. "I want to get to our resting spot so we can kiss some more."

Wind lashed at me as he sprinted, and I laughed.

It didn't seem to take too long before he stopped.

"We will rest here," he said firmly.

The bright light of the cavern seemed to make my head thump a little worse, but I determinedly ignored it as Drav eased me to my feet.

"Was this the place you had in mind or are you improvising because you want a kiss?"

"Improvising." That was the last word he said before his lips claimed mine.

The heat of his kiss burned away thoughts of headaches, bombings, missing family, and hellhounds. Nothing else existed but me and the man whose hands smoothed down the curve of my back to cup my butt. I let him explore, reveling in the feel of his firm touch. All his caresses sent sparks of fire into my already heated blood.

His lips left mine, and he looked down at me.

"Wherever you go, I will follow and keep you safe. Whatever you need, I will provide it for you. I am yours Mya, in every lifetime."

He said the words with such burning intensity, my insides melted further. How could someone so different come to mean so much to me? I didn't know.

"And I'm yours," I said, heart pounding.

I loved the way he kissed me and touched me and knew he felt the same. Yet, everything was so new to him, and he probably had no idea what he liked. Eager to learn more about him, I slipped my hands under his shirt and slid my palms up the flat plains of his stomach. He made a small sound, a mix of exhale and pained groan.

"Do you want me to stop?" I asked.

"No. You have my permission to touch me how you like."

I grinned and slid my hands up further, my fingertips brushing his flat nipples. They pebbled under my touch, and his fingers twitched on my back. Circling the softer skin, I watched his expression. His gaze grew hungrier, and he claimed my lips for another searing kiss that made my toes curl.

Pushing his shirt up, I waited for him to break the kiss then moved my attention to his broad chest. He slid his hands from my back to my hips, and he gripped me firmly as I pressed my lips against his sternum. The smooth feel of his skin and his racing pulse notched my need for him higher.

He arched into me, pressing the bulge of his erection near my bellybutton. His size brought a moment of worry.

"You won't take more than I'm ready to give, right?"

"I will take nothing you do not give freely."

Reassured, I traced the indent between his pectorals with my tongue. A hiss escaped him when I veered to the right and circled around his nipple.

"You still okay?" I whispered against his skin.

"Yes." The rough word grated with need, his breathing ragged.

"If I do something you don't like, let me know, and I'll stop."

"I like everything you do," he said.

While I kissed my way to the left side, I slid my hands lower to the waist of his pants. His breathing stopped.

"Keep breathing, Drav," I whispered just before I lightly nipped his nipple and grasped his erection.

His groan echoed in the cavern, and he pressed firmly into my hand. The urgency in which he tipped my head back and kissed me hard, stole my air and fed my hunger.

He arched against me again, a demand and a plea. Wrapping my hand around him, as much as his pants would allow, I firmly stroked him. After thousands of years alone, that single touch undid him. With a cry, he stiffened and held me to him. I could feel him pulsing under my palm.

His fingers threaded through my hair, and he kissed me deeply until I was breathless.

"Magic did not die in your world because you still live," he whispered against my hair.

I HAD NEVER BEEN to the ocean but was familiar with big lakes. Oklahoma had a lot of them. However, the sight before me proved more stunning than anything I'd seen before. No waves or wind disturbed the still surface. Not even a bubble. Small patches of crystals on the vast ceiling above the water and those underneath the surface illuminated the body from both sides, making the liquid a glowing crystal-blue. It appeared unnatural, but beautiful, with the rock formations and vegetation surrounding the lake reflecting back on its surface.

Drav led us into the surrounding trees, much smaller than those in their city but not like the orchard trees, either. These had large grey leaves that draped over a silver trunk with no branches. A brown ivy with tiny leaves grew up the trunks, completely covering the tree. Between the thick vines that dropped down amid the large leaves of the trees, I caught glimpses of round, yellow globes that looked like some type of fruit.

As pretty as everything was, I had a hard time staying focused on our surroundings instead of Drav's firm ass ahead of me. After his happy ending during our explosive little make out session, I'd insisted we rest like we were supposed to. However, I had actually fallen asleep instead of just giving him enough time to recoup. When I'd woken, it had been to him already carrying me to our final destination. I'd decided to play it cool and wait, but after hours of fantasizing what we might end up doing once we'd reached the lake, I'd had to ask to walk when I'd caught myself eyeing his chorded neck.

Now, I was only waiting for him to point out where we were bedding down for our stay.

Drav stopped walking, and my hope surged until he pulled some of the fallen ivy from the ground.

"What is the word for this?" he asked.

"Looks kinda like ivy to me."

"We need to collect some for the fish."

I wrinkled my nose but pitched in to gather what he needed. When Drav declared that we had enough, we moved closer to the lake's edge where he sat down and indicated for me to join him.

"So what are we doing?"

"We will build a net."

Drav stuck two thick sticks in the ground before us. Then, he reached into a small pouch from his belt and pulled out a wooden tool pointed on one end with a small shaped hole near the top. He set it next to me and pulled out a second one.

"We will use the tools to make nets. Here."

Drav grabbed the ivy and began to wrap it around the tool he had set next to me. After watching him for a bit, I picked it up and followed suit. Once they were wrapped, Drav demonstrated what to do next. It was a lot of the same work over and over. While he labored with a practiced ease and patience, I grew bored and kept thinking back to our prior rest.

I grinned slightly.

"You are happy?" he asked.

"Mostly. I was thinking of last night."

His lips curved.

"We will finish the net, feed you, and kiss some more."

His hands flew through the weaving pattern he'd attempted to show me. Once he had a completed net, he stood, handed it to me, then pulled the string to his pants.

"Not that I'm complaining, but what are you doing?"

"We will be going into the water. It will take a long time for our clothes to dry if we do not remove them." He punctuated that statement by dropping his pants and tugging his shirt over his head.

Drav held out his hand for the net, but I couldn't take my eyes off him.

"Come, Mya. We must fish."

"Right." I tore my gaze from his impressive length and handed over the net.

Drav walked to the edge of the water and waded in. He stopped once the water reached his waist and looked back at me expectantly.

Flushing, I pulled off my shirt and unbuttoned my jeans. Drav watched with rapt interest as I slid them down my legs. When I reached behind my back, he turned in the water so he fully faced me. The tender way his gaze swept over me from head to foot eased some of my nerves. I unclasped my bra and shrugged it off my shoulders.

"You are beautiful, Mya," he said with awe.

"Thank you. You are too." With my underwear still on, I stepped toward the edge.

"You should take that off or it will get wet."

"I'll risk it."

His lips twitched.

"Don't laugh. I don't trust what's in that water."

"Nothing will harm you. Come." He held his hand out, waiting for me to join him.

The water was warmer than the river, but it still wasn't like climbing into a relaxing hot tub. I took Drav's hand when I reached him, and I was glad I did because I slipped on a rock and stumbled forward, right into his chest. Without his hold, I would have landed face first in the water.

"Oof, sorry," I said, balancing myself against him. He held my hand steadily and allowed me to use his chest to right myself.

"Are you okay, my Mya?"

"Yeah, I'm good." I saw some strands of Drav's hair had come out of his braids and brushed away the ones that had dropped over his forehead.

"We must stay very still. We will scare the fish."

"I sincerely hope these are not the same fish I encountered when we first arrived."

"No, you are safe."

I began to ease backwards but Drav tightened his arm around my waist and kept me close.

"We cannot move."

Water lapped at my bellybutton.

"How will we catch fish then?" I whispered.

"Don't worry, I will catch us dinner."

"I don't like raw fish."

"You need to eat."

"There was fruit in the trees."

"Shh..." he said softly, his gaze shifting to the right.

I stiffened as I glanced over. A small school of fish swam closer to us. More specifically, our toes. Drav released his hold around my waist and moved in a blink of an eye.

The water splashed around us, spraying me. When I opened my eyes, I found Drav holding the net out proudly. Inside thrashed several dripping wet see-through fish.

"That's amazing, Drav!"

I leaned forward, in awe of their translucent bodies, and slipped slightly again. I caught myself on his chest, but in the process, my breast brushed his arm. My nipple pebbled at the contact, and I shivered. He growled, dropped the fish net, and held me to his chest.

His intense gaze captured mine as he reached up and stroked a finger over my hard nipple. A small gasp escaped me. Warm heat spread from his fingertip down to my belly. His focus shifted to my parted lips as he continued to tease my breast.

"So soft," he said a moment before he dipped his head and brushed his lips against mine.

Another shiver ripped through me, spreading the heat further south. He inhaled against my skin and deepened the kiss, his tongue seeking entrance. I opened and dissolved into his embrace. His mouth and fingers made everything disappear except for the growing need burning inside me.

Something jumped in the water beside us, a reminder of our location. I pulled away to breathe, and Drav pressed his forehead against mine.

"You dropped the fish," I said.

"It was worth it."

"We don't have dinner now."

"There is fruit in the trees."

I laughed and pressed another quick kiss on his firm lips.

When we finished the fruit he'd quickly collected, Drav made us a bed from the large fronds. He lay down naked and stretched out on his back, his erection proudly exposed. Moisture still glistened on his skin. Between the dip in the lake and the humidity in the air, he'd been right. It would have taken a long time for my clothes to dry. As it was, my wet underwear still clung to me uncomfortably.

"Are we really safe in here?"

"Yes. The blue and green crystals both exist here so there is never darkness. No hounds will enter here."

Taking a steadying breath, I hooked my fingers in my underwear and pulled them off to hang them over a nearby frond. When I turned around, Drav observed me with an intensity that made me nervous.

Neither of us moved for several long minutes.

"I won't touch you if you've changed your mind," he said, softly.

"I haven't changed my mind. I'm just crazy nervous."

He sat up and held out his hand.

"If I do something you don't like, let me know, and I'll stop."

An ache grew in my chest at hearing those words. Taking his hands, I stepped closer. His gaze dropped to the patch of hair that had so fascinated him at the cabin then back up to my face.

"Will you snuggle with me, Mya?"

I nodded and lay down beside him.

His fingers skimmed over my skin from belly to breast as he leaned over to kiss me. His tongue teased mine until I forgot to be nervous and panted for air. When his mouth left mine and his kisses trailed down the column of my throat, I turned my head to give him better access. The entire time, his fingers never stopped moving. They drifted over my navel, then lower. I grinned slightly, knowing his curiosity was killing him.

His lips closed over my nipple, obliterating humor with a burning need between my legs. I curled my fingers in his hair. His lips moved to my other breast, and his teeth gently nipped me as his fingers slid over my folds.

Panting, I opened for him. Conscious thought fled as his lips trailed lower. His breath fanned against my bellybutton before going further south. My gasp echoed in the cave when he kissed the sweet spot between my legs. I involuntarily bucked under him.

"Do you want me to stop?" he asked, pulling back.

"Please don't," I panted.

He kept going, his tongue teasing and stroking every inch of me until I pulsed and cried out in a long, low wail.

Limp and relaxed, I twitched under Drav's lips as he kissed his way back up to my breast, where he set his head.

"That is how my heart raced after you touched me," he said softly. "Sleep, Mya. When you wake, we will snuggle some more."

With him half draped over me, I closed my eyes and reveled in the feel of his light touch as I drifted off to sleep.

In the morning, Drav lay beside me, a piece of fruit in his hand.

"Thank you," I said, sitting up with a wince. The headache from the day before had only grown worse. Not wanting it to wreck our remaining time, I brushed away his concern and let him show me how to peel and eat the fruit. As I nibbled, so did he. But not on the fruit. It was, by far, the best meal I'd ever had and helped distract me from the thumping behind my eyes.

The relief didn't last beyond the final fading tremor, though.

"I'm not feeling really good. I wish I would have brought my bag," I said, thinking of the pain reliever I had in the first aid kit.

"Dress. We can go back."

"You don't want to snuggle more?"

"Not when you don't feel well," he said with a kiss to my temple.

I was mildly disappointed then reminded myself the sooner we returned, the sooner we could head back to the surface for some privacy with a real bed.

He packed up the tools he had brought with him but left the fish net. Without needing to ask, he lifted me and took off toward the city.

The motion didn't help. Not only did the pain in my head grow worse, but my stomach started to roll. When he stopped for the resting period I didn't sleep as soundly. My stomach cramped continually, and I moved restlessly. Drav worried the whole time. Obviously, the fruit we had eaten wasn't sitting well. As soon as the cave's crystals dimmed, we started toward the city, and I tried to ignore the increasing pain in my stomach.

Hours later, the wall appeared, and the door opened well before we reached it. Drav went right through.

"Do you want to walk for a bit?" Drav asked, concern in his tone.

"Yeah. Maybe it'll help my stomach."

It didn't. I changed my mind about the illness stemming from weird fruit to possible period cramps. I couldn't remember how many days it had been. Too much had happened.

Drav laced his fingers between mine, and we walked to the city. It definitely buzzed with more activity and men who stared at me with curiosity.

Drav picked me up when we arrived at our tree, and he ran up the steps to our burl. The relief I felt at the welcome sight of our home died when Drav entered.

Molev sat on the bed. The white cords of the iPod's earbuds stood out starkly against his black shirt. He stared down in rapt interest at the glowing iPod cradled in his large hand.

"Put me down," I said to Drav, pissed.

Molev noticed us and stood, tugging the earbuds out of his ears. He nodded in greeting.

"Thank you, Mya. Your language is very interesting to learn."

CHAPTER FOURTEEN

In full blown bitch mode, I marched up to Molev and grabbed the iPod out of his hands. The battery icon blinked in the corner. How long had he been listening? I flipped through the list of previous books and cringed. All romance novels. I wanted to swear.

"You didn't have permission," I said.

"I apologize. I was returning the clothes that Grio and Limar washed and was curious about you and your world and looked at your things. I meant no harm. When I accidently turned this on, my curiosity only grew stronger. I'm glad I found it and learned your language, though. I have many questions for you, Mya."

His calm sincerity and lack of any perverseness defused my anger. However, the pulse of my headache grew more pronounced.

"I'll answer what I can," I said, placing the iPod back in the bag and digging out the first aid kit. The sight of two foil pain reliever packets comforted me. Both men watched as I ripped one of the packets open and downed the pills. Setting the bottle of water aside, I got cozy on the blankets and looked up at Molev.

"What's your first question?"

Drav sat beside me and began to soothingly rub my back and

shoulders. I loved him touching me. It was both a reassurance and a comfort. I couldn't seem to get enough of him.

Molev resumed his relaxed position by the entrance and studied us for a moment.

"When you went to the source, it didn't give you a life crystal, but something else. Tell me, what did you see?"

I repeated the story of the history I'd been shown, and how the deer coming back to life started it all. When I finished, Molev nodded slowly.

"We are connected with the magic here. Phusty's death proved that."

"Connected, but should you be? I think the magic here changed you. Your skin. Your eyes. I'm not saying it's bad, just that you've had to adapt to live in a place you maybe weren't meant to live."

"From what Kerr has told me while you were away, the surface does not sound like a better place to be."

"That's because you didn't know it before the earthquakes and the hellhounds and the infected."

"Tell me what it was like before."

I thought of the woods by the cabin and the peaceful sound of the birds and the wind. Before I could open my mouth to tell him about all the quiet beauty, other thoughts intruded. Pollution. Prejudices. War. Our world did have beauty, but it had a lot of ugly, too. Well, it had beauty. How much remained now?

With my sorrow, the ache in my head consumed my thoughts.

"Can we talk some more later? My head is really hurting."

"Of course. Rest." He stood and moved toward the entrance.

"Can you take some of these lanterns with you? I think the light's making it worse."

Molev nodded, took several, and walked out.

"Can I get you anything, Mya?" Drav asked.

"No. Can you just keep rubbing me until I fall asleep?"

I closed my eyes and let the gentle swipe of his hand lull me into a slumber where I dreamed I lived with Drav in his underground world forever and eventually forgot about my brother and parents.

When I opened my eyes, the complete darkness puzzled me as did the brush of fingers over my bare breast. When the fingers reached the peak, they gently pinched my nipple, explaining the growing ache between my legs.

"Drav?"

"Yes. I am here. Does your head still hurt?" His fingers continued their slow assault.

"No, not really. Why is it so dark in here?"

"The light seemed to bother you, even in your sleep, so I removed the lanterns and used some of the material to block the rest of the light."

His hand covered my whole breast and gave it a kneading squeeze before moving to the other side. I licked my lips and struggled to focus on my next question.

"Okay. Do I want to know why I'm naked?"

"You undressed."

"I did?" I said, breathlessly. I was brilliant even in my sleep.

"Yes. You threw the clothes across the room, but I don't think you really woke up. I wasn't going to touch you, but you put my hand here."

His fingers circled the circumference of my breast, then skimmed over my pebbled nipple. Unable to help myself, I arched into the touch.

"You've slept a long time."

"And you've been touching me the whole while?"

His fingers stilled.

"Was that wrong?"

"No," I said quickly, not wanting him to stop. "It's okay. I'm just thinking your arm must be tired. I'm sorry I—"

His mouth crashed down on mine, searing me with his unrestrained kiss. My head swam and the tingle of need burned hotter, igniting the aching flesh between my legs. With a groan, I tore my mouth from his. The intention to demand he ditch his clothes, too, died when he kissed his way down to my breast. The heat of his lips and the brush of his tongue tore a gasp from me.

He lifted his head.

"Mya?"

"Don't stop," I panted, grabbing his head and guiding him back. My fingers brushed the long tips of his ears. He groaned and kissed his way to my other breast.

"Drav," a voice called just before dim light flooded the room.

"Shit." I grabbed the nearest bit of cloth, which turned out to be Drav's shirt. Not caring, I yanked him over me for cover.

"Are you fucking?" Molev asked in a calm, curious tone.

"Oh, come on!" I buried my face in Drav's shoulder, appreciating the irony of my current wish to disappear in a deep, dark hole.

"That is not what this is." My words were muffled.

"Then what were you doing? Were those your breasts? What do they taste like, Drav?"

"Kill me now," I mumbled.

Drav growled fiercely and tensed over me.

"No one will kill you."

"Not literally," I said.

He relaxed slightly.

"What do you need, Molev?"

"Solin has just returned. More are on their way from the old orchard hole. Fyllo came back while you slept and said the rest of his group has passed through the gap near the black lake. I would like you both to be there when everyone arrives."

"We will," Drav said.

The light left the room. Neither Drav nor I moved.

"No one will kill you," he repeated with quiet ferocity.

"That's not what I meant. I was just embarrassed he'd seen us making out."

Drav shifted slightly, his weight settling a bit more firmly between my legs. His lips skimmed mine.

"I would like to do more."

"I bet you would, but one interruption is enough. I'd like to get dressed and go figure out when we get to leave."

With a sigh, he rolled off me. Before I could find a replacement cover, light flared in the room. I turned my head and saw Drav standing just inside the entrance, holding a lantern. His wistful gaze swept over me, and I could feel myself start to blush. I sat up and crossed an arm over my breasts.

"Can you turn around? I can't get dress with you watching."

"I don't understand why that makes you uncomfortable. I watched you at the lake."

The lake where we'd been the only two people. Not a tree crawling with men who didn't know how to knock.

"The way you move and the pretty paleness of your skin is so pleasing to me. I would watch you for hours if you let me."

Drav studied me with such intensity that it reminded me of when we first met. Before I was terrified of his reptilian eyes but now I felt pretty, wanted. The raw desire in his expression had me throwing aside my caution, dropping the blanket, and standing. He didn't move from his position near the door as I picked up my underwear. He did, however, make a slight noise when I stepped into them.

His focus never wavered as I dressed piece by piece, in a slow show that would have felt embarrassing with anyone else. The complete fascination in his gaze had me doing things I didn't normally do to get dressed...like smoothing my hands over my breasts and down my sides.

By the time I finished, he looked pained, probably due to the massive erection tenting his pants. He crossed the room and pulled me close.

"When we return, will you take your clothes off again?" he asked, kissing my temple then nuzzling the place below my ear.

"I'll think about it," I said with a small grin, already knowing I would.

I craved his attention more than I cared to acknowledge.

Drav carried me down to the communal table where many men had already gathered. I'd thought there'd been a lot of them before. Their numbers had easily doubled. Men crowded into the lantern strewn clearing, the throng of muscular bodies filling the stump area and spilling over into the surrounding undergrowth.

"Is this everyone?" I asked softly.

"This is more than half, but not all."

Nearby men noticed our arrival and conversation slowly quieted, drawing the attention of Molev, who stood near the communal table. He started our way, his eyes never leaving me.

"If he mentions what he saw, I'm punching him," I said under my breath. Drav grunted.

"Hello, Mya," Molev said when he reached us. "Thank you for joining us. Come. We will eat while we wait."

Relieved, I followed him through the crowd to the three empty stumps near the center. He motioned for me to sit. He and Drav took seats on either side of me. A bald man approached with a leaf stacked with cabbage rolls. He held out the leaf to me first.

"Oh, I'm not falling for this again. Last time I helped myself, people got hurt."

"That won't happen again," Molev assured me. "Eat."

I glanced at Drav, who nodded, before helping myself to two rolls.

"Thanks," I said to the man.

"You're welcome." He turned and offered the rolls to Molev then Drav.

"Thank you, Limar," Molev said.

I did a double take at the man as he walked away.

"Is he being punished? Is that why he's serving dinner?"

"The lowest serve and train until they prove themselves worthy of more," Molev said. "It is not punishment, but protection for them and us."

As I munched, other men brought food to the communal table. Once offerings heaped the surface, Molev stood and turned to me.

"There is more to eat. Come choose," he said.

Drav nudged me until I stood and picked a few things from the table. Molev grabbed some food, then Drav. One by one, the men approached, and I began to notice a slow change in their general appearance. By the time the last bald man helped himself from the picked over remains, I understood the length of their hair related to their social standing. Drav's reaction when I'd put my hair up back home took on a whole different meaning.

A commotion near the far side of the clearing drew my attention. The men stood aside, making it possible to see the new arrivals, who stood out starkly from the rest. Dust coated their grey skin and dark hair, and several of the men had rips or scorch marks on their clothes.

With a weary droop to their shoulders, the travel worn group progressed to the center of the circle where they hungrily helped themselves to what remained of the food. I felt a surge of pity for them and what they'd likely endured on the surface. It conflicted with my impatience to hear the news they brought so we could be on our own way.

A few of the new arrivals noticed me and stared, catching the attention of the rest.

"Tell us what you learned," Molev said, without addressing their curiosity.

Since only Drav and Molev spoke English, I sat between the two of them and listened to the gibberish pouring out of each speaker's mouth. Sometimes, Drav would translate or Molev would ask a question in English so I would get an idea of what was being said.

The men had come from the old orchard and told stories of unintelligent beings who craved flesh and of birds whose shit destroyed anything in a flood of flames. That description of planes, by far, won as my favorite. The men produced different items, explaining their purposes. One man showed a broken cell phone that he said used to glow. Another showed a lighter, which he'd actually figured out how to operate. My amusement ended, though, with the guy who dumped a bag full of canned food on the feast table.

He picked one up and squeezed it, popping the top right off and causing a mass of brown to come squishing out. He brought a finger full to his mouth and, after eating it, explained that he had seen some intelligent beings above who didn't crave flesh. They had eaten what the cans provided.

Drav stood and took one of the cans, which he brought to me.

"Eat," he said.

I looked down at the can of dog food I held, a feeling of devastation overwhelming me. While I safely hid underground, people were up there struggling to survive.

"What happened to the people? The ones eating this?" I asked in a tight voice.

Drav translated the man's answer.

"He killed them and took the cans."

My silent tears fell onto the label.

"I'm sorry, Mya," Drav said softly.

"Tell them what happens when our heads are ripped off. Tell them we don't resurrect from the dead. Tell them they are taking away our lives forever."

Getting angry, I looked up and glared at everyone.

"Those unintelligent people were once like me. But when the

hounds came to the surface and started attacking, people got sick. Those uninfected, healthy people you killed were scared and just trying to survive, and you killed them so you can bring fucking dog food down here for show and tell." I threw the can, almost hitting one of the bystanders. It didn't appease my anger.

"I thought this was about sharing real news. All of this is a waste of time. You want real news that won't be at the expense of some innocent person's life? We're just as fucking important as you are. You had no right."

Tears tried to clog my throat.

"No right to kill them, and no right to keep me down here where I'm no help to anyone."

The tears won.

CHAPTER FIFTEEN

DRAV TURNED ME INTO HIS COMFORTING ARMS. HIS HOLD SOOTHED my tears, but not my anger or the increasingly painful thump in my head.

The rational part of me understood Drav, too, had killed humans. That none of these men had known better because they'd lived thousands of years in a place where death did not exist. And, although I understood all of that, I couldn't forget or just "get over" what had been done.

When the tears slowed, I pulled back from Drav and looked at Molev.

"Your people were trapped down here. You had no choice in that. Now, you do have a choice. You know the earthquakes set the hellhounds free on us. Your men have seen what they do to humans...how unprepared we are. Stop hiding underground. Go to the surface and fix the mess you made. And, it is your mess. You ate the cursed deer, which created the hellhounds. Whether accidental or not, the hellhounds exist because of you. Help my people, like yours should have been helped so long ago."

I turned to Drav who'd held me through my speech. The soft

lantern light played on his concerned gaze and made my head ache worse. Crying hadn't helped, either.

"Please, can we leave now?" I asked. I desperately wanted to get back to the surface and start the search for my family. Drav bent, as if to pick me up.

"No, you will stay," Molev said. His gaze swept over my tear-stained face.

I opened my mouth to tell him to stick it—Drav and I were going back no matter what—when he cut me off.

"Please. I need you here to help clarify what these men are sharing. Your world is vastly different than ours," he said.

So he wasn't trying to keep me in his world, just at this meeting. I sighed, about to agree, when a jolt of stabbing pain shot right into my head. I hissed a sharp breath and pressed my fingers to my temples, trying to sooth the ache. It didn't help. Instead, a wave of nausea twisted in my stomach. I closed my eyes, hoping it would all fade away, but it didn't. The cramping grew worse.

Perhaps leaving would need to wait for a few hours so I could lay down and rest first.

Drav touched my arm.

"Mya?"

At the anxious concern in his voice, I forced myself to open my eyes and drop my hand to my side. Drav didn't look reassured.

"I'll be fine. Let's hurry up and get this done."

As much as I hated hearing about my people dying unnecessarily, I needed to learn everything I could about the state of the world above before we left.

"We will continue," Molev said after I sat.

The men seemed a little more cautious when they approached us. Some watched me warily as if making sure I didn't have anything nearby to throw at them. Their garbled language became background noise that I began to ignore.

"Mya..." Drav said.

"Hmm?"

"Sain said there was a weapon the intelligent ones were using that made a lot of noise, and something went into his chest and stomach. It took him until he arrived here to heal."

The man in question pointed to the two bloody holes in what remained of his shirt.

"You were shot," I said, amazed that he was still standing. "The humans were using guns to protect themselves."

I felt a stirring of pride toward the other human survivors out there. They weren't helpless, even if these guys could heal quicker or weren't the real threat. As I thought it, another man stepped forward.

The dark fey wasn't dirtied like the rest, and his hair looked a little wet still. He spoke a stream of words which didn't quite sound like their language. It had a familiar ring, but I couldn't place it.

"Fyllo says there were no birds with explosive shit on the surface where he explored," Drav said. "The skies remained clear and the cities whole and quiet."

I frowned, not understanding where he was going with this.

"No bombs?" I asked. That sounded promising. "What did he mean when he said where he explored?"

"The other hole that opened," Drav clarified.

Fyllo took a step forward and hesitantly produced a can of food. He didn't pop it open but handed it to me whole.

He spoke as I looked at the can, and Drav translated.

"He said he found it on the shelf of a building full of food."

I took the can from him realizing he was implying he did not kill anyone for it. I turned the can over, half expecting it to be dog food. Instead, I saw an unfamiliar label with a bright blue background and a plate of sausages on a table. It read, "4 Munchner WeiBwurste." The words he spoke, and the words on the label, clicked into place. German. Of course. They'd suffered quakes, too. My stomach sank a little at the realization it wasn't just our continent that had been affected.

"That other hole leads to Germany? What's happening over there?" For a moment, my headache took a backseat to my curiosity. "Are there any safe places? Did you see any normal humans? Not the infected kind?"

"Yes. Humans," Fyllo said.

"You saw humans?"

Fyllo looked worried, and his gaze darted to Molev then Drav before he spoke again. Drav set his hand on my leg and squeezed it reassuringly. I doubted I would like hearing the translation.

"He said there were many people, most of them infected. He did find a group of humans travelling together, though. He followed them for some time until they arrived at a human stronghold."

Had the Europeans fared better than us? If they weren't dropping bombs there, then perhaps they thought it better to preserve our Earth. Considering we only had one planet, it made more sense to find a solution that didn't involve bombing the hell out of everything.

"What else can you tell me about what's happening over there?"

Fyllo spoke again, but this time, Molev translated.

"He said he followed the humans until they arrived to a safe point, but that is where he got his injury and the news to return."

"Did you notice anything else?" I asked, swallowing hard against my roiling stomach. "Were any of the humans gathering to go look for others? Any military movement to suppress the infected without the use of bombs? Any hope at all that they have a chance of killing the hellhounds on their own?"

"No," Fyllo said clearly.

Drav moved his hand so he was rubbing my back, and it helped ease some of my tension. It didn't matter. I didn't listen to more after that. My mind dwelled on the wasted time since Drav drug me down here. Drav and I could have been up there searching and helping anyone we found. But what could two people do against the mess on the surface? The struggle wasn't just mine or Drav's. It concerned Drav's people, too. They needed to see that. Living down here wasn't living. It was existing.

When the last man finished showing what he'd brought, the rest drifted to speak in smaller groups. Loud chatter came from most of them, along with a few bursts of boisterous laughter here and there. Most likely due to some retelling of tales of their time above ground. Were they laughing at the weak humans? At their struggle to survive when the shadow men could so easily outrun hellhounds and rip off the heads of infected?

Drav rubbed my neck gently, and I realized my hands were clenched into fists.

"Molev, you need to return to the surface. Now. Today. It's where you belong."

"No, down here is safer. We do not have a final death like your people on the surface."

"Safer, but is it better? Do you really want to spend your lives down here like you have been? Now that you've seen the surface and females like me? This isn't where you belong."

"This is where we have lived for thousands of years. This is our home. For now, we will stay. We will revisit this conversation when the birds that shit bombs are gone, and the hounds are far from the crater."

I opened my mouth to argue more when my head blossomed with a pain that would have knocked me off my feet if I had been standing. Black dots clouded my vision. I closed my eyes and gripped my head between my hands.

"Mya?"

Drav's quiet voice sounded like thunder. Bile pooled under my tongue, and I slowly shook my head.

"Home." It was the only word I could manage.

"Yes," Drav said before Molev could get a word in.

A strong set of arms scooped me up. Cradled against a familiar chest, I turned my face into the wind, seeking any sensation to distract from the pain threatening to explode my skull. Within seconds, some of the pain eased. I exhaled slowly and tried to relax as Drav ran, hoping the rest would go away too. The majority of the pain stubbornly remained.

The sensation of Drav racing up the tree stopped along with the wind. His growl had me opening my eyes. Men crowded the branch which held our burl. Some moved to and from other burls further out, others lounged outside the burls, talking to one another.

At our appearance, someone called out Drav's name and everyone's attention turned to us.

Drav didn't put me down but moved right for the entrance of our temporary home. No material covered the opening like before. The pile of "blankets" no longer waited inside on the wooden bed either.

Drav growled again.

"Where did everything go?" I asked. I wanted to block out the weak crystal light, burrow under the blankets, and fall asleep until my head stopped hurting and I didn't feel like hurling my rolls.

A voice come from behind Drav, who grunted then translated.

"They needed to replace damaged clothing." He turned. "Can you hand Mya the bag?"

The man standing nearby picked up the bag and handed it over.

"Thank you, Nero. You may use this place. If Molev looks for me, tell him I went to my village."

"Village?" I just really wanted to sleep.

"My home outside of the city."

Outside of the city meant closer to the wall and the way home, so I didn't argue.

We left the burl, and I closed my eyes, ready for the trip down. The wind continued after we stopped descending. I opened my eyes, anyway.

"How long will it take to get there?"

"Not long. Close your eyes. Rest."

I wouldn't have thought rest possible but managed some, until the steady motion of Drav's running stopped abruptly.

Pulled from my light doze, I opened my eyes and found my head felt a little better. It probably had something to do with the lack of light. We'd stopped close to the wall. No lanterns hung nearby, and the dim light from the larger cluster of crystals suspended above the now distant grove didn't reach far over the fields that stretched out behind us.

Turning my head, I focused on the four stone huts we faced. The structures seemed to emerge from the city wall. Nothing about them looked inviting, except their completely vacated state.

Drav walked to the one on the far left. Once again, no door or covering protected the entrance. Drav's village home didn't look much different than the city dwelling. The builders had used stone to create seating along the walls. Other than the entrance, there were no other openings to see beyond the immediate area just inside the door.

"Stay here, and I'll get a lantern so you can see."

He gently placed me on the bench and left me sitting in the dark. I didn't really mind. It gave me a minute to think.

Resting my head against the stone, I considered everything I'd learned after the arrival of the remainder of Drav's people. The bombings decimating the surface weren't happening worldwide. It gave me hope there might be something left to call home when we returned to the surface.

The news about the infected still roaming didn't surprise me.

I thought of my family and wondered how they were surviving. Were they eating canned dog food? I hoped not. I hoped jackasses like those at the bridge weren't taking all the supplies from the cities and starving out the survivors.

I also hoped the rest of my headache would go away after a nap so we could leave.

Soft light preceded Drav's return and cast enough of a subdued glow to see the rest of the room. I groaned just as he entered.

"Are you in pain?" he asked in concern, moving to my side.

"I'm going to be. Do we really have to sleep on that?" I asked, pointing at the stone bed protruding from the back wall. A furred hide covered the center of the platform with a thickly woven matt at one end.

"You didn't really sleep on there, did you?"

He glanced at the bed.

"Yes," he said, meeting my gaze.

"We must seem like a bunch of marshmallows to you."

"I don't understand."

"Soft and weak."

He feathered a finger over the curve of my cheek.

"Soft, yes. Not weak. Fragile."

I turned my head to kiss his hand.

"Good answer."

He grunted, set the lantern aside, and sat beside me. Leaning into him, I stared at the stone slab, and imagined all the nights he'd lain there. How long would I call his place home?

"I might never see a real bed again," I said quietly. "All those bombs...I wonder if they'll really stop with the cities. Will it be towns next? What will be left when they're done?" I exhaled heavily. "Probably piles of stone and ash. And, I bet there will still be infected."

"Yes. But I will keep you safe."

Of course he would, because we'd be together up there. I patted his leg and lifted my head, looking around at the few items resting on the opposite bench and hung from pegs protruding from the rock. Three hardened gourd looking things hung from a leather strap. Several woven baskets were stacked upside down underneath them.

There wouldn't be much to leave behind when we left.

"Has this place always been your home?"

"Yes."

"You don't have much. Not that it's a bad thing, but you've been here a long time. I thought you would have collected more stuff."

"I don't need anything more than what I have right now." He said the words while sliding his fingers up my arm.

I smiled slightly and leaned against his shoulder once more. His considerate attentiveness made my chest ache in a sweet way. Yet, as much as I wanted to return the sentiment that I had everything I needed, I couldn't. Although I did need Drav, I also needed to get back to the surface, too. I wouldn't just abandon my family.

A yawn broke through, and Drav suggested I lay down.

"I will look for some covers and return soon."

I went to the bed and lay down on the hide. The barrier didn't cushion me from the stone, but it did stop the cold from seeping into my bones.

Closing my eyes, I willed my partial headache away, along with the thoughts of Kristin, Dawn, Mom and Dad, and Ryan.

CHAPTER SIXTEEN

A HOWL PENETRATED MY TROUBLED DREAMS. IN THAT PLACE BETWEEN asleep and awake, I thought it just my imagination and snuggled more closely to Drav. Then, I heard it again. Long and low, the howl echoed nearby. I jolted upright with a gasp.

Baying and barking began in a frenzy. Drav sighed and sat up with me.

"Did they get inside?" I asked, my heart pounding.

"No. They are outside the wall."

Focusing beyond my racing pulse and panting breaths, I listened. Those hounds didn't sound outside the wall. They sounded like they were only yards away.

"How do you know?" I whispered.

"Because we aren't dead."

I smacked him.

"That is not reassuring."

A horrible scraping reverberated through the stone near my head. I squeaked and looked at the wall. The scraping, snarling, and howling grew louder.

"They're right on the other side, aren't they?"

Drav ran a soothing hand down my arm.

"Yes. They have very sharp hearing."

"Shit."

"I'm sorry, Mya. I didn't mean to frighten you. They truly are outside the wall and can't get in."

I could barely think over all the noise they were making.

"Are you sure?"

"I'll show you."

He picked me up and had me outside before I could say "no, thank you." With a leap, he jumped onto his hut's roof. A rackety looking scaffolding, made out of branches the size of my wrist, extended up to the top of the wall.

"Would you like me to carry you over my shoulder or climb by yourself?"

I swallowed my first choice of answer—neither—and said I would climb.

He followed closely, his fingers brushing my ankles and guiding me to the next secure footing. At the top, I stood on the lashed branches and peeked over the edge. I couldn't see a thing at first. Then Drav uncovered a lantern that had been placed on the thick stone ledge.

Yips and yowls sounded below as dozens of hellhounds retreated into the darkness beyond the lantern light.

"We can leave this lantern uncovered until the city crystals brighten again."

As he spoke, red dots moved in the distance like a swarm of angry fireflies.

"There are so many out there," I said softly.

"Not so many, but enough. They must be returning from the surface, as well."

I frowned as I considered what that meant. My family would be safer with the hounds down here, but how would we possibly make it back to the surface now? Drav remained quiet a moment when I voiced my concern.

"Returning will be difficult," he said.

"But we're still returning, right?"

He stared out at the sea of red dots for a long while before answering.

"If it is safe, we will return to the surface."

"What? Bullshit. Not 'if it is safe.' It will never be safe again if you guys don't get your asses up there and do something about the mess those things made," I jabbed a finger in the direction of the hellhounds, ignoring the throb of pain growing behind my eyes. "I am going back to the surface, Drav, as soon as it's light again."

However, that didn't happen. The next time the cavern's crystal brightened, my head hurt too much to move more than a few steps on my own.

For two rest periods, we stayed at Drav's village. Not that I got much rest. With mournful howls and aggressive snarls, the hounds rallied outside the wall each time the city crystals dimmed. Drav brought more of the crystal lanterns to line the wall, but it only stopped them from scratching the stone near my head. They knew we were there and wanted in.

My headache and poor mood grew worse. Drav patiently rubbed my head or back through the worst of it and removed the lights from the hut so we sat in the dark. Usually, it helped. But it never lasted.

"I think something's wrong with me," I said in the dark. The city lights hadn't yet dimmed so I lay in the warmth of Drav's arms, relaxing as he played with my hair.

"What do you mean?" With each new headache, his worry for me had only increased.

"I've never gotten headaches like these before. Not one right after the other. I think being down here is making me sick. Humans are supposed to have sunlight. It keeps us healthy."

"You're not eating much," he said. "Perhaps that is the reason."

"I'm not eating because I'll throw up if I do. My head hurts too much."

"Does it hurt now?"

"Not as much when we're laying in the dark. It hurts a lot when I try to move around, or we would have left already." I sighed and tried not to think about the passing time. Instead, I focused on the feel of his hands on my head.

"It feels good when you run your fingers through my hair."

He grunted and kept doing it. I didn't know how his arms never tired, but I sure appreciated his stamina.

"Close your eyes and rest before the hounds come."

THE PAIN in my head pulsed in time with the beat of my heart before I even fully woke. Groaning, I gagged and rolled to the side just in time. Nothing came up but bile because I hadn't eaten since the prior resting period. I lifted my head and tried to open my eyes. The light from a crystal the size of three basketballs pierced my skull. I closed my eyes and swallowed back another urge to gag. That light needed to go.

Through sheer determination, I lifted myself from the slab, dragging a blanket with me. Step by painful step, I approached the mini moon in the center of the hut.

My attempt to flip the blanket over the crystal threw me off balance, and I fell forward and landed against the crystal. Pain lanced through me like a thousand needles had pierced me at once. I screamed.

"MYA! MYA!"

Drav's voice pulled me from the darkness into the excruciating light. My skin felt raw and bruised, and the touch of his arms when he attempted to lift me made me want to die.

"Stop," I begged with tears burning my throat.

"Please don't cry. Tell me what's wrong."

I swallowed a gag and panted in pain.

"Take the crystal out," I managed between breaths.

He immediately set me on my side of the bed. Every movement, no matter how gentle, hurt. He made soothing sounds, and the light disappeared. Curled in a ball of misery, I breathed in and out, focusing on the cool rock beneath me. A hot spot on my side where I landed on the crystal was flush against the rock, easing the sting a miniscule amount.

"Mya?" Drav said softly. "Are you hurt?"

His fingers gently smoothed over my hair.

"I hurt all over."

"Can I bring a lantern in to check you?"

"No." The idea of being near a crystal made my stomach turn. "No more crystals. Every time I'm near one for too long, the headaches get worse. I accidently touched the big one and thought I was going to die. They're making me sick, Drav. I need to leave."

"Are you sure it's the crystals?"

"Yes."

He stroked my hair for several quiet minutes before speaking again.

"We need to return to the city."

I groaned. The idea of going anywhere just now made me want to puke. Yet the idea of waiting longer filled me with a certainty that I was going to die down here.

"Why? Why can't we just leave?" My eyes started to tear up. "Why are you doing this?"

"We will need help."

He slid his arm under me, attempting to pick me up, and I cried out. He immediately stopped.

"Can we wait a little while?" I panted. "How much time until the hounds get here?"

"Not long."

"Let's rest until then."

He lay beside me, his heat warming and soothing me. With a sigh, I relaxed against him and waited for the throbbing in my head to ease up.

It never did.

Drav's fingers rubbed the base of my skull. The kneading movement had eased some of the pain before, but it didn't help now.

"Drav," a voice called from outside.

I groaned at the sound. The voice called again, and Drav slipped from the bed.

"I will be back."

He left and spoke softly to his visitor.

The howls of the hounds started and pierced my skull. Knowing that it would be time for us to go soon anyway, I slowly sat up. My body ached all over. My stomach rolled as I swung my legs over the edge of the bed. I paused to take a few steadying breaths.

"Mya." Drav stepped back into the house, his body silhouetted the entrance way. He rushed over when I pushed off the bed, trying to get to my feet.

"How do you feel?"

"Terrible."

I shivered. Drav frowned, and I brought my hand to his cheek.

"I need to get away from the crystals," I said. "I need to go home."

"Yes. Ghua has returned from the surface. He will accompany us to the city."

"I thought we could skip that part," I said, glancing at Ghua, who had followed Drav in.

M.J. HAAG & BECCA VINCENZA

"No, Mya. We need help to reach the surface safely."

Of course. He was right. How could he defend me from a hound when he had to carry me?

"Okay, we can go. But, I'm not sure I'll be able to stand up."

Drav didn't waste another second before he had me in his arms. He looked down at me, gauging my reaction to being held. I ached but tried not to show it.

"I'm fine," I said.

Drav's gaze swept over my face once more before he stepped out of the hut to where Ghua now waited for us. Ghua had a couple of scratches on his arms that were healing and a multitude of scrapes and bruises on the exposed skin of his shirtless chest.

"Hey, Ghua. What the hell happened to you?" I asked.

"Hounds."

Just more evidence of how much help we would need to travel through hound infested caverns.

"Why did you return so much later than everyone else?" I asked.

Ghua smiled, his canines flashing. He had a twinkle of mischief in his eyes, but not before his smile dropped and sorrow replaced it.

"There is much news."

"Come. We will return to the city, share the news, and see who will join us," Drav said, leading the way with me in his arms.

He and Ghua spoke softly in their language as we traveled. It didn't bother me anymore. Nothing bothered me but my head, stomach, and the clawing need to get back to the surface.

Ghua glanced at me a couple of times, his gaze filled with sympathy and worry.

"Mya, okay?" Ghua asked.

"No, not really."

The pain and sickness grew progressively worse the closer we got to the city due to the lanterns that lit the pathway every ten feet. My stomach began to cramp so badly I wrapped an arm around my middle. Drav caught the move and watched me with increasing concern.

"Just get us there and get us help," I said softly.

Within the towering timbers, the city seemed to be a flurry of activity. Others hurried past us, some nodding in acknowledgement, some carrying weapons and travel bags over their shoulders. A few stared at me, curious, but most seemed to have become accustom to my presence. I could have sworn I even heard a couple say a few things in English.

Drav and Ghua quieted as we drew near the common area. The low tones of Molev's distant voice drilled into my brain. I rested my head against Drav's chest, my achy body tired and demanding more sleep. I didn't sleep, but I shut my eyes in the hopes that the pounding in my head would calm. Or even that my stomach stopped twisting in knots. Anything to give me some type of relief.

"Mya," a familiar voice said, much too loudly.

I opened my eyes to see we'd reached the lantern lit common area. Molev stood in the center of a large gathering and waved us forward through the crowd, closer into the heart of the poisonous light.

Although packed with hot bodies, the area felt cold. Cold enough that I exhaled to test if I could see my breath. Struggling not to shiver uncontrollably in Drav's arms, I closed my eyes briefly and swallowed down my bile.

"You do not look well, Mya," Molev said.

"She's not," Drav said, answering for me. "The crystals are making her sick. She needs to return to the surface."

"Are you certain it's the crystals?" Molev asked.

"Just coming here has made her worse. Before this, she accidentally touched the large guard crystal I'd taken inside the hut before bringing it to the wall. She fell over after touching it."

"I think I'm dying," I whispered.

As if reacting to my words, shivers wracked my body.

"We need more time," Molev said. "Another rest for those who just returned to be ready."

"We don't have more time. Look at her. We need to leave now."

Molev grunted, and Drav held me more firmly to his chest.

"Those who are ready," Molev said loudly, "will leave now. Those who are not ready will meet us on the surface in one rest. We also need men to stay and guard the city. If the humans do not welcome us as Mya has, we will need a place we can return to."

"What of Merdon and Ririn, and the four who have not returned?" Ghua asked.

"We will search for them when we reach the surface and hope our brothers aren't gone, and the traitors are."

A universal agreement ran through the crowd.

"Drav, please," I rasped. Everything hurt so much. Talking. Thinking. Even breathing.

"We leave now," Molev said. "The return of the hounds will make the journey dangerous. Be ready."

The crowd, who had been quiet, broke out in a hub of noise.

The racket added to the pain, and I whimpered. My stomach cramped painfully, and a gag caught in my throat.

"Mya?"

"I don't feel well, Drav," I mumbled. "It's so cold here."

His lips touched my forehead.

"You are not cold. You're hot," he said.

Figured. Fever in hell. Part of me frowned at that thought. Not hell. Drav's home.

"You're hotter than you've ever been. Your heart is racing."

I gagged again.

"What do I do, Mya?"

"Fevers need to be cooled. But it won't help. We need to leave. It's the crystals."

Drav ran.

CHAPTER SEVENTEEN

EACH STRIDE RATTLED MY TEETH, DESPITE MY CLENCHED JAW. NEVER in my life had I felt so cold or hurt so much. I could barely think past the pounding in my skull. It just needed to end. Now.

"P-please, just r-rip my head off," I stuttered to Drav.

"No, Mya. You will die."

"I'm already dying."

He growled fiercely and ran faster. I burrowed my face in his shirt, desperate for some heat. Some relief. Tears gathered as I thought what would happen if I died. My family would be left always wondering what had happened.

We suddenly stopped moving.

"I'm sorry, Mya."

That was all the warning Drav gave before he jumped. Icy spears lanced through me as we plunged into the river. The shock of it kept me from gasping until our heads popped back up.

I choked on a curse and shivered uncontrollably.

"Just a little longer," Drav whispered in my ear, holding me when I would have flailed in the direction of the bank. "We need to cool you."

If I'd thought the air cold before, the water robbed me of every ounce of heat, sucking my energy until I could barely cling to Drav. His lips brushed my forehead, cheek, and mouth.

"You're cooling. Hold your breath one more time."

"N-n-no."

"Three. Two."

I inhaled quickly and held it.

"One."

He dunked us under again. I wouldn't have thought my head held any warmth after the first submersion. However, I was proven wrong the second time the icy water enveloped us and stole what remained of my heat and strength.

We broke the surface, and Drav surged out of the water onto the bank. Cradling me in his arms, he sat and gently rocked me. Some of the pain in my head had eased. That or the water had numbed it. For a moment, I let myself float in the almost nothingness that waited at the edge of my consciousness.

Drav's hands wiped over my face, and his lips brushed mine repeatedly between softly spoken pleas for me to open my eyes.

I felt so tired. Yet, hearing his gruff demanding voice, I forced myself to try. As soon as I opened my eyes, he kissed me hard.

"Do not do that again," he said when he pulled away.

"T-that's my l-line."

He hugged me close, melting my anger with his body heat. We stayed like that until the worst of my tremors stopped. In the darkness by the river, the pain in my head didn't return full-force. It didn't fade either. A steady thumping persisted, reminding me that we needed to leave these caverns, no matter what.

In the distance, the faint sounds of baying echoed. Between the crystal poisoning and the gathered hounds, the journey to the surface wouldn't be an easy one.

"Drav, I need you to promise me something."

"Anything."

"If something happens to me, you need to find my family and

tell them everything. From the moment we met until the end. Except for the boob grabbing and kissing. That would upset my parents."

"Nothing will happen to you," he said, before pressing another kiss to my temple.

"Drav, I'm sick, and we still have caverns filled with hellhounds to fight our way through. If something happens, I want your word you will try to find my family. I have a picture of them in my bag. I know it's asking a lot, but I can't leave them just wondering. And, they need your help to live."

"Nothing will happen, Mya. You will see your family again. I give you my word."

I sighed and closed my eyes, knowing that was as good as I'd get from him. The stubborn man wouldn't give up on the idea of both of us making it to the surface alive and well. What would happen then?

"It's not going to be easy once we reach the top," I said. "The infected will still be roaming. The hounds will likely follow us. And, everyone will probably want to kill you." I rubbed my head against his wet shirt. "I wish there was a safe place for us to just... be."

"We will find a place. Your world is very large."

"It is. And a lot emptier now. Maybe we can find a farm in the middle of nowhere. We can grow things like you do down here. Maybe even raise chickens or something...if we can find any."

"We can do anything you want, as long as we're together."

I lifted my head and met his worried gaze.

"Together," I agreed, ignoring the sinking feeling in my stomach.

He kissed me softly then tucked my back against his chest. We stayed like that until Molev found us a while later.

"We are ready. Is Mya all right?"

Drav stood with me in his arms.

"For now. I will meet you at the gate. We can't risk lit caverns. Mya grows too sick in the light."

"But the hounds."

"I know. Make sure to let everyone know what we face and that any lanterns must stay away from Mya."

Molev glanced at me. Was he wondering if I was worth all the trouble? I hoped not because I couldn't think of a reason to support my worth at the moment.

"We will meet you at the gate," he said finally. "We will keep you safe, Mya."

"Thank you. Can someone bring my bag? It has things in it that I still need." Mostly, the picture of my family. Just in case.

"I will bring it," Molev said.

Drav set off at a run. The breeze made me shiver, but I didn't complain about the wet clothing. The cold helped numb the body aches. Closing my eyes, I tried to rest. It worked until we reached the outer wall. The sound of Drav's running attracted the hounds on the other side. Snarls and growls increased in volume and number as he ran.

"Maybe we should run through the fields," I said.

"No. The light will hurt you."

"So will all the hellhounds that are following us to the gate."

Drav grunted and glanced at the fields. The lantern light didn't hurt my eyes, but it would hurt my head once we drew closer.

"It'll be a good test to see how close I can be to the lanterns when we're out there. Better to know now when we're safe, right?"

My reasoning seemed to decide him. He veered inward and wove his way between the lanterns. The baying fell behind, remaining near the point of the wall where they'd last heard us.

"How do you feel?" Drav asked after passing by several lanterns. He kept at least ten feet away.

"It's not getting any worse when we move between the ones

with smaller pieces of crystals. I can feel the ones with bigger chunks, though."

He pressed his lips to my forehead.

"You're starting to warm again."

The hot grittiness I'd felt in my eyes hadn't returned since our plunge in the water, so I couldn't be too bad, yet. A sudden thought occurred to me, and I jerked my head up to stare at Drav. The move made my head pound a little more noticeably.

"If I get too warm again, promise you won't jump in any fish infested waters to cool me off once we're outside the wall."

"I promise I will care for you and keep you safe."

I set my head back on his chest.

"Not the promise I was looking for."

He kissed the top of my head.

"Rest. Sleep while you can."

Unfortunately, I hurt enough that resting proved impossible. But I closed my eyes and pretended for his peace of mind.

While he ran, I listened to the sounds of the hounds fade and swell in waves. Although I knew he stayed in the fields, based on the pain I experienced from the nearby lanterns, the creatures still gathered at places outside the walls. Probably near the tiny village stations the men used to guard their city. I could only imagine how many hounds we would have attracted if we'd stayed running near the wall. Hopefully, my suffering now would keep us safer when we left. And I certainly did suffer. The pulsing energy from each crystal seemed to burrow into my bones and twist me from the inside.

By the time we reached the gate, my stomach churned nauseatingly; and the sounds of the hounds outside grew.

"Do you have her water bottle?" Drav asked, slowing.

I opened my eyes to see a large gathering of men before us. Those nearest the gate held lanterns, glowing with large chunks of crystals. I could feel the energy from where we stood and winced.

Drav caught the look and stepped further away. The men not carrying the lanterns held bows and spears. Some had knives strapped to their legs.

Molev moved forward. He carried a spear along with my bag.

"I thought you only used your weapons for hunting," I said, the words coming out slightly slurred.

He handed me the bottle.

"I'm not thirsty," I said.

"You need to drink, Mya. Please," Drav said.

I sighed and took a tiny sip before passing the bottle back.

"Leaving with lanterns is usually enough to keep the hounds away. However, we generally hunt in the crystal caverns. This time, we will travel through the dark ones. We will need both the lanterns and the weapons to keep you safe."

"You say that as if you don't like the idea of killing them." The effort of the words had me closing my eyes briefly.

"Because, even with weapons, we can't kill them. We can only slow them and make it take longer for them to heal."

Leaving the city walls should have terrified me. Instead, I only felt relief. We were finally making our way to the surface. To my family. To the survivors who needed our help.

Drav looked up at the men. "The larger crystals poison her quicker. She can endure the smaller from a distance."

Molev nodded.

"You will carry her at our center. Those with the lanterns will form a circle around us in the open caves. In the tunnels and cross ways, the lanterns will move to the front and the back. Those of us with spears will guard the lantern bearers. Those with arrows will remain closest to Drav and Mya."

I shivered slightly in Drav's arms.

"We must leave," he said. "She's warming again. No stopping. No rests."

"No rests? Won't you get tired?" I asked.

He met my worried gaze.

"Resting in dark caves is too dangerous, and I fear what resting in crystal caves would do to you."

All good points, which made me feel guilty as hell.

"If you get tired, don't be stubborn. Ask someone else to carry me for a bit."

He grunted, and I knew he'd never willingly let someone else carry me.

"Are you ready?" Molev asked.

Drav nodded. The two men by the gate removed the brace. The barking outside the wall grew more intense. Two other men scurried up the ladders and uncovered lanterns on top of the wall. Yipping and snarls drew further away, and the men by the gate started pulling the rock slab open. Those with lanterns crowded near the gap.

In the darkness beyond, I could see the multitude of glowing red eyes, and my heart started to thump heavily in my chest.

"I will keep you safe," Drav vowed, pressing a kiss to my head.

I said nothing, just watched the first of the lantern carriers slip outside the wall followed by the men with spears. When more than half the group had left, the rest stood aside. Drav walked forward. I closed my eyes against the feel of the crystals on the wall as we passed through the opening. Part of me considered keeping them closed, but I had to know what we faced. What I saw terrified me.

A sea of blinking red dots circled our group, kept at bay by the weak light of the lanterns and the sharp ends of spears. As Drav moved forward, so too did the lantern bearers at the front.

"Is everyone out?" Molev asked. He held a position near the front, spear in hand.

"Yes," someone said from behind us. I looked back and saw we stood in the center of a lantern circle. The gate rumbled closed behind us, and the lanterns disappeared from the top of the wall.

"We run and we don't stop," Molev said.

CHAPTER EIGHTEEN

Drav started running and the sixty men around us moved with him, a protective barrier against the growing mass of writhing black bodies hungry for flesh.

A hound, keeping pace just outside the circle of light, darted in toward a lantern carrier. The creature screamed in pain as the crystal's glow bathed its coarse fur, but didn't stop its charge. The carrier saw it coming. His gait remained steady until the last possible second when he jumped mid-stride. A spear pierced the hound's side. The spear bearer, who I hadn't noticed, hoisted the hound and threw it off the end of the spear into the dark.

Seeing one of their own wounded and tossed aside sent the rest into a frenzy. The baying and snarls grew deafening. More darted in, attempting to bring down the lantern bearers and extinguish the light. The men with bows and spears kept the hounds at bay.

Molev yelled something into the din, but I couldn't make it out.

A moment later, two of the lantern bearers at the front moved closer to each other while the next two stopped altogether. It took a second to understand why. We were running through two enormous columns. The two who'd stayed behind stood on the outside of the columns, keeping the darkness and hounds back as the rest passed through.

After the columns, nothing separated us from the first dark cavern. Almost as if the hounds sensed they were losing their prey, half their number darted forward toward the abyss.

"Do not let them reach the cavern first," Molev yelled.

Drav tensed and leaned into his run, picking up speed. The lantern bearers in the front did their best to reach the cavern entrance first, but missed it by at least a dozen hounds. Red eyes glowed in the darkness ahead as the men continued forward. The men waved the lanterns, forcing the hounds back. The hoarse yowls echoed around us as the light hit them.

The hounds behind kept a healthy distance from the crystals, not that I blamed them. The lanterns, even though a distance from me, still made my head ache and my stomach twist.

Despite the agony it caused them, a few hell hounds charged forward, sharp, yellowed teeth flashing in the green light before a spear or arrow whistled through the air. A meaty thud followed. The men kept their pace, veering to the right, out of the dark lush sub cavern and into the barren cool darkness of a cavern void of crystals.

Although I felt an immediate degree of relief, I couldn't enjoy it. I knew where we were. This stark cavern belonged to the hounds.

A pained yell came from behind us. I itched to glance over Drav's shoulder, but his words stopped me.

"Do not look back, Mya. He will rise at the pool and join the others."

I heeded Drav's warning and lay my head back on his shoulder. The fever still lingered, and I felt exhausted. Drav held me securely against him, but it didn't stop the throbbing pain that shot through my head with each stride. Although, the darkness eased the worst of my pain, the crystal lanterns that surrounded us guaranteed my fever would slowly return.

Drav misstepped and lurched forward. Bile rose to the back of my throat at the movement, and I fought not to throw up.

"Are you all right?" he asked, not stopping.

"Yes. If you need the lanterns closer—"

"No. I can see well enough. There's another entrance ahead."

The men picked up speed together and raced for it, creating distance between us and the pack of hellhounds.

As soon as we emerged from the other end of the passageway, all sounds of pursuit abruptly ceased. I shivered and wondered what that meant while I struggled to see where we were.

This cavern, too, had no crystals. The absence of that stronger light continued to prevent the pain in my head from increasing, despite the smaller green shards around us. However, those shards proved too small for the complete nothingness in this cave.

The darkness swam in, like an unsuspecting fog. It rolled around us until we were submerged. From the echoing glow of the furthest crystal, I could only see shadows outlining Drav's chest and my hand, if I brought it close enough to my face.

The silence settled around us. Even with the sound of the men's feet hitting the compact floor, the quiet heightened my anxiety.

A hollow howl suddenly came from behind us a moment before the burst of noise echoed off the stone walls. The never-ending sound boomed in my ears. I stiffened in Drav's arms, but he didn't even flinch. The hounds had entered the cavern and passed through whatever barrier had kept their pursuit quiet from us.

A few of the lanterns swayed haphazardly before I spotted the first set of red eyes.

The hounds surged forward, a mass of angry predators closing in on their prey. The first scream made me jump. More yells from the men who fought filled the cavern.

I watched another lantern bearer fall away into the dark. The man behind him, ran faster to fill in the space and close the circle around us.

"Keep moving forward," Molev called out from nearby.

The men didn't stop running. But the darkness remained unchanged as if we didn't make any progress at all. Slinking shapes kept pace in the lanterns glow. Exaggerated shadows of the hounds stretched and twisted. One moment, there; the next, gone.

The men switched directions, avoiding the shadows when they appeared. An arrow whistled in the air, and I tucked myself closer to Drav.

Two men suddenly went down, seemingly yanked into the darkness by nothing. A howl followed their disappearance. There were shouts from the back of the group, and we began to slow down. The scrape of nails against the stone ground and heavy panting surrounded us.

I peeked over Drav's shoulder and saw a flash of red eyes. The hounds were herding our group, trying to separate us from the two who had fallen.

"Keep moving," Molev called out again, his voice heavy with regret.

One of the men let out a cry cut off by a wet gurgle. I shuddered, knowing the sound would haunt me in my nightmares.

"The men will return to the pool, inside the city. They will be safe," Drav said.

"Will they remember their deaths?"

Drav didn't answer, and I knew they would. Being ripped apart by a hound would be a terrible thing to remember for eternity.

The hounds' efforts grew more intense in the next cavern.

Molev ran up next to Drav and spoke to him quietly in their language. I hated that they were keeping things from me, but I was still too tired to protest.

"No," Drav said firmly.

"What's going on?" I asked.

"Molev wishes to take a detour through one of the lit caverns."

I thought of the number of hounds following us and the men we'd lost. They were picking us off slowly. It would only be a matter of time before the hounds tried something braver. Although I understood the fallen men weren't really dead, the thought of Kerr, Shax, or Ghua getting hurt before we reached the surface worried me.

And then, of course, there was Drav. The thought of something bad happening to him broke me. I couldn't bear it. If his safety meant I would have to be in a bit more discomfort for a while, I could stand it.

Besides, the men were the ones that would get me to the surface. Without them, I would be lost.

"It's the smartest idea."

"No, you are still hot."

"I'll be okay. All these dark caves have helped. Passing through a light cave will win us some safety and breathing room. I promise to tell you the moment I start to feel worse."

Molev ran next to us, listening to our conversation.

"If Mya is okay with it, the men could use a rest."

I didn't know how long we had run. It was impossible to tell in the darkness. But after losing men, I could understand the group's wariness to continue.

"I can handle it for a while," I said to Drav, who nodded to Molev.

Molev called out, and the group changed directions. Hounds darted forward, trying to catch the outermost runners with a bite. Those within the circle let arrows fly into the rushing hounds.

"Almost there," Drav said.

Turning forward, I saw a lit cavern in the distance. Sparse vegetation grew on the outskirts of where the illumination reached. Jackalopes sprinted from the growth toward the light before we even came close, the baying alerting them of the danger.

I squinted against the increasing brightness. The men raced forward, the lantern holders moving to the side to let those without light through first.

Drav rushed into the passage with the rest following, and I exhaled in relief at the hounds' wailing at the loss of prey.

"Are you all right?" Drav asked, slowing.

"Yes. So far so good." And I was. The cavern wasn't as huge as the city's, meaning the crystals in the ceiling were smaller, too. Although my head still thumped, the pain didn't seem to grow terribly worse.

As a group, we made our way through the well-lit cavern's thick vegetation to the center. Men plopped to the ground, sides heaving.

"Can you put me down, please?" I asked, knowing Drav had to be tired, too.

He eased me to my feet but kept a hold on my arms. The support kept me steady on my numb legs.

"Mya?"

"Hmm?"

"How do you feel?"

"I'm okay for now. Honest. How much longer until we reach the old orchard?" I asked, my gaze drifting to the men around us. Molev walked among them, speaking to a few here and there.

"Not long," Drav answered. "One more resting period."

"Is that how long we ran?"

"No. Not quite half of that."

Crap. Worry pooled in my stomach, and I began to count men.

"We lost seven," Molev said, coming up to us. "The crystals in this cave are still strong. We can rest for a while but should leave well before the light begins to dim." He studied me for a moment. "Are you well?"

"I'm holding it together for the moment. I can feel the crystals, but the run through the dark caves helped settle the worst of it," I lied. "So I should be fine in here for a bit."

"Good. Thank you."

As soon as he walked away, Drav convinced me to sit in the tall grass.

"Stay. I will get your bag. You need to eat and drink something."

"Thank you." The thought of food still didn't appeal to me. However, I kept quiet because Drav would worry if I said something.

A wave of exhaustion swept over me, and my eyelids fell heavily. When Drav returned with food and nudged me, I couldn't bring myself to open my eyes. Splashing of the water and quiet whispers lulled me to sleep.

DRAV'S WARMTH left my back a moment before I felt myself lifted into the air.

"She's growing warm again," he said. "We must go."

Around me, I listened to the slight rustle of noise as the men stood and started moving.

"I'm fine," I tried to say, but the words came out a slurred murmur. "They need more rest."

"You are not fine," Drav said. "And we've rested as long as we dare."

I didn't have the energy to argue.

We made our way toward the next cavern's entrance. The sudden temperature drop and complete darkness gave a welcome respite. I hadn't been aware of just how badly my head hurt, until the pain began to ease.

My head and stomach settled enough that I closed my eyes, and I dozed on and off as Drav and his men ran tirelessly through caverns. Occasionally, the volume of Molev's voice would rise and rouse me. But never for long. The steady swaying motion of Drav's gait and the strong sure hold of his arms always pulled me back under, and the much-needed rest worked wonders.

When I next opened my eyes, my head no longer beat in time with my pulse. My stomach didn't feel the greatest, but the sensation of being on the verge of vomiting had faded.

"It seems quieter," I said, glancing up at Drav's tense jaw.

"It is. How are you feeling?"

"Better. My head and stomach only hurt a little."

"Good."

"Do you want to take a break? Could Kerr or Shax carry me for a while?" I asked only because I worried for him. I saw how tired the others had been from running full out. And I didn't want Drav weak or exhausted if the hounds attacked.

"No."

"Please, Drav. I'm okay with it. I don't want you to—"

"Mya, I am fine."

Before I could argue with him, a long, lone howl split the air. It sounded different than the normal baying. Close, but not frenzied.

The men immediately picked up their pace.

"What was that?"

"Hunting call," Molev said from nearby. "It's to let the others know prey has been spotted."

Howls started up around us, all coming from different directions. I twisted in Drav's arms and spotted a looming sea of red in the darkness.

CHAPTER NINETEEN

THE HELL HOUNDS CAME AT US LIKE A SWARM, BLINKING OUT OF sight here and there because of the columns hidden within the depths of the cavern.

Ahead, one of the leading lantern bearers said something I didn't understand. However, whatever the guy had shouted couldn't have been good because Molev swore in English.

"Tighten the circle. Channel ahead. Watch from above," he called out.

"Above?" I said.

"We should turn back," Drav shouted to Molev over the baying and snarls.

"If you could look back, you would know that's not an option."

I looked over Drav's shoulder, and my mouth dropped open. Very few of the lanterns remained. Even as I watched, a sleek black body leapt forward and silently brought another man down.

"We can't go back," I said to Drav. "We're running out of lanterns."

He ran faster.

"Close your eyes," he ordered.

My stomach churned with fear. Just what the hell was going to happen? I looked ahead. Numerous stocky columns rose out of the darkness. The hounds racing ahead of us scrabbled up the rocky sides. One reached a peak before we entered the maze of pillars.

From atop its perch, the hound launched itself into the center of our group. Mad eyes fixed on a hunter not far from us, the hound salivated and snarled as it fell. It yelped in pain when the light of the crystals touched it but didn't twist to avoid the brightness.

The hunter hefted his long spear and braced himself. The hound skewered its body onto the pole without a flinch. It clawed at the shaft, trying to pull closer to the hunter. Meanwhile, other hounds were winning their way to the tops of other pillars.

Now I understood why Drav wanted me to close my eyes.

We were all going to die. Only, there was no resurrection pool for me. I clung to Drav as we passed between the first two pillars. Hounds began launching themselves at will, reducing our numbers in seconds. Blood spattered my jean clad legs. As much as I wanted to close my eyes, I couldn't.

This was the cost of returning me to the surface. Closing my eyes to it wouldn't make it any less real.

Screams and roars echoed around us. The thump of the men's feet on the ground as they ran was non-existent in the noise.

Turning my head, I caught movement high to our right. A hound's eyes met mine from above just as it leapt toward us.

I gasped and cringed into Drav.

"Molev," Drav shouted.

Then he threw me. I screamed, sailing through the air, looking back to see the hound bring Drav down. Another converged on him.

I screamed his name.

Strong arms caught me, and the forward momentum jerked me, interrupting my view. When I saw again, there was nothing but a pile of black bodies where Drav had stood.

"No!" The cry ripped through me. I didn't care if he had resurrected a million times before, I didn't trust fate to bring him back to me now. Not after everything I'd seen.

I looked up at Molev's shadowed face.

"Stop! You have to help him!"

Molev didn't slow. He veered, avoiding another leaping hound.

"Ghua," he yelled.

Yet again, I found myself sailing through the air. Molev shouted out several names as Ghua caught me and tucked me under one arm, carrying me like a flailing football. I lifted my head and squinted at the bright glow of the lantern he carried in his other hand. Four more lantern bearers moved to surround us, all running at the same breakneck pace as Ghua. The light of the crystals they held, the only thing keeping the beasts at bay.

A shout from behind us distracted the circling, snapping hounds, though. Their numbers thinned, opening a path to the next dimly lit cavern.

"Ghua, please," I panted. "You have to help Drav."

"I am," he said.

He continued forward, toward the dim light of the cavern. As soon as we exploded through the passageway, the noise of the fight behind us couldn't be heard over the sound of the group's harsh breathing. Ghua fell to his knees, taking me with him.

His sides heaved with great, gasping breaths as did those of the men around him.

Ignoring the pounding behind my eyes, I scrambled to my knees and looked back at the black entrance. For a moment, I heard and saw nothing. Then the faint snarls and growls reached me. The hounds were already turning away, knowing the light in the cavern would be too much for them. But, they'd gotten what they'd wanted.

Tears flowed down my cheeks, and a sob caught in my throat. Slowly, I wrapped my arms around my aching middle.

"He will swim in the pool and come back for you, Mya. Do not doubt that." Ghua's hand gripped my shoulder, a small comfort to my breaking world.

None of the men spoke as I continued to cry through my pain. A numbness crept in. I swallowed hard and wiped the back of my hand across my dripping nose. After a few calming breaths, I looked up at Ghua who squatted beside me, studying me with concern.

"How will we ever reach the surface with just the six of us?" I asked, my voice still rough.

"We need to stick to the light caverns."

"That will only work until the old orchard. It and the cavern leading up to the surface are both dark," I said.

He nodded.

"We'll wait until the old orchard is lit. We will be safe. But I will need to carry you and run, Mya."

"I know."

He stood and offered me his hand.

"Come. We must keep moving. The light is increasing here and will give us more time."

I stood and let Ghua pick me up. It wasn't the same as running with Drav. He didn't hold me as closely, for which I felt very grateful.

We ran through the lit cavern, my heart feeling heavier with each step.

A distant sound stopped Ghua before we reached the next entrance. He turned back, looking the way we'd come. I saw nothing in the soft light but the swaying long purple grass. Another anguished howl-like yell echoed distantly.

"Is it the hounds?" I asked, my heart beating hard. They shouldn't have been able to enter, not with the light.

"No," Ghua said. He started walking toward the sound. "It's your name."

I tilted my head and listened. This time, I heard it. The long, drawn out syllables of my name.

"Is it—?" My throat tightened with hope.

"I can't tell." He turned back and started to jog, the other's falling in around us.

From a distance, I caught the shape of four men. Just four out of the sixty who'd left the city with us.

"It's Molev, Drav, Kerr, and Shax," Ghua said.

I started to cry. Ghua picked up the pace, and we met them near the base of one of the spindly trees. I pushed myself from his arms and went running to Drav, who was being half carried, half dragged by Molev and Shax. Blood covered every inch of his skin, along with bites and ripped, gaping wounds. He seemed blind as he yelled my name again, and swung his head from side to side.

"She's right in front of you. Stop your yelling," Molev said. He released Drav, who fell to the ground.

I ran to him.

"Does anyone have my bag?"

Kerr set it beside me. His bloody hand caught my attention. I looked up and noticed, in a glance, they all looked just about as bad as Drav.

"You heal faster in the caverns, right?" I asked.

Molev collapsed to the ground beside Drav.

"Yes. We will need a rest period. Maybe two."

I grabbed my water bottle and dribbled some onto Drav's ravaged face. His eyes were too swollen to tell if he really had been blinded.

"Everything will heal?" I asked, worried.

"Yes. We keep the scars until we are reborn."

"Mya," Drav gasped, his hand reaching up and closing around mine.

"I'm here," I said, afraid to touch him. "Lie down. I'll lie with you."

"No. Must leave. Crystals."

"It'll be okay," I said, giving him a gentle nudge. "Ghua is here and will wake us before I get sick. It'll be just enough time to let you heal."

Drav eased down to the ground and pulled me close. His bleeding had already stopped. Within seconds, he slept.

I looked up at Ghua, my head already pounding. However, I couldn't be sure if it was from the scare and the tears or the crystals.

"Don't wake them up until everyone can run. None of us will survive if we have to carry the injured."

He nodded slowly, and I closed my eyes.

SOMETHING cold and wet pressed against my forehead, and I tried to push it away. I could barely lift my arm, though.

"Mya?"

"Stop." My word slurred with sleep.

"Mya, you must wake."

"No, too tired."

Drav shook me lightly.

"Your fever is back. You must wake."

"Stop, I'm awake."

"Then open your eyes."

With a great effort, I managed to crack my eyelids open a bit. The light was gone, replaced with darkness again. A lantern was nearby, and I cringed away from it.

"We are getting close to the crater. We need to keep moving, Drav," Molev said from somewhere right beside me. Drav pulled away the cloth he was using to wipe down my forehead. How long had I been out? I groaned from the pain radiating in my body.

"Ghua is going to lift you. Are you ready to move again?"

Honestly, I wanted to tell him no, I wasn't. But, I knew I wouldn't be getting any better here. A hound howled, and it sounded too close for comfort. Ghua picked me up as gently as he could, but the fever and the accompanying pain made everything worse. I bit back my cry of pain and turned my head to look at Drav.

His face looked less swollen. But, when he stood, he did so with a grimace and stepped back with a limp.

"You need more rest," I said.

"I'm sorry, Mya," Ghua said. "You do not look well. I had to wake them."

He took off running, and the agony that jolted in my head pulled me into a pain-filled darkness.

"WE ARE CLOSE."

"She needs help."

"Once we get to the surface, we will find her people. Someone will help her."

Drav and Molev's conversation grated on my nerves. Every sound seemed heightened, and I wanted them to stop talking.

I groaned and tried to open one eyelid. I only caught a glimpse of our surroundings before it closed. Darkness surrounded us, but the ceiling had seemed familiar. I tried again, and Drav noticed.

"She is awake. We must move now," Molev called out.

Drav held me tightly, his fingers running through my hair. I wanted to ask what was wrong, but he had me up in his arms before I could.

"You must hold onto me."

I did as he asked but had no strength in my grip. Drav ran forward and there was a pressure in my ears as they popped loudly and painfully. I winced. We'd just passed through the barrier. We were almost there.

I spontaneously threw up on myself, and weakly choked on it.

"You will be okay, Mya. You will be."

Muscles moved under me. I drifted off, knowing he was wrong this time.

Molev's quiet voice roused me again. Something was tied around me, anchoring me to Drav.

"Drav," I rasped. "Remember. Family. Promise."

"I remember, Mya. I promise you will see them again."

I wouldn't. I couldn't see anything. But, I tried again to open my eyes.

Just when I thought it wasn't working, I saw the stars. They glittered above me with a dazzling beauty rarely seen even at the cabin. I wanted to cry. The twinkling stars above us seemed too spectacular to be true. My fever had to be making me delusional.

"We are here," Drav said, untying me. He lay me on the cool ground. Instead of stars, I stared up at his ravaged face.

"Where?" I rasped.

"The surface," he said.

I sighed and closed my eyes. He'd done it. He'd returned me to the surface like I'd asked. But far too late.

"Thank you, Drav. Don't forget your promise."

With that, I let the darkness take me once more, barely hearing Drav's anguished cry.

"No, Mya! I will not lose you."

DEMON ASH

CHAPTER ONE

EVERYTHING HURT. THE STEADY THROBBING IN MY SKULL PENETRATED my disoriented mind, creating a dark dreamscape filled with terrors I didn't believe real. Skeletal black bodies with glowing red eyes swarmed around us. A single flashlight and four spear-bearing men with grey skin kept them at bay. A man with a mangled face whispered that I would have no second life, that I needed to cling to the first.

I didn't want to cling to anything. Pain enveloped me when I tried. So I let go, but I couldn't drift.

The clamor of sound, echoing howls and incomprehensible shouts, tormented me almost as much as the jolting cadence rocking through my body. I wanted to escape into an abyss of darkness. But every time I came close, something jostled me. Then, the whispers would start again.

The words began to change, along with the light. A brightness crept in that made me whimper and turn my head, despite the pain.

"It's the only safe place," a voice said.

"It will likely house humans," another answered.

I wanted to tell the voices to stop. To be quiet and just let me sleep. But, opening my mouth only produced a mewling whine. Something brushed my forehead, hurting me further.

"Good. They might be able to help her."

"We don't heal the same here. We need to watch for those guns. Do not let them touch you."

"I know," yet another voice said. "You stay. We go."

"Do not kill them. Mya will not like that."

Frustration and confusion got the better of me. I opened my mouth, again, to yell. Nothing more than a groan emerged.

"Shh...my Mya. You are safe. We will find help."

After that, things grew blissfully quiet, and the light faded. I floated in the void of nothing, the pain gradually easing. In its absence, a chill crept in. Even though I couldn't see, I could imagine my breath misting in the air and ice forming on my skin. I shivered uncontrollably, each shudder punctuated by a rapid series of muffled bangs.

"We need to cool her off. She's too warm."

I wanted to cry. Why couldn't the voices just leave me alone? Or say something that made sense. Who would want to cool off when it felt ready to snow?

More pops sounded then silence returned.

"They are angry," a voice said.

Fingers grabbed me with bruising force, and I cried out.

"I don't care," another said. "They will help her. Where are they?"

"Barn. Tied to chairs."

"Take her to the house. Find a bed that is soft. I will be there in a moment. And do not touch her or try to look at her pussy. She will be angry if you do. And so will I."

The rocking started again. I groaned, hating this dream and wishing I could wake up. Instead, I pulled away from the light, the voices, and the pain and found a dark, quiet corner to hide from their persistent presence.

Something gently smoothed over my hair, and the warm wetness on my forehead left only to be replaced by a cooler wetness. I sighed and snuggled deeper into the pillow.

"I've sent Ghua back to the hole. He will wait for the others," a familiar voice said.

"Good. What about the ones in the barn?"

"They still only swear and spit at us. Are you sure they are intelligent and not infected?"

"I am sure."

Groaning, I tried to roll away from the voices.

"Shh...Mya. Do not move so much."

"Then shut up," I mumbled.

Arms wrapped around me suddenly and squeezed me too tightly.

"Stop," I panted, my head starting to throb again. "Hurts."

Lips brushed my cheek and the corner of my mouth.

"You're awake," a voice said.

"No." If I was, I sure as hell didn't want to be.

A clank came from nearby. The arm under my shoulders lifted me slightly as something touched my lips.

"Drink, Mya."

I did, gratefully. The water slid down my dry throat. The first swallow hurt, but the ache left by the third gulp.

"Good," the voice said, taking the drink away. "Are you hungry? I have chicken noodle soup."

"No."

The arm eased me back to the bed, and I slept.

AWARENESS CAME IN SLOW INCREMENTS. The low murmur of voices. The soft pillow behind my head. The clatter of dishes.

The smell of chicken noodle soup had me opening my eyes. I blinked twice, not sure if I still slept.

Blankets covered the room's two windows, muting the light. I could still see well enough. I lay on a bed in an actual bedroom. A ceiling fan hung above me, its blades unmoving and the light off.

The memories of the last few weeks crawled through my mind. Earthquakes, hellhounds, people becoming infected, looking for my family, finding Drav, the bombings, going to Drav's world. All of it swirled in a confusing jumble until the memories settled and clicked into place to complete a big picture. I'd almost died trying to get to the surface. Not just me. Drav.

A man walked into the bedroom. He bore healing scratches on his face and arms.

"Molev," I said. Panic and worry started to rise. "Where's Drav? Where are we?"

"I'm here," Drav said from behind me. A weight moved on my waist. I reached down and touched his arm under the blankets as I turned my head to look at him.

"We are in a house on the surface," Molev said.

I barely heard. I couldn't stop staring at Drav. He still bore signs of his hellhound attack, but his eyes were no longer swollen, making it easy to see the earnest worry with which he watched me. A scar ran from the top of his left eyebrow, over the bridge of his nose, to his right cheek.

I lifted my hand and gently caressed the new mark. My eyes watered for what he'd endured to save me and for what I felt for him.

"Hey, handsome," I said softly. "Don't throw me like that again. I thought you'd died."

He leaned forward and pressed a kiss to my temple. I frowned at the vague memory of a dream.

"Did I have a washcloth on my forehead?" I asked.

"Yes. You had a fever."

"Thank you for taking care of me."

"Would you like this soup?" Molev asked, reclaiming my attention. "I warmed it on the stove."

My stomach growled, answering him. I shifted my feet under the covers and wrinkled my nose. They'd tucked me into bed, fully clothed. Shoes and all.

As much as I didn't want to leave Drav or our warm bed, the shoes bothered me.

"How about we go to the kitchen?" I asked.

Molev retreated toward the door as I pulled the covers back and sat up. The abrupt change from laying down to sitting up caused my head to swim, and I waited a moment for the sensation to pass before swinging my legs over the edge of the bed.

"How do you feel?" Drav asked. His warm hand soothed my lower back.

"Weak, but my head doesn't hurt. Ugh! Why do I smell like puke?" I stood and looked down at my stained shirt. I vaguely recalled throwing up during our race from his world.

"Do we still have my bag? I need a new shirt."

"There are some in here," Molev said, opening a door to a small closet.

An assortment of men's button up shirts mixed in with several lady's dresses. Not in a position to be picky, I took one of the long-sleeved dress shirts from the hanger.

"Your bag is here." He pointed to the bag on a nearby chair. "I did not touch your things."

"No one did," Drav said.

"Thanks. Can we meet you in the kitchen?" I asked Molev, hoping he'd get the hint and leave.

He smiled slightly and retreated from the room, taking the mug with him. My stomach rumbled again, and I hurriedly ditched the dirty shirt and put on the clean one. I briefly thought of washing myself up, but just standing was taking more effort than I cared to admit to myself.

Yawning, I went to my bag and checked for my phone. It was there but dead. I pulled out the charger and plugged it in. As soon as I could, I needed to try my brother's number.

When I turned, I found Drav sitting on the edge of the bed and watching me.

"You worried me," he said as he stood.

He wrapped me in a loose hug. The feel of his strong arms gave me a sense of peace. Of safety. I rested my head on his chest and closed my eyes. He held me closer, his hand pressing my lower back so we were flush, front to front. The contact made me shiver and remember our time at the lake. Had that only been a few days ago?

He pressed a kiss to the top of my head and loosened his hold slightly.

"You stopped breathing several times," he said, quietly.

Holy shit.

"I did?" I looked up and met his tormented gaze.

"Yes. You moaned and cried once we brought you up here. I wanted to take you back."

"I'm glad you didn't. I do feel better now."

He leaned in and brushed his lips over mine before setting his forehead against mine.

"You are still the best thing here."

His quiet confession made me ache for all the worry he'd endured.

"And you make my heart race in the best way," I admitted.

My stomach growled again. This time he released me fully and took my hand.

"Come. You need to eat."

I almost told him that I'd changed my mind and wanted to go

back to bed, but I didn't want him to worry more. Instead, I let him lead me from the room. The short hall led past another bedroom with twin beds. Blankets covered the windows in that room, too, leaving just enough light to see Kerr and Shax each laying on a bed, their eyes closed.

We quietly continued along the hall and down the steps. At the bottom, Drav turned left. I followed a few more steps to the kitchen. My hands shook, and my legs felt weak.

The mug of soup waited on the table along with a multitude of open cans.

"How long have we been here?" I asked as I sank into a seat.

"Several hours."

"That's it?"

I looked at the cans again. Food remained in some of them. Like the can of peas. Others, like the tin of quail eggs and the cans of tuna, were completely empty.

"It looks like you guys ate well."

Molev walked into the kitchen just then, followed by the others I recalled running with Ghua.

"Thank you for keeping me safe and bringing me to the surface," I said.

The men nodded in acknowledgement and continued to watch me.

I lifted the mug of soup and took a sip, not as uncomfortable with their scrutiny as I once had been. My stomach cramped greedily with the first swallow

"This is really good. I needed to eat."

They remained quiet as I consumed the rest of the soup. Once I set the mug aside, Molev sat next to me. I fought to stifle a yawn and lost.

"What's the plan now?" I asked. "Are we safe from the infected and the hellhounds here?" I no longer felt safe in a house after seeing how the hellhounds had brought down the men in the caverns. I looked around the kitchen, wondering what, other than blankets, they'd done to make this place safe for us.

"We wait for the others to join us then help you search for your family," Molev said. "Do you think there are more women who are still healthy like you?"

"I hope so." I yawned again. "How long will it take them to get here?"

"Another day, perhaps. Your skin's color is changing," he said.

The abrupt change in subject had me glancing at Drav. He looked worried as he studied me.

"What do you mean?" I asked.

"It is losing its pinkness," Drav said.

"You mean I look pale?"

"Yes. Very pale."

"Yeah, I think coming downstairs might have been pushing it."

"Then we will return," Drav said. Before I could protest, he picked me up and moved toward the stairs.

"You're limping. I can walk up the stairs on my own. Or have someone else carry me. I don't want you to hurt yourself."

He reached the top step before I finished speaking.

"Stubborn," I mumbled.

"Desperate to hold you."

I set my head against his shoulder and sighed.

"Ditto."

He set me on the mattress, and I quickly kicked off my shoes. I felt a twinge of guilt that we'd messed up the sheets but knew we'd be moving on soon enough anyway, and no one would likely stay in the house again anytime soon. Before I lay down, I checked my phone. It had a charge, but no signal. I hadn't really thought it would. Turning it off, I settled into bed.

Drav snuggled in beside me and covered us.

"Sleep, Mya."

I closed my eyes.

WHEN I NEXT WOKE, the light from behind the blankets had faded considerably. Drav lay beside me, sleeping peacefully. I reached up and gently touched his healing cheek. His fingers twitched over my bra clad breast, and I smiled. Even looking like a homeless woman and smelling faintly of vomit, he wanted me. I melted a little knowing just how much.

Wanting him to rest, I eased from the bed and tucked the covers back around him before sneaking from the room.

My growling stomach led me down the hall, past where Shax and Kerr still rested. At the bottom of the steps, I turned to the right and peeked into the living room where Molev lay sleeping on the couch.

As I looked at the fading light sneaking in from behind the blanket covered windows, vague flashes of memory intruded. Images of hounds chasing us and only the flashlight from my bag keeping them at bay. I shook my head and focused on the growing dusk. Night approached, and that meant the hellhounds would return if they were still around. Blanket covered windows wouldn't be enough to keep them out.

The men looked like hell and needed more rest. I could give them another hour before I needed to wake them.

Heading to the kitchen, I jumped in surprise at seeing two fey men sitting quietly at the table, studying closed cans of food.

"Hey, guys," I said quietly. "Are you hungry?"

I reached for one of the cans. Another tin of spam.

"You guys like meat more than the vegetables, so you'll probably like this one." I popped the lid open and handed it over before taking the empty cans to the sink. Underneath, I found a garbage bag and started throwing the trash away while the two men shared the spam. It felt good to move. To do something useful even if there wouldn't be any garbage man to pick the bag up. I figured it didn't hurt to tidy up. Cleaning beat just leaving a mound of used cans on the table for the duration of our stay.

When I finished with the empties, I looked at what remained. The fey hadn't wasted too much. Dumping an assortment of vegetables into a large bowl, I stuck it into the microwave, for the first time noticing the rumble of a generator coming from somewhere outside.

The microwave beeped, and I sat at the table with the guys and started eating the mix of random canned veggies. It didn't taste the best, but given the number of closed cans still on the table top, I wasn't going to be a picky brat. The food was cooked and not going to kill me. Down the hatch it went.

Before I finished, the stairs creaked. Drav's worried gaze found mine.

"Why did you leave?" he asked.

I lifted my spoon. "Hungry."

"You need meat."

"Heck no. I know how you serve up meat."

"I will bring more cans so you can choose something you like."

"That's okay. I'd rather you sit down and tell me what's happened since we reached the surface. I think I might have been awake for some of it, but I'm not sure."

He sat in the chair beside me, resting his hand on the back of my neck. His fingers teased my skin as he spoke and I ate.

"We ran north. A pack of the hounds caught up to us just after we left the broken buildings of the city behind. There were too many to keep away with just our weapons and hands, so we used your flashlight until we saw more light in the distance. That light led us here."

"Yeah, I can hear the generator running outside. Were there people here?"

"Yes. Four. With guns."

Surprise lifted my brows, and I struggled to swallow my mouthful of veggies.

"Really? You didn't kill them, did you?" I asked.

"No. They shot at us, but we ignored their challenge and did not remove their heads."

One of the other men said something, and Drav grinned.

"Yes. We are regretting not removing their heads."

"Why? Where are they? I hope you took away their guns."

"The men are tied to chairs in the barn," he answered. "The guns are hidden there with them."

More of my scattered memories solidified. Gunshots. Worried whispers. Swearing.

"I want to talk to them," I said, setting my food aside.

"Are you sure? They usually don't say more than 'fuck off' and spit at us."

I stood. "I'm sure. Let me shower first so they don't mistake me for one of the infected." Other than the clean shirt, I looked like hell. Blood still spattered my jeans.

"Do you need help?" Drav asked, standing.

Although the last time we'd been in the water together had been fun, I knew I didn't have the strength for that.

"Nope. Just my bag."

I expected a frown of disappointment. However, he only nodded and threaded his fingers through mine before leading me back upstairs.

CHAPTER TWO

AFTER DRAV BROUGHT MY BAG, I CLOSED MYSELF IN THE NEAREST bathroom and started the shower. Hot water almost immediately rained down on the old porcelain tub. Eagerly stripping from my clothes, I wrinkled my nose at the dirty spot on the top of my foot.

"You're so nasty," I said to myself.

I opened the linen closet and grinned. A stack of wrapped toothbrushes, razors, and new deodorants sat next to bottles of shampoo, boxes of bar soap, and tubes of new toothpaste. Way too many of the same kind of supplies neatly stacked together to belong in a normal house.

Leave it to Drav to find the home of some kind of prepper. Shaking my head, I grabbed a razor, toothbrush, and toothpaste.

The shower felt like heaven. Water beat down on me, washing away the remaining aches. I soaped my hair, then scrubbed every inch of my body. The mark on the top of my foot didn't come off. I figured it might be a bruise, but it didn't really hurt. Shrugging it off, I shaved then rinsed.

By the time I finished, I felt like a new person and grinned at myself in the mirror until I noticed a mark near my collar bone. It appeared to be the same greyish purple as the one on the top of my foot and, like the other spot, didn't hurt when I pressed on it. I dried, did a slow turn in front of the mirror, and found another spot on my lower back.

"Drav?" I called.

"Do you want me to come in?" he asked from the other side of the door.

I wrapped the towel around my torso before saying yes. When he entered, his gaze swept over me, lingering on the exposed parts. I could feel myself flush, and my stomach danced distractingly. I let my gaze sweep over the grey skin of his familiar face. The healing scars didn't change my level of attraction one bit. I still wanted him for keeps.

"I have something weird to ask. Can you put your hand by my foot?"

He immediately squatted down and did as I asked. When he looked up at me—well, not quite at me, more like my crotch—his gaze heated. Before I could say anything, he pressed a kiss to my exposed knee. My concern about the grey patches of skin faded as a tingle spread. He kissed my thigh, right where towel and skin met, then buried his face in the towel over the V of my legs.

My knees went weak, and I gripped the sink with one hand.

"Was this just to get me close to your pussy? Can I kiss it again?" he said, pulling back to look up at me.

"Geez!" I clapped a hand over his mouth. "Can you stop saying that word?"

"Kiss?" he questioned, the word muffled by my hand.

"No. And I'm not saying it. And no, I wasn't asking you to squat down so we could make out. I'm not sure I've recovered enough for that."

His hand snaked up the outside of one leg and back down again, tempting me beyond belief to reconsider. I cleared my throat and focused.

"I'm worried, Drav. Look at your hand and that spot on my foot. They look close to the same color, don't they?"

He glanced down again and rubbed his thumb over the mark before meeting my gaze.

"They do."

"That's what I thought. I think I was changing, like you had, but wasn't strong enough. Maybe because I have no magic. I don't know. But, I do know I was dying. No matter what, I can't go back down to your caves. I think I got out just in time."

Drav frowned, his thumb sweeping over my skin again and again.

"We will not go back," he vowed.

I smiled slightly.

"Thank you. Do you want to shower while I get dressed?"

Before I even finished, he stood and dropped his pants.

"You are shameless," I said, looking my fill. "Not that I'm complaining."

He leaned down and kissed me gently. My heart fluttered, and I lifted my hand to his shoulder to steady myself. A puckered bit of skin under my fingers had me pulling back instead of pressing in for more. Dirt and grime covered him as much as it had me. And blood. A lot of dried blood.

"Get cleaned up. I'll be waiting for you in the bedroom."

Only after I said the words did I realize how they might sound. He stepped into the shower, his hot gaze not releasing me until he closed the curtain and turned on the water.

With a deep calming breath, I picked up my bag and, in just the towel, left the bathroom. Molev saw me in the hallway, his curious gaze traveling the length of me.

"Not happening, Molev," I said. "Towel stays on."

He chuckled and stepped into Kerr and Shax's room while I entered the one I'd shared with Drav. Seeing Molev had helped remind me of the task at hand. I needed to talk to the men the fey had in the barn. Dusk was falling, and I didn't know how safe we were here.

After closing the door, I dug in my bag, looking for a fresh pair of underwear and a clean pair of jeans. Fate spared me with the underwear, but not the jeans. I took what I could get, found a pair of sweats in one of the dressers and a t-shirt in another. Still looking like a hobo, but a clean one, I gathered up my clothes and went in search of a washer, hoping we would be able to stay long enough to use it. If not, I'd raid houses along the way.

When I finished, I returned to the bedroom and found Drav dressed and waiting for me.

"Ready?" he asked.

I nodded and squeaked when he scooped me up into his arms.

"I can walk," I said.

"Yes. But I like carrying you."

"Yeah, I know. Cuz I jiggle."

He pressed a soft kiss to my lips that made me yearn for more.

"And I don't want you to lose your pink coloring again," he said.

He left the room and carried me downstairs. With Molev, Shax, and Kerr close behind, we left the house.

Dusk had already come and gone. The brightness from several portable stadium-type lights, which I'd mistaken for daylight, illuminated the fenced-in yard and barn. Curled barbed wire topped the chain link fence, and I shivered.

This wasn't the home of a prepper. This went way beyond prepping. The people who owned this place were not messing around. The additional height of the barbed wire above the fence brought the top close to level with the second story windows. Definitely taller than normal. Hopefully, the fence and the light would be enough to keep the hellhounds out.

Drav stepped over to the large, red-painted barn. Deep furrows marked the boards facing the house. Hellhounds. Shit. I hoped that was before the fence and lights went up.

"You put the humans in here? You didn't hurt them, did you?" I asked.

"No. They would like to kill us and challenge us continually. We've ignored them and kept them safe for you but are willing to accept their challenge if you are not against the idea," Molev said.

Whoever had been here first had really rubbed the fey the wrong way.

"I'm against it."

"You can let me down, Drav. I promise on the way back you can carry me."

Drav grunted but set me down as Kerr and Shax stepped forward to open the large door. Enough of the light filtered in to reveal a large filled space. It wasn't until I fully entered that I understood what type of place the fey had found. Not a home of hoarders or preppers but a secured location for a group of looters.

Pallets and racks full of supplies created two columns of aisles extending into the shadowy depths of the building. My eyes widened as I walked over to the nearest pallet of neat layers of bathroom supplies stacked one on top another. My thoughts went back to my shower and all the supplies in that cupboard.

Wood scraped against the floor, drawing my attention to the four men tied to chairs just inside the door. Based on appearances, they ranged in age from Ryan to my dad. All four watched us with varying levels of fear and hostility. I couldn't blame them. They didn't know Drav's people and being tied to chairs by them certainly didn't make a good impression.

"Hi," I said.

One man curled his lip back in distaste while the rest of them remained silent. I stepped closer, and Drav reached out to stop me from approaching the men.

"No, Mya."

"It's okay."

He didn't seem convinced but released his gentle hold on my

arm. I moved toward the men, giving them a friendly smile. One turned his head away, refusing to look at me.

"I'm trying to find my family. We lived in Oklahoma. I was away at university when the hellhounds attacked. I got one call from my brother in the brief window when they turned on communications for the bombing warnings. He said my family had been evacuated to a safe zone, but he didn't know where. I need to find them."

The man in front of me scooted back in his chair, sitting a little straighter. A surge of hope grew inside of me. His lips twisted before he opened his mouth and spat at me.

Drav picked me up and moved me further back, growling a warning at the man.

"Challenge her again, and you will deal with me," Drav warned.

The man scowled at us but remained quiet.

"Please," I said, trying again. "Where are the safe zones?"

"Fuck off, slut," one said.

That's why they were spitting at me? Because I was with the fey?

"You fuckers brought back those damned hounds," another said hotly. "The bombing nearly wiped them out."

Guilt nipped at me. The bombings had successfully driven the hounds from the surface. Yet, herding them back to Ernisi wasn't any fairer to the fey than siccing the hounds on the humans.

"The hounds would have returned no matter what." I glanced at the supplies crowding the inside of the building. "This can't all be just for you. Please, tell us where we can find a safe zone. These guys can help with the hounds."

"Help with the hounds?" the one who'd spit sneered. "Like the two who helped drive the infected in here?"

"What two?" I asked, glancing at Drav.

The rude man on the chair made a sound of disgust.

"Get a little demon cock, and you think they can help?" he said.

"They're all the same. Killers. It's better to die than to let one of them touch you."

Anger flushed my cheeks. I understood the men were scared and lashing out with their crude words, but knowing that didn't make them any less hurtful.

"You're going after the wrong people, here. I'm not the enemy. These guys aren't the enemies. The hellhounds spreading the disease that created the infected are the real enemies."

"If these guys aren't the enemy, then why are we tied up?" the younger one asked, a slight quaver in his voice.

"Because you shot at them. They aren't stupid. They know you'd do it again in a heartbeat, given the chance."

"Damn straight, demon whore. We know our side," the older one said.

Drav's grip around my waist tightened, and his free hand curled into a fist.

"What is the point of all this slut shaming and name calling? What do you think it's going to accomplish? You're wasting time and proving you're an asshole. That's it."

"You are changing colors again, Mya," Molev said. "Maybe it's time for you to return indoors and rest some more."

I debated leaving. So far, the men had acted exactly as Drav and Molev had said. All they did was spit and curse. I couldn't force them to talk. Letting them calm down seemed like the smarter thing to do. Hopefully, they would see the fey men posed no threat, given time.

"You're right," I said to Molev. "I should rest."

Before Drav could pick me up, a new sound rose over the rumble of the generator. The oldest man stilled, and a smile crossed his lips at the roar of an approaching engine. A tingle of worry erupted in my stomach.

"Are there more of you?" I asked.

He continued to smile slightly and remained silent.

Turning my back on the bound men, I went to the barn entrance where Shax was standing. I was glad he made it out of the caverns whole, his hair still intact.

I patted his arm and smiled up at him as I walked past.

"Mya, it might not be safe," Drav said from right behind me.

Outside, a big black truck idled on the other side of the gate. My heart slammed in my chest at the sight of a shadowy, long line of people further down the road. The mass moved with single-minded purpose toward the truck. Infected. The idea of a truck full of more gun-toting humans did worry me, but not as much as leaving the humans to fend for themselves outside the gate with those oncoming infected.

I opened my mouth to say we needed to let the truck in when the driver's door swung outward. My mouth stayed open at the sight of Ghua as he walked toward the fence and unlocked it.

"Good. Ghua has returned with the others," Drav said from behind me.

Without preamble, Drav lifted me in his arms and began moving toward the house. I twisted to look at the people still on the road. They didn't stagger and waver like the infected.

Ghua saw me, raised a hand in greeting, then got back into the truck. It rumbled forward up the drive.

"Can you put me down?"

"You said I could carry you back," Drav said, shifting my weight in his arms.

"Yeah, but I want to talk to Ghua. I want to know what it's like out there."

"Barren, except for infected and hounds," Drav answered without stopping. "The men will be tired from traveling in the sun for hours. You can talk to them after they rest."

With the truck out of the way, the fey wearily filed into the yard. My heart squeezed at the sight.

"Tired and probably hungry," I said. "I'm betting that barn has a lot of soup. After you drop me off inside, can you go back for a few cases? Soup will be quick and easy to heat up."

Drav nodded and set me down inside of the house. While I searched for pots in the kitchen, he left to get the food. Molev, Shax, and Kerr came in before he returned.

"Thank you for thinking to feed them, Mya," Molev said. "They are tired from making their way out of Ernisi with the remaining hellhounds chasing after them."

I placed four pots on the stove. It had looked like at least forty men following behind the truck.

"No problem. Can you two go help Drav with the soup? I'm guessing we'll need a lot."

Molev nodded to Shax and Kerr. Those two left, and he sat at the table. A few moments later, the kitchen door opened again, followed by heavy footfalls.

With a wide smile on his face, Ghua stepped into the room. He looked untouched from the hellhound attacks but still tired and dirty.

"Food then rest," Molev said. "Sit and tell us the news while you wait to eat."

Ghua sat, and I went to get him a glass of water. He thanked me, drained the cup, then looked at Molev.

"The hounds have abandoned the crater. That is a good thing for the men who still need to leave the city. They have divided into three more groups. A group of ten is waiting in the old orchard to direct the others to our location. As you asked, a group will remain behind to guard the city."

Molev grunted in acknowledgement. I inhaled, ready to ask Ghua where the heck he'd learned so much English, but the arrival of Drav, Kerr, and Shax with cases of canned soup distracted me. Directing the men to set the cases on the table, I began sorting the cans while Ghua continued.

"Twice while waiting, I saw a lone human. The first one stayed back as if afraid to approach. However, when I went to greet it, I could smell the decay and see the wounds from a hound. The second ran before I could tell if it was one of the intelligent ones or not."

"It sounds like the bombs really did decrease the infected numbers if you only saw two," I said, removing anything tomato based or with peas from the variety of soups they'd brought.

"Yes, in the cities. But, not outside of them. We killed many groups of infected on the way here. The lone sightings were different."

Drav helped me open the cans. I dumped all the chicken based soups into a separate pot from the beef based ones and turned the heat all the way up.

"Any injuries?" Molev asked.

"Yes. Dax and Tor were hurt. Hound injuries from the caverns. They had reached the surface shortly after us. I found them when I went back. They slept in the bed of the truck, under a cover, while we waited."

"They will heal," Drav said, catching the sidelong look I gave his injuries. "So will I."

"I know. The soup is almost ready."

"Ghua, let the men know to come in. They can rest anywhere inside the house, except the bed in the last bedroom. That is for Mya and Drav."

Blushing, I walked away to change over the laundry while listening to Ghua leave. I added a dryer sheet and started the machine, grateful for the generator, before returning to the stove.

Ghua walked back into the kitchen a short while later followed by the first of the men who'd traveled with him.

Once the soups were warm, I pulled out dishes from the cabinets and began ladling out portions. Drav set the first two servings in front of Molev and Ghua before coming back for his own.

Cup in hand, I ladled another serving and swayed unexpectedly on my feet. Drav was right there to steady me.

"You need to rest," he said.

I nodded and handed the cup off to one of the men waiting for his portion.

Drav lifted me into his arms and pressed his lips against my forehead. I set my head on his chest and let him take me upstairs.

CHAPTER THREE

DRAV'S FINGERS STROKED THE SKIN OF MY STOMACH, WAKING ME. Feeling much better than the day before, I snuggled closer and smiled sleepily as his hand drifted lower. Movement on the floor beside our bed reminded me we weren't alone, though. I grabbed his wrist as I opened my eyes and shook my head at him.

He exhaled heavily but stopped his tempting assault. Mutually disappointed, I gave him a quick kiss on the cheek and quietly sat up. At least ten men had found space to sleep on the floor.

Ghua lay right beside the bed on my side. He opened his eyes and looked up at me then winked. I shook my head and tossed a pillow down at him.

"Don't get weirder," I whispered. "Skootch over so I can tip-toe out of here."

Half the men in the room opened their eyes and sat up.

"Sorry." I quickly stood and made a beeline for the door. Drav followed closely behind.

When I glanced back, I saw Ghua move from the floor to my spot in bed. I couldn't blame him. Sleeping on the floor sucked.

In the hall, I stepped around more bodies. Some fey even leaned on the stairs. There were far more men present this morning than there had been when Drav had taken me upstairs. They lay in any open spot. Even in the kitchen. Those who slept in there stirred as soon as I entered the room.

I motioned for Drav to follow me outside and felt bad when his eyes began to water in the early morning light.

"I was thinking I could cook something for everyone. Or at least try to. How many men do you think are here? A hundred?"

"At least."

"Come on. Let's see what we can find in the barn."

Before we even made it halfway across the yard, I heard muffled yells from within the building and hurried my steps. Drav beat me to the door and went through with a growl. I peeked around him and almost laughed.

The four men still sat in their chairs, but gags now stuck from their mouths. The one on the right rocked from side to side, his face beat red in his agitation.

"Hey, guys," I said to the fey standing guard. "What's going on?"

The human men all started yelling behind their gags, and one of the fey began speaking to Drav. Walking up to the rude guy who'd spit at me yesterday, I pulled the gag from his mouth.

"I'm going to fucking shit my pants," he yelled at me.

"Yeah, that wouldn't be cool."

I looked at one of the nearby fey.

"What's your name?" I asked him.

"Anizo, Mya."

"Anizo, will you please untie this man—"

"My name's Bud, bitch."

"—and take him outside so he can relieve himself?"

"Yes," Anizo said.

I turned away from the pair and found Drav glaring at the man who'd just called me a bitch.

"It's not worth getting angry over, Drav. They're scared, and they don't understand. Honestly, tying them to chairs isn't going to help win them over either."

"Nothing you do will win us over, you grey-skinned piece of shit," Bud said with venom.

"For Pete's sake." I turned on the man. "Did you like the gag in your mouth? Do you want to crap your pants? Do yourself a favor and shut your pie hole." I looked at Anizo. "After Bud's done, take the rest outside, too. Don't retie them, but keep a close eye on them." I studied the dirty human men. "If you want, come inside, clean yourselves up, and get something to eat. Do yourselves a favor, though, and stay away from any form of weapon. The fey will see it as a challenge. And, trust me, you'll lose if they decide to take you up on what they perceive as a challenge."

Shaking my head at their continued angry glares, I moved down the aisle of racks until I found one with boxes of mac and cheese.

"Don't touch our fucking food, demon whore," one of the men yelled.

I heard a slight thump of flesh on flesh and shook my head again.

"Idiot," I mumbled under my breath. No doubt, Drav had hit the man. I just hoped he'd held back a little.

Grabbing one of the nearby laundry baskets, I knocked at least fifty boxes of mac and cheese in, then went to look for the spam and tuna fish. Once I had a full basket, I joined Drav, who stood at the end of the aisle, watching the men slowly walk around. Two of them were standing close and whispering.

"Don't be stupid," I said, moving toward the door. "Because the fey aren't."

Outside the barn, Drav took the basket from me.

"Why can we not remove their heads?" he asked, his tone indicating sincere puzzlement.

"Because there are so few healthy humans left. Because you

guys aren't cruel and know now head removal would result in a final death."

Neither of those reasons seemed to be an answer for Drav.

"Because I'm asking you not to," I added.

He grunted, and I grinned.

In the kitchen, those who had been sleeping now milled about. One said something to me that I couldn't understand. I looked to Drav to translate.

"He's wondering if he can help."

I nodded. Others offered to help too, creating the whole "too many cooks in the kitchen" scenario. Not wanting to hurt anyone's feelings but needing to create some space to work, I came up with another idea.

"Actually, I have a different task for anyone willing."

They moved aside as I made my way to the television in the living room. As I'd hoped, a shelf of DVD cases hung from a wall. The titles ranged from kids' classics to adult action films. Selecting one that looked like it would have plenty of words and a family friendly rating, I went to the TV.

The number of men who had crowded into the room made maneuvering a little cozy. Molev now sat up on the couch, freeing additional space for others.

"This," I said, holding up the DVD, "will help you all learn some English." They quietly watched me put the DVD into the player and turn on the television.

"Only I am allowed to change the movie," I said, straightening.

"Why?" Molev asked.

"Movies can be different things. Some are real, but most, like the ones in this house, are make-believe. The only human you've ever really known is me. That means, so far, my behavior has been the sole basis of your opinion of humans. Some of these movies have humans pretending to do things most humans would never do.

We're not going to have an easy time convincing the rest of my kind how good you guys really are. And, I don't want you watching stuff that will have you giving up on the humans before you give them a chance. Because I don't want you to get the wrong ideas about us, I don't want you to watch those kinds of movies. Make sense?"

"Yes," Molev said. The rest echoed him.

"Now, get comfy. Most movies last between an hour and a half to two hours. This one has a lot of pretending in it, but not bad stuff. It's more silly than anything. If you see or hear something that doesn't make sense or seems unbelievable, ask me about it. By the time this is done, I should have something ready for everyone to eat."

Just as I finished speaking, Bud came walking in with Anzio. He glared at me and went to stomp off in the direction of the bathroom.

"Door stays open," I said. "No razors. Just the soap. And if Anzio doesn't trust you, he'll probably open the curtain. You'll get used to it."

Bud mumbled something under his breath and kept going, Anzio close on his heels. I started the movie, which was about a father who accidentally shrunk his children, before going back to a much emptier kitchen. Drav stood by the stove, staring at two large kettles of steaming water.

"Is this right?" he asked.

"Yep. Next, we start opening these boxes."

With the help of a few others, we had a meaty version of mac and cheese ready to feed the multitudes by the time the movie finished.

Molev joined us in the kitchen and waited for me to scoop out three bowls. I handed one to him, one to Drav, and kept one for myself, understanding their routine now. We sat at the table and ate while the rest of the men slowly filed into the kitchen. The ones with the shortest hair stood by the sink and washed plates as the others finished.

Drav, Molev, and I took our time.

"If the humans here don't know where the safe zones are, we'll need to find them on our own," I said to Molev. "I doubt we'll find another setup like this, though. Safety from the hounds...a lot of food..."

He nodded thoughtfully.

"They mentioned two others of our kind," Drav said to Molev.

"You think those are the two who killed the man in your world?" I asked.

Molev let out a long breath. "Yes. It is unfortunate they have not given into a final death up here. We will watch for them as we search for your safe zones."

"The hellhounds and infected will make traveling at night harder with a large group of men and you," he said. "Perhaps we send scouts out during the day. They can look for other humans and report back before nightfall."

"That's a good idea," I said. "We can keep playing movies so the ones who leave will be able to talk a little. Not all humans are jackasses like the ones you found here."

"I heard that, bitch," a voice yelled from somewhere beyond the kitchen. The yell was immediately followed by a solid thump.

"Remember you guys are stronger than humans when you hit him," I called out. "Don't break bones. It's not fair."

"Yes, Mya," a voice returned.

A moment later, Bud walked into the kitchen. The pissed off look on his face hadn't mellowed with his shower.

"Come sit," I said.

He opened his mouth to respond but closed it again when every fey in the room stopped what they were doing to look at him.

Sullenly, he sat in the fourth chair.

"Where are you from, Bud? Around here?"

"I'm not answering any of your questions."

"Why not? You've already proven what an asshole you are. No one is going to contest that. And the answers you have aren't any kind of state secret. I'm just trying to figure out what I missed in the last week or so. How bad were the bombings? Are there any cities left? Any hope for us survivors to rebuild our lives?"

He snorted.

"Rebuild? What do you think you're going to see in your lifetime? A shopping mart open on the street corner? That's not going to happen. That world is dead."

I nodded slowly, understanding what he meant.

"Yeah. It is. How many of us are left?"

"I'm not telling you that."

I rolled my eyes.

"Probably because you don't know. I saw a bunch of guys like you on a bridge north of Oklahoma City. The douchecanoes were taking supplies from people still leaving. Is that how you got all your supplies? Jacking other people's stuff?"

"Hell, no. We cleaned out the evacuated town ten miles from here. Lost two guys to the infected before the bombing. Another one to the two grey-skinned fuckers that came after."

"I'm sorry. They aren't with this group."

He snorted in response to that.

"Are there less infected now, after the bombing?"

"Shit no. At least not that we can tell. Out here isn't so bad, but we still see them on supply runs." He got quiet for a minute, looking down at the table. I waited and was rewarded when he looked up at me with just a pinch less anger in his gaze.

"Our men should have been back by now. If you're sending these guys out, I want to go and look for them."

"Honestly, that would be helpful. But, you wouldn't get a gun or any other kind of weapon. Do you still want to go?"

The anger returned.

"Do you think I'm some kind of idiot? I'll die out there with nothing."

"I haven't had a weapon since this started. Do I look dead?"

He glared at me and looked pointedly at my boobs. Drav growled beside me.

"He wasn't looking at me with interest," I said, patting his hand. "He's hinting that you guys have only kept me safe because I'm a girl, which is true." I focused on Bud again. "That also means they will keep you safe because I'm asking them to. Well, safe as long as you don't do something that puts them in danger."

"Why do you love them so damn much?" the man asked with contempt.

"Haven't you figured it out yet? Beyond the fact that they're actually nice, they are our only hope against those hellhounds. Have you ever seen one die? No," I said answering for him. "Because they're that hard to kill. But these guys know how to fight them without dying themselves."

At least, I hoped they did.

CHAPTER FOUR

"FINE. I'LL GO," BUD SAID.

After that, I listened to Molev give orders, in English, to the men who wanted to go out.

"Hey, Bud, would you happen to have a dozen pair of sunglasses?"

He stared at me like I was insane. I held his gaze until he relented.

"We might have some," he said.

"Good." I looked at the nearest fey men. "Can you bring Bud out to the barn? He will show you where to find the glasses. They'll help with the sunlight."

The fey who were willing to scout for the day led Bud through the kitchen door. I stood and pulled back the blanket to watch them through the window. Bud's friends were being escorted to the house. The two groups stopped for a minute as the humans spoke to each other. I nibbled at my lip, uncomfortable with the mistrust swelling inside me.

Bud and his friends could plot all they wanted, and it wouldn't likely do any good. But, the fact they still wanted to plot sucked.

That meant we weren't doing a very good job of finding any common ground. I wished I would have been awake when we'd arrived. The tension would have been lower by now if the men hadn't spent a day and a night tied to chairs.

The human men looked at the house then back to Bud and nodded before they resumed walking toward the house.

"We should tell the scouts to watch for a new, safe place further north of here," I said, returning to my chair. "We'll need to keep moving as we look for the safe zones. I think staying in one place for too long will be dangerous."

Molev grunted in agreement just before the men entered. The youngest of them immediately glanced at the small portion of leftover food in the pot on the stove.

"You're welcome to it. Or you guys can make something else if you want. Shower. Use the toilet. Do whatever you need to do." I hoped my offer to let them in the house would help gain their trust.

The men didn't say anything, but one separated from the rest and went to the bathroom. The other two stood near the sink, considering the leftover food.

"What are your names?" I asked.

"Fuc—"

Molev and Drav growled. The fey watching the movie in the living room grew very silent.

"Might want to watch your language," I said. "They understand."

"I'm Jerry," the silent, younger one finally said.

The guy with the sailor mouth glared at the kid.

"Learn to keep your mouth shut," he growled.

The third human returned to the kitchen, and sailor mouth left the room in a temper.

"Friendly," I said with an eye roll. "I'm Mya." My hope to start willing introductions was rewarded.

"Tucker," the new arrival said.

"And your friend with the temper?"

"Butch."

"Thanks. Is there anything you can tell me about other survivors?"

Jerry and Tucker exchanged looks. When both remained silent, I stood up from the table.

"Think about it. I have to change over the movie."

Drav stood and walked with me to the living room. Most of the fey were sneaking glances at the guys in the kitchen. While I protected the fey from negative influence with the movie choices, there wasn't much I could do about real life negative influences. And, I hated that.

Plucking another movie off the shelf, I faced the men crowding the living room.

"Any questions so far?"

"Is there really a machine that will shrink people?" one asked.

"No. Not that I know of."

"Do all married people have children?" another asked.

"No. Some choose not to."

"Will you and Drav have children?"

"Okay. Time for the next movie," I said quickly, turning around once more to change the disk out.

Just as I moved toward Drav, Butch stepped out of the hall from the bathroom and bumped into me. I stumbled a step. Drav steadied me with an arm around my waist at the same time something thudded.

I glanced up to see one of the fey pressing Butch into the wall. Butch's eyes widened further as the gray fist wrapped around his t-shirt and lifted him to the point his toes barely touched the floor.

"Ease up," I said. "It was an accident."

The fey didn't step back. I absently brushed away Drav's hold and went to the fey.

"It was just an accident," I repeated. "Not a challenge or a disrespect or whatever. No harm done, I promise."

The fey reluctantly released Butch. From the look he gave the man, the fey still itched for a fight.

"Go join the others in the kitchen," I said to Butch.

Butch glanced at me, then the fey I had coaxed off of him, before nodding and heading to the kitchen.

"Mya? What is this?"

I turned toward the unfamiliar voice to find an almost bald fey holding up a clean pair of my underwear.

"I took it from the machine that stopped making noise," he said.

I snatched the garment out of his hand, fighting not to turn red. Drav watched me closely, probably trying to determine if the fey had upset me. The last thing I needed was more man-drama, though. So when I answered, I kept my tone free of the annoyance and embarrassment I felt.

"That's my laundry. Thank you for letting me know it's dry."

The fey nodded and retreated to the kitchen. Drav frowned after the man.

"I'm going to go upstairs and put my stuff away. I'll be back down in a bit. Keep an eye on things for me and make sure there's no fighting," I said to Drav, but the entire room answered with a "yes, Mya."

I grabbed my laundry from the dryer down the hall then went upstairs. With the departure of the scouts and the movie playing, I found our bedroom blissfully empty. Exhaling slowly, I closed the door and pulled the blankets off the windows.

Sunlight streamed into the room and warmed my skin. I stood there, looking out without really seeing the barren trees beyond the backyard's fence. The impossibility of the task before me weighed heavily on my shoulders. How would the fey and humans ever find common ground?

If the vision I had was true, the fey had as much right to this world as the humans, if not more. Although the release of the hellhounds had caused the zombie apocalypse, the fey weren't to blame. At least, not these fey. And, we couldn't even fully blame their ancestors. Our damn mining broke the barrier and released the creatures the exiled fey had inadvertently created. I saw the injustice in all of it, but would the rest of my race?

After a moment, I became aware of my idle staring at the woods, and my gaze shifted to the right. My stomach plummeted when I saw something other than a tree. The woman dressed in a torn, dark brown business suit almost blended with the surrounding barren forest. The mangled stump of her right hand pressed against the nearest trunk as she stood there. The utter stillness of the infected sent a shiver of fear racing down my spine. She reminded me of the woman stuck in her seatbelt, waiting for someone to get close enough. This one waited just outside the fence. How long had she been standing there? Had removing the blankets from the window caught her attention?

"Drav?" I called.

The sound of my voice seemed to startle the infected because she took off running. I frowned. They'd never done that before. Noise always drew them closer.

Feet pounded on the stairs.

"What's wrong, Mya?" Drav said, stepping into the room.

"There was an infected outside. Just there," I said, pointing.

I'd barely finished speaking before three fey came into view in the backyard. I pushed the window open and directed them to the spot where she'd stood.

"She was on the other side of the fence. Standing there. Not moving, just staring up at me."

One of the fey remained where she'd been while the other two disappeared. I watched a group of fey search the other side of the fence until Drav pulled me away from the window.

"You are safe, Mya. Let's go downstairs."

"I know I'm safe. It was just really creepy."

"You always find them creepy."

I did, but this time felt different.

We waited in the nearly empty living room with the movie paused. Molev said nothing until the majority of the men returned.

"What did you find?" he asked.

One of the original three stepped forward.

"We found an infected and took his head off. He wasn't alone. There were other tracks. We did not follow those."

"There is no need if they are outside the fence," Molev said.

Before my thoughts could linger on the whole incident, a commotion broke out in the kitchen. I hurried through the door to find a fey and Butch glaring at each other. Kerr's restraining hand on the fey's shoulder had probably saved Butch's life, by the looks of things.

"What happened?" I asked.

"This demon-fuck tried to attack me," Butch said.

"No, Mya," the fey said with an earnest glance in my direction.

"Butch, you obviously did something that challenged him in some manner," I said.

"No, I didn't," he snapped a little too quickly.

"He insulted you, Mya," the fey said.

Behind me, Drav growled. I raised my brow at that but didn't scold him or the other fey. Their protectiveness warmed me.

"He is fucking lying," Butch said.

"Watch your language," I said too late as the fey lunged forward again.

"Stop!"

The men all froze and looked at me. Drav stepped forward and wrapped a protective arm around my waist. No doubt, if the fighting continued, I'd find myself upstairs in the bedroom before I could blink.

"We really need to find a more peaceful way to resolve issues that arise. Molev, I get that your way involves death-match challenges, but you understand why that won't work on the surface, right?"

"Yes," he agreed, giving the fey a hard look.

The man stopped trying to go after Butch, but his open hostility remained. I sighed, wracking my brain for another option.

"Arm wrestling," I said suddenly with a wide smile. "It'll be perfect."

"Are you serious?" Butch said. "What the hell is that going to prove?"

"It's physical and pits the strength of the two opponents against each other. Their current way of handling disputes is to see who can rip the other person's head off first. You want to try that?"

He glared at me. Ignoring him, I focused on his companions.

"Um...Jerry? Tucker? Do you mind showing them what arm-wrestling is while I explain?"

The two men stepped over to the table and sat down. They rested their elbows on the surface and clasped hands. All the fey paid close attention as both men strained for a moment before Tucker's arm gave way and slammed against the table.

"The object of the challenge is to overpower your opponent using only the strength in your arm. If you rip off your opponent's arm, you lose. If you make your opponent bleed or break any bones, you lose."

Butch snorted, obviously not believing either of those scenarios a possibility. For a brief moment, I wished I hadn't said anything and let him find out for himself. However, that wouldn't help the whole demon-human relations thing I was trying to fix.

I continued as if I hadn't heard him.

"If your hand touches the surface first, you lose. If your elbow leaves the table, you lose. And you can't pull your opponent's elbow from the table, either. That's cheating, and you'd lose. The only way to win is what they just demonstrated. Any questions?"

No one spoke up.

"Okay, this will replace your death challenges while you are up here. And, not just against humans," I said with a glance at Molev, "but against each other."

Molev nodded his agreement.

The fey, who'd heard Butch talking about me, took the seat Tucker had abandoned and motioned to Butch. Butch glared but took a seat as well. I could see the determined glint in his eye. He wanted to best the fey. I felt bad knowing I'd set him up with an impossible task. The pair clasped hands like Jerry and Tucker had demonstrated.

Drav's fingers brushed against my skin just under the side of my shirt. I leaned back against him, hoping the fey would use caution with the humans.

Butch glared at his opponent, and it wasn't until I saw the vein in Butch's forehead pop out that I realized they had already started. The fey looked bored and glanced over at me, as if wondering if he should begin. I nodded. He smiled, his fangs flashing, and slammed Butch's hand down on the table. Butch looked dazed, then his face turned red.

"Rematch. I demand a rematch."

The growing heat from all the bodies jammed in the kitchen had me shaking my head.

"Not in here. There's more room out in the barn. I'm sure there's something you can use out there for a table."

Fey and human alike quickly left the house. Even Molev went to watch, leaving Drav and me alone for the first time since waking here.

Drav seemed to have the same thought because he leaned down and brushed his lips against the exposed skin of my neck. I shivered at the sensation and threaded my fingers through his hair, encouraging him. It didn't stop my mind from circling around what had just happened.

"I have to ask...they went from challenging me for eating first to acting all overprotective of me. Why?"

"Because they understand you are the key to finding more women like you. Without you, the humans will not give us a chance." He turned me in his arms. "Does that bother you?"

"Nope. Not even a little. I've gotten to know you, all of you, and see you act with more honor than most humans. Any girl would be lucky to have one of you interested in her."

"Does that mean you're lucky to have me?"

"Very lucky." I stood on my toes and pulled him down for the kiss I'd been wanting since we woke.

He hungrily pressed against me, his tongue sweeping over my bottom lip before dipping inside. He gripped my hips and pulled me flush to his length. I groaned and lifted my hand to his hair, my fingers brushing over the tips of his ears.

He growled and swept me up in his arms, breaking the kiss to bolt upstairs and close us into our room. A shiver of anticipation rippled through me as he set me on my feet and snagged the hem of my shirt, pushing the material up over my ribs. The slow drag of his fingers created a blazing trail of need. Panting, I helped pull my shirt off and backed him toward the bed.

"Ready to learn something new?" I asked, heart hammering.

"Yes."

He sat on the bed and didn't resist when I robbed him of his shirt and pushed him onto his back. His heated gaze remained locked on mine as I placed a knee on the mattress to the right of his hip and crawled forward until I straddled his waist. I let my fingertips graze the dusting of hair just below his navel as I settled my hips to his. He grunted at the contact and experimentally arched into me as his fingers dug into my hips. A zing of pleasure arced between my legs. Part of me wanted to ditch the pants and go straight to the good stuff, but there was so much he didn't know. So much I wanted to show him.

"It gets better," I whispered, bending down to place a kiss on his throat then chest.

His fingers stroked over my skin, skimming down my spine then coming around to try to cup my breast as I slowly made my way down to his belly button. His breathing grew harsher with each press of my lips. Sliding my fingers under the waist of his pants, I guided the material down until he sprang free.

He growled but held still as I brought my mouth to the tip of him.

"Do you want me to stop," I whispered.

He growled louder. I grinned and opened my mouth, barely touching the hot, smooth skin with the tip of my tongue. The feral sound Drav emitted made my heart race. I wanted him as much as he wanted me.

The sudden pounding on our door acted like a cold bucket of water dumped over my head and sent me scurrying for my shirt. Drav roared so loudly, the windows shook.

"What are you doing in there?" Molev called. "Drav said we should not open doors when you close them, but he sounds angry."

Shaking from the adrenaline spike from almost being caught, I stifled my laugh by pulling my shirt over my head. When I emerged, Drav stood before me, his pants still loose. Passion raged in his eyes.

I reached out and tied his waistband again.

"We'll pick this up again when we're alone," I said softly

"No."

"This isn't something most humans do with other people around, Drav. It's meant to be private. Like at the lake. Now isn't the best time." I planted a quick kiss on his chin before stepping back and picking up his shirt to offer him.

His disgruntled expression didn't change as I moved to open the door.

"We were just spending some alone time together," I said to Molev and the few other men standing in the hallway. "Did you want me to start the movie again?"

Molev nodded, his gaze going to Drav, then dipping lower. I flushed and quickly escaped, knowing that Drav's leather pants did very little to hide the evidence of his continued erection.

After getting the fey situated with a new movie, a pouty Drav accompanied me to the barn to search the storage for something to make for lunch.

Most of the fey stood within the open door, trying to avoid the sunlight. Those without the sunglasses Bud had produced before leaving, blinked against the tears in their eyes as they focused on the current arm wrestling match. The three human men were standing back watching, shouting encouragement as the two competing fey struggled.

More of the fey men were lined up to try. I called out a warning, reminding them they couldn't rip each other's arms off, and heard a chorus of "yes, Mya," throughout the barn.

Grinning, I walked down the aisle, looking for something the fey might enjoy eating. I kept remembering how Drav had spit the pizza out.

"How about this?" Drav pulled out a box of instant potatoes.

"That might work. Let's see if we can find some meat and gravy to go with it."

Drav and I gathered a bunch of boxes into the laundry baskets, and I added cans of anything that looked like it would make a good stew. When I looked up and caught Drav watching me hungrily, I knew we needed to head back to the house.

In the kitchen, we set the baskets on the tables.

"How can I help?" he asked.

He brushed my hair back from my face, his hand lingering on my cheek. I brought my hand up to cover his and pressed a kiss to the palm of his hand.

"You already are."

CHAPTER FIVE

THE SUN HAD ALREADY STARTED TO SET BY THE TIME WE HEARD shouts from the front gate. My heart kicked up a notch from where I was snuggled against Drav on the couch.

"The scouting group is back," he said.

"Come on." I stood, anxious to learn what the group had found.

Outside, the gate was just grating open for the line of fey on the road. As the men jogged into the crowded yard, I noted the clean paths on their dusty cheeks, evidence that their eyes had watered throughout the day, despite the sunglasses.

I frowned at the sight of Bud flung over the last fey's shoulder.

"What happened?" I asked over the sound of the gate closing behind them.

"What happened," Bud answered, "is that these assholes wouldn't let me set the pace."

The fey carrying Bud dropped him like an unwanted sack of potatoes. Behind me, I heard a few soft "arm wrestle" comments and almost grinned.

Bud grunted and climbed to his feet with an angry glare.

"You didn't tell me how fast they would want to run. As soon as

I couldn't keep up, one of them tossed me over his shoulder without giving me a choice. I couldn't see shit that way."

"No sign of Will or Tubby?" Jerry asked.

"None," he said bitterly. Bud started off toward the barn and the rest of his men quickly followed. I looked at the nearest fey.

"Would you be willing to follow them? Keep your distance, but watch what they do and listen to what they say, if you can."

He nodded. Three of his friends went with him. Once they left, the group's mood turned from tension to open reunion as those who'd been out scouting welcomed the fey who'd joined us since they left. There had to be close to two hundred of the fey on the surface now.

"Ghua, what news?" Molev asked over the greetings.

"We passed several cities. Some whole. Some destroyed."

"Any signs of humans?"

"No. We did find a new safe place, though, north of here. It's just outside a city Bud knew. He called it Ardmore. The large building has a lot of land with a high fence around all of it. Safe enough to stay for a night or two as we scout further."

I hated the idea of more sitting and waiting just because Bud and his friends wouldn't talk. I glanced at the barn where they'd disappeared inside.

"Did you tell Bud we were looking for a new place to stay?" I asked.

"No. He thought we were looking for humans."

"What are you thinking, Mya?" Drav asked when I continued to stare at the barn.

I sighed. "I'm thinking that it would be dangerous to let those guys know we're leaving or where we're going. I wish they would just tell us if they knew something, but I understand their fear. I'm going to try talking to them again and see if Bud's attitude can be persuaded to change." I put my hand on Ghua's arm. "Thank you for scouting and putting up with Bud. I'm betting it wasn't easy."

Ghua grinned slightly. "His mouth tempted me to leave him to the infected when they trapped us inside the warehouse."

"They what?" I said, dropping my hand.

The image of the infected woman outside my window popped into my head, and a tingle of apprehension shivered over my skin.

"Let's go inside," Molev said. "The scouting party can sit and eat while Ghua tells his story."

Once inside the house, Drav and I scooped out four portions of stew and brought the bowls to the table. We sat to listen to Ghua as the rest of the men began serving themselves.

"How did you get trapped in a warehouse?" I asked.

"The first time we came up here, the stupid ones moved around as if they were lost until they heard something. Then, they ran. The second time I came up to tell everyone to leave the surface, they seemed less lost. This time, they don't seem as stupid."

"When we reached the first town, a line of cars stretched across the road and far into the trees on both sides. Bud moved toward the cars, not seeing the lone person standing in the road further away. Farco reached out to stop him. Before he did, the infected made a noise. It wasn't a word, but a long, loud groan. More infected swarmed from the woods. Only twice our number. We removed their heads while Bud cried and yelled. The infected down the road had disappeared by the time we'd finished."

"That's disturbing," I said. "More than disturbing, really, but I don't know that I would really describe that as being trapped, though."

"We were trapped in the warehouse, Mya, not the street."

The way he said it almost made me grin.

"I'm sorry. Continue."

"After that, we didn't see any infected until we reached Ardmore. Standing alone in the road was the same infected. He wore a red shirt and only had one shoe. He didn't call out this time. Instead, he turned and ran. We followed, chasing him into a warehouse. The door closed behind us. Bud was yelling because it was dark, but we could see and smell. Decay soured the air in the building from the hundreds of infected waiting within. It was good that Bud could not see all of them."

My stomach dropped at Ghua's description, and I sincerely hoped this was like a fishing story. One embellished to make the retelling more interesting.

"What did you do?" I asked, leaning forward, food long forgotten. Most of the men in the kitchen lingered to hear the end as well.

"I considered throwing Bud to them, but we climbed the metal logs supporting the ceiling and ripped open the tin roof."

"Why didn't you just rip open the door?"

"I wanted to see what the infected would do."

"And?"

"They didn't do much. They couldn't climb like we could. After the warehouse, we left the city and found the fenced-in place. The return trip was much quieter," Ghua finished.

"Eat, Mya," Drav said softly, nudging the bowl toward me.

I picked up my spoon and ate a few bites as I considered everything. Although I trusted Ghua's word, he knew very little of humans, uninfected or otherwise. Maybe what he'd thought was a sign of intelligence was just his lack of understanding. Or maybe I just didn't like the idea of smarter infected.

"I need to talk to Bud," I said, pushing the bowl aside.

"Why?" Drav asked.

"I don't like the idea of shuffling around from place to place in a blind attempt to find the safe zones. I'm hoping after a day with Ghua and the others, he might be more willing to share whatever information he knows.

"I'm also thinking about telling him we're leaving. Part of me thinks that's a bad idea. That they'll go running to whoever they'd thought had shown up when Ghua arrived. Yet, the other part of me feels...I don't know. Worried maybe? They have two men out there who haven't come back. How long will four humans last against the infected and hellhounds, even with this fence protecting them?"

"I think you should tell them," Molev said. "If they go to tell other humans, then your people will find us."

"Yeah, that worries me. You saw how they destroyed the cities. I'm worried they will try to do the same to you if we can't find and talk to them on our terms."

Molev shrugged. "I still see no reason to remain quiet. Perhaps they tell other humans, and we find women sooner. Perhaps they come with us, and we must look longer. We cannot know the outcome until we make the choice."

"All right," I said, standing. "I'll go talk to them."

Drav stood, too.

"Together," he said.

"Together," I agreed.

His company came in handy when we walked into the barn to an openly hostile one-sided argument between Bud and the four fey who'd been keeping an eye on the men.

"Is there a problem?" I asked Bud, interrupting his tirade about privacy.

"Yeah, tell them to get lost."

"They're keeping an eye on you because I asked them to," I said, walking toward the aisles of supplies.

"Why, and what are you doing?" he asked, angrily following in my wake. "Leave our supplies alone. You've taken enough."

"You're right. We have." I turned to look at the man. Drav stood inches behind him, the intensity in his gaze a bit awe-inspiring. Bud wouldn't even be able to sneeze in my direction without immediate intervention by Drav.

"We're leaving. Tomorrow morning, if I have my way."

"Good," he said with a satisfied smile.

"Is it? You said you're missing two men. How long do you think just the four of you will be able to stay here on your own?"

"Long enough."

"That's such a macho bullshit answer. The real answer is not long."

"We'll last plenty long if you give us our guns back."

I shook my head, not in denial but annoyance.

"You'll get them when we leave and not before." I glanced past him to his men who watched us and listened. "If any of you want to come with us, you'll be welcomed and protected." I looked at Bud again. "What happened in the warehouse?"

"How the fuck would I know? Those idiots ran into a pitch-black building. I couldn't see a damn thing."

"What about what you smelled or heard?" I asked.

"I didn't smell or hear nothing."

The steady almost daring way he held my gaze told me the truth. Ghua hadn't embellished.

"Right. You weren't stuck in a building filled with infected who only wanted to rip you apart so they could taste fresh human flesh. I get that you're not worried about you. That's fine. But think of everyone else out there. You wouldn't be standing here right now if it weren't for the fey. There are other survivors out there who need their help. Please, tell me where they are."

His eyes narrowed.

"There ain't nothing to tell, demon whore," he said with menace.

Drav growled low behind him, and I had the pleasure of watching Bud pale.

"Fine. We'll see you again in the morning. Enjoy your night," I said, walking past him to Drav. Drav wrapped an arm protectively around my shoulder and led me to the others.

"Keep watch," I said. "All night. I don't trust them." I didn't bother to lower my voice.

Outside, Drav scooped me up into his arms.

"Why do they keep calling you something you are not?" he asked, pressing his forehead to mine.

"They use insults to try to make me as angry as they are. By staying calm, I'm robbing their insults of any power. Next time, ignore them. It will make you the bigger man."

"I already am the bigger man."

I grinned knowing he meant that literally.

"Let's go to bed, big guy. We have a long day ahead of us tomorrow. There's no reason to stay here if everyone who's coming from the caves has joined us. It's time to start seriously looking for my family."

No one stopped us as we made our way to the bedroom. Most of the men already lay wherever they could find an open spot. Ghua once again rested on the floor beside our bed.

Drav didn't say anything about all the bodies crammed into the room. He just set me on the bed and snuggled close. I toed off my shoes and closed my eyes.

Tomorrow, for better or worse, we would leave this place.

CHAPTER SIX

The smell of bacon tickled my nose. I sat straight up in the mostly dark room and inhaled deeply, not believing what I smelled.

"No way."

I bolted from the bed, and like a pro hurdler, I cleared the bodies on the floor. Drav called my name as I sprinted down the steps, waking up the men along the way with my racket. The sun hadn't yet kissed the horizon so I whispered "go back to sleep" as I passed.

Rounding the corner to the kitchen, I found Jerry at the stove, guarding three pans full of the greasy meat. Molev watched from the table.

"That smells like heaven," I said, moving close to Jerry. "Where did it come from?"

"The freezer on the back porch. It's full of meat."

"Damn."

"Bud was glad you didn't notice it. But I figured if you're leaving today, you might want something that reminds you of home." He shrugged as if what he'd done was no big deal.

I studied him, noting the worry in his face. Likely for me. He knew what to expect out there. He'd been living it for weeks. And, I had no real idea, but I did know the fey would keep me safe.

"Come with us," I said softly. "You spent all day with these guys yesterday. You had to learn a little bit about them in that time. They're no better or worse than us. They have faults, but they have strengths too."

"I know. I'm not staying because I don't trust them. I'm staying because my friends need me. We've lost too many already, and I can't do that to them." He set his fork aside. "Now that you're awake, I better get back out to the barn before Bud notices. He's been arm wrestling most of the night." A slight grin followed that statement.

"Thanks for the bacon," I said, watching him as he walked away.

Drav entered the kitchen to the sound of the door closing behind Jerry.

"Good morning, Mya. Is this the food you crave?" he asked, standing behind me and wrapping his arms around my waist.

"Oh yeah. Bacon and eggs. I never thought I'd eat that again."

He watched me nudge the bacon around the pans while I waited for the salty meat to finish cooking. Once it was crisp enough, I removed all of it from the pans and set a heaping plate full on the table. Neither Drav nor Molev seemed too impressed when they tried a piece. I didn't mind. It meant more for me.

Men slowly trickled into the kitchen and tried bits of the bacon before going outside.

"We're leaving this morning, right?" I asked, looking at Molev.

"Yes. According to Ghua, we should be able to reach the building before the sun is too high."

"Good. The humans are going to stay here. We can't leave them defenseless. Where are their guns?"

"In the back of the barn next to the sacks of rice."

"In plain sight?"

"Yes."

"How did you know they wouldn't find them and try to use them?" I asked.

"Someone was always with them. They wouldn't have gotten close."

I didn't argue, but he probably saw the doubt on my face.

"I'm going to head upstairs, shower, and pack. It shouldn't take me too long to be ready."

Drav followed me upstairs.

"You should see if any of the clothes in these dressers fits you. It doesn't hurt to have something clean to change into," I said as I set my bag on the bed. While he looked through drawers, I pulled a clean set of clothes out of my bag.

He didn't say anything when I left the room.

In the bathroom, I brushed my teeth and looked at myself in the mirror. I didn't look different. Not really. But I felt so different. Older. More tired. More determined, with a clear goal. Find my family and a way for all of us to rebuild our world, together.

Turning from the mirror, I started the shower and stripped. Not wanting to waste time, I stepped into the chilly spray and began washing. Physically, I felt recovered from my time in the caverns, which was a good thing. Even though Drav would likely carry me the whole way to the new place, I would still need my strength and wits about me in the days to come. Because, while my goal might have been clear, how to achieve it still remained a mystery, especially given the reaction of the humans to the fey.

The water had just begun to warm when the door opened. I rinsed my face and stuck my head out of the curtain to catch Drav in the process of stripping.

"Uh...what are you doing?"

"Showering with you."

My gaze shifted to his erection.

"I'm not sure that's a good idea. Molev wants to reach the

building before the sun gets too high. Showering together is going to slow us down."

"No, it will save time." He swept the curtain aside and stepped in with me.

My pulse jumped at the first brush of his fingers over my water slicked skin. I should have said no, but I couldn't. Not when he took the soap from me and ran his foamy hands over my shoulders in slow gentle sweeps. I closed my eyes and let him wash me, relishing the feel of skin on skin. Each soapy caress over my breasts made my breath catch. He didn't rush, and I didn't want him to. As he washed my chest, he nibbled his way from my collarbone to my jaw. I wrapped my arms around his neck and waited for his lips to meet mine.

Instead of kissing me, he coaxed me to release my hold and turn around. The spray of the shower rinsed my front as his hands slid over my shoulders and down the long line of my back. I held still as his hands swept over the curve of my ass and cupped me, but I ached for more than just a washing.

He reached around me and set the soap on the ledge. Before I could turn to rinse again, his hands gripped my hips, and he pulled me against his chest. One hand anchored me to him while the other slid over my abdomen and down to my curls. I reached up behind me, digging my fingers into his hair.

"I love the sounds you make," he murmured in my ear as he parted me.

I tried not to make sounds. Really, I did. But when his finger brushed over my sweet spot again and again, I came apart with a pained-sounding mewl. I turned my head up to him, and he kissed me hard, capturing most of the sound.

Trembling with aftershocks, I kissed him in return until he pulled away, turned me, and placed his forehead against mine.

"I love you, Mya."

Tears welled in my eyes for the beautiful, sincere man holding me. My heart ached for what I felt for him. Was it love? I thought so. But the fear I had for our future fought so hard to stifle it.

"We better finish up, Drav, before Molev bursts in again."

Drav didn't seem to mind that I hadn't returned his sweetly worded sentiment. When I took the soap and helped him wash, I paid all his parts as much attention as he'd paid mine. Kissing him didn't keep his growls quiet, though.

His release echoed in the bathroom, and I didn't stop touching him until the last shudder wracked through him. He kissed me tenderly, and I was glad I hadn't fought showering together. Even though he'd never left my side, I'd missed him like he had left me. We'd needed this.

Someone knocked on the door.

"We are meeting in the yard," Molev said through the wood.

"Okay. We'll be just a minute," I called back.

Drav kissed me hard then turned off the water. Pushing the curtain open, Drav grabbed the waiting towel and handed it to me before getting his own.

We hurriedly dried and dressed. Well, I dressed. Drav left the bathroom without wearing a stitch of clothing. No one in the hallway seemed to even notice.

Drav put on a clean shirt and the same pants in our room while I brushed and braided my wet hair in the bathroom. We both walked downstairs a few minutes later. Most of the fey had left the house. The few remaining ate soup in the kitchen.

Stepping outside, we found the majority of the fey milling about the yard in the pre-dawn light. Molev called Drav's name, gesturing him over toward the barn where he stood with some other long-haired fey.

"Go. I'll walk around before we have to leave," I said, waving him off and shouldering my bag. He pressed a kiss to my forehead and went to join Molev.

I wandered over to the gate. I didn't think we were that far from

Irving, which meant we had a lot of road to cover to get to the new place. It wouldn't take the fey long, though, at the speeds they traveled.

While the others wandered about, I watched the trees through the fence. Shadows danced among the barren trees, the branches rustling in the wind, creating creaking groans as bark scraped against bark.

The woman from the day before and Ghua's story rose to my mind again. How many infected lurked in those trees lining this road and the next?

Suddenly, I no longer felt so eager to leave.

I stepped back, ready to turn away from the fence when something in the trees caught my eye. A trace of red amidst the brown. I leaned forward, focusing on the spot. There it was again. A small figure moving through the forest. I watched the uneven way it moved, and my heart broke. As much as I wanted it to be a fox or some other creature, I knew it wasn't. A child had become infected and now wandered the woods, forever alone.

The figure stumbled from the trees into the road, tottering closer with each uneven step. Close enough that I could see its tousle of black hair. A little boy, no more than three or four years old, lifted his head. I caught a glimpse of his baby blues as he stumbled then threw his hands out to catch himself.

My hands gripped the chain link gate, and I gasped, not believing what I was seeing. Blue eyes without a trace of cloudiness. The child was not infected, just thin and dirty. How was he still alive out there?

The boy regained his feet and wobbled forward, each step a monumental struggle. I finally saw why. A heavy, thick loop of rope had been tied around his waist. The end trailed after him and disappeared into the trees from where he'd emerged.

Fear gripped me. Who had tied him?

I reached out and grabbed the fey beside me.

"Do you see the human?" I asked, not taking my eyes from the boy.

"Yes, Mya."

"Go get him. But be very gentle. There's a rope around his waist. I don't know why. Hurry and be careful."

The fey jerked the gate open and sprinted toward the boy. The child stopped walking, shocked at the sight of the big grey man coming his way. The toddler's bottom lip wobbled.

The rope behind him moved. The slack began to tighten. Something held the other end.

"Quick," I yelled. "The rope!"

The fey reached the boy and quickly untangled the rope from his tiny waist. A loud gurgle sounded beyond them.

From the trees, a herd of infected emerged, racing toward the fey and the boy. The number of infected spilling from the forest stunned me. Amidst the chaotic movement, one stood still. A woman in a torn and dirty brown business suit. The woman I'd seen outside my window. She held the other end of the rope.

Terror coursed through me as the fey lifted the child into his arms and sprinted toward the gate, barely ahead of the infected.

Across the yard, Bud started yelling, demanding their guns. I hoped the fey were smart enough not to give the humans the weapons.

"Get Mya away from the gate," Drav shouted.

Strong arms wrapped around my waist and yanked me off my feet. As I was carried away from the gate, I couldn't stop watching the scene play out.

The fey and child made it into the yard with the herd of infected right on their heels. Men tried to force the gate closed as the infected crashed against the fencing, the sound of grunts and groans filling the air along with eager yells.

I swatted at the arm holding me.

"Stop. Put me down." The fey listened, but he stayed close to my side.

"Get the kid to the house," I yelled. The man, who still held the boy in his arms, heard me and sprinted in that direction.

The rest of the fey moved toward the fence, ready. On the other side, the infected pushed harder against the metal barrier. One fell. The infected behind him stepped on his back, reaching closer to the top.

Metal groaned. Fear clawed at me as the gate's hinge twisted under the weight of so many infected. Infected spilled into the yard. The nearby fey met them with a brute strength that sent the first infected head flying from its body.

"Protect Mya and the child," Molev's voice called out from somewhere in the fray.

The fey beside me nudged me back toward the house as infected swarmed the men nearest the gate. I couldn't tear my eyes from the fight as fey began to disappear under the swell of bodies pouring through.

Bud continued to yell for weapons. Weapons wouldn't help against these kinds of numbers. Only the fey could.

Not a single infected made it a step in the direction of the house—my direction—because of the number of fey lined up to meet them. The sickening sound of tearing flesh filled the yard. Heads began to sail through the air as the fey pressed forward, clearing infected from those in the front. Heads weren't the only thing flying. With a thunderous yell, one of the fey sent a body flying over the chaos. The limp headless infected landed outside the fence.

In the melee, I saw an infected slip between two fighting fey and go for Bud. I opened my mouth to call out a warning at the same time Bud saw the infected. The man grabbed Butch and pushed his friend toward the creature.

The infected pounced on Butch, and Bud turned to sprint into the barn.

In horror, I watched Butch struggle with the woman. Bodies blocked my view for a moment, and the fey with me nudged me further toward the house. There were still infected pouring in through the gate, though.

"Go help them. I only need one of you. We can't afford to lose any of you. Go!"

Half the fey guarding me broke off to help their friends. I caught sight of Kerr racing toward Butch and the infected that had him pinned against the barn. He ripped the infected away from the man by grabbing the infected woman's hair and shoulder. His biceps bulged as he separated head from body. As Butch slowly slid down the barn's wall, Kerr turned back to the fight.

Within minutes, the fey eliminated the remaining threat. Bodies littered the blood-stained ground, and the fey began tossing infected parts over the fence.

I shuddered at the sight and focused on the men by the barn. Bud had reemerged, and Butch still sat on the ground, a hand pressed to his shoulder.

I strode over to them.

"What happened?" I asked. Blood seeped through Butch's fingers and shirt.

"Nothing, demon-bitch," Bud said.

"He was bit," Jerry said.

"Fucker pushed me," Butch panted, pulling his hand away to reveal the bite on his shoulder.

Gnarled, torn flesh flapped against the remaining skin and blood poured from the wound. I held in my gag and focused on Butch's face. I didn't know what would happen to him. Every person who had turned infected that I'd witnessed since this thing started had been because a hellhound had killed them. But I knew from Charles, a bite from an infected caused the sickness to spread, too.

I squatted down in front of Butch and met his pained gaze.

"How long do you have?"

"Not long," Jerry answered for him.

I reached out to put a comforting hand on Butch's leg, but Drav stopped me with a hand on my shoulder.

"No, Mya."

I hadn't even realized he'd joined us.

"What happens now?" I asked.

"Give us the location of the guns so we can put this fucker out of his misery," Bud said.

I stood and looked Bud in the eye.

"I saw what you did. I wish I had the strength to hit you in the face and break your damn nose." No sooner had the words left my mouth than Drav's fist darted forward and made my dreams come true.

Bud howled in pain as blood poured from his nose.

Ignoring him, I squatted back down by Butch.

"Thank you for that," he said.

His breathing hitched, and he groaned in pain. Drav jerked me back, well out of the man's reach.

A moment later, Butch hunched over. He clutched his stomach and threw up. The other men jumped backwards as bile and breakfast splattered on the ground. Butch kept dry heaving.

"Butch?" Jerry stepped forward, but Tucker stopped him with a hand on his shoulder.

"Don't, there isn't anything we can do."

"FFFFFuuccck," Butch moaned, straightening enough to lean back on the barn.

His eyes watered, and tears fell down his cheeks. My stomach became queasy as I noticed blood coated around his mouth. In a moment, he fell forward onto the ground. He made no noise, and the area around us became utterly silent.

"Butch?" I said.

A muffled groan came from the fallen body at our feet, and slowly Butch got back to his feet. His milky white gaze swept over us, his mouth opening and closing listlessly.

CHAPTER SEVEN

Drav stepped protectively in front of me and immediately removed Butch's head. Crisis averted, he tossed the head to Kerr and turned to me. For a moment, my brain couldn't process how quickly Butch had gone from a person with an attitude to a mindless abomination. There were so few of us. One bad decision, one bite, just took another. At a loss, I stared at Jerry and Tucker as a nearby fey stepped forward and removed Butch's body.

"You wanted to know what the world was like?" Bud demanded in a nasally voice. "What you missed? That is what you missed."

Something flickered in Jerry's gaze. Anger. Maybe hate. I felt the same toward Bud. Without acknowledging the asshat's comment, I addressed Jerry and Tucker.

"You're both still welcome to come with us; but if you decide to stay, watch your backs around him. He'll push you next if it means saving himself."

I turned to go to the house and stopped short at the sight of Drav and Molev standing in front of me. Blood and gore caked their hands and arms.

"You guys are a mess. Do you want to shower?"

"No. It will take too long, and we will probably need to do this again before we reach the next safe place," Molev said.

I nodded slowly and glanced at Drav.

"You're not carrying me like that."

"I'll shower."

We walked together to the house. The sight that greeted me in the kitchen made my eyes water. The fey, with a content look on his face, stood in the center of the room, holding the little boy he had saved. The boy's head rested on the big man's shoulder. One arm looped around the fey's neck, and his little hand gripped the man's braid. He sucked the thumb of his other hand, his tear-streaked face turned toward us.

His gaze kept flicking between me, Drav, and Molev.

"Go get cleaned up," I said to Drav. "The less people in here right now, the better."

Drav went upstairs, and Molev retreated outside once more. The boy sighed gustily, the exhale hitching a bit from his recent crying.

"Hi there," I said softly. "My name is Mya. What's your name?"

He stared at me for a moment before pulling his thumb from his mouth just long enough to say, "Timmy."

"I'm so glad we found you, Timmy. Because this house has a lot of food, and we need some help eating it. Would you like to help me?"

He shook his head no.

"That's okay. I'm just going to make some food, and if it looks good, you let me know."

I went to the sink and wet a clean washcloth, which I handed to the fey.

"For his face and hands if he'll let you. We need to get any infected blood off or he might turn, too."

The fey frowned and took the cloth.

Turning back to the cupboards, I searched until I found some peanut butter, jelly, and crackers. At the last second, I put the peanut butter back and just fixed a plate full of jelly crackers and set them on the table. My luck, the kid would have peanut allergies or something.

The fey still held the washcloth, and Timmy didn't look any cleaner.

"Here," I said, holding out my hand. The fey gave me the cloth.

"What's your name?"

"Byllo," he said.

"Okay. Timmy, Byllo's arms are getting tired. Can you sit in a chair for just a few minutes?"

Timmy lifted his head and looked Byllo in the eyes.

"They are not tired," the man said. "I could hold you forever."

"Not helping, Byllo. What do you say, Timmy? If you sit in the chair, you can have some of those crackers I made."

The boy looked at the table, and his eyes lit up at the sight of the crackers. He wiggled in Byllo's arms, and the man bent to set him on a chair.

"Hold on, Timmy. First, we need to wash your hands and face, right?" The boy held his hands out to me and waited patiently while I wiped them and his face.

"There's a spot on your face this washcloth isn't getting. Is it okay if Byllo lifts you up so you can wash in the sink?

"Yes."

Byllo carefully picked the boy back up and held him steady while Timmy and I worked together to wash his hands and face with soap at the sink. By the time we finished, Timmy's stomach growled continuously.

"While you eat those, I'm going to see what we have to drink."

Based on how the boy looked, he'd been without food for a while, and I worried it would be the same for fluids. I poured a cup of water and set it in front of him.

"Byllo, can you go to the barn and see if there are any cans of evaporated milk and maybe a bag you can use to carry them? Ask Jerry. We'll need some for Timmy."

The fey left. Timmy paused his eating to stare at the door.

"Byllo will be right back," I said, sitting. "He's going to get some stuff so you won't be hungry or thirsty at the next place we stay."

The boy shifted his gaze to me, concern lighting his eyes.

"How old are you, Timmy?"

He held up four fingers.

"That's pretty old. I bet you know a lot of stuff. I know a lot, too. Have you noticed how some people are sick and not acting very nice?"

He nodded.

"My mommy, daddy, and sissy got sick."

"Aw, Timmy..." Struggling not to cry, I cleared my throat and gently smoothed my hand over his head. "I'm really sorry about your family getting sick. Byllo can't get sick. He's strong and fast and very nice. So are all his friends. After you're done eating, we're going to go look for the rest of the people who aren't sick."

"Do I have to wear a rope?"

"No. Never again." I wanted to ask him about that but doubted it would do anything more than scare him. "Would you like some peaches or pears to eat next?"

"Yes, please."

I smiled and grabbed a can of each.

Drav entered the kitchen one slice before Timmy polished off his can of pear halves.

"Drav, this is Timmy. Timmy, this is my friend Drav. He's really nice like Byllo."

"Hello, Timmy," Drav said, approaching us.

"Your eyes are funny," the boy said, staring up at Drav.

"Not funny," I said. "Just different. He can see better at night."

A look of terror crossed the boy's features when I had said night.

"It's okay, Timmy. You'll be with us now. We'll keep you safe." The words barely left my mouth when Byllo came in, followed by Bud, Tucker, and Jerry.

"Like hell you're taking the kid or the fucking supplies. Both stay with us," Bud said.

Timmy stared at him with wide eyes. Byllo set the two cases of evaporated milk on the counter and came to stand beside the boy.

"If the fact that you just pushed your friend into an infected to save your own skin isn't enough of a reason to disqualify you for child care, the fact that you swore is. Leave, Bud, before one of these guys makes you."

Bud stormed out.

"You're welcome to whatever you need," Tucker said. "We'll be pulling out right after you do. We've got a place we can go."

He didn't need to say it was a place where we wouldn't be welcome. I could see that in his eyes.

"I hope you get there safely. Tell them everything, Jerry. And be honest about it."

"I will," he promised before heading out the door.

"We need to leave, Mya," Drav said.

"I know." I looked at Timmy. The boy had a smudge of jelly on his chin. Much better than infected blood.

"You ready, sweetie?"

His nod set in motion a swift departure. Byllo carried Timmy and stayed close to Drav, who carried me. No one spoke as they sprinted out the corpse-riddled gate and down the road. All of the men remained alert as we passed the discarded rope and trees.

The sound of an engine roaring to life behind us made me cringe. After what we'd just gone through, I couldn't help but feel on edge.

Molev motioned to Ghua. Ghua nodded and, along with five others, broke off from the group and slipped into the trees. Staying true to the ingrained need to remain quiet out in the open, I said nothing.

The sun rose and some of the tension left me as miles swiftly passed under the fey's feet. It wasn't just our progress that soothed me, but little Timmy. Having him with us worried me, but it also made me feel so much less alone. I looked over at the boy as he sucked his thumb and dozed in Byllo's arms. The man kept glancing down at the kid, too. He wasn't the only one. They all did with a mix of curiosity and awe in their expressions. I couldn't imagine what it would be like to only know adults and then discover an adorable tiny version existed.

We traveled for almost an hour before Timmy woke and started fidgeting. I called a stop, helped him go to the bathroom, and gave him something to drink. Byllo was right there to pick him up again when it was time.

The boy never really made a sound. Seeing someone that age so subdued felt unnatural. What had the child gone through before we'd rescued him? Still, not a single bite marked him. That, along with the rope, could only mean one thing. The infected had known to use a healthy human as bait.

When we reached the blockade of cars outside of Ardmore, blood smeared the faded blacktopped surface. The wide path of red veered to the left into the trees.

Molev slowed the group, keeping well back from the vehicles, and silently motioned left and right. Twenty men broke off in each direction. Just as they left us, a single person stepped into view further down the road. The creature emitted a creepy as hell sound that made me want to run the other way. In seconds, grunts and groans came from the woods on either side of us. However, nothing emerged.

A creak of metal drew my attention to the line of cars. The trunk of a vehicle slowly opened. The back door of another unlatched.

"Byllo, turn Timmy away so he doesn't see this," I said softly as the first fey man stepped forward.

Molev didn't mess around with the infected crawling from the blockade. He ran forward into the line of cars, pushing the two central ones wide apart. He didn't stop there. Gaining speed, he ran for the infected leader while the remaining fey cleaned out the cars.

After hearing Ghua's story about how they'd been led into a trap, I appreciated Molev's foresight to kill the apparent infected leader immediately. He tossed the head aside and motioned for us as the fey dispatched the final infected from the cars.

The men who'd disappeared into the woods reappeared, dirtier than before. One had a bit of gore stuck to his cheek, and I hoped the new place we were headed had more than one bathroom.

It took hours to reach our final destination. Hours of moving quickly and quietly. Hours of watching the trees beside the road for signs of infected. However, other than that first group, we never saw any more up close.

All that effort seemed such a waste as I studied the building before us. Sure it had a protective fence and space enough where we could all fit and be safe during the night, like I'd specified. However, the cold distribution factory was far from the cozy farmhouse we'd left behind.

Molev led us up the drive to the gated entrance.

I glanced at Byllo, who walked nearby with Timmy draped against his shoulder. The boy's sleep relaxed face made me smile slightly. He obviously felt safe with Byllo. I just hoped the little guy wouldn't freak out when he woke and saw our new temporary home.

The clatter and groan of metal drew my attention back to the gate where Molev and a few others forced their way in.

"Wait here," he said.

He motioned for a group of ten. They moved toward the

building and disappeared inside through the main doors. I felt safe enough in the open, held securely in Drav's arms, but I wasn't so sure how I'd feel inside.

The place felt creepy in its abandonment. Semi-trailers sat forgotten at docks that would never again be used. Cars remained in the parking lot for owners who would never return. Nothing moved except the dried grass that had grown up around the fenced perimeter. No sound reached my ears except the soft shuffle of the fey's feet as they kept watch.

While we waited, the sky began to cloud over. Without the sun, the temperature dropped. I shivered in Drav's arms and knew Timmy would be getting cold, too.

Not long afterward, one of the scouts returned.

"We removed a few infected. Molev says to come in," he stated.

A couple of the men stayed behind to close the gate while the rest of us entered the building. The high ceilings of the warehouse produced an echo of our footsteps as we passed the metal shelving lining the factory floor. Untouched by the chaos outside its doors, the shelves in this place still had boxes and boxes of now useless electronics.

The fey fanned out, checking out our temporary home. My eyes swept the large room again. With so much space, I worried about spreading out too thin. As we learned at the last place, a fence only provided so much protection if the infected found us.

I glanced up at the second-floor platform and saw windows with blinds. Likely an office.

"I think it's safe enough for me to walk," I said, glancing at Drav. "I want to explore upstairs."

Drav grunted, put me down, and followed me to the old office. Our footsteps echoed loudly on the sturdy metal stairways bolted to the wall.

At the top, I looked out over the vast warehouse and spotted a couple of different entrances.

"You'll want someone posted at each exit," I said, pointing them out.

Seeing the fey try to find places to sit and rest, I realized not only would there be no showering, there would be no food or comfort either. Not until we went out to find some supplies.

We had all traveled extremely light, most with only the clothes on our backs. We needed food, water, warmer clothes for Timmy, clean clothes for the men, soap, towels...the list of supplies kept getting longer. I chewed my bottom lip, knowing we would have to head into Ardmore to get supplies.

On the way here, the glimpses I caught of the town showed it free from any bomb destruction. That meant an infected infestation. Although the fey had swiftly dealt with the infected on the road, the idea of going into any area where there would be even more infected worried me. As it should, I supposed.

Turning away from the view, I opened the office door. Paperwork still covered the desk, waiting for the manager who had probably assumed he would be back the next day to finish. It felt odd to see that there were pockets of the world I'd known still untouched by devastation. Quiet little pieces suspended in time. The thought left an open wound in my heart. Our old world was gone.

Drav moved behind me, reminding me of our task.

"This wouldn't be a bad place to sleep. Some of those empty boxes from down below will keep us from getting cold on the floor. We could bring one of the chairs down for Timmy to snuggle in, too." I rolled out the comfortable looking chair from behind the desk, and Drav took it from me, lifting it easily.

"We need to get supplies. It would be good to find some sunglasses for you guys if we are going to continue traveling during the day. We need food and some lightweight basics like soap and clean socks for Timmy."

I frowned as I thought of what else we needed.

Warm hands framed my face, and Drav pressed his forehead to mine.

"We will find these things. Rest your mind."

His words helped calm my rampant thoughts. In this new world, Drav was my anchor. My reality and my safety. I wrapped my arms around him, taking a moment to soak up the comfort I found simply in his presence.

He made a satisfied sound and held me close, his hands rubbing over my back. It felt heavenly, and I didn't want to move. Part of me wanted to ignore the world and just steal as much quiet time as I wanted with Drav. But I knew better. This world didn't give the unprepared any quiet time.

I sighed and pulled away.

Any thoughts of gathering supplies fled from my mind the moment I noticed Drav's hungry gaze focused on my mouth.

CHAPTER EIGHT

"My Mya."

The way Drav said the words set my heart racing. He changed his hold on me, reaching under my shirt so his fingertips brushed my skin.

I shivered at the contact.

He smiled slightly and lowered his head.

"Mine," he said just before his lips touched my mouth.

He kissed me tenderly, and I basked in his attention and playfully nipped his bottom lip.

He growled against my mouth, and the kiss changed, becoming more demanding. The hot palm gripping my side trailed upward until just under the curve of my breast. His fingers traced the edge of my bra then lightly moved over the cup. He teased me, circling my breast before he deftly found my nipple. I groaned into his mouth as he toyed with it through the material. His free hand gripped my butt so he could press his hips against mine, a slow rolling grind that had me gasping for air.

Just as I gripped his shoulders to pull him closer, he withdrew his hand.

"Tell me what we need, and we will find it."

I almost told him I needed him to finish what he'd started, but a burst of sound from below brought back reality. I exhaled slowly and wrapped my arms around his waist, holding him while letting my pulse settle. After a moment, I could focus on what we needed to do and left the office to go talk to Molev about our need for supplies. Drav carried the executive chair down the stairs.

Molev had remained in the open part of the factory, watching the fey explore the place while staying close to Byllo and Timmy, who was draped over his shoulder.

"Drav, can you break the backrest off of the chair? We can use it as a bed for Timmy."

Drav snapped the chair in half like a twig and set the large, well-padded back on the ground. Byllo put Timmy down on it. The boy curled into a small ball and continued to sleep.

I stared at the child for a moment. At four, he shouldn't need so much sleep. But, given what he'd been through, I could understand why he might want it. Still, it worried me. He needed proper care.

"I want to take a small group out and scout the surrounding area for supplies," I said quietly, stepping away from Timmy.

"I will send out twenty men."

"I need to go, too." Not that I really wanted to go. I knew there'd be infected all over the place.

"No, Mya," Drav said. Molev agreed with a nod.

"It would be better if you stayed here, Mya."

"The men have learned some English, but they won't know how to read signs or know what supplies they are looking for. I can read and know what we need."

Molev looked at Drav. I did, too.

"I'll be safe with you, right?"

Drav sighed.

"Very well."

I snagged my bag and searched until I found the snack packs of applesauce I'd tucked inside.

"Here," I said, handing the containers to Byllo. "If Timmy wakes up, have him just sip this from the container. One should be good for now, but I will leave the rest for you in case he wants more. We'll bring back some better food for him. Oh, and make sure he stays in sight at all times. Little kids can get into trouble quickly without even realizing it. They are as clueless about this world as you guys were when you first came up. Only they don't learn as fast. Be patient, kind, and gentle with him. If you think I'm fragile, children are even more so."

"We will take good care of him, Mya," Molev said. "The sun is starting its descent. You should go now."

I nodded.

Molev called out for volunteers; and, within seconds, Drav and I walked outside with our group. Although the sun still floated high in the sky with no clouds in sight, I knew daylight wouldn't last much longer. The men's eyes watered as Drav picked me up and took off south, heading back the way we'd come.

The surrounding area to the left of the highway had more abandoned and ransacked buildings, so the men moved quickly, running alongside the road.

Cars, some with doors still hanging open, littered the long stretch of blacktop. The fey kept their distance from the vehicles, which I appreciated.

The highway billboards didn't help as much as the store signs towering far above everything.

"Drav," I said, careful not to speak too loudly. "Go that way. We need to follow that road."

The fey ran past several fast food restaurants, heading further into town. After seeing the home goods store to our left, the buildings slowly began to thin out again as if we were already heading out of town. Only the signs indicating a hospital ahead kept me from telling the fey to turn around. I couldn't help but look back, second guessing myself though.

Behind us, something moved. The steady cadence of the fey's running had attracted attention.

"Infected," I said to the fey behind Drav.

A couple of the fey separated to take care of the infected. The rest of us kept going until the buildings grew thicker again. We passed more restaurants, but I ignored them. Most would have had fresh or freezer food that had long ago spoiled if the buildings had lost power.

A pharmacy on the corner of the next intersection gave me hope.

"Which way, Mya?" Drav asked.

"Go left. We'll run that way for a little bit, and if we don't find anything promising, we can turn around."

Within another block, I saw a bright blue sign that belonged to a huge chain super-center in the distance.

"There," I said softly, pointing.

Cars waited in the parking lot. Only a few had their doors open. I scrutinized the complete stillness of the surrounding area. The well-spaced business buildings remained quiet. Where were the infected? Probably near their homes. If this area had been struck at night, like everywhere else, I doubted there would have been many people in the shopping district.

Despite the logical explanation, I still felt nervous as we made quick time to the front entrance. Broken glass covered the ground, both doors smashed by looters. I hoped we'd still be able to find what we needed.

The fey's deer hide boots crunched on the debris as they stepped inside. The opaque panels in the ceiling gave just enough light to see. Other than the glass on the floor and missing items from the nearby shelves, the store seemed normal enough. The fey were cautious, though. As a group, they paused and listened. Nothing moved or made a sound as they waited.

"Check the store," Drav said. "Shax and three others stay with me."

"If there are healthy humans in here, please don't hurt them," I added.

The rest of the fey nodded and quietly moved into the store's interior.

"Can you put me down?" I asked, looking around.

I could see the produce section to our right but doubted there'd be anything worth saving there.

"Do you think it's safe to start looking for things?

"As safe as it will be."

I nodded and started forward. Shax and Drav walked beside me with the others loosely spread around us. I explored the food aisles closest to the entrance, disheartened by the sight of so many nearly bare shelves.

A sudden commotion came from further back in the store, and I looked at Drav.

"We will keep you safe. What do you need?"

"We need bags to carry the supplies in," I said.

I made my way further down the aisles toward the center of the store. The weak light from overhead caught on three carousel displays of mostly untouched sunglasses.

"We need to grab all of these. You guys should each pick out a pair to wear now and bring the rest back for everyone else."

Drav went over to the first rack of sunglasses and pulled off a pair of reflective avatars.

"Very dashing," I said sincerely.

Drav gave me a toothy smile and slipped the glasses on. Shax grunted and pulled off a similar pair to try on.

"You can use the mirror to see what you look like," I said, pointing to the reflective triangle.

He ducked down and caught sight of his reflection. He grinned and moved aside so the rest of the guys with us could try some on, too. The men who'd checked the back of the store joined us before we moved on.

"We removed a few infected. The rest of the store is quiet," one of the men said.

Drav nodded, and I watched with growing humor as the newcomers tried on several pairs of sunglasses each, checking their reflections often.

Knowing our limited time, I turned away from the fun and started toward the other side of the store.

"Where are you going?" Drav asked.

"While you guys do that, I'm going to grab some other necessities."

"Necessities? What do you need?" He removed his glasses, ready to retrieve whatever items I might require. The driven way he wanted to take care of me made me feel cherished beyond belief. It also made him even more adorable in my eyes.

"You know...socks, undies, tampons. Things that will probably save my life someday," I said, unable to resist a little teasing.

His expression of idle curiosity changed to one of complete seriousness.

"I'll help you find these tampons." He strode forward with a determined gait while I trailed behind him.

"Will you carry my tampons for me?" I asked with barely contained amusement.

"I will not let them out of my sight."

I didn't have the heart to tell him they wouldn't actually save my life.

Drav and I navigated through the untouched greeting card section to the slightly raided health and beauty area. The mangled mess of what remained of the pharmacy shelves gave me little hope we would find much in the section. However, the items available surprised me. I found children's pain reliever, vitamins, and toothbrushes. Near the pharmacy, I also found some reusable shopping bags. While Drav held one, I stocked up on the things I thought we'd need. Soaps, shampoos, conditioners, toothpaste, razors, and tampons.

"This is good," I said. "Go ahead and set that by the front doors, and I'll check out the clothes."

"No. We stay together."

"They checked the store."

He continued to give me a "not happening" stare.

"Fine, but we need to hurry. I want to be safely in our building by dark." I started walking toward the front doors with Drav following closely behind.

"What are some of the names of the fey who came with us?" I asked.

"Tihr, Bauts, Gyirk..."

"Okay, how good is your hearing?"

"They will be able to hear you if you need them."

"Tihr, Bauts, Gyirk, Kerr, and Shax, could you guys join us when you are done?" I couldn't help but raise my voice a little. Almost as soon as I finished speaking, the men joined us.

"Yes, Mya?" Shax said.

"Can one of you find us a couple more bags like these?" I lifted my bag holding my spoils. "Or better yet, find some duffle bags or backpacks. Something you guys can carry on your backs as we travel."

They nodded and took off. Drav and I set the first two bags by the doors then walked further into the store. I found the toys and stopped short. The shelves remained fully stocked. Of course they would be. Who would think of toys with infected and hellhounds running around? Me. I couldn't help but recall the sad look in Timmy's eyes as he lay his head on Byllo's shoulder.

"Can you go just a few more aisles down and look for blankets?" I asked Drav. "I just want to grab a few things for Timmy."

"No, Mya. We stay together."

Shaking my head at his protectiveness, I started down the aisle.

I ignored all the toys that made noise or lit up and found a box of eight crayons, a coloring book, and a small stuffed animal. It wasn't much, but for a boy who had nothing, it might just mean the world.

Turning, I handed everything over to Drav then paused to look at a brightly colored ball. Timmy would probably like it. But runaway balls led kids into streets with cars, or in this case, with infected. It would also make noise when bounced. Our new world sucked.

With one last regretful look, I moved away from the ball and led Drav to the bedding.

I loaded up his arms, and my own, with any non-bulky blankets I could find. Hopefully, the guys had located some decent bags to carry everything because the further north we traveled, the colder it would get.

Thinking of that, I moved off toward the clothing section. We crossed paths with the men. Each carried some kind of bag.

"Those are perfect," I said. "Can you go back to the food section and load up on whatever is left in cans?"

"Yes, Mya," Shax said.

"Would two of you be willing to run this stuff to the front of the store?" I hefted what I held, and two of the fey jumped forward to relieve me of my burden. They took the blankets stacked in Drav's arms, too.

"Thanks, guys. Just a few more things then we're done."

As they ran off to gather the food, Drav and I veered toward clothing.

"Timmy needs everything," I said. "He said he's four. I'm no expert on kids, but he seemed kinda small to me for that age. So I have no idea if that's actually right or not. To be safe, let's get clothing that says 5T." I showed Drav the marking on the hanger as

I spoke. "He can always grow into them and have room to layer to stay warm." I held up a shirt and studied it for a moment. "Yeah, I think this will work."

"Grab five shirts and three pair of pants," I said, moving away.

"Mya," Drav said with low warning.

"I know, I know. Stay together. I'm not going anywhere. Just looking at jackets."

I found a jacket, then socks, and cute little superhero underwear. Before I knew it, I had drifted further away to grab an armful of bras for myself from the women's department. Drav stood in the men's department, stocking up on the large shirts there. I was glad he'd thought of that. Most of the men were messy from the infected run in on the road. A clean change of clothes—

Something moved quickly across the floor toward my foot. My first thought was a rat, and I jumped a little before focusing on the red toy ball.

Frowning, I bent down and picked it up. The cold wetness coating the toy surprised me, and I jerked my hand back. I turned my wrist to look at my palm. Blood covered my hand.

CHAPTER NINE

HEART HAMMERING, I STRAIGHTENED, SEARCHING FOR DRAV. THE semi-milky, pale gaze of an infected met mine over the top of the clothing rack. It lifted a hand to its mouth and began chewing on its pointer finger. The way it tilted its head to study me, like a cat toying with a mouse, sent a shaft of terror through me.

Where the hell had it come from?

Something moved to my right. From the corner of my eye, I saw another one stand from where it had crawled between the displays of clothing. Stalking me.

With a desperate yell, I gripped the rack between us and rammed it forward to knock the first infected onto its back. Not stopping the momentum, I swung the rack around to the side. The second infected caught it in his hand and pushed back. I stumbled.

Drav yelled my name. The infected on the other side of the rack tilted its head at the sound, though its gaze never left me. It shoved the rack back at me, and I turned and sprinted in the other direction.

Drav roared behind me. As I dodged around clothing racks, I thought of Drav's stubborn insistence we stay close. I should have listened. My lungs burned from my ragged breaths. Everything blurred in my panic, and I ran almost blindly, not sure where to go.

Turning the corner to an aisle of cookware, I skidded to a halt. An infected stood swaying from side to side on the other end. When it spotted me, it gave a low, moaning yell and raced toward me. Spinning around, I took off in yet another direction.

Drav yelled my name again.

"I'm here," I screamed.

I shouldn't have. Several moans came from different areas of the store. They were hunting us. Not us. Me. They'd seen me look at the ball and thought to use it as bait, just like they'd done with Timmy. The infected were getting far too smart.

I continued to run, the sounds of my feet giving away my location, but I couldn't stop.

Something stepped out in front of me, and I collided with it. Arms immediately closed around me, and I struggled to get free.

"Shh..."

I looked up into Shax's eyes and almost passed out in relief. Movement from the top shelf, just behind him, caught my attention. An infected, previously laying perfectly still, rolled off the shelf and onto Shax, who pushed me out of the way. I stumbled backwards. A moment later, arms closed around me again, steadying me.

Exhaling shakily, I relaxed as Shax gripped the infected's head before it could bite him.

The fetid stink of rotting flesh hit me a half a second before a low moan echoed in my ear. Horror filled me as I realized my mistake. I thrashed in the infected's hold. It didn't help. It was too late.

Teeth bit into my left shoulder, and I screamed.

The pain and fear of what would come made me crazy. Reaching back, I gripped the infected's head and bent forward with a heave. The creature flipped over my shoulder, his bite dislodging with the move.

I grunted against the pain but stayed on my feet.

Shax caught the infected and, in a blink, the creature lost its head. Not that it mattered. It had already gotten what it wanted. A taste of human flesh. The luck that had kept me alive until now had finally run out.

Shax looked up at me. His gaze immediately went to my shoulder. Before I could say anything, Drav came running around the corner, followed by three other fey. Red bathed their hands and arms.

Drav took one look at the infected laying on the ground and started giving orders.

"Search the store again." The three fey took off running.

Shax stayed, watching me with sad, guilty eyes. My stomach clenched, and fear made it hard to breathe.

Drav strode toward me, gripped my arms and leaned his forehead against mine.

"Mya," he said, ignorant relief echoing in that one word.

"I'm sorry," I said, tears welling. "I should have listened. I should have stayed right by you." A sob choked my last word.

"Shh..." he said, wrapping his arms around me. "It's okay."

My heart broke, and I shook my head slowly.

"It's not, Drav. One bit me."

He jerked in my arms and pulled back to look at me. His gaze swept over my face then settled on my left shoulder. Fear and panic spread over his features.

"Tell me what to do," he said.

I reached up and placed my hand on his cheek. Regret made my tears fall faster.

"You saw Butch. You saw what happened. There's nothing you can do but listen." I gripped his face between my hands. "You have a child with you, now. You need to protect him. You need to find my family. You need to help the humans destroy the hellhounds and clean up the infected. You can do all that. I know you can."

"Not without you," he said, leaning his forehead against mine once more. "You are the best thing here. Without you, the surface can go to hell."

"It already has. You need to save it, Drav. Please. For me."

A sudden wave of pain speared my stomach, I groaned and wrapped an arm around my middle.

"Children need a lot of care," I said, panting. "Timmy's meat has to be cooked. If you feed him raw meat, he'll get sick. Don't touch him when you're coated with infected blood, and wash his hands often with soap because he sucks his thumb."

The pain grew so intense that my knees gave out. Drav eased us to the floor and held me in his lap, tucking my head under his chin and smoothing back my hair.

"I don't know how Timmy didn't get infected already, but I want to spare him this," I said clutching Drav's shirt.

He rocked me gently, making small sounds of comfort. Exhaling shakily, I closed my eyes and tried to memorize the feel of his arms, the smell of him. We'd been through so much together. I didn't want to leave him. I wanted us to see this through to the end. Not just our journey to find my parents, but the journey of us.

Something wet dripped onto my forehead. His tears spurred my own grief.

Opening my eyes, I caught Shax's gaze. He stood back, quietly watching us, sorrow and guilt pulling at his features. I hated that I was about to add to both.

"Shax, when it's time, send Drav away and take my head. I don't want him to have to do that."

Drav growled and held me tighter, making me cry out in pain. He immediately loosened his hold and pressed a kiss to my brow, right where his tear had landed.

"No, Mya. There is a way. You said things can save you. Tell me what to do."

"Drav, there's nothing."

My insides twisted, knifing a new level of agony through me. I cried out and turned my head just in time to empty the contents of my stomach onto the cold tile floor beside us.

"No," Drav yelled, the sound echoing with each of my gagging heaves.

He held me, soothing a hand down my back again and again until I finished, then gently settled me against his chest. His ragged breathing tore at me. He knew as well as I did that the end hovered just in sight now.

I set my hand on his chest over his heart and struggled for a few beats to catch my breath. My eyes burned, but not from tears. It felt like a million needles jabbing into them. As much as I feared what was happening to me, I feared what would happen to Drav once I left.

"You're the best thing that has ever happened to me," I said. "You terrified me at first. Then shocked the hell out of me with all your boob grabbing and pussy talk. I hate the word pussy, by the way." I pulled back and looked up at him.

The moisture in his eyes added another ache to my chest, and my effort to smile proved futile. It hurt too much. Physically and emotionally. Instead, my gaze held his.

"And, I love you, too, Drav. More than I would have ever thought possible."

He made a pained sound and brought his mouth to mine. His lips brushed mine tenderly, pouring so much into the contact it could no longer be simply defined as a kiss. It was our bittersweet goodbye to a happily ever after...to a future together, good or bad. It was a last memory he would hold onto as he walked away.

When it ended, my whole body shook.

"I'm sorry, Drav. We should have had a lifetime together." I lifted my hands and touched his cheek gently.

"You're breaking my heart, Mya," he whispered. "Do not leave me."

I closed my eyes, unable to stand the pain any longer.

DRAV...

MYA's pale skin grew paler. The blood seeping from her bite slowed as did her shaking.

"Mya, open your eyes," I said, brushing my lips over each eyelid.

She didn't do as I asked. Her exhale tickled my chin. I pressed my lips to hers again. She didn't respond. It took a moment to understand she no longer breathed. That her heart no longer beat.

Pain greater than any cursed hound bite ripped through me.

"Mya! Do not leave me!"

"Drav," Shax said quietly, "she has already left." He set a hand on my shoulder, a show of sharing in my pain. But I shrugged it off and rocked her, desperately breathing in the scent of her hair and memorizing the soft feel of her body against mine.

"You should go now," Shax said again. "I will do as Mya asked."

"No. I will see her open her eyes again."

"You would let her become what she feared? You would dishonor her wishes?"

Not all of them. Every infected and hound on the surface would die by my hands. But I would never stop protecting Mya.

I wrapped my arms around her, holding her tightly as I tipped my head back and let the world know my grief.

The building rattled with the thunderous echo of my cry.

MYA...

A HEAVY PAIN gripped my chest then eased enough that I felt the unsteady beat of my heart. I inhaled, needing air. The ringing in my ears suddenly stopped.

"She breathed, Drav. Leave, now." Shax's worried voice penetrated my confused awareness, and I struggled to open my eyes.

"You will not touch her," Drav said, anger lacing his words.

I tried to lift a hand to reassure him, but it was too heavy. My pulse thumped in my ears twice before the memory of the last few minutes clicked into place. An infected bite. My shoulder.

I gasped and forced my eyes open. Drav stared down at me, the vertical slit of his pupils wide in his grief.

"How did I ever think your eyes anything but beautiful?" I asked, my voice a rough rasp.

"Mya? You are not dead or infected," he said, raining kisses over my face.

I frowned and focused on how I felt. The pain twisting my insides didn't seem quite as bad as before.

"I don't understand. How long was I sleeping?" I asked.

Shax moved toward us.

"You were not sleeping, Mya. You were dead. Why are your eyes not white? Why are you still smart?"

"Quiet, Shax," Drav said. He demanded my attention by planting his face right in my line of sight. "Mya is smart and beautiful and alive. That is all that matters."

He kissed me hard and pulled away to stare at me again as if not quite believing it. I felt the same way.

"How? How am I still alive?" I pulled away from Drav's hold and gingerly felt my shoulder. It hurt like a bitch.

"Does it matter how?" Drav asked.

"It might. I don't know. Can you find me a mirror, Shax?" I asked.

The man ran off and returned a few moments later with part of the sunglass display. I hadn't realized we were that close to the front of the store. I took the mirror and angled it to get a look at the bite through my shirt. The infected's top row of teeth had created a deep crescent-shaped puncture but the bottom row had only left a darkening bruise on the already grey patch of skin. My mouth dropped open as a possibility came to mind.

"What happens when the infected bite you?" I asked Drav.

"Nothing," he said.

"Nothing because you had adapted with the crystal's help. Because your world is all part of the curse that created the infected. The crystal was changing me. That change was killing me, but it might have also saved me."

I had no other explanation than the time in his world had made me immune to an infected's bite.

The rest of the fey joined us and looked down at Drav and me with curious, confused expressions.

"The infected have been cleared," Kerr said. "We found a few hiding on the tall shelves."

I looked up at the shelf, remembering how the infected had hidden there and noticed the fading light.

"Drav, we need to get moving. We can't be out at dark. I'm not ready to try surviving more bites."

He stood with me in a fluid move.

"What does she mean? More bites?" Kerr asked, his gaze landing on my bloody shoulder.

"She was bitten and survived," Drav answered. "Stay close. I will not risk Mya again."

He strode toward the front of the store.

"Wait. Before we leave, I should clean and bandage the bite," I said. "All the supplies I need are back where we found the toothbrushes."

"We have the supplies you already gathered. It's not safe here."

I didn't point out that I hadn't grabbed peroxide or bandages.

"Drav, it's a risk to wait. I might have avoided turning into an infected, but there's a possibility I could still get sick in other ways."

Drav immediately veered in the correct direction.

When we stood in the pharmacy area, he set me on my feet and helped remove my shirt. I didn't care that they all watched us. Modesty went out the window after kissing death. Plus, I felt a lot safer with all of them nearby.

Shax grabbed the bottle of peroxide that I pointed out, and Drav held me as I doused the bite with the cool liquid. I gritted my teeth against the sting and kept pouring until I'd rinsed all the blood from my skin.

"Kerr, can you grab as many of those bottles as we can fit?" I said. "And all the bandages. Maybe some of those cleansing wipes, too."

The first-aid supplies were barely touched by the looters, which made sense. They'd likely passed them by for the same reason I had. Anyone hurt wouldn't likely need first aid after fifteen minutes. Anyone except for me.

While I added salve and gauze, Kerr handed Drav some of the wipes. Drav quickly cleaned his face and hands, removing any trace of infected blood.

Once I had gauze taped over the bite, I looked down at the dirty shirt we'd removed.

"Here is a clean one, Mya." Kerr held out a man's pink, long-sleeved t-shirt that had #survivor on the front.

I snorted a laugh.

"That's perfect. Thanks, Kerr."

Drav helped me ease it over my head. Although my shoulder ached, it didn't burn with pain like it had before I'd closed my eyes.

In fact, other than the awful taste in my mouth, I didn't feel like a recently bitten person.

As soon as Drav tugged the shirt into place, he pressed a kiss to my forehead and lifted me gently. He started toward the entrance, but I stopped him when I spotted the pre-pasted travel toothbrushes on the aisles end cap.

"Shax, can you grab all of those and hand me one?" I said, pointing.

He tossed me a pack and loaded the rest into a bag.

While I scrubbed the taste of death from my mouth, Drav strode toward the entrance. The men picked up the supplies we'd gathered and followed us out the door.

CHAPTER TEN

THE SHOCK OF BEING BITTEN SETTLED OVER ME AS DRAV RAN. Although I breathed and thought normally, I struggled to believe I'd actually survived. That one moment...that single, stupid mistake of not seeing who had held me had almost robbed me of everything. Life. A chance to see my family again. A chance to show Drav what family meant and why they were so important to me.

I looked up at him, realizing it wasn't just my family who held that level of importance in my life now. When I lay dying in Drav's arms, I'd worried about him, too. Without me consciously realizing it, he'd made a place for himself in my life. He was my family now, too. And, he needed to know that.

He caught me looking at him.

"Are you in pain?" he asked, running faster.

I ducked my head into his shoulder to hide from the wind.

"No. The bite feels tender but doesn't really hurt." I pressed a kiss to his collarbone to reassure him. It didn't seem to work, though, because he didn't slow his pace.

With the rest of our party forming a protective circle around us, Drav ran tirelessly. The distribution factory came into sight, and I exhaled with relief seeing the fence just as we'd left it. I didn't like these new, smarter infected.

The men on guard opened the gate for us. One of the men from our group stopped to talk to the lookouts, likely to warn them about what the infected had done. Drav and the rest of the group continued their jog until we reached the main area inside the building.

"Welcome back," Molev said when Drav stopped.

While the rest of our group began emptying the bags out on the floor, Drav continued to hold me close. I didn't mind. I wasn't quite ready to let him go, either.

Resting my head on Drav's shoulder, I watched Shax sort the things we'd collected, and I studied the slow-growing piles with a sinking stomach. There hadn't been a lot of cans or dried goods left on the shelves I'd seen, but I'd hoped they'd found more while Drav and I had been collecting clothing. Seeing the cans now, though, compared to all the men who lounged around the factory floor, I knew we'd only managed to gather a small amount of food.

"You brought back more supplies than I thought you would," Molev said, studying the piles with me.

"Less than I'd hoped. We'll need more. But, we only hit one place."

Drav growled, and his hold on me tightened. Molev's gaze shifted between the two of us.

"What happened while you were collecting supplies?" he asked.

"Found a supercenter. Found some infected. Same old, same old," I said. My flippant response didn't fool Molev or calm down Drav.

"Some infected had set another trap, waiting out of sight on shelves. One bit Mya."

Molev looked at me.

"Show me," he said.

I pulled the neckline away to reveal the gauze.

"I already disinfected it and shouldn't remove the bandage until I'm ready to clean it again."

"It broke your skin, though?"

"Yeah."

"Her heart stopped beating," Shax said. "She stopped breathing."

A tremble ran through Drav's arms, and a low rumble began in his chest.

"If it's all right with you guys, I think I'm ready to lay down for a bit." I looked up at Drav and gently set a hand on his jaw. The contact warmed my chilled hand.

"I'm okay," I said softly. "Really."

Drav's gaze held mine for a moment, then he leaned down and kissed me tenderly.

I'd completely forgotten our audience until he tore his gaze from mine to look at Molev. Flushing, I focused on him, too. Molev smiled, flashing his fangs.

"Go rest. I'll tell the others to leave you alone."

Kerr handed me one of the wrapped quilts as Drav turned.

"Thank you."

Kerr nodded.

The blanket almost slipped from my arms as Drav took the stairs to the office two at a time. His rush to get me alone worried me. I'd seen Drav angry enough to not want to be on the receiving end of it. Now, he had plenty to be angry about. He'd told me repeatedly to stay close, and I hadn't listened.

"You can put me down," I said when we arrived at the top of the stairs.

Instead of listening, he stepped inside the office with me still in his arms. The door ominously clicked shut behind us. My stomach churned, and I struggled not to let my guilt or worry show.

"Seriously, Drav. I can't make our bed if you're holding me."

He finally set me on my feet, but he didn't release me. I peeked up at him, ready to apologize again. Instead of anger in his gaze, I saw desperation and fear. He gripped my sides and pulled me close. I could feel the tremble in his hands as he set his forehead to mine.

"I can't lose you, Mya." The anguished rumble of his voice almost broke me.

How many times had he told me I was the best thing here? He'd proven time and again that I was his world. My death would have destroyed him. The thought of it still tortured him.

"You won't, Drav. Their bites won't turn me. I'm safe."

My words didn't change his grip or his shaking. He was in a dangerous place, and I wasn't sure how to help him move past what had almost happened.

I lifted my hands to his face, cupping his cheeks.

"I'm here, Drav. In your arms." I tipped my head up and gently kissed his lips. "I'm not going anywhere." I kissed him again, trying to prove my words.

His hold loosened, and his lips moved under mine. My heart leapt as I understood what he needed. I pulled back and met his tormented gaze.

Any hint of lingering doubt left me. Simply loving Drav wasn't enough. I needed to show him that he'd become my world, too.

"You're my family now, Drav. And, I'm yours."

"Mine," he echoed.

His lips crashed upon mine, demanding proof that I meant what I'd said. I gave it willingly.

When we finally broke apart, we both panted for air.

"Just a minute," I said, escaping his hold.

I moved to the windows and pulled the cord to release the blinds then went to the door and did the same. When I turned, Drav still watched me with the same desperate intensity.

"Mya..."

I walked to him, framed his face with my hands, and brought his lips to mine for another searing kiss.

"I love you, Drav," I whispered against his lips. "No matter what the future brings, I love you."

He growled low, but I knew it was his fear of losing me, not my words.

I walked away from him once more to spread the quilt out on the floor. Kicking off my shoes, I sat down on the unforgiving, makeshift bed. Drav still hadn't moved from his spot. The panicked glint still darkened his eyes, and his hands still trembled. He needed me as much as I needed him.

"Can I use you as a pillow?" I asked, holding out a hand.

As he knelt beside me, I got to my knees and wrapped my arms around his neck. I leaned in and pressed a small kiss right below his ear.

"Do you trust me?" I whispered.

"Yes."

"Then, love me back."

Drav growled and gripped my hips.

"Mya."

I couldn't help the smile that spread across my lips at the heated warning.

"Trust me," I whispered before kissing my way to his mouth.

I nipped his bottom lip. He groaned and gripped the back of my head with one hand. When his tongue traced the seam of my lips, I opened with a throaty moan. His kiss demanded everything and left nothing untouched. It started a need that grew too consuming to ignore.

Breaking the kiss, I ran my hand down his cheek, drawing my fingers over his neck until I reached his shirt.

"Your shirt needs to go," I said.

Gathering the material in my hands, I tugged it upwards. He

helped, snatching the end and pulling it over his head in a quick movement.

His gaze held mine as he reached out, his fingers sweeping under my shirt and brushing over my stomach to leave trails of fire in their wake.

"Yours, too."

I reached for the bottom of my shirt, but Drav stopped me from removing it; instead, he carefully eased the material up, showing extra concern for my bandaged shoulder.

My heart melted as he removed my shirt then slipped off my bra. Bared from the waist up and still on my knees, I held still as he looked at me. Heat and hunger like I'd never seen before filled his gaze.

He reached out and reverently covered one breast with his big hand. I closed my eyes, reveling in the feel of his gentle caress. The warm, firm squeeze he gave made me ache for more. His lips settled on mine as he explored with his hands. The combination of his kiss and rough texture of his fingers heightened the sensation of each touch. I moaned as his fingers found my nipple, and gently plucked at the sensitive peak.

Slowly, he lowered us to the blanket. His lips left mine to graze kisses in a searing trail down my throat. My breath caught at the touch of his tongue to the skin over my collarbone. An ache started in my breast. His fingers, his hands, were no longer enough.

I reached up and threaded my fingers through his hair. His lips skimmed lower. I held my breath, waiting.

A second later, his mouth latched onto my tight nipple. I moaned and arched into his touch, desperate for more.

He sucked and played with the aching peak until I felt each tug in my very core. Releasing my nipple with a lick, he focused on its twin. My hands clenched in his thick hair as his mouth closed over the tip. His tongue flicked, circled, and teased, and he gave a low rumble of approval as he paid the other breast the same attention as the first.

The heat of his touch consumed me and spread lower. I slipped my hand from his hair down his back, exploring the muscled planes until I touched the waist of his pants. He growled, the vibrations doing things to my nipple and making the ache between my legs grow.

He gently pushed my hand away.

"Drav." I arched my hips, needing him to understand.

A moment later, his fingers plucked at my jeans, freeing the button and easing down the zipper. His mouth left my skin, and my heart thumped heavily in my chest as he reverently slid the material free.

Tossing my clothes aside, Drav sat back and looked at me. I swallowed hard and parted my legs slightly. Desire darkened his eyes to a forest green.

"Mine," he growled.

He stood and removed his pants. The thick erection twitched as I stared. He knelt beside me, his fingers and gaze sliding up my legs. When he reached the V, he stopped and braced a hand on each side of me. With care, he settled his weight over me. A breathy sigh escaped as his hips touched mine.

He kissed my chin and reached between us, his thumb brushing my curls and parting my folds.

"Drav..." It came out as a plea as I opened for him. His exploring fingers found my sweet spot and circled the tender flesh slowly. Bliss shuddered through me.

"I trust you, too, Drav," I said, setting my hands on his back.

He hissed out a breath, his fingers delving deeper and parting me. A moment later, he positioned himself at my entrance. His gaze remained locked on mine as he slowly pushed forward.

Each minute thrust kindled the desire growing inside me. Once he filled me, he stopped moving. I ground my hips against his, eager for more.

"You're going to need to move, or I'm going to do it for you," I said.

He grinned wickedly, his fangs dimpling his bottom lip. Then, he moved. The first stroke of his withdrawal left me breathless. The next thrust made my eyes roll closed. He set a slow, steady rhythm, and I moaned unable to keep my satisfaction to myself.

Drav rumbled his approval and moved faster. The friction sent waves of pleasure through me, pushing me toward the place where I knew even more waited. I panted and wrapped my legs around his waist. Tension coiled inside of me, building to a breaking point. I hovered there, grasping for the release that waited just over the edge.

Drav slid a hand under my hip, changing the angle of his thrusts. The hot, hard length rubbed the top of my channel, and the tension exploded in a release of pleasure, ripping a scream from me. As I arched in ecstasy, his mouth latched onto my nipple. The suction of his mouth sent another wave of pleasure through me, my walls clenching around his engorged length.

He released me and thrust deep with a roar that I was certain the remaining fey back in Ernisi heard.

Drav kissed me hard then slowly withdrew. He didn't collapse on top of me but turned us so we lay on our sides, facing each other.

"I love you, my Mya."

I brushed a kiss to his chest.

"I love you, too."

The exhaustion of the day, and being cradled in Drav's embrace had me fighting to keep my eyes open.

STILL UNDRESSED, I stirred from sleep, my skin covered in goosebumps. I curled closer to Drav, seeking his warmth.

His hold tightened around me, and he pressed his lips against my forehead.

"I'll go get another blanket and some food, now that you are awake."

"No, I'm okay."

I reached for the edge of the quilt we laid on and pulled it over my exposed back.

"Your stomach has been very loud in its demand for food," he said softly, his fingers finding their way to the skin covering the insistent organ. It growled loudly again.

"Fine, but you're going to have to hurry because you're the only thing keeping me warm."

Drav sat up and tucked the blanket around me.

"I'll return quickly," he said.

Completely nude, he strode out the door.

I shook my head and fought not to blush. Hopefully, there wouldn't be too many fey awake. Sitting up, I wrapped my arms around my knees and placed my cheek against them. I sighed contentedly and reflected on what we'd done. I didn't regret it. Not a single moment. Although I still wanted to find my family, Drav was my world now. My future. There would be no going back.

Drav returned a moment later with a blanket and two cans of food. I lifted a corner of the blanket and he joined me, covering us both with the new blanket as well.

We shared the food, even though I tried to push the tuna away. Our meal didn't last long before our hunger turned into a different kind.

As soon as the sun rose, we dressed and left the office. If the men had heard us, they didn't mention anything when we joined them on the main floor. Probably because they were too focused on the new arrivals who still slept on the cardboard piles near the shelves.

"When did Ghua get back?" I asked Molev softly.

"Not long before the sun brightened the sky." He picked up a can. "Will Timmy eat this?"

I looked at the can of fruit and nodded.

"We need to make sure we feed him a balance of foods. That's a fruit. It's good for him. But he also needs some kind of protein, like meat, beans, cheese, or milk." I picked up one of the cans of evaporated milk. "He should have one of these a day, for sure. Oh, and he needs to brush his teeth. Twice a day. You all should, now that you don't have your leaves to chew on." I caught myself before I let the conversation distract me from the question I should have asked when we'd first arrived.

"Where did Ghua go?"

Molev gave me a slight smile.

"He and a few others followed the humans when they left."

Excitement filled me. Why hadn't I thought to suggest that?

"And?" I asked.

"They stopped at a place further north and east from here. There were more healthy humans at this place."

Relief coursed through me. Now we wouldn't be wandering around aimlessly in search of a safe zone.

"That's great. Did Ghua say how long it would take for us to get there?"

"He thought we should reach the next human place just after the sun is at its highest."

"How long does he need to sleep?"

"They can wake now," Molev said.

"No, that's fine. Let them sleep. We need to divide up the

supplies we brought back and repack and do a few other things before we're ready."

He let me take charge of that. I handed out the regular toothbrushes we'd grabbed, explained how to use them with toothpaste, and pointed to the employee bathrooms. Little Timmy scampered after Byllo, who also carried a child's toothbrush for the boy.

Drav stayed beside me, tracing lingering touches down my arms or over my shoulders as I inspected our final haul from the superstore. We distributed the items so if we lost a bag we wouldn't lose all of one thing. It also helped keep the bags evenly weighted, even though Drav assured me that wouldn't be an issue.

As soon as the men finished brushing, I ducked into the bathroom to clean myself up as best as I could and to check the bite on my shoulder. The whole thing had already scabbed over but remained tender to the touch.

I stared at the wound unable to believe I was still me and not some mindless infected. I thought of Drav and what would have happened to him and my family if things had gone differently. Nothing good rose to mind. Thankfully, I'd survived. Something I seemed to be pretty good at. Something I resolved to stay good at. I had a lot to live for.

Thoughts of the previous night filled my head again, and I let go of my shirt to study myself in the mirror. I still had no regrets. My family would accept Drav because I did. The rest of humanity worried me, though. The dark fey deserved to be welcomed, not shunned or subjected to suspicion. Yet, that was what they were likely to encounter. I couldn't help but wonder what else we would need to confront at the new place.

Nervously, I smoothed back my hair and re-secured my ponytail.

I wouldn't let the fey be so easily dismissed. Not this time.

CHAPTER ELEVEN

THE SAFE ZONE DIDN'T LOOK LIKE MUCH, JUST A CLUSTER OF METAL buildings in a large parking lot surrounded by a fence on steroids. Different forms of temporary housing had been set up near the perimeter. A few military-style tents rustled in the wind, and a weird little weather vane on top of one of the RVs shifted direction and let out a low creak. Nothing else moved. At least, not that Drav could see or hear from our current distance.

The majority of the fey waited behind the barn that belonged to the house across the road from the safe zone, a good half a mile away, while Drav watched and listened and described everything to me from a small group of trees much closer to the base.

Since arriving, Drav hadn't seen any human movement. However, Ghua assured us that Tucker and Jerry had driven right up to the gate, and it had opened for them.

Drav picked me up and sprinted back to the barn followed by the few fey who'd accompanied us close on his heels. Molev listened to Drav's description of the place.

"Do you think the humans are still there?" Molev asked me.

"Yes. I think they're just hiding. I want you guys to stay here," I said. "Just Drav and I will go forward. When they see us, they'll come out." Probably heavily armed, but I didn't say that. "Drav, you'll need to walk behind me."

"No, Mya," Drav said, gently cupping my shoulder because of the bite. "Your body is not meant to protect me. Mine is meant to protect you."

I sighed.

"Would you listen if I said I'd rather you not come with me at all?" I asked.

"No. I won't. We will walk to the gate together."

"And we will follow at a distance," Molev said. "Not all humans are like you, Mya."

Molev and the fey hung back by the trees midway between the house and the fence while Drav and I approached the gate.

"Stop there!" a voice yelled when we stood within twenty feet.

"My name is Mya," I called. "This is Drav. We're looking for the safe zone where people from Oklahoma City would have been taken. I'm trying to find my parents."

"We know who you are," the voice called back. "You need to leave."

"Leave? Are you kidding me? Do you know what I've gone through to get here?" I took a step toward the fence, but Drav scooped me up in his arms and turned his back to the gate.

"You put me down right now, Drav," I said. The anger in my tone wasn't meant for him, but the asshole yelling at me.

"He has a gun pointed at you," Drav said.

"Leaving isn't an option. Please, Drav."

He scowled stubbornly.

"Will you at least turn around?" I asked.

He did, and I looked for the speaker but didn't see anything.

"If you really did know me and who I'm with, you wouldn't bother with a stupid fence and guns. Ask Tucker and Jerry how well that worked for them. We don't want your damn supplies or whatever else you have in your buildings any more than we wanted theirs. I just want to find my parents."

"Can't help you. Leave."

"No. You want me to leave? You'll have to shoot me."

Drav growled very loudly but held his ground.

"And I can promise you shooting me will be the biggest mistake of your life. You don't want to see these guys angry."

"We already have. Two of them took out three units in less than a minute."

I didn't believe him. Ghua would have told us about any altercations when he'd returned. The fey weren't shy about killing or talking about it. I opened my mouth to call the disembodied voice out on his lie then remembered the two exiled fey.

"The two that attacked you aren't with these guys," I called out. "Those two are outlaws, the men these guys have been looking for."

"Yeah right."

"What part don't you believe? That these guys have outlaws, just like we do, or that they are looking for the outlaws, much like our own FBI looks for high-profile criminals?"

Silence answered me.

"Throughout the history of our world, fear and intolerance of differences have led to countless wars, segregations, and violence. That world is dead. We don't need to repeat the old world's mistakes in this new one."

"What do you want?" the voice said, finally.

"For you to listen and try to understand. These men have been here longer than any of us. In fact, we are descended from their people. They have been locked away beneath the surface for thousands of years. The quakes from our drilling released this shit storm on us. Not them. They had nothing to do with the hellhounds coming here or the attacks by the two men they have been hunting.

"Since I've met Drav, the man holding me, he's kept me safe from all of it. The infected, the hounds, even my own people. You have no valid reason to ask us to leave, other than fearing what's different."

The bay door to the largest white building rolled open, and a uniformed man strode out. He walked part way to the gate.

"Old world or new world, I can't just give you another safe zone location and risk countless lives because you say your intentions are good. You want us to trust you? You need to prove you aren't like the other two."

"How?" I asked.

"Jerry and Tucker told us about the supplies they left behind with Bud. We have seven vehicles ready right now. Some of these demons can help us retrieve the supplies. The rest can tell us more about their race. How many there are. Where they come from. And just how fast and strong they are."

"First, they aren't demons. They're fey, like from our legends. Second, do you really think they should tell you all their strengths and weaknesses and get your supplies for you just to prove they're trustworthy?" I gave a harsh laugh. "You've got this so backwards it's just sad. You should be the ones proving you're trustworthy." I lowered my voice and glanced at Drav, who still held me.

"Let's go."

He turned, more than ready to take me away from what he perceived as a threat. The man stopped us.

"Fair enough. You help us with the supplies, and I will help you find your parents."

Drav stopped walking and looked down at me.

"I don't trust him," I said, honestly. "He's dressed like some branch of military. Last guy like that tried to shoot me in the head to save me from you."

"Yes. But without his help, how will we find your family? Your surface is much larger than our caverns."

I sighed. "Can you put me down? It's hard to negotiate when you're carrying me like a child."

"This is how you carry children?"

"Sometimes. Are you going to put me down?"

He considered me a moment then did as I'd asked. I immediately faced the man by the building.

"Drav and I can't make this decision alone. We'll need some time to discuss it with the rest of our group."

"We leave in ten minutes."

"Fine." I looked at Drav. "We better hurry then."

Drav picked me up, ran back to the trees, and started speaking to Molev before I even knew what was happening.

"The man said he knows where Mya's humans are and will tell us if we protect them while they get supplies from Bud's house."

"That's not what he said." Both men glanced at me.

"That's what he meant," Drav said.

"Are you against us protecting them, Mya?" Molev asked.

"No. I'm against them using you, and you guys getting hurt in the process."

Molev grunted. "Let's go talk to this human."

The whole lot of them, including Timmy, came with us when we returned to our previous position not far from the fence. The man inside hadn't moved.

Molev stepped forward.

"My name is Molev," he called.

"I am Commander Willis."

"In exchange for helping us find Mya's family, I will send half my men to protect your people while you gather your supplies. The other half will remain here to protect Mya and Timmy until our men return."

"You have yourself a deal, Molev."

Molev turned toward his men. "The supplies stay with Mya and Timmy. Kerr, will you go?"

Kerr nodded and stepped to one side. More men joined him until the group seemed roughly split in half. From within the fence, the sound of engines roared to life. Huge military trucks, like the ones that had evacuated us from the dorms, pulled out from the white building behind the Commander.

"Be careful, guys," I said as the gate rolled open.

"Be safe, Mya," Kerr said.

The rest of the fey stood back while the trucks rolled through. Kerr's group of fey fell-in around the vehicles, keeping pace with an easy jog. I turned toward the gate as it started to close and only made it a step before a gun was lifted and aimed at my head.

Drav growled low behind me, his hand resting on my shoulder. "What the hell? We had a deal."

"The deal is that they prove we can trust them, and we help you find your parents. We never said we'd let you in."

Had it only been me, I wouldn't have cared. But we had Timmy.

"It's too cold for a four-year-old to sleep out in the open."

"We'll find you a tent." With that, the commander turned and walked away.

Byllo watched me. The look in his eyes said he'd rip down the fence and get whatever I thought Timmy needed. The little boy in Byllo's arms watched me with solemn eyes, too. I gave them both a reassuring smile.

"We'll be fine. Let's find something to eat and drink. Then, I have a surprise for you both. Do you know how to color, Timmy? I bet Byllo doesn't."

Timmy and I squeezed into the tent while Drav and Byllo stood outside. Having them so close was a comfort, but I would have rather had them be able to stay in the tent with us.

I finished tucking Timmy into one of the sleeping bags the

others had brought with us then lay down beside the boy. His eyes remained locked on me as he sucked his thumb. I stared at him, too, so he would know I was awake and watching and, hopefully, feel safer because of it. Gradually, his blinks became long and heavy until his eyes finally stayed closed and his mouth grew slack.

After pressing a kiss to the boy's brow, I crawled out of the small popup tent. Drav offered his hand and helped me to my feet while I looked around. The sky had darkened considerably since I'd gone into the tent. Most of the men lay in groups on the ground, apparently at ease with sleeping in their clothes under the stars.

"Is everyone settled?" I asked.

"Yes, Mya. Is Timmy asleep?" Byllo asked, his bright yellow gaze on the tent.

"Yeah. Just."

Byllo continued to watch the tent.

"If you think you can squeeze inside, you can check on him."

Byllo nodded and crouched low to unzip the tent and crawl inside. He barely fit.

"Are you ready to sleep?" Drav asked me, his voice carrying through the night.

I shook my head.

"I need to visit the bushes first," I said softly.

"I will take you." He threaded his fingers through mine and led me toward the copse of trees a fair distance from where all the fey men had bedded down for the night. The same exact spot I'd visited a few hours ago in daylight. Now, the light from the fenced-in area barely reached this far.

I released Drav's hand, ready to step into the trees on my own, but he stopped me with a hand around my wrist.

"No, Mya. I will check it first."

I stood on my tiptoes to press a quick kiss to his lips.

"Okay. But please hurry because I really need to go."

He walked into the trees, disappearing for several long minutes during which I bounced on my toes. When he finally emerged and gave me the go ahead, I rushed into the darkness without another thought.

The struggle with my button gave me a moment of worry before I dropped my pants and squatted. I tried to pee quietly so I could still listen. It proved impossible, though. Commander Asshole was going to get an earful when I saw him tomorrow. Had he even given one thought to what it would be like for a healthy human female outside the fence? Probably not when he simply needed to unzip and wave it around to relieve himself.

A breeze stirred some dead leaves behind me. I frowned and turned my head. No breeze touched my skin. A dark shape moved in the trees with me. I opened my mouth, ready to scream when another shape came from behind me. I struggled to finish my business as the two collided with barely a sound. The disgustingly familiar wet sound of a head being removed heralded the end of a threat. How many times would this man need to save me?

Shaking, I quickly zipped and buttoned then flew at Drav as the body fell to the ground. He tossed the head aside and turned just in time to catch me in his arms. I didn't hesitate to pull him down for a kiss. He bent willingly toward me.

My fingers touched matted hair. A tiny alarm went off in my head. That alarm grew louder as the man stiffened at the first press of my lips to his.

I jerked back, almost falling into the puddle I'd made. He caught me with an arm around my waist and pulled me upright before releasing me. We stared at each other in the dark. Well, he probably stared, I could barely see the outline of him.

"You're not Drav," I said softly.

His teeth flashed white then he just disappeared.

"Mya?" Drav said from further away. "Did you call me?"

I stumbled toward the sound of Drav's voice. He caught me in his arms, and I clutched him tightly.

"What is it? Are you hurt?"

"No. An infected was in there."

He growled and picked me up, quickly removing me from the trees.

"It's dead. A fey killed it. I thought the fey was you." I looked up at him feeling slightly sick. "I kissed him."

He stopped walking and looked down at me.

"I thought it was you," I said again, my voice catching.

"Shhh." Drav leaned his head against mine. "Do not cry. We will find who tricked you, and I will remove his head."

I sniffled and half-laughed.

"You can't. He would die."

"I will not share you."

"No. I don't want you to either. I think I startled whoever that was as much as I startled myself when I realized it wasn't you. He took off as soon as I released him. As long as you're not mad at me, let's not make a big deal about this. It was a mistake. That's all."

Drav opened his mouth to say something more, but never uttered a sound.

A lone howl echoed in the air. Gooseflesh exploded on my arms, and I stared up at Drav, panic coursing through me.

He picked me up in his arms and ran toward the fey.

CHAPTER TWELVE

AN ALARM IMMEDIATELY BLARED FROM THE MILITARY BASE.

"Condition Alpha! Hellhounds!"

A set of lights inside the fence went dark with a loud pop followed by the sound of broken glass hitting the ground.

The fey, who had been lounging moments ago, jumped to their feet.

"Don't shoot the fucking lights!" someone yelled from inside.

The three remaining lights went out rapidly, plunging everything into darkness.

Drav growled and didn't stop running until he reached Timmy's tent. I set my hand on Drav's chest, seeking comfort while trying to figure out what the hell was going on.

Around us, a soft blueish glow emerged from the dark as the fey's crystals began to come to life. The fey stood ready, studying the darkness. My gaze shifted toward where they watched. My eyes adjusted quickly, picking up the dark shape of the trees and the distant building across the road. I realized I saw far more than I thought I should have been able to see.

Over the ringing of the siren, I heard the men yelling from inside the fence.

"Meyrs, get the replacement bulbs. Davison, get the ladder."

"I knew we couldn't trust those grey skinned bastards!"

"We aren't shooting out the lights," I yelled back before turning my face toward Drav. "Are we?"

"No."

"Bullshit," an angry voice called behind us. "This is a fucking arrow shaft. We use guns."

"Find them," Molev shouted.

Several groups of fey ran off into the darkness surrounding the camp just as another howl ripped through the air, barely audible under the siren's wail.

The idiots were already dealing with hounds and possibly the two outlaws. They needed to shut the siren off before the infected came, too.

Byllo emerged from the tent, holding a very frightened Timmy. I reached out and patted the boy's back.

The sirens stopped. In the distance, an eerie howl rent the air followed by a chorus of others.

"Sounds like they found us," I said softly. I worried for the fey who'd left. They had spears and bows while the humans behind the fence had guns and didn't trust us.

The growls grew louder. The group of remaining fey tightened their circle around Drav and Byllo. I stayed still in Drav's arms, trying to hear over the pounding of my heart.

Drav and Byllo's gazes searched the dark, watching for the telltale flicker of red against the black of night. Off to the side, toward the trees, I thought I saw movement. But nothing emerged.

Pops sounded behind us, and I flinched. The fey looked unfazed.

"What are they shooting at?" I asked.

"A hellhound approaches from the other side."

As soon as Drav said the words, I spotted a dark shape trotting from the dark. The flashes of light that punctuated each pop of a fired bullet didn't faze the beast. Either the shooters were missing or the bullets hitting its flesh didn't faze this hound, just like the one back at the stadium. With its gaze focused on the shooters, the monster growled low and charged the fence.

Six fey moved to intercept. I clutched at Drav in fear for them as the guns continued to fire.

"Stop shooting!" I yelled.

The fey didn't wait. They ran at the beast while the Commander yelled for his men to hold their fire. The gunfire quieted before the hound clashed with the first fey. Grunts and growls filled the air as the fey struggled to grip the beast. The hound sunk its teeth into a man's arm. The other fey used the distraction to impale the hound with a spear and pin it to the ground. The bitten man punched the beast in the throat, still fighting for release.

Another howl came from the trees to our right.

"How many are there?" I asked, my eyes moving from the thrashing hound to the trees.

"I hear three. Do not fear, my Mya. No harm will come to you or Timmy."

As he spoke another dark figure crept out of the woods. Its glowing red eyes seemed to lock onto mine. Dread formed a murky pool in my stomach. The hound lowered its head as if getting ready to charge.

Six fey broke away to face off with the second hound. Before they could reach it, another beast stepped from the barren undergrowth. This one growled loudly and sprinted toward the fight.

Three of the fey jumped forward, trying to tackle the beast. The other three stalked the first hellhound, waiting for it to charge. It didn't, though.

The burst of gunfire flared nearby us, and I ducked my head. When I looked up, I saw that the hound near the trees was trying to creep around the fey. The beast's eyes were locked on Timmy and me, but the fey kept blocking the hound's attempts to go around. As the hound snapped its teeth in warning, another lone howl came from the darkness.

"Shit," I said under my breath.

"Get those lights working!" someone yelled from inside the fence.

The dozen men fighting the hounds wouldn't be enough. I'd seen how a pack of hellhounds could slowly peck away at their numbers. Numbers we couldn't afford to lose. While the main group of fey stood around Timmy and me, the rest struggled. They needed to help their men.

"Drav, Timmy and I have to get inside. We'll be safer there and the rest can go help."

The tussle of Timmy's black hair moved in the blanket Byllo had wrapped around him. Byllo's gaze met Drav's, and Byllo nodded before he sprinted for the gate.

Drav pressed a kiss to my temple and followed. At the gate, the humans posted as guards lifted their guns, aiming it at Byllo and Timmy. The fey roared at them.

"Lewis. Eldridge. Hold your fire," a loud voice barked from behind them.

The guards immediately averted their weapons. However, no one moved to open the gate when Byllo reached it.

"You have to let us in," I yelled, only a little behind them. "The fey will be able to focus on the hounds better without Timmy and me out here."

The commander nodded sharply, and the gate rumbled open just enough to let Byllo slip inside. Drav and I quickly followed.

While Byllo took Timmy further in, I asked Drav to stop. We watched the fight outside the fence.

Some of the fey who had guarded us had split off toward the downed hellhound. The first spear had snapped, and a second spear held the hound in place as the men continued to stab the beast repeatedly. The thing didn't stop growling or trying to bite them.

"Why isn't it dying?" I asked.

"Our weapons do not kill them."

His words sent a spike of fear through me.

I thought back to the hounds I'd seen Drav fight on the surface. He'd run while both of them still moved. Likewise, I hadn't witnessed what happened to the hounds who'd chased us when we met up with Kerr before returning to Drav's home. Did that mean the hounds couldn't die in the caverns or up here?

The group of fey fighting the two hounds to the right kept the creatures at bay while the rest worked to try to kill the pinned one. My gaze swept the darkness, searching for more glowing red. They were out there, somewhere, along with the groups of fey who had left to hunt them.

A flash of movement drew my attention to the left. A fey had caught the crazed animal by its neck, reached around, and ripped its lower jaw off in a disgustingly familiar move. The hound continued to make sounds and struggled to lunge for the fey as if unaware it could no longer bite.

The fey fell upon the beast, hacking at the creature. I wanted to turn away but couldn't. It was brutal to watch, but they had to find a way to kill it. If they couldn't, there was no hope for us humans.

Something slammed into the fence right in front of us, jolting my attention. The volume of the hound's snarls competed with the sound of its claws against the fence as it tried to climb its way in. Drav stepped back and growled in return. The men around us opened fire until the hound bled from multiple wounds. The report of gunfire didn't cease, each bullet mangling the beast's flesh further until I could see inside of it.

A light flashed in the dark cavity of its body. Not a normal bright light, but an unnatural dark glow. A shiver raced through me as the sinister non-light shimmered again.

"Did you see that?" I said to Drav.

He grunted.

"Keep shooting at its chest," I said. "Where the heart should be."

Tissue disintegrated under the fire until I saw bone, and the dark peeked through the mangled mess.

"Molev, look at its heart," Drav said.

Molev and another fey rushed forward. The firing stopped, but the hound didn't. It continued its attempt to claw its way through the fence unaware or uncaring of the two men approaching. The fey crashed into the wounded hound and knocked it over. The hound tried to jump back up, but Molev threw his arm around the beast's neck, pinning it while keeping a safe distance from its snapping jaws.

The second man plunged his hand into the creature's chest cavity.

"Hurry," Molev barked.

The fey tugged twice before finally jerking back and pulling out a rugged, black rock from the hound. The object pulsed with its darkness. The hound continued to struggle, unfazed by whatever they'd removed.

"What is that?" I asked.

"It looks like a crystal," Drav said.

Molev strained to keep his hold, the muscles in his arms and neck bulging.

"Break it," Molev said.

The fey wrapped his hands around the stone. His arms flexed and the crystal on his wrist flared blue. With a crunch, the black stone dissolved to black dust, and the hellhound stopped moving in Molev's arms.

"Their hearts are their life crystals," Molev bellowed. "Remove them, and destroy them."

While he tossed the dead hound aside and got to his feet, the fey dealing with the speared hound ripped out the same black stone and crushed it as well.

The floodlights flared to life behind us. The remaining hellhounds yipped and ran back into the night.

The relief I felt in the destruction of the two hellhounds didn't last long, though. With the light, I could see the men. The hellhounds had left their marks on so many of the fey. So had the bullets of the humans within the fence.

"Put me down, Drav."

He'd barely done as I'd asked when some asshole pushed him from behind. Drav pivoted, facing the man.

"What the fuck do you think you were doing?" the man shouted.

"I accept your challenge," Drav said with deadly calm.

"No, you don't!" I quickly tried to step around Drav, but he held me back with an arm.

"No challenge issued, right?" I insisted, looking at the man.

The guy didn't take the hint as his challenging gaze stayed locked on Drav.

"Fuck if there wasn't. You almost got us killed. Why? To prove you could kill the hounds?"

"What are you talking about?" I demanded. "You assholes hid behind this fence while the fey did all the work. How does that translate to them almost getting your cowardly asses killed?"

The man held up several broken arrows.

"They took out our lights and brought the hounds."

"Enough," Commander Willis said, striding toward us. "Go check the back fence." He held out his hand for the arrows. The man surrendered them and walked off stiffly.

The Commander looked down at the broken shafts.

"We use guns," he said.

"And they use spears and arrows. So what? I've already told you, they have two outlaws up here. Those arrows weren't fired by these fey, right here."

"And you expect me to believe it was their outlaws?"

"Expecting anything in this world seems pretty pointless, but I'm telling you the truth. These fey have traveled by day to avoid the hounds because of me and Timmy. They wouldn't shoot out lights and risk us. And none of this would have been an issue if you'd let us in the fence where you could have clearly seen what we were doing, which was trying to sleep on the hard ground."

The commander sighed, a soul-weary sound, and scratched under his jaw as he looked at the bodies of the fallen hounds.

"Infected we can handle if there aren't huge waves of them, but those hounds...nothing we have slows them down, aside from a well-thrown grenade. But they're usually already out of the way before it detonates."

He faced me.

"Collect any supplies you have and bring in your injured. We'll set you up in the training gym. We don't have enough beds for you all, but we've got a good supply of cots."

"Open the gates," he called.

While the fey helped their wounded inside, Byllo joined us. Timmy was still draped against the man's shoulder, one little hand resting on Byllo's neck.

"Are you okay?" I asked the little boy.

He shook his head.

"Did those dogs scare you?"

He nodded.

"Me too. But we don't have to sleep outside anymore. We'll be safer inside, okay?"

He nodded once more, and I wondered if he had any hope of growing up normal.

"This way," the commander said when the men were inside.

He led us toward one of the larger buildings, stopping soldiers along the way with orders for them to round up all the unused cots and bring them to the training gym.

When we arrived, a few cots already waited.

"We house traveling families or groups seeking shelter until we can get them to a better equipped base. Rest up. We'll talk in the morning. More soldiers will be in with cots."

After that, the man left.

The fey spread out, the wounded taking the cots. I searched through our bags for the first aid supplies and went to work cleaning cuts, bites, and the occasional bullet hole. Drav followed me around quietly, not trying to stop me from using what we'd gathered.

While I worked, Molev spoke to a couple of groups who nodded and went outside.

"Where are they going?" I asked Drav as I dabbed a cut over a fey's eye.

The man held himself completely still and kept glancing at Drav. They'd all done that. I didn't try to send Drav away, though. Having him near comforted me, even in the midst of the fey who I knew would protect me to the last man.

"To guard the entrances. Molev does not trust the humans here."

"I don't blame him."

I added a bandage and stepped back from the injured fey.

"The cut probably needs stitches, but I don't know how to do that. Keep an eye on it. If it starts oozing anything nasty, tell me." It was the same thing that I'd said to all of the fey I'd treated.

I turned, looking for anyone else who needed help. The men lay spread out on the cots that had slowly appeared, courtesy of the commander. Those without cots sat propped against the outer walls. Most already slept. No one else seemed to require my attention.

My eyes burned with the need for sleep, and I shuffled closer to Drav, leaning into him.

"Come," he said.

Drav led me over to two cots pushed together and encouraged me to lie down. I didn't need much encouraging.

"Stay with me?"

"Of course, my Mya." He lay beside me and held my hand.

I drifted to sleep with his thumb rubbing up and down the back of my hand.

"COMMANDER WILLIS WILL WANT to know more about the hounds and how to kill them," I said before taking another bite of my plain oatmeal.

Byllo sat at the same table as Molev, Drav, and me. He carefully fed Timmy each bite from their shared bowl. Once the boy chewed and swallowed his current bite, he immediately opened his mouth for more. I was pretty sure Byllo hadn't eaten anything yet.

"He saw how to kill them. The humans do not have the strength," Molev said.

"Sure. We know that. But, it'll take a while for them to come to that same conclusion."

As if mentioning the commander had summoned him, the man walked through the door. As he strode across the room, he addressed Molev.

"Your people can continue to rest here until the patrol returns with the supplies. Meanwhile, I'd like to discuss a few things with you."

Molev's gaze shifted to me briefly before landing on a few of the fey.

"Azio and Ghua, come with me."

The two fey stood and walked out with Molev and Willis.

I finished up with breakfast and glanced around the room. The fey were resting, Timmy was in good hands under Byllo's watchful eye, and we weren't under any immediate threat.

"I wonder if there's anywhere to shower," I said, looking at Drav. The bathrooms attached to our building just had toilets and sinks.

"Most of the humans here smell like soap," Drav said.

I grinned.

"Then let's see if we can find one."

I stood, and Drav followed me outside. I asked a soldier watching our building where I could find a shower. The man led us to a different building.

Inside, not far from the entrance, the soldier opened the door to a locker room type space. He pointed out the stock of supplies and the towels that filled a shelving unit just inside the door, then left with the warning that he'd check on us in ten minutes.

Drav and I took a quick shower together. It felt good to really clean myself, but I hurried to rinse and dry, not wanting anyone to walk in. Especially not with the healing bite still on my shoulder. Once dressed, we left the shower room.

I thanked the man, who'd waited just outside the door, and Drav and I went to rejoin the others in their dining hall.

The fey we'd left there no longer sat at the tables quietly eating a meal I knew they found disgusting. Instead, the bowls had been collected and stacked on one unoccupied table while the majority of the men gathered around a different table. Human soldiers were crowded in with the fey, all focused on something I couldn't see clearly.

Shouts of encouragement and a low murmur of conversation echoed in the room as I pushed my way forward, through their numbers, already suspecting what I'd find.

Four fey sat on one side of the table with four humans on the other. Each pair had their hands clasped above the table's surface. Grins plastered the participant's faces.

"Go!" one of the humans yelled.

The men were at a standstill for several seconds until the first fey grunted. As one, the fey began pushing back on the humans.

Sweat dotted the forehead of each human. Several bicep muscles quivered with effort. They didn't stand a chance. Not in arm wrestling. Not in any physical sport against the fey. In short order, each fey brought his opponent's hand to the table. The fey grunted and grinned while the pairs shook hands. The contenders switched out so four new sets could test each other's strengths.

At the end of the long table, Byllo sat with Timmy. In front of Timmy waited an open coloring book and a couple crayons. Byllo had a crayon in his hand and followed Timmy's gaze to the men arm wrestling.

Timmy twisted in his seat and mimicked the men further down the table, lifting his tiny elbow on the table and held his hand out for Byllo to take. Byllo set his crayon down, gripping the toddler's hand.

Timmy grunted loudly just like the men further down the table. Byllo grunted and let Timmy knock his hand down to the surface. Timmy's delightful laughter filled the room, catching the attention of the other fey. Soon more fey and even some of the humans came over and "challenged" Timmy.

I smiled. Maybe there was hope that human and fey could co-exist, after all.

CHAPTER THIRTEEN

The distant rumble of engines and a growing commotion outside our building woke me. Drav's cot beside me lay empty but still retained his heat. Whatever was going on had woken him, too.

I got up and stepped outside while redoing my ponytail. Many of the other fey stood near the building's entrance, blocking my view. Nudging my way through, I found Drav near the front. I stood behind him and took in the sight of the busy enclosure.

Human men poured from the white building and ran toward the fence where the gate was in the process of sliding open. Just beyond the outer fence the convoy of seven vehicles, along with their fey escort, approached. No infected trailed behind them.

The vehicles and fey cleared the gates, and I smiled at the sight of Kerr's familiar face. With Drav at my side, I hurried toward the gate to welcome the fey back. The commander already stood nearby with Molev.

While the humans looked tired and dirty, the fey appeared well enough and no dirtier than when they'd left. They'd fared much better than we had.

Kerr saw us and jogged over.

"How did it go?" Molev asked.

"Bud is dead. I'm sorry, Mya," Kerr said.

"Can't say I'm really sorry about that. He was an asshole. What happened?"

Kerr shrugged. "When we returned, the gate stood open. A trail of cans led from the empty barn into the woods where we found Bud's remains and several waiting infected. We cleared the infected and helped gather the supplies the infected had left in trails all over the woods."

I didn't like the sound of that. More baiting and traps. Drav's fingers brushed over my side in a comforting gesture.

"Was anyone hurt?" I asked.

"No. One gun misfired, but the human survived."

"Misfired?"

Kerr nodded.

"If you will excuse me," the commander said, "I need to talk to my men."

The four of us watched him retreat into the white building with the driver from one of the vehicles. The gates closed and the men, human and fey, began to unload the supplies. I hoped the commander would deliver on his promise after talking to his men. We'd delivered on ours.

"What happened?" Molev asked Kerr.

"One of their men shot at me while we were clearing the infected. When I said I accepted his challenge, he said it was a misfire. An accident. It was not, but I kept the peace," he said, meeting my gaze.

I smiled at him.

"I bet it wasn't easy, but thank you for not giving Commander Willis a reason to withhold information from us. Hopefully, we'll find out where my parents are soon."

"And more women?"

"I hope so." Except for me and Timmy, uninfected women and

children seemed pretty scarce. "I'm going to go check on Timmy and make sure he's been fed," I said.

"Byllo fed him twice already. The child was hungry during the night. He's sleeping again," Molev said.

Drav walked with me back to the building, and I stopped to peek in on Timmy. The little boy slept curled against Byllo's side on a single cot. The fey just lay there, eyes open, watching the entrance of the building. When he saw me, he nodded.

"Timmy ate and relieved himself then wanted more sleep."

"That's just fine. Kids that age might still need naps, but I'm guessing everything he's going through is just taking a little bit more out of him."

Byllo frowned, concern on his face.

"Taking what out?"

"It's just an expression. It means he might be more tired than normal."

Byllo grunted, and I left the pair to gather the supplies the fey had brought inside our first night. With nothing left to do but wait, Drav and I returned to our position near the gate. Molev still watched the soldiers.

"No news yet?" I asked.

"Willis has remained in the building," he said.

The newly acquired supplies disappeared into the reinforced shed, and the trucks were parked inside the white building before the commander finally stepped out and strode toward us.

"There's another safe zone in Missouri," he said without preamble. "Whiteman Airforce Base. Your family is there."

Hearing those words squeezed my heart in the best possible way. Mom, Dad, and Ryan. Finally.

"We've radioed them and shared what you did for us," he continued. "They're expecting you."

He held out a folded map with the route already marked.

"Avoid the places crossed out. There are too many infected there to go in for supply runs."

"Thank you, Commander Willis," Molev said.

The commander gave a slight nod and walked away.

"Ready to head out?" I asked Molev.

"Yes. Lead and we will follow, Mya," he said with a glance at the map.

Drav scooped me up, and I smiled.

"Tell the men we're ready then. And tell Byllo to try not to wake Timmy when he picks him up."

The fey retrieved our supplies from where we'd left them inside the building. Within minutes, we were on our way north. The clearly marked map showed we needed to head up Highway 69, but not to go into the city of McAlester itself.

"Molev, we need to leave the highway before we reach the next town," I said as our group sprinted over the blacktop.

He called out for the group to slow and came over to look at the map with me. I pointed out the area that defined the city of McAlester and the highway cutting through it. Then, I drew my finger along the back roads that would take us far out of our way.

He considered the map in silence for several moments.

"Humans fear the infected because they can become infected. We cannot. You cannot. We are strong, silent, and fast. I think we should stay on your road and go through the city without stopping," Molev said.

"I'm not just worried about Timmy and me; I'm worried about you guys, too. Half the men from last night are still healing, and the commander marked it as heavily infected."

"We will be well, Mya. My instincts are telling me to go through."

I glanced at Drav.

"Molev is the strongest and oldest because he has good instincts."

They both waited for my decision.

"All right. I trust you guys." I reached up and gently traced the scar running across the bridge of Drav's nose. "But, we need to be careful."

He kissed me softly, and a moment later, our group continued toward the city. For the first stretch, we passed wide areas of grass and trees and quiet industrial buildings.

I watched the road and the structures around us. Knowing that the infected had evolved enough to try to bait humans worried me. I could ignore cans of food or a lone figure in the distance, but what if they tried using a kid again? I couldn't ignore that. Thankfully, I didn't see any sign of humans from the highway.

"Do you hear that?" Drav asked softly, still running.

"What?" I strained to hear what he had. Nothing but the whisper of boots against blacktop reached my ears, though, until we approached the city's shopping district. The faint wail of a car horn drifted on the light breeze.

Within moments, a shopping center came into view on our right. In the parking lot, an RV sat in the middle of a swarm of infected. The vehicle rocked as the creatures slammed into the sides, trying to get in.

Molev lifted his arm, and our group slowed.

"It's probably a trap," I said softly.

"Yes," Molev agreed. "But the infected seem to want whatever that thing is."

"It's an RV. A mobile home that people use when traveling."

"So there might be humans inside?"

"Yes. Hopefully, healthy ones."

A scream rang out, proving that uninfected humans were trapped inside.

"We need to help them," I said.

Half the group split off, racing toward the motorhome. The infected didn't notice the fey until the first infected's head flew through the air. The horn quieted, and the infected turned as one, attacking the immediate threat to their existence. It didn't matter that the infected now worked together. The herd of at least seventy infected posed no challenge for the fifty fey. Blood bathed the exterior of the RV by the time the last one fell.

In the silence, the fey watched the camper. The door stayed firmly closed.

"We need to go down there, Drav. If there are humans inside, the sight of you guys is probably scaring the hell out of them. They'll never leave the RV."

Drav grunted and led the way from the highway to the parking lot. The fey moved out of the way so Drav stood near the front of the group, just on the outskirts of the dead bodies now surrounding the RV. The stink of rotting flesh almost made me gag before the wind shifted, bringing cleaner air.

"Can you put me down? I look more like a captive than a willing..." What was I? I glanced at Drav, and found him watching me knowingly.

"I look more like a captive than a girlfriend."

He smiled slightly and let me down. With a blush covering my face, I focused on the camper.

"I really hope you're not all infected in there," I said in a normal voice. "And I really hope you can hear me without me needing to yell because I don't want any more infected chasing us."

One of the windows slid open an inch.

"We can hear you," a man said. "And no one in here is infected."

"Good. What happened? Why are you here?"

"We're on our way to the McAlester Ammunition Plant and stopped for supplies."

"The commander from McAlester said they don't come here because of too many infected." As I said that, I heard a distant call.

A moan like we'd heard on the road when the infected had tried to ambush us.

"The infected know you're here. Can you start the RV?" I asked.

"No. We came out with supplies, and it wouldn't start. Something got to the engine."

A trap.

"We need to get out of here. You have two options. Stay in there and face the infected on your own, or come out and let these men carry you out of the city."

"What are they?"

"They are the men who can hunt and kill infected and the hellhounds."

"You going to McAlester?"

"No. Whiteman. Honestly, McAlester isn't that safe. We just came from there. They had a hellhound attack the night before last. The whole thing would be filled with newly made infected if these guys hadn't been there."

The door opened, and a young woman with greasy blonde hair stared over her shoulder while the other inhabitants started yelling at her to close the door.

"I'm fucking tired of this shit," she said, not addressing us. "Everything wants to kill us. She's cleaner than I am and standing there telling us these guys are safe. Either they are or they aren't. Either they kill us or the infected do. I'm done."

She faced us and saw all the infected bodies for the first time.

"Holy shit."

"Yeah, stay where you are," I said.

I glanced at the men around me. Most of them had infected blood on them.

"Same rules apply to these humans as Timmy. If you have infected blood on you, stay away."

Some of the men grumbled, and others chuckled.

I looked at the girl again.

"If it's okay, one of these guys will carry you. They can run much faster than we can."

"Sure. Whatever."

I called out the names of a few men who had been around me enough that they weren't overly weird.

Ghua, still clean, stepped toward the girl first and picked her up.

"Hi," she said nervously, looking up at him.

"I will keep you safe," he said.

She exhaled shakily. "I'd really like that."

An infected called out again, sounding much closer.

From the shadows, another girl stepped forward. "I don't want to die here."

"How many are inside?" I asked.

"There's twelve of us, total."

"We need to hurry. Molev, who else can carry someone?" I asked.

Drav scooped me up, and Molev started calling out names. When a woman with a young girl stepped forward, I knew the woman wouldn't want to be separated from her daughter.

"It will be harder and less safe if one of these guys tries to carry two people," I said before she could ask. "But whoever carries your daughter will stay right beside you the entire time." She reluctantly handed over her whimpering daughter and squeaked a little when the next man picked her up effortlessly. She glanced at me, and I gave a half smile.

"You'll get used to it."

The human men were last, hesitating on the steps.

"We can walk," one said.

"We don't have time for that," I said.

An older man with white hair nudged the other man out of the way.

"Speak for yourself. If one of you wants to carry me, I'm willing to take the lift."

I grinned and watched Azio move forward to pick up the man.

"Azio, be extra careful. Humans with white hair tend to be more fragile."

The older man snorted.

"Come on, Mary, your chariot awaits," the man said.

An old woman stepped down and looked over the men.

"Oh my," she said. "I don't think I've seen this much bare chest since watching the Summer Olympics."

I chuckled, already liking Mary and the older man.

An infected came from around the side of the RV. The already bloody fey moved to create a protective circle around the humans and beheaded the infected.

"That's so gross," one of the girls said, turning her head away.

"Gross but effective." I looked at the remaining human men lingering by the RV. "It's now or never."

In short order, each of the twelve RV inhabitants occupied the arms of a fey. The group set off at their normal sprint, heading north out of town. A few of the fey hung back and dealt with any infected that tried to follow.

Once we cleared the city limits, I asked Molev if we could stop. He immediately lifted an arm and the group slowed.

"Good instincts, by the way," I said, giving his arm a pat after Drav placed me on my feet.

He nodded, and I turned to the humans who the fey were also putting down.

"My name is Mya. This is Molev and Drav."

The mom stepped forward. "I'm Jessie and this is my daughter, Savannah. Savvy for short." She went through the rest of the introductions quickly, nodding toward the older couple first. "That's James and Mary, then Finley, Ollie, and Aaron." Each man raised a hand when she spoke his name. The girls did the same.

"And that's Hannah, Emily, Taylor." They all looked close to my age. The two remaining boys, Caleb and Connor, looked about twelve or thirteen.

"Thank you for helping us," Jessie added.

"I'm glad we found you. You're welcome to travel to Whiteman Air Force Base with us. We were told my family is there."

"Yes. We'd like that."

"Good. Byllo, can you bring Timmy's bag and let Jessie use some of the wipes to clean up Savvy?"

He brought Timmy over to the woman, and another fey followed with Timmy's supplies. While they quietly cleaned up the kids and got them something to drink, I motioned for the other humans to move a little further away. The fey stayed loosely positioned around us. Drav and Molev remained with me. There would be no private talk to help explain things.

"Drav found me the first night this craziness all started. He didn't know a word of English then but kept me safe. Through all of it. The hellhounds, the infected, the bombs. I'm not telling you this so you trust him. I'm telling you this so you understand why I trust him and the others. Why I'll take their side over yours if it comes down to that."

Aaron slowly shook his head at me as if I'd lost my mind.

"They will keep you safe as long as you don't do something to jeopardize my safety or the safety of any other woman or child," I said.

"Why just women and children?" Aaron asked.

"Because they don't have any of their own."

"Seriously?" Taylor said under her breath, looking at the fey with partial awe.

"Yes. They'd never seen a female until me or a child until Timmy. This is still very new to them."

"So they are stealing women and children?" the older woman asked, horrified.

"No. I'm not stolen and neither is Timmy." Technically we kind of were, but I wasn't going to get into that. "We were both rescued. They're helping me try to find my parents. Along the way, they're also looking for any humans who aren't infected. But, I'll be honest. They're mostly interested in any female who would be interested in them."

"You mean interested-interested?" Taylor asked.

I nodded.

"Drav and I are very happily together. The rest see what Drav has with me, and they're hoping for the same. They are kind and gentle. They will ask you if you want to be carried...unless you're in danger. Then you don't get a choice. They are loyal and very protective. But they are also a little clueless about some things. Because of that, we need to set some rules so there are no misunderstandings."

"Jessie, you might want to cover Savvy's ears. Timmy, too," I said to Byllo. As soon as the children's ears were covered, my gaze swept over the fey. I knew what I needed to say, but could already feel my face heating.

"Humans are typically modest. We like staying covered, so no asking..." I swallowed uncomfortably. "No asking to see someone's pussy. And no more using that word."

"What word should we use?" one of the fey asked.

"Nothing. You don't need to talk about that part."

"Then how can we ask to see it?" another asked.

"You don't!"

There were unsatisfied grumbles around me, but I ignored them and addressed the humans once more, my face burning.

"These men don't know much about us or our culture. But don't mistake their naivety for lack of intelligence. If they do something that makes you uncomfortable, tell them. Nicely. If you're rude to me, they take offense. Don't use nasty words or slang. Not only are there children present, but these guys take things literally."

The girls, including Jessie, continued to watch the fey with a mixture of doubt and fear. I turned my attention back to the fey. Other than their open, hopeful expressions, they didn't have much going for them. Infected blood covered the majority of them. If I wanted the new girls to look at the fey in a different way than they did now, I needed to figure out how to get the guys cleaned up. But, first I needed to finish the rules so they didn't ruin their chances before they even got started.

"Any female under the age of eighteen is completely off limits for anything other than respectfully keeping her safe. Humans are still considered children until eighteen."

I glanced at the twelve newcomers.

"Do any of you have any questions about the rules?" Most of them shook their heads. "No? Good. Any fey with questions can ask Drav privately." I didn't want to deal with their pussy complaints.

"Now, we need to find a place for these guys to clean up."

"We're out in the open, and you want to stop for a shower?" Aaron asked angrily.

Savvy, who'd been dozing in her mother's arms, jerked awake with a cry.

The old man hushed Aaron; and Mary moved closer to Jessie, who held her daughter to her chest and bounced the child, trying to ease her back to sleep. The dark circles under Jessie's eyes stood out, another indicator of her exhaustion as her bounces became slower.

"Jessie, dear, give me the girl for a bit. Let one of those handsome men carry you for a moment or two," Mary said with a wink.

"I will carry you, Jessie," echoed around us as many of the fey spoke up at the same time and stepped forward.

The woman immediately took a step back and clutched her daughter a little closer.

"Back off boys, please," I said stepping forward. "We'll get the guys cleaned up first. But, maybe in the meantime, we can all walk. With this large of an escort, we're safe." I gave Aaron a pointed look.

The group surrounded around the humans, and Jessie moved over to where Byllo walked with Timmy in his arms.

CHAPTER FOURTEEN

THE HUMANS WE HAD SAVED CONTINUED TO BE WARY OF THE FEY AND tended to stay as far away from them as they could. That meant the group was spread out in its plodding pace with the humans in the center. Caleb and Connor, the young teenaged boys, dragged their feet against the ground in exhaustion. The girls walked in a group, leaning on each other. Jessie struggled to hold her daughter, changing her from hip to hip in an effort to find relief. And, Mary and James had fallen behind the rest.

We'd already walked for a couple of miles when we came up to a large lake. The water looked murky, but I didn't think the men would mind. The humans needed the rest, and the fey needed to bathe in order to continue carrying them.

"This is a good place to wash up," I said to Drav.

He grunted in acknowledgement and set me down.

"Are we going to rest for a bit?" Ollie, one of the older men with tired eyes and grey at his temples, asked.

"Yeah, we can rest while they wash up."

The fey who walked at the front dropped their pants without warning and went into the lake. The trio of girls gasped. Hannah's eyes went wide, but she didn't glance away. Taylor just gawked. Emily squeaked and turned away. Then she squeaked again.

I turned around to see more of the fey men pull the strings to their pants and drop them where they stood. Those standing near Mary looked at her before confidently and slowly walking past.

"Oh my!" Mary exclaimed as she got an eyeful. Most of the fey smiled proudly at her examination.

"Mama!" James called.

"Oh hush it, Pa. This is good for the blood." She winked and continued staring at the men who walked passed her.

Drav growled behind me.

"What?" I asked, turning around to him. He stood, watching the others walking naked to the lake.

"I do not like you looking at the others."

I smiled slightly and stepped close.

"Drav," I framed his face with my hands. "I only want you." I pressed a quick, chaste kiss to his lips. "And, as I recall, you had no problem with me seeing their bathing when we were in Ernisi."

He grunted, and water splashed as more fey made their way into the water.

"So stop worrying about what I'm not even remotely interested in and give me something I do want to look at."

He smiled and wrapped his arms around my waist.

"Join me?"

I glanced over at the brown water and the steam rising from the men already washing. I was no fool. That lake had to be as freezing as their underground river.

"I think I will pass."

Drav grunted then stepped back to pull off his shirt and drop his pants. I shook my head at his shameless walk into the water.

"You're a lucky woman," Mary said, ogling Drav's firm butt as he walked away.

"I am."

Mary's eyes went big as one of the fey left the lake. The afternoon light caught on his wet, chiseled chest.

"Mary," the fey said acknowledging her.

"New rule. No flirting with married women," I called.

"Oh, hush," Mary said.

"What is married?" a fey called.

"It's when two people are committed to each other and no one else."

"How do we know if a woman is married?" another fey asked.

"Married women usually wear a ring on the third finger of their left hand. If in doubt, politely ask if she's married."

A few of the freshly bathed men strode past the girls. Taylor nodded to them, taking their bath in stride. Jessie, who sat near Byllo, Timmy, and Savvy, kept turning her daughter back to her coloring book instead of the parade of naked fey.

The human men stood off to the side, talking quietly and ignoring the fey who had stripped down and washed off.

I walked toward them, curious about what they were so quietly discussing.

"We need food. The women haven't eaten in days. I know Jessie gave all of her rations to Savvy," Finley said.

Aaron hushed him and stared at me. I moved away from their conversation and went to the water's edge to wait for Drav. He, Molev, and I needed to talk. There wasn't enough food in my bag to feed everyone. We only had enough small portions to last Timmy and me a day. Just enough time for us to reach Whiteman, according to the map that the commander had given us.

Drav saw me, dipped underneath the water, then started toward shore. He emerged, water trickling down his body as steam rose from his skin. My mouth dropped open a little as I stared. He'd definitely given me something to look at. He was mine. All mine. My chest tightened as my eyes dipped lower. When I looked back up, Drav's eyes locked onto mine, and he smiled.

I tried to suppress my own smile and shook my head at him. I had to keep my thoughts on the humans who needed us, not the delicious expanse of Drav on display.

Unable to resist, I peeked one more time as he walked toward me. I licked my lips in appreciation, and he rumbled in satisfaction at my response.

"We need to focus," I said, stepping back as Drav stalked toward me.

"I am."

He stepped closer, his body brushing against mine.

"What did you want to talk about?" he asked, leaning in to kiss the side of my neck.

I shivered at the feel of his cool lips on my skin.

"Mya."

"Huh?" I was too distracted by his lips to remember his question.

Drav laughed quietly as his lips continued to blaze a path to my mouth. When he reached my lips, I made a sound of agreement and tugged my fingers through his hair, bringing him closer. His tongue traced the seam of my lips then delved inside, making me forget time and place. Only the two of us existed, and one of us had too many clothes on.

He pulled away, and when I finally opened my eyes, he wore a proud grin on his face.

"That was some kiss," I breathed.

"Did it help ease whatever worry filled your mind."

"Huh?"

"You came over with that look in your eye. What was troubling you?"

I shook my head, trying to gather my thoughts that had fled with his kiss.

"The humans haven't had anything to eat for days. We need to feed them."

Drav looked over my shoulder, and I turned to see Molev standing dressed behind us.

"Small groups can go out and scout for houses with food," he said.

I considered all the potential problems with that plan. The fey knew cans had food in them. But, they wouldn't know what kind of food because the fey couldn't read. While we didn't really have any right to be picky, I wanted to at least try to avoid feeding our new friends dog food.

"It would be best if each group took a human or two with them while gathering the food. Someone able to read the labels."

"We will take the human men."

I looked over at the younger boys, Connor and Caleb. I had already explained to Molev and Drav that they hadn't come into their manhood. Although I didn't want the kids out there, sending the older men worried me. It took most men time to warm up to the fey, and I didn't want anyone doing anything stupid while out scavenging.

"Maybe it would be better if I went out with a single group. If we don't collect enough in one trip, we could go out again."

"No, Mya. That would take too long. We will take Connor, Caleb, Aaron, and Finley. We will protect them."

"Okay. But, be careful. And, no challenges while you're gone."

"They will not be gone long, Mya."

I nodded. While Molev went to speak to a few of the fey, Drav quickly dressed. By the time he finished, four groups of five fey had split off to speak to their assigned humans.

Connor and Caleb enthusiastically listened to the fey who explained the boys' roles in the hunt for supplies. When two of the fey turned around so the boys could climb up their backs, neither boy hesitated.

Not everyone in the group was as excited as Connor and Caleb, though. With a worried frown, Jessie watched the boys leave. Byllo reached over, set his hand on her arm, and spoke quietly to her. She nodded and rubbed her daughter's back as the girl colored with Timmy.

Finley and Aaron didn't get the same consideration the younger boys had. The fey told them they needed their help then threw the men over their shoulders and took off.

Some swearing trailed in the group's wake.

"Where are they going?" Hannah asked, stepping over to where I stood with Drav. Shax joined us, studying Hannah avidly. Interest sparked in his gaze.

"They're going to gather food," I said.

"It's not that we aren't hungry, but it's getting later. Are we going to be traveling at night?"

"No. We'll probably need to make camp somewhere."

Shax moved closer to Hannah, inhaling deeply through his nose. Her eyes cut over to him.

"What are you doing?" she asked warily.

"Smelling you. You smell different from Mya. But still good."

"Excuse me?" Hannah said, taking a step back.

Shax shadowed her move.

I smothered a grin at her expression.

"Think of it as their way of flirting," I said, trying to ease her worry.

Hannah's eyes went big as her gaze darted between me and Shax.

"Sniffing is flirting to them?"

"I am Shax," he said before I could answer.

He stood inches from Hannah. His hair, wet from bathing, stuck close to his neck, its length just brushing his shoulders. Hannah's hair was about the same length but in tight ringlets. Shax lifted his hand as if to run his fingers through the curls.

Hannah took a quick step back.

He tilted his head to study her, not at all bothered by her retreat.

"You have no penis," he said.

Hannah made a pained sound and glanced at me for help.

"Shax, that's not something we like having pointed out. We're very aware we're not made the same as you."

Hannah quickly retreated, and Shax stared after her.

"Did I say something wrong?" Shax asked, still watching her.

Hannah joined the other human women, who were moving closer to Jessie.

"You might have come off a little strong," I said.

"What does that mean?"

I patted his arm.

"It means no more penis talk."

Shax's gaze swung back over to Hannah. Determination lit his eyes. I cringed, wondering what he would do next.

Drav, who'd quietly watched the exchange with me, laughed and wrapped his arm around my shoulder.

"The men will not stop," he said.

"I know. Just trying to give them some pointers."

While we waited for the raiding parties to return, the rest of the fey spent the afternoon attempting to converse with the women. Mary willingly talked to each fey who spoke with her. She seemed to understand their curiosity about females and didn't appear to fear them like the other girls. Any time one of the fey approached one of the younger girls, they only responded with short, quiet phrases.

Drav and I remained nearby, ready to keep the fey in check. However, none of the fey pushed too hard with their flirting. Their attempts ranged from the obvious, "you have boobs" to the men challenging each other to brawls in front of the women.

Byllo ended up taking Timmy, Jessie, and Savvy to the edge of the lake, away from the commotion. The remaining human men stood back and watched the fey as well.

As the afternoon dragged on, I began to wonder what was taking the fey so long to scout for food. I tried to see the positive in the delay. With so much time together, the other women gradually grew more relaxed with the fey's presence. However, the fact that none of the groups had returned by the time the sun touched the horizon worried me.

James and Ollie, the oldest of the men, began walking the edge of the area. They picked up small branches and made a pile of them near the center of our gathering. It made sense that we'd want a fire once the sun set and the night turned cold. We humans would need the warmth. That thought just made me worry more. Would the fey know that Caleb and Connor would need extra warmth?

"The sun's almost down. Where are they?" I said to Drav.

"Do not worry, Mya. They will return soon," Drav said. "I can hear the young ones."

I followed the direction of his gaze. The group was walking the road in the distance, with Ghua at the front. Caleb sat upon the shoulder of one of the fey.

When the group reached us, the fey pulled Caleb from his shoulder and set him to the ground. The boy beamed with happiness and pride as he raced toward his friends. He barely reached the others before he started telling his story.

"Zoihm went first into the house we found and just chucked out a zombie's head. Then Hanno ran in to help, but Zoihm had taken care of all the zombies waiting inside. Once it was clear, we all went in. The guys let me pick out the food. Said I was the only one who could." Caleb spoke fast, pointing to the fey. "Hanno said they aren't hungry. That means there's enough for all of us to eat."

The other groups slowly began to return, too. Although the food they brought back wasn't abundant enough to feed the whole group, it would feed the people the fey had saved until we reached Whiteman. The humans lit the fire and started warming cans of food over the low flames as night descended.

The fey spread out in a protective circle surrounding us. Those who'd gone out to scout for the food lay down to sleep while those who'd remained behind stayed awake and vigilant. Both sets quietly watched the humans eat, listening and learning, and likely thinking of their possible futures with one of the girls.

The fey were finally living, not just existing.

CHAPTER FIFTEEN

A PLANE FLEW OVERHEAD. WHILE THE OTHER HUMANS GAVE RELIEVED laughs, I worried. I'd witnessed the destruction those planes could bring, if they chose, and thought their presence more of a warning than a comfort. I didn't know how the people of Whiteman would receive us.

My gaze tracked the progress of the plane until it disappeared up into the clouds.

"How much further, Mya?" Mary asked.

"According to the map, we should only have a few more miles to go."

"That's a shame," she said. "I rather enjoy being carried."

I glanced at the fey who currently held her. He winked down at Mary, and she giggled.

"Woman," James called, "don't forget who you're married to."

She grinned and winked at her husband, who smiled back.

The speed of the fey ate up the miles quickly, and only a few minutes later, we heard the faint reports of gunfire. The men immediately slowed down.

"We need ten who are willing to scout ahead," Molev said. "I will lead." Nine other men stepped forward, and Molev nodded to Drav before taking off again.

The men continued to carry us, but they walked, letting Molev's group scout ahead. No one complained about the pace or continued protection.

It didn't take long for Molev's group to return.

"I think the sounds are coming from the place we want. It is a fence that stretches very far. Men dressed like those with Willis stand inside the fence. Infected surround the barrier. The humans are using guns to shoot them, and the sounds are drawing in more infected."

"Did you see a gate or a way in?"

"Yes."

The hesitation in his eyes made my stomach dip.

"What aren't you saying?"

"They are many people at Whiteman. There are even more infected outside."

The worry congealed in my stomach, and I looked off in the direction of the base. We were so close.

"We should bait them like they've been baiting us," Ollie said.

"What do you mean?" I asked.

"They're still distracted by sound, right? Let's get a car or two and race up to the gate. Honk the horn. Rev the engine. Whatever it takes to get them to follow the car. Lead them away so the rest of our group can get in."

Everyone else got excited about the idea while I dwelled on Ollie's words.

"Wait," I said, looking at Molev. "The infected are attracted to sound. They have been since the beginning. The military would know that. How many infected bodies are laying outside the fence?"

"None. The bullets are missing their heads."

I glanced at the humans.

"You think they brought the infected to the gate on purpose," James said, watching me. "Why?"

"Exactly. Why? We helped McAlester during a hellhound attack. If not for these guys, the McAlester safe zone would be filled with infected already."

"How do we know it isn't?" Aaron said. "All we have is your word that you helped. Maybe that's why Whiteman is blocking its gates. Maybe they know you didn't help. Maybe these guys are the spread of the infection."

"Keep talking like that, and I'm going to tell that nice man to drop you on your head," Mary said with a scowl and a pat on her own carrier's arm. "You just ignore him. We know you helped."

The fey grinned at her.

"So what do we do?" Jessie asked.

"I'm not sure. What if Aaron's right? Not about our help, but about their doubt of it? Maybe Commander Willis didn't let them know we were coming like he said he would. Maybe the plane that flew overhead saw us headed toward Whiteman and told them a large group of grey-skinned people was headed their way. How did you feel when you saw these guys? If Whiteman wasn't warned, they're probably feeling the same way."

"If you helped, why wouldn't that commander share the information? I saw what those hounds can do. Bullets didn't seem to bother them. If these guys can take care of them, we need their help," Taylor said.

I rubbed a hand over my face, wishing I knew what to do.

"Mya," Molev said. "We can get you inside."

"How?"

"The infected are easy to kill. We will leave you here with—"

"Nope. Not happening," I said. "They have guns, and I don't trust them not to use them on you. If you're so sure that you can clear the infected, then I'm going with you."

"Us, too," James said.

"Safety in numbers," Emily added.

Jessie looked at her daughter and Timmy before meeting Byllo's gaze.

"I will keep you all safe," he promised.

She smiled at him, a telltale blush spreading across her cheeks.

"We go together, or we don't go at all," I said, looking at Molev then Drav.

When no one else said anything, I took a settling breath.

"All right. Let's do this."

Molev assigned an extra man to each human. Shax moved beside Drav with a nod to me.

"Protect the humans," Molev said. "Even from their own."

A shudder ran through me at his words. I really hoped it didn't come to that again.

"You will be safe," Drav said, pressing a quick kiss to my temple.

"I know. But will you?"

With a signal from Molev, the group started on our last stretch. Anticipation and worry battled in my stomach. I desperately wanted to see my family again but not at the expense of Drav.

The firearm discharges grew louder and more frequent as we neared. The little ones covered their ears and looked scared, but they didn't shed a tear or make a sound. Ahead, the fields gave way to a road then grass leading up to the long length of zombie lined fence, just as Molev had described.

The gate, what I could see of it, looked like a dual system. A long, wide channel of more fence separated the exterior gate from the interior gate. Both of them were firmly closed.

As soon as we came into view, the gunfire stopped.

In the sudden quiet, the infected lost some of their drive to claw at the fence. The forward push from those still arriving slowed then ceased. The almost silent thump of the fey running over the earth drew the attention of the infected.

They began to turn toward us.

"Do not stop!" Molev yelled.

The sound of his voice started an infected charge. The mass of them poured toward us, crashing into the fey at the front of our protective circle. Without pausing, the fey ripped off heads, clearing a path toward the main gate. Bodies fell, and the fey ran right over the top of them.

Drav held me tightly, sprinting toward the place of supposed safety. A place still firmly closed to us.

"Mya!"

I barely heard the voice over the noise of the infected and shouts of the fey. Through the fence, I caught sight of people running toward the group of uniformed men impassively watching us.

"Open the damn gate! There's people out there. Kids!"

The cried demands from inside didn't change anything.

With the gate still firmly closed, the fey fought their way through the infected. Once the first of the fey reached the metal barrier, the men spread outward, killing the infected trying to press in at the sides. The forward momentum didn't stop until those of us in the center stood at the gate, a half-circle of fey protecting us.

Most of these infected didn't seem as smart, their movements not as coordinated. However, a few groups worked together, targeting a single fey and trying to pull him away from the rest. The other fey didn't allow that to happen. They kept the infected at bay, beheading one after another in a bloody spray of gore.

A hum filled the air, and the outer gate began to move. Byllo rushed through with Timmy first then the fey who held Savvy. Drav waited until all of the fey carrying humans had wedged their way through before he moved forward into the press of bodies. Slowly, the remaining fey followed. I saw the problem right away. We wouldn't all fit. Still, the rest of the fey backed toward the opening, keeping the infected from reaching us.

The hum filled the air again, and the outer gate began to close.

I twisted around in Drav's arms and looked at the men. They had their guns poised, ready to fire. But at who? Us? The fey still outside? The infected?

"If they start firing on the rest of our group, we need to stop them," I said softly to Drav.

"Yes."

The outer gate barely closed when the inner gate swung inward.

"Move quickly!" a man shouted.

Drav tensed. I waited for the first bang to sound. Instead, a man stepped forward and started waving for us to hurry.

"Move!" he said again.

Byllo sprinted forward, the rest of us following. But not far. A circle of heavily armed men surrounded us. Drav stopped and turned back. We watched Molev and the rest continue to fight. My pulse raced as an infected bit down on his arm. The last fey ran from the space of safety between the two gates, and the inner gate swung shut.

I looked back at the men with the guns then Molev. The man shoved the infected back and ripped off his head before turning and dealing with another.

The outer gate began to hum once again. The remaining fey backed into the opening, a solid front against the infected. A garbled yell came from within the mass of milky-eyed bodies, renewing the frenzy of the creatures.

"Get in position!" someone yelled.

More men ran forward, passing around our guards to stand five feet from the fence, their guns aimed at the infected and the fey now trapped between the two gates. The fey didn't stop fighting until the last infected within the enclosure with them fell to the ground.

DEMON ASH

No one opened fire on the infected still outside the fence. The gate didn't open either.

"Timer!" someone yelled.

"Three minutes," someone called back.

"Put me down, Drav," I said.

He started too, but a shot into the air and a yell stopped him.

"Do not move!"

I looked over his shoulder anyway to the man who was doing all the yelling.

"What the hell are you doing?" I asked. "They just killed a quarter of the infected out there."

"And they were bit. Some of you could have been bitten, too. Timer," he said again.

"Four minutes and thirty-seven seconds," another man answered.

"So you're waiting to see if some of us will change? These men won't. Didn't Commander Willis contact you?"

"He did. And I surely hope that these fey men can do what he said they could."

For the next eleven minutes, we all just stood there with guns trained on us. I honestly didn't mind so much because, beyond the lines of men with weapons, there were lines of people fearfully watching us. The guns were meant to protect them, the survivors.

"Time's up!" the man with the watch yelled.

There was a long moment of silence then the inner gate made a noise and swung open for the remaining fey to enter the base.

"Now, which of you is Molev?" the man in charge asked.

"I am," Molev said, stepping forward.

"Welcome to Whiteman. You and your men are sorely needed. Will you follow me so I can explain our situation?"

"No," I said before Molev could move.

"No?" the man asked.

"Who are you? And, where are my parents?"

"I'm Matt Davis."

"No title?"

"None that would really matter anymore."

The way he said it set a lead ball in my stomach. As bad as it had seemed out there with the infected getting smarter, I'd hoped that was just my skewed perception. Having someone in charge of a safe zone say something like Matt just had, meant we were as screwed as I'd thought.

From the sea of uniformed military personnel, two people rushed forward.

"Mya!" my mom yelled.

Drav immediately set me on my feet.

"Mom! Dad!" I ran toward them, meeting them halfway. Their arms encircled me. Mom sobbed and held me tightly. Dad pressed several kisses to the top of my head.

"I can't believe you're here," Mom said, pulling back to look at my face.

"Me either," I studied her just as hard, memorizing the new worry lines creasing the corners of her soft brown eyes.

"Where's Ryan?" I asked.

"Cleaning up infected at another gate," she said.

Drav moved behind me, drawing her attention. I realized he had Dad's attention, too.

"Mom, Dad, this is Drav. He's the reason I'm alive. He found me that first night and kept me safe even though he had no idea what I was."

"You smelled good," Drav said.

I grinned and blushed slightly. Mom's gaze flicked between us.

"I see."

"And there are your parents, as promised," Matt Davis said. "If it's all right with you, I'd like to speak to Molev."

I glanced back at Matt.

"They need to clean up first. Although the infected blood doesn't bother them, it could contaminate others."

"I understand your concern," Matt said. "However, I'm hoping they will be willing to leave again. We need to clear the infected from the fence line so we can do a supply run."

"You were using your guns before, use them now."

"The sound draws them in."

"Yeah, which makes me question why you started using guns after your plane flew over and saw us coming."

He glanced at everyone around him then back at me.

"We had to know if what Commander Willis said was true."

"And what did he say?" I asked.

"That these men fought like demons and could kill anything."

"They can and have been. First showers, then talking."

I looked at my parents. Mom still silently cried. Tears of joy that broke my heart a little. I wanted to hug her some more. Both of them. But I knew that Drav and Molev needed me more at the moment. Matt had plans for them, and I had to be sure those plans wouldn't lead to their annihilation.

"I'm so glad to see you," I said quickly. "Let me clean up and listen in on the talks, then I'll come find you."

Mom nodded and waved me off. Dad hugged her.

I turned to Matt.

"These men are not your new weapon. They might be your new allies, though."

He nodded.

"If you'll follow me, I'll show you to the showers myself," he said.

The other humans in our group walked beside their newly made fey friends. Matt didn't question their presence, relieving me a little. When we reached a large building, he pointed toward the two labeled doors.

"Ladies to the left and gents to the right," he said. "We

converted this building for temporary public showers to accommodate all the families, which you'll see when we tour the zone. It's rustic, but it will do the job. You'll find what you need inside."

"I'll stick with them," I said, taking a step toward the men's room.

Matt started to frown, but I held up a hand.

"You needed proof to trust. I'm no different."

"Fair enough."

I stepped inside and studied the ceiling while giving basic instructions for turning on the showers, adjusting the temperatures, and rinsing away the infected blood.

"Rinse your clothes out, too," I said. "You'll probably need to wear them around wet. Sorry guys."

As soon as everyone finished, we stepped back out into the light. My parents had joined Matt in waiting.

"Mya, I thought you might be more comfortable with your parents showing the rest of your group around while we speak."

Mom gave me an encouraging nod and glanced at Drav again. I turned to Molev.

"You okay with the rest of the men going with my mom and dad?"

"Yes."

I focused on the group behind me. "These are my parents. Remember the rules. No swear words in front of them. No asking the questions you know you're not supposed to ask. No challenges until after you get back. No matter what. We clear?"

A bunch of "Yes, Mya," followed.

"Mom, do you have more daughters?" one of the guys in back asked.

"Are you married to Dad?" another asked.

"New rule. No questions at all until you get back," I said.

"Mya," Mom scolded with a hint of amusement, "they can ask us whatever questions they want."

"No, they can't." I felt on the verge of a heart attack just thinking of one of them asking to see her southern parts using the p-word.

I gave the men a hard look. "I mean it."

Matt cleared his throat.

"Follow me," Mom called. The men walked after her, and I could already hear her talking about the base.

"They will keep her safe, Mya," Drav said.

I smiled and shook my head.

"I know they will. I'm more worried about what they're going to say."

Drav, Molev, and I followed Matt to another building where he had maps pinned to movable boards.

"What is all this?" I asked, looking at the colored pins placed here and there.

"Bombed cities, clusters of infected, fallen safe zones, remaining safe zones, and sightings."

"Sightings?"

"Of the two men you're hunting and of the hellhounds. I won't go into the boring details of how we know all of this—"

More like he still worried the fey would somehow use those details against them.

"—but I wanted to show you what we face so you understand why we need your help. The black pins are bombed cities. The red pins are fallen safe zones. The green pins are functioning safe zones. The yellow pins are high volume areas of infected. The white pins are sightings. We're here," he said, pointing to the lone blue pin.

Black, white, and red dominated the area around us. McAlester had a red pin in it.

"Commander Willis?" I asked, touching the pin.

"On his way here in an armored truck. The infected breached his fence this morning."

"They're getting smarter," I said.

"They are," he agreed. "But, a bullet to the head will still end them."

"So, what do you need from these guys?"

"Their help. We need to end the most aggressive source of the infection. The hounds know we're here and want in. Without the perimeter lights, the fence is useless to keep us safe. But, if we can eliminate the hellhounds, we might have a chance. Not just here but worldwide."

"Do you know how many hellhounds there are?" I asked.

"We're estimating over one hundred here and almost as many overseas."

I looked at Drav and Molev. Why had it taken them so long to catch onto the fact that eating the deer made them monsters? Sighing, I faced the board again.

"What's the plan?" I asked.

"The hounds hide during the day. Usually in abandoned buildings. We're hoping if these guys go in after them, they can pick them off when they are at their weakest."

"We will help you," Molev said.

"Thank you." Matt's relief showed in the droop of his shoulders.

"I was thinking we could divide your men into three groups to attack here, here, and here," he said, pointing at white pins on the map.

"When?" Molev asked.

"Just after first light tomorrow."

"We will meet you at the gate."

Matt extended his hand, and Molev looked down at it. I reached forward and shook Matt's hand. Matt gave me a surprised look but caught on when he glanced at Molev and found the fey studying our hands. Molev shook his hand after I let go.

Although we'd just reached Whiteman, I knew the world outside the fence wasn't going to give us a break because we were tired and wanted to rest. The fey needed to go. And the fact that I didn't like it one bit didn't matter.

"Make sure the men who go with you come back," I said.

Matt nodded and resumed his study of the board as we walked out.

CHAPTER SIXTEEN

Mom and Dad were just outside the door, waiting.

"Where are all the fey?" I asked.

"We left them with their friends. They're figuring out the tent assignments. We thought you might want to join them. But, maybe we could talk first?"

"Yes, I'd like that." I hugged both my parents again then followed them as they led the way down a road.

"This part of the base is still used for the planes and pilots and whatnot. Toward the back, in the open areas, the military set up tents for the survivors when this first started. There's a lot of room now," she said sadly. "A week ago, one of those hellhounds got in and killed quite a few people before leaving again. It took a while to clear the infected out. Last night, another hound showed up. It didn't get as many. We all sleep with guns now."

It felt surreal hearing my mom say that.

She continued pointing out areas of interest as we walked our way across the fenced-in base. When we spotted the tents, I saw immediately that the fey had a table set up and were arm wrestling some humans.

I made a noise of exasperation.

"Oh, be nice," my mom said. "It's obvious they are trying to fit in. And they are so nice."

Dad snorted.

"What?" I asked, suspiciously. "What did they do?"

"Oh nothing. Your father is still miffed that one of them asked to see my pussy."

"Oh, God." Both my worst nightmares had come true. They'd asked the question they weren't supposed to and my mom just said the p-word.

"Mya, don't you dare scold them. It's obvious they're curious about us and are just trying to learn. Here we are," Mom said, stopping in front of one of the drab green tents. She pulled back the flap and motioned for us to enter.

I went inside the square canvas tent and looked around the dim interior. The space wasn't huge by any standards; but there was a small stove to the side for heat, a cot across from it, and two more shoved together against the back wall. As my parents sat on the doubled cots, Drav and I settled on the ground, our backs to the unlit stove.

Guessing the single cot belonged to Ryan, I glanced at the opening of the tent, half hoping he'd suddenly show up. I needed to see him.

"Ryan'll be back shortly. His shift at the gate is almost done, sweetie," Mom said, catching my gaze.

I nodded.

"We've worried about you every minute since the attack. Will you tell us what happened? How you two met?" Dad asked.

"Yeah. I guess I should start from the beginning."

I told them everything but glazed over some of the details of how Drav and I met. My parents listened raptly, not interrupting at all. Mom did sniffle, though, when I told them how Drav and I had been only a step behind them during the week before the bombings started.

Drav grabbed my hand and rubbed his thumb against mine when I spoke of his world and our time there. My parents gripped each other's hands when I described what happened to me at the superstore, and my heart broke at the sight of Mom's silent tears.

She waited until I finished before she slid off the cot and held out her arms.

"Oh, baby," she sniffled against my hair.

"Quite a tale, Sis."

I looked toward the entrance of the tent. Ryan stood there, the afternoon light shadowing his features. Since I had last seen him, shaggy brown hair had been replaced by a short, almost military cut.

I swallowed hard and untangled myself from Mom to rush to my brother. He hugged me hard in return as my hands brushed the rifle strapped to his back.

"I wasn't sure we'd get to see each other again," he said, still holding me.

"Your messages helped. Thank you."

He gave me a brotherly pat then released me. I really looked at him. He had worry lines around his eyes now, too, and he looked much leaner. I tugged him further into the tent.

"How long have you been standing there?" I asked.

"Long enough to hear about your time down under and the trouble you've been brewing since you came back."

His gaze went to Drav, who still sat on the ground.

"This is Drav," I said, taking a step closer to the man who'd stolen my heart.

Drav stood and nodded toward Ryan.

"Sorry about the welcome you received at the gates. But, thank you for bringing Mya to us. For keeping her safe. Keeping her alive."

Ryan held out his hand to Drav. Drav glanced at it, then at my brother, before clasping his forearm. Ryan returned the gesture.

"She is the only good thing up here," Drav said. "I will always keep her safe."

Ryan didn't try to stifle his laugh this time.

"You'll fit in just fine."

Dad stood and repeated Ryan's thanks and handshake. Seeing all the people I cared about finally together warmed my heart.

"So what happened to you guys? I want to hear everything."

We all settled back into our seats, Ryan joining Drav and me on the ground.

"Ryan started talking nonsense about hounds in Germany," Dad said. "He was so worked up, we had already agreed to pack up and head to the cabin before we even heard the first howl. Ryan figured out real quickly that the lights kept those monsters away. We stayed in the house with every light on until after the hounds swept through the city. Then, we loaded up the car, rigged floodlights on the roof, and headed north. We made it to the cabin with no problems. But, it helped that we arrived after the hounds had already gone through."

I nodded. "We saw Doug."

Dad sighed, and Mom made a small sound of grief.

"When the military came and told us we needed to leave, that infected were coming, Doug never answered his door. They didn't give us time to check on him ourselves."

I was glad they hadn't. If they'd tried, they might not be alive now.

"The military escorted us to Tinker during the day. The infected were everywhere in the city. They came out in droves at the slightest sound.

"Once we got to Tinker, we searched the crowds for you, hoping you were already there. We ran into some other survivors from Oklahoma City. They told us the same story about the university evacuation that you did. We never thought we lost you, though. You are too smart. But, every day more survivors came, and there was no word from you." Dad swallowed hard. "We tried to stay at the base as long as possible. They were flying out survivors during the day and digging in at night. The whole time, those hounds seemed to know right where we were, attacking anyone they could reach. The military forced us out here two days before the bombings started.

"So much has changed since the bombings. This wasn't the only base the military set up for civilians. The people in charge then had the survivors spread out, living and working in different safe zones. We kept in contact with several of them. Getting reports. Coordinating military efforts. But, more bad things started happening.

"The infected started setting traps. Less military personnel were returning from supply runs. Then, some of the safe zones stopped answering. Flyovers showed them overrun by infected. More convoys of survivors started showing up here. However, that stopped when the hounds returned a few days ago.

"McAlester was one of the last nearby safe zones. Our long-range communication is spotty. Nothing better was turned back on. From what I know, we have only spoken to Europe once since the world went to hell.

"We don't know what's still left of the world or its leaders."

"What happened to the military leaders at this base? At McAlester, Commander Willis was still in charge. His men seemed like true military personnel. It doesn't seem like that here," I said.

"That's because so many of the people left are civilians. Evacuees. Families who escaped. People who don't know how to be military but still need to do their part in protecting this place. We're all adjusting. We work hard. We're surviving."

We were silent for a moment after that statement. The new world was not kind. The humans here were surviving; but given what Dad had just said, they wouldn't have survived for much longer. This safe zone would have fallen like all the other safe zones. My hands trembled at the thought, and I clasped them in my lap.

Drav and I were here now, and the fey would keep them safe. But, the hounds and the infected weren't the only issues we faced.

Winter was on its way. The weather had gotten colder since we'd returned to the surface. Cold weather meant finding ways to keep warm. The little stove in the tent was a start, but I'd already noticed there was no wood. We would need supplies to survive. We would need to leave the safety of the fence.

"You are thinking very hard, Mya," Drav said, leaning toward me to press his lips to my temple.

"There's a lot to think about."

"There is," Dad agreed.

"How about we go get some dinner? We'll look for an extra cot so you can stay with us, Mya," Mom said.

Drav's hand twitched on my thigh. I set my hand over his, likely thinking the same thing. Seeing my family again had been amazing. I couldn't believe they'd made it here safely. That they were still alive. But, the fey had become more than friends to me. They felt like family, too. And, Drav felt like so much more.

"I'll be staying with Drav and the other fey."

"All right," Mom said with a small, disappointed smile. "Let's go eat. I'm sure Ryan is starved after his shift, and I bet you two haven't eaten in a while."

"No, we haven't."

As the four of us made our way through the encampment, I paid more attention. Everywhere I looked, I saw the same thing. People pushed to the point of exhaustion. They shuffled toward their tent, then the flap closed behind them.

"Where did you go this time?" Mom stopped to ask a man

passing us. His lifeless blue eyes stood out against his weary, dirty face.

"We tried for the superstore in Sedalia. Almost made it. Another trap. The infected took out half of our supply party this time." The guy's voice didn't change in pitch while sharing the news.

"Emery?" Mom asked quietly.

"Gone. I kept my promise to him when he was bitten."

The man walked away and closed himself in a tent.

"Who was that?" I asked.

"Emery's father. He's lost everyone now," Mom said.

My parents' words came back to me. *We are surviving.*

Were they? Making through one day to the next, dying a little inside each day? I wasn't sure that counted as surviving.

We didn't stop to speak to anyone else as my parents led us to the mess hall. We joined the line of silent people slowly shuffling into the building.

Further inside the door, a hardened woman stood at the counter, scooping out food to each person who passed by her. Another woman, with a kind smile, handed out rolls.

When my parents reached the stack of trays, they each grabbed one then stepped toward the counter. The woman scooped some kind of steaming stew mixture on their trays. It looked amazing, and I eagerly stepped up with my tray.

With a scowl of dislike, the woman fixed her gaze on Drav.

"Some of your kind was here earlier. Said they'd only eat meat. I got Spam."

"Spam will be fine," Drav said.

The lady grunted, grabbed two small cans of spam from under the counter and plunked them on Drav's tray. She plopped a scoop of stew onto mine.

"Don't mind Bertha," Mom said as we walked away. "There are

a lot of people who are having a hard time adjusting, and accommodating everyone isn't possible. She's a little touchy."

"It's fine, Mom. This looks great. Far better than what I've had to eat in a long time."

"Don't get too used to it," Ryan said. "This is it until there's a successful supply run."

We sat at an empty table and quietly ate our food. I savored each bite of my hot meal while trying not to pay attention to Drav enjoying his gel-covered Spam. When we finished, we took our trays to another counter where a different pair of women worked, washing their way through a tall stack of dirty trays.

"We all have jobs here," Mom said as we left the building.

"I bet I know what your job will be," Ryan said, reaching out to give my hair a playful tug.

Drav growled.

"It's okay, Drav. Ryan's just teasing me. It didn't hurt."

Drav grunted and gave my brother a warning look. I grinned at Ryan and arched a brow.

"You're not playing fair," Ryan said.

I shrugged and turned to Mom and Dad, who watched me closely.

"Drav and I really need to check on the rest of our group."

I wasn't overly worried about the fey. But, in a lot of ways, they were like children. They didn't know much about the human world, and I didn't want them to get into any trouble.

We found the fey at the far end of the encampment where they had been assigned the tents closest to the fence. With the help of the humans we'd rescued, the men were settling into their new homes.

Savvy and Timmy chased each other. Byllo and Jessie stood together watching the children.

"These men are just amazing with children," Mom said.

"They really are."

"Come on," Dad said. "I'm sure whoever is in charge has a tent for you somewhere around here."

As we walked, I noticed tent numbers and names already written on tape near the openings. Three fey had been assigned to each tent. We kept walking, looking for a tent with Drav's name on it. Before we found it, we found Molev talking to a man with a clipboard.

"Mya. Drav," Molev said in greeting.

"Hey, Molev. What's going on?" I asked.

"We're setting the fey up in these tents by the fence," the man said.

"Why's that?" I asked. I already had figured out the reason, but I wanted the man to say it aloud.

"To protect all of us from the hounds," the man answered.

"And to keep them as far away from the rest of you as possible?"

The man looked down at his board briefly before meeting my eyes.

"I think most of us would take a lion as a house cat if it would keep us safe."

I sighed. It would have been foolish to expect open acceptance. The fey were too different for that. But, I knew after the people got to know the fey, their attitudes would change like mine had.

"Your tent is not by the fence," Molev said to me.

The man nodded. "Tent H11 has been assigned to you and Drav. The H-row is the fourth from the fence."

Drav threaded his fingers through mine as we followed my parents toward our assigned tent. Two sleeping bags and my backpack waited inside by the cold stove.

"This one looks nice," Mom said. "No cots, yet. Your Dad and I will see if we can find you some."

"Thanks, Mom." I hugged them both before they left. A chorus of "Bye, Mom," echoed through the tents.

Ryan grinned at me.

"I better go, too. I have another shift for body removal before I can sleep. I'll talk to you tomorrow. Find me in the morning, okay?"

I nodded and gave him a hug, too.

Drav put an arm around me as we watched him walk away. Byllo, Timmy, Jessie, and Savvy moved to a tent just three down from ours. I smiled when I realized they would be sharing. It made sense. Timmy and Savvy had slept together almost every night since they met.

Mary and James walked around from the tent just in front of ours.

"This is some place," James said. "Big from the sound of things. Most of it's not used because it's too hard to defend. Heard there are some real houses on the other side."

"With real beds," Mary said.

"Would you rather stay in the houses?" I asked, wondering what they were getting at.

"No, no," James said quickly. "We feel safer here."

"But it seems a shame that all those mattresses are going to waste."

I smiled, understanding.

"I'm sure any fey you ask would be willing to take you to a house and get a mattress for you. Maybe even a whole bed. There's no reason for you two to have to sleep on a cot."

"Cot?" Mary laughed. "They gave us sleeping bags."

She was right. Why let good mattresses go to waste? I looked up at Drav, and he started to call out names. The fey immediately jogged over and nodded when he asked if they would help Mary and James.

A group of ten fey left, two carrying the couple.

Since I'd explained marriage, all the fey respected Mary's relationship with James. But they still flirted with her like crazy. I heard several tell her that if she ever got mad at James and desired another, she could come to him. She'd laughed each time and gave the speaker a wink before sending him away so she could eye his backside.

I turned back toward our tent and stared at the clean sleeping bags.

"What are you thinking, my Mya?" Drav asked.

"That I really want a shower before bed."

"A good idea," Drav said, stepping around me to pick up my bag.

We walked to the communal showers where Matt had taken us earlier. Drav held my hand the entire way, neither of us talking. The day's events still ran through my head. The infected at the gate. Seeing my parents. Matt's request that the fey help them in the morning. It still felt surreal that we were really here. That my family was still alive and so close.

As I'd guessed, my family accepted Drav because I did.

At the showers, I took my bag from Drav.

"I better go to my own side this time," I said. I stood on my toes and gave him a light kiss on his lips before entering the women's showers.

By the time I finished, it was dark outside. I shivered at the chill of the air on my wet head.

Drav, who'd been waiting for me outside, noticed the movement and scooped me into his arms.

"You grow cold too easily," he said, already jogging back to our tent.

I snuggled against him while denying his claim.

"My tolerance of the temperature changes is pretty standard for humans. But I'm sure glad you don't get as cold as I do."

Drav ducked into our tent, set me down, and closed the flaps. I looked around in mild surprise. A mattress now took up a large portion of the canvas floor, along with a little table that held a lit glass jar candle. The bed had been made up with real sheets and piled with three quilts.

"I really like Mary," I said, knowing this had to be her doing.

Drav's arms circled my waist, and he held me close from behind. Snuggly in our tent and out of the chill, the heat of his chest pressed against my back warmed me. As did the light trail of kisses he placed from the base of my neck to my jaw, where he stopped.

"Are you happy, my Mya?"

I turned in his arms and looked up at him.

"I am. Are you?"

"Yes." He brushed his fingers over my cheek and down my throat. "With you, I am always happy."

The sincerity in his gaze only made my feelings for him stronger.

"I'm so glad you found me. I love you more than I ever thought possible."

"My Mya," he said, cupping my cheek gently.

His mouth settled over mine in a slow kiss that stole my breath. Each tender touch of his lips melted my heart further.

Wrapping my arms around his neck, I melted into his kiss. He growled softly, and the mood of the kiss changed as he gently cupped my breast with his warm palm. A jolt of desire shot straight through me, and I couldn't stop the small sound of enjoyment that escaped.

Drav pulled back, his thumb brushing over my nipple before he released me and tugged his shirt over his head. Tossing it aside, he waited, his intense gaze asking what his mouth wouldn't.

I smiled slightly and kicked off my shoes. He didn't move. I tugged off my shirt then eased the straps of my bra over each shoulder. His sharp gaze followed the movements as I freed my breasts. My bra hit the floor beside his shirt. Reaching for the clean jeans I'd just put on, I released the button and listened to the rasp of the zipper.

With his focus entirely centered on my hands, I slowly worked the jeans over my hips and saw the moment he realized I wasn't wearing any underwear. The sound of his breathing increased, and I smiled. Naked, I walked to the bed and glanced over my shoulder at Drav.

The hunger in his gaze stole my breath. He tossed his pants aside and strode toward me.

CHAPTER SEVENTEEN

Drav kissed my temple and eased away from me. I rubbed my eyes and rolled to my side to watch him move in the dim light of the burned down candle.

"What are you doing?" I mumbled, still too tired to fully form words.

"I must meet the others by the gate," he said softly. "Rest."

There was no chance of that knowing he planned to leave.

"No. I'm up. I'm coming to see you off."

He sat on the mattress and watched me dress. His appreciative gaze traced over every curve I possessed. I loved the way he watched me. Smiling to myself, I tugged my shirt over my head then stepped into my boots.

"Let's go," I said, holding out my hand.

His fingers curled around mine. Instead of standing, he tugged me down on top of him. I landed with a squeal and a giggle.

"I love the sounds you make," he whispered just before kissing me lightly. "You will make them for me again when I return."

"Bossy," I said, teasingly.

"Yes," he agreed. "You are."

"Hey!"

He smiled and stood with me in his arms.

"I will carry you until I have to leave."

"Fine. But just this once."

He winked at me, and I leaned my head against his chest as he stepped out of the tent. The longer we spent together, the more human he behaved. Just the good stuff, though. The teasing and the laughing. I supposed that made sense. His life before me had been all fighting and surviving.

At the gate, most of the men already waited. Molev and Matt spoke together near the vehicles. No infected waited outside, just the stained, dried grass showing where they'd once stood. A plume of dark smoke rose in the distance.

"Good morning, Mya," Matt said. "That's the clean-up crew's fire."

"Good morning. Any word from Commander Willis?"

"Complete silence, which likely means he is infected now, too."

The man didn't pull any punches with his news. While hearing the information sucked, I also appreciated the complete honesty.

"How long do you expect these guys to be gone?" I asked.

"Everyone should return before dark. Group one will clear a smaller overrun safe zone to the north. Groups two and three will check nearby sightings."

I looked up at Drav.

"You be careful out there," I said.

He kissed my forehead then turned to Matt.

"I want your promise that you will keep Mya safe while I am gone."

"You have my word," he said.

I rolled my eyes.

"Drav, he has to keep several hundred other people safe, too."

He ignored me and pinned Matt with his unblinking gaze.

"I will hold you to your word."

"If you're done being adorably overprotective, it's my turn," I said. "Molev, make sure he comes back whole and healthy."

"Yes, Mya."

I tilted my head up to Drav. "Time to put me down."

He kissed me hard and set me on my feet while I was still dazed and grinning stupidly. The gate rolled open, and Drav stepped in with the first group of fey.

I waited there until the last truck rolled through and the groups started off. Drav gave me a lingering look and raised his hand in farewell before sprinting away, his long braids moving in the wind. It wasn't until I turned that I saw Kerr standing behind me.

"What are you still doing here?" I asked.

"Molev needed Drav, not me," he said with a shrug.

"Bullcrap. They left you behind for a reason. Why?"

He didn't say anything.

"Tell me why, and I'll find out which girls here might be interested in hooking up with a hot demon man named Kerr."

"Drav wants you safe," he said immediately.

I grinned, missing that sweet man already.

"Come on, let's go find my brother."

"I thought we were going to find the girl who likes me."

"Patience, Kerr. Girls don't like guys who seem desperate."

After at least an hour of asking and walking around, we found Ryan by the east gate.

"About time you showed up," he said, catching sight of me.

His dark hair lay plastered to his scalp, and his shirt had sweat stains under the arms and down his chest. He strode over and gave me a huge hug.

"You stink," I said, returning the hug before pulling back.

"I'm conserving supplies by skipping deodorant." He grinned widely.

"And soap from the smell of it. What are you doing to get so sweaty?"

"Just finishing clean up." He pointed a thumb over his shoulder at the dead infected on the ground outside the gate. "We load them up, then the armed group takes them to the burning grounds."

"That sounds gross."

"It is. But it's worse if we leave them lying there. Not only do they smell, but the infected are getting smarter and have started using the bodies to climb the fence."

"Ew. How much longer do you have to work?"

"I'd get done faster if you helped."

"No, Mya," Kerr said immediately.

I rolled my eyes and gave Ryan a shrug.

"I promised I would stay inside the fence."

Ryan looked at Kerr and offered his hand. Kerr took it immediately, surprising me. It shouldn't have though. The fey learned quickly.

"This is Kerr. Drav went out to help clear a safe zone, and Kerr got stuck babysitting me."

"Not stuck, Mya. I volunteered."

"I'm Ryan. I hear you guys are pretty strong and fast. Any chance you want to take over for me so I can spend some time with my sister?"

"Please?" I asked.

"Yes, I will take over. Where will I find you when I'm finished?" Kerr replied.

"Shooting range," Ryan said. He hooked his arms around me and started tugging me along. With a grin and a wave to Kerr, I willingly obliged.

"Why are we going to the shooting range?" I asked once we were out of sight. "And did you even get to sleep last night?"

"I grabbed a few hours. But, there's a lot of work to be done. Which is why you're going to spend some time on the range. You have to be able to shoot to go on a supply run with me this afternoon."

I stopped walking.

"I promised Drav I wouldn't go outside the fence."

"I know. But I also know you'll break that promise."

"Why?"

"I know you've been paying attention, Mya. Even with everyone helping, we're dying here. There aren't enough of us experienced supply scavengers left. If you don't help out, it'll be some kid too young to hold a gun or some older person who can barely walk. We need supplies. You and I have to be a part of those who go, or the people here will starve.

"I get that Drav cares about you. Do you think Mom and Dad don't worry every time I go out? We can't hide behind the fence."

"You suck," I said, knowing he was right. "And Drav's going to be so mad when he finds out."

Ryan grinned, and we continued to the indoor shooting range where he showed me how to use the gun I would be assigned. I wasn't that good, but he told me that with all the infected the fey had killed, there would be less around for the supply run.

When I finished emptying my current clip into the target, I engaged the safety and set the gun back down. Taking off my earmuffs, I studied the odd pattern of holes around the head I'd been targeting.

"When do we leave?" I asked, turning to Ryan.

Kerr stood just behind my brother.

"Where are you going?" Kerr asked.

I shifted my gaze to Ryan, who looked far too amused.

"Ryan, where are we going next?" I asked, hoping the change in wording would ease Kerr's mind.

"Well, you're going to go back to your tent to take a nap like a good little ward, and I'm taking Kerr to meet some of my crew."

I glanced at Kerr. "He means friends."

"Will there be females?" Kerr asked, losing his frown.

"Yep. Not sure they're worth your time, but I'll let you be the judge of that," Ryan said with a shrug.

Kerr grinned widely, showing off his very pointed canines.

"Whoa," Ryan muttered.

Kerr didn't hear. He was busy promising me that he would not ask to see anyone's pussy or boobs.

"You know what? You're with Ryan, now, and his responsibility. Have fun."

I left Ryan with Kerr and started my way back to the temporary housing. I knew darn well Ryan hadn't meant for me to actually nap; besides, the tent would be too chilly without Drav to warm me. But, with nothing else to do, I went there anyway, wanting some time to think.

Around me, people moved with the same weariness as the day before. Some were armed. Some carried things from one building to another. Ryan was right. I needed to pitch in. To help ease some of the strain. Supply runs were a start. After he and I returned, I would talk to Matt to find out what more I could do. Not just me, but the fey, too. These scouting missions were fine, but the fey needed to integrate and become part of the community. Their presence might be what the survivors needed to give humanity hope again.

I'd just reached the tent I shared with Drav when Mom found me.

"Hi, sweetie. Want to come with me and help with laundry?"

"I'm not sure if I have time. Ryan said he wanted me to go with him on a supply run."

Her expression went from happy to troubled.

"Well, if you're going with Ryan, you won't have time for laundry. Promise me you will be careful," she said. "I worry every time Ryan leaves. I understand he has to go, but I still can't stop wishing it were someone else."

I stepped close and hugged her. "I get it. But, we'll be smart and watch out for each other. When I get back, I'll see what I can do to start helping around here."

She hugged me tightly in return then released me.

"You'll need to talk to Matt. He'll add you to the work schedule."

"I've been wanting to ask, what's the story with him? I know Dad said the military is more relaxed because of so many civilians helping out, but why just Matt and not Commander or some kind of title?"

"We haven't had much luck with people in charge here."

"What do you mean?"

"He's the eleventh leader. All the ones before him have died in some tragic or unnecessary way. Infected. Hellhounds. Suicide."

"Suicide? Now?"

"I know. To make it through so much and then give up." Mom shook her head. "Knowing that something purposely allowed those hellhounds in shook everyone."

"What do you mean?"

"You saw the lights all over this place. They keep the hounds away at night. Over a week ago, someone shot the lights with arrows. The hounds broke through the fence, and well, I already told you the rest.

"Anyway, after that incident, the commander in charge decided living wasn't worth it anymore. There was some dispute about who was next in line. No one wanted to be that person. Matt stepped up and said we needed to change. That military rank no longer mattered. That we were a ragtag group struggling to survive in a world that had either forgotten about us or that had already given up. He said we'd probably all die within a week, but he wasn't ready to give up a day of that remaining time without at least trying. Most of the people agreed we weren't going to make it. But, we all wanted to keep trying."

"How long ago was that?"

"Five days," she said with a sad smile. "Our numbers have been cut in half since then."

Matt had been in charge for four days before we arrived. I thought of his desperation to talk to Molev right away, the maps in his room, and all those color-coded pins.

"When we heard from McAlester that there might be a way to kill the hounds, that help might be coming...well, that lit a new fire in everyone's hearts. Everyone's but Matt's. He cautioned us not to believe in something we hadn't seen for ourselves."

"That's why he drew all the infected in?"

"Yes." She glanced over my shoulder. "Here comes your brother."

I turned to look at Ryan.

"Where's Kerr?" I asked.

"Talking to Julie."

"Oh, Ryan. That poor man will be stuck there for hours," Mom said.

"Who's Julie?" I asked.

"A lonely woman grieving the loss of her entire family. She'll talk to anyone who will listen."

"Kerr said he wanted to meet her," Ryan said.

I shook my head, knowing he'd made the introduction to distract Kerr.

"We better get going," I said to Mom. Now, more than ever, I wasn't going to let Ryan go out alone. I knew what might be waiting out there.

"Be careful," she said.

"We will," I promised. She hugged us both then walked away.

Ryan and I jogged across the compound. My heart hammered the entire time. I half expected Kerr to show up and tell me I couldn't go. However, Ryan seemed to have found the perfect distraction because we reached the gate without spotting Kerr.

Two military trucks with several armed men already loaded in the backs waited near the gate.

"Thought you weren't going to show," one of the men called to Ryan just as the inner gate swung open to allow the first truck to enter.

Ryan and I jumped into the back of the second one. The man near the back reached out and pulled the metal grate up and pinned it in place, creating a clever cage that would keep us safer from infected.

"Not a chance. Mya, this is Tom."

Ryan introduced me to the rest of the guys in the truck, twelve including us, then asked where we were going.

"Warrensburg," Tom said.

"I thought it was marked," Ryan said.

My stomach sank.

"The town is. But, there's a high school and a few gas stations on the outer edge. We'll scout the school first and if it seems clear, hit it and hopefully find enough food to last us a while."

The truck rolled through the gate, and I looked out at the wide unprotected expanse of field.

I didn't know how far Warrensburg was from Whiteman, but I hoped we'd return before Kerr noticed me missing.

CHAPTER EIGHTEEN

Trees lined the sides of the road, their barren canopy creating a creepy tunnel. No one spoke over the rumble of the engine as we stood in the back, watching the roadsides. Ready for anything, each man had his gun aimed outward through narrow windows in the steel grates.

Nervous energy made me feel twitchy. Yes, I had volunteered for this. The people at Whiteman needed food. And, I didn't want Ryan to go without me, not when I could see how exhausted he and most of the other men were. But, knowing I needed to help didn't make me feel any better about leaving the security of the fence. Drav would be furious with me.

The truck rocked as we hit a pot-hole.

"Is this the safest route?" I whispered to Ryan.

"Nothing is really safe anymore, Sis. You should know that."

Yeah, I did know. Ryan nudged me playfully with his shoulder.

"So you and the big gray dude, huh?"

"Shut up," I whispered, almost smiling. Only Ryan would bring up my love life at a time like this.

"Debris in the road," Tom said, keeping his voice low. "Watch the trees."

The truck slowed, and I glanced at Ryan.

"We'll probably be able to drive over whatever it is."

A series of pops went off from the lead truck.

"One from the trees," Mark, who watched the front, said. "He's down now."

The rest of us kept our eyes on the trees as the first truck went through whatever the infected had tried to put in our way. Branches based on the sounds. Our truck rolled over the debris next without another infected sighting.

I glanced back at the trunks of the two large trees laying in the road, and anxiety coiled in my belly as we drove on. It didn't feel right that only one infected had been out on its own. Not with that kind of trap laid. The thought that the infected were getting smart enough to not attempt an attack because we didn't stop made me shiver. Hopefully, there was a different route home.

It didn't take as long as I had expected to reach Warrensburg. Other than the trees, we didn't run into any more obstacles.

"Is this the first run to this place?"

"Nah, we've hit Warrensburg before. We went to a preschool the first time. General store another time. We try to pick locations on the outskirts. It's too dangerous to go further in because of the noise of the vehicles," Ryan explained.

It took a few more minutes before I spotted the high school. The large building dominated the surrounding acreage while the parking lot sat barren and ghostly.

How long had it been since students walked Warrensburg High's halls? Around a month now, I figured. School felt like a lifetime ago. Ryan had been a senior. Would he ever graduate, now? I glanced over at him and doubted it. He wasn't that kid anymore, and our new lives didn't require diplomas.

The trucks cruised through the parking lot straight toward the side entrance where they stopped and cut the engines.

"In and out guys and girl," Tom said quietly. "If you see an infected, try to avoid it. If you have to shoot, shoot to kill and get out before more come. Truck one has the cafeteria. We're here for the routine things. Sanitary items. Let's move."

Two of the men quietly opened and lowered the back gate. The first man jumped out of the truck and headed toward the doors, which opened without a sound.

A crackle of static came from the cab as I waited my turn to climb out the back. I glanced at the cab as the driver picked up the radio and spoke quietly. He turned to look back at me through the window.

Tom went around to the driver, and Ryan nudged me so I would get moving. Mark remained, closing the gate and guarding the truck.

I checked the safety on my gun and started toward the side door with Ryan when a hand came down on my shoulder.

"You weren't supposed to come, little lady," Tom said.

It felt like a rock settled in my stomach. A radio call from the base meant that Kerr knew I was missing.

"We need help, right?" Ryan said before I could speak for myself. "We all pitch in to stay alive."

"Just keep an eye on her," Tom said, before moving past us into the building.

Ryan nodded his head for me to follow.

Inside, the lights didn't work. The hall we stood in wasn't completely dark, but several of the men held penlights and shined them up and down the hall's length. The school looked normal, just empty.

"Look for supply closets near the bathrooms. Grab what you can and get back to the truck," Tom said.

The eleven of us split into two groups. Ryan and I went to the right with three others. If we hurried and got what we needed, I'd be back before Kerr could really freak out. Hopefully.

My group walked down the hallway, one of the men's penlights helping to illuminate the way. Light filtered into the hall from closed classroom doors. We came to a set of stairs.

"We'll go up and start a sweep of the second floor. You two finish up down here. There has to be a bathroom somewhere."

Ryan nodded. I hesitated. I wanted to get back to base quickly. Splitting up would be the fastest way to make that happen. But, it didn't feel like the safest. I looked up and down the hallway. There were no blockades or other signs of infected traps.

"You good?" the guy asked me.

I nodded and watched them slowly make their way up the stairs. Ryan motioned for me to follow, and we started down the hall again. Near the end, where the hall branched off to the left, we found bathrooms and a supply closet. Ryan tried the nob. It didn't budge.

"Shit," he said softly.

A brush of noise came from behind us. I looked down the hall but saw nothing. Neither Ryan nor I moved as we waited to see if the sound would repeat itself.

The sudden pop that echoed through the halls made us both jump.

"Come on." I tugged on Ryan's arm, ready to lead him away from the gunfire.

"It's okay, Mya. In a town this size, there is bound to be an infected roaming in here. Hopefully, it was the guy with the keys to the supply closet."

Several more shots rang through the hallway, followed by a scream that bounced down the halls. Ryan's wide eyes met mine.

"Time to go," he said.

He clicked off his light and held his gun between his hands.

"Which way?" I asked.

Ryan paused, looking down both hallways. At the very end of the one we'd already walked, a person staggered forward, stopped, and turned in our direction.

Ryan switched his grip on his gun and grabbed my hand, pulling me down the opposite hall. A groan echoed after us. I didn't dare look back as we ran side by side.

A door opened just as we passed. An infected lunged out and grabbed for Ryan, the momentum taking them both to the floor. I stopped and aimed at the infected, watching its jaws snap at Ryan as my brother held it back with a forearm to the throat.

I exhaled and pulled the trigger. The boom of the shot rang in my ears as the infected fell to the side. Rushing forward, I hauled Ryan to his feet. He picked up his gun.

"Come on." I grabbed Ryan's arm and pulled him down the hallway.

The sound of staggering footsteps reverberated off the lockers from all directions. More infected.

My heartbeat pounded in my ears as I searched for an exit. Something moved in the shadows ahead.

Ryan tugged me into a classroom then quietly shut the door behind us. We were silent as we backed further into the classroom. Unfortunately, the room only had small windows up near the ceiling. No exit that way. Unless...I looked at the desks, wondering if Ryan would have enough upper body strength to—

The doorknob rattled. We both lifted our guns, ready.

The door quickly opened and a head poked in. I recognized the face. The driver of our truck. His pained blue eyes swept over us before he limped inside and closed the door. Panting and sweating, he slowly slid down the wall beside the door and sat on the floor.

"Greg?" Ryan said. "Were you bitten?"

The guy looked like hell, but I couldn't see blood anywhere.

"Fuck, I don't know. I don't know." He closed his eyes, wincing.

Ryan kept his gun trained on his friend, but his hand shook.

"It's okay, Greg," I said in a calm tone, keeping my gun steady on the man.

"It ain't. I knew there wasn't somethin' right about just one infected on the road. Shoulda turned around. Fucking shoulda turned around." Greg groaned and wrapped his arms around his stomach before puking.

"What do you mean?" I asked.

"Fuckers followed us here."

He retched again then looked up at me with bloodshot eyes.

"I can see it in your eyes. Fuckers bit me, didn't they."

"Yeah," I said.

"Then kill me now. End it."

I exhaled slowly.

"Kill me!"

A bang rang out, and I flinched. Red exploded onto the wall behind Greg's head, and a dot dripped down his forehead. Slowly, he fell to the side.

I looked at Ryan, who held his gun pointed at the spot where Greg's head had been a moment before.

"Start making a barrier with the desks," I said, touching Ryan's arm to get him to lower his weapon. "Don't drag the desks. I'll check for a radio on Greg. Maybe we can call for help."

Ryan nodded and lowered his gun. I rushed forward to start patting the pockets in Greg's jacket first. Metal scraped over the tile behind me. I flinched at the sound but didn't scold Ryan. Our position had been compromised when Ryan fired.

Finding nothing in Greg's jacket pockets, I tried his cargo pants pockets. My hand hit hard plastic, and I withdrew the radio.

A low moan came from the other side of the door just as Ryan wedged the first desk against it. Pocketing the radio, I rushed to help him, both of us lifting and stacking desks as the moans increased in volume.

The heavy metal desk that belonged to the teacher still sat over in the furthest corner from the door. I motioned to Ryan to help me move it under the windows. We'd just positioned it there, and he'd stepped on the surface when something hit the door. His eyes went to mine, then the window still just over his head. He lifted his gun and hit the glass. It spidered but didn't break out.

"Shit." He hit it again and again. The mesh in the glass wouldn't give.

He jumped from the desk.

"Tip it over," he said.

We hunkered down behind it, and Ryan glanced at the radio in my back pocket. A fleeting look of hope flashed over his face.

I pulled out the radio and pressed down on the button.

"This is Mya and Ryan. We're trapped in a classroom at Warrensburg High School. We need help. Is anyone there?"

I released the button. Static crackled back. I pressed the button again.

"Is anyone there?"

More static.

"Hello?"

No one responded.

Cold fear coiled in my belly and tears stung in my eyes. Help wouldn't be coming.

I turned to Ryan and wrapped my arms around him, holding him tight.

"I'm sorry, Sis."

"The end of the world isn't your fault."

Ryan leaned his head on my shoulder, and I stroked his hair. It felt like we were kids again, riding out a tornado.

More footsteps shuffled outside the door. Something hit it again. This time hard enough to nudge the desks.

I hugged my brother closer.

"Love you, Ryan."

"Love you, too, Mya."

The moaning and groaning in the hall became deafening as the door opened a bit. A hand reached in, the thick, pale blood-stained fingers gripping the door. I pulled back from Ryan so I could aim my gun. Ryan did the same. Together, we waited for the infected to push through.

We watched the pile of desks slide backward an inch at a time until the barrier fell with a loud crash. Three infected shoved through the door, semi-milky eyes locking on us as we fired. As their bodies fell, more came, tripping over the fallen and making it harder to aim for a headshot. Sweat coated my forehead. I kept aiming and firing.

"I have only one more clip in my back pocket. After that, I'll be out," Ryan yelled.

How many shots did I have left? The implication of the few moments we had remaining hit me hard.

The moans grew frenzied in the hall, and scuffling footsteps escalated as more infected pushed through. Ryan stopped shooting briefly to reload.

I kept firing until my gun clicked. Numb to the reality of what would happen next, I tucked myself behind the desk and listened to the mixture of Ryan's shots and the infected moans. Ryan would turn. I wouldn't. The infected would eat me alive.

The shooting stopped, and Ryan crouched down next to me.

"That's it," he said.

I took in a deep breath and held his hand.

"It hurts," I whispered. "But not for long."

He frowned at me. I didn't know how else to comfort him, though.

"Someone's calling your name," he said.

"That's not funny, Ryan."

"No, seriously. Someone is calling your name, listen."

I heard it. A voice echoing down the hall as it called out my name. Then, another voice joined in, calling my name, too.

"Mya!"

Hope coursed through me. The fey were here, searching for me. I looked over at Ryan. He nodded.

I stood, drawing the attention of the infected, who'd paused in the doorway at the sound of the voices in the hall.

"Drav," I yelled.

Two of the infected lunged toward us. Unable to think of anything else, I threw my gun as hard as I could. It hit the first one in the head, and he jerked to a stop.

Ryan pulled out a desk drawer and hit the second one with it again and again. Infected blood spattered me at the same moment a roar shook the room.

It was the best sound ever.

Heads flew off of the infected crowding the doorway as Drav tore into the room like a storm. The infected who'd entered because of my yell turned toward Drav. He took their heads in a fury, moving so fast that the first head hadn't hit the floor before the next head parted from its body. Blood coated most of the room by the time the last body fell.

Drav stood in the middle of the mess, dripping with infected blood and looking like an avenging angel of death.

"Mya," he said, looking at me for the first time.

I climbed out from behind the desk and threw myself at him, half-crying, half-laughing, and fully shaking.

He caught me in his arms and held me.

"My Mya," he said again and again as he stroked my hair and kissed my head.

I heard Ryan behind me.

"Thank you, Drav."

Drav growled loudly and released me.

"You should not have let her leave," he roared at Ryan.

I stepped in front of Ryan, ready to defend my brother.

"It's not his fault. I had to come, Drav. I can't selfishly hide behind the fence while other humans go out to get food and supplies that I'll use, too. We all have a responsibility to pitch in if we want to not just survive, but live."

"No, Mya. Matt Davis gave his word that he would keep you safe. That promise was broken. We are leaving. Now."

He picked me up and stalked through the door. I looked back at Ryan, who followed behind us, along with several other fey.

Outside the school, Drav stopped to speak to Molev, who studied me with a frown.

"The school is clear," Drav said. "I will take Mya back while you gather the supplies they were willing to risk Mya for."

CHAPTER NINETEEN

EXTREME GUILT WEIGHED ON ME AS I LAY ON OUR BED, SNUGLY WARM in Drav's arms. He hadn't loosened his hold on me all night, which I completely understood. I'd scared him. But, did he honestly think it justifiable to keep me inside the fence when everyone else had to go out?

I tried moving a little.

"No, Mya," he said gruffly.

His words tickled the hair on the back of my neck and sent a shiver through me. The reaction prompted him to groan and kiss the tender spot just below my ear. His palm brushed over my still sensitive nipple.

This wasn't the first time he started something since we'd returned yesterday.

"We can't stay in here all day, Drav."

"Yes, we can." His hand slid down my stomach, and I knew I wouldn't win. I wanted him to touch me as much as he did.

As if sensing my surrender, he nudged me to my back and covered me with his very naked warmth. He stared down at me for a moment while settling his hips over mine.

"You're selfish when you risk yourself," he said softly.

"What do you mean?"

"I've told you, you're the best thing here. Without you, I have no reason to help these people. Without you, we would return to the safety of the home we know. If you care for these people so much, do not risk yourself."

His words were proof that he'd listened to what I'd been trying to say last night. He'd heard me, but he hadn't agreed. While I might not agree with him, either, I knew better than to push just now. Besides, I could be useful in other ways inside the fence.

"I won't. I promise." I leaned up and traced the curve of his lower lip with my tongue.

His hips pressed against mine and, with a groan, he took over the kiss with the consuming energy of a drowning man. The stroke of his sure fingers started a fire beneath the surface of my skin that blazed just for him. He rocked against me in a slow rhythm that showed his love and passion for me.

For the next thirty minutes, the world outside the tent faded away as Drav proved his need for me.

In a sweaty heap, we lay together afterward. Underneath the blankets, his fingers stroked over the bare skin of my stomach. I lay my head against his chest and traced little circles on his skin with my fingertip.

"I don't want you to stay mad at Ryan," I said softly after my pulse slowed.

"Then he shouldn't have told you to go outside the fence."

"How do you know he did?"

"Because that's what you told your mother, and that's what she told Kerr."

"You do know that I could have said no. But I didn't because I understood what Ryan was saying. We're all taking risks just by being alive, and we all need to help out."

"No. Not for things outside the fence. That's why you wanted my people to come here. We aren't as fragile as you. As you pointed out to Molev, the hounds exist because of us. We will take care of them. Your job is to stay inside the fence, so we have a reason to return."

I shook my head and exhaled. "You are stubborn, and I love you."

He kissed my temple. "I love you, too."

"Drav," Molev called from outside the tent. "It is time."

"I am staying today," Drav said, his hold on me tightening.

"No, you aren't," I said firmly. "You've made yourself very clear, and I've given you my word that I will not leave the protection of this fence. Now, it's a matter of trust. Do you trust me to keep my word?"

He sighed and studied my face.

"Yes."

"Then go. We all need you to keep us safe."

"I will leave a few more men today," Molev added through the tent, obviously listening. "To watch over the humans who stay behind and to help with any supply groups that leave."

"Thank you, Molev," I said, holding the blanket to my chest as Drav slid from bed.

"I will meet you at the gate, Molev," Drav said.

"Do not take long. We go further this time."

A moment later, Molev's voice called out a greeting from further away, and I knew Drav and I were once again alone. In silence, I watched him pull on his pants.

His gaze shifted from lacing his leather boots up to me. The hunger in his eyes made me smile.

"Will you come with me to the fence?" he asked.

He held out his hand, and I slid from the blankets, grinning even wider at the way he looked at me.

"Of course I'll come see you off. And I'll be here waiting for you, just like this, when you come back." I held out my arms and did a quick turn so he understood.

When I faced him, he wrapped his arms around me and pulled me to his chest for a thorough kiss.

"I do not want to leave," he murmured as he trailed kisses along my jaw to the side of my neck. "I want to stay here and listen to you pant yes again and again."

An embarrassed flush consumed my face.

"I say stuff during sex?"

"Oh, yes. Many things for different places." His fingers traced my collarbone before he nipped my skin, right below the almost healed infected bite. A tingle of need spread through me, and I almost groaned his name.

"Molev said not to take too long," I managed to say, instead.

He grunted and stepped back from me after one more kiss.

"I'll wait outside."

After I dressed, I walked with him to the gate and waved as the men left. The fey who remained watched me like I was going to climb the fence and go running around screaming for infected to come get me.

"Relax guys. I have no plans to leave. In fact, I'm going to go to the dining hall and see if I can help there. I heard they're going to use the potatoes you guys pulled from the school yesterday. With all that butter from the coolers, my mouth is watering big time."

The fey disbursed when I walked away, likely to find their own ways to occupy the time.

A few people were already working in the kitchen when I arrived. Some scrubbed pans. Some stirred pots. Everyone seemed to be avoiding the pile of potatoes. I walked right up to the mound, picked up a peeler, and got to work.

While the others finished their various tasks and walked out without an offer to help, my pile of peels slowly grew. A few times, a fey would poke his head in and say hi but never stay long. I knew they were just checking to make sure I was still where I was supposed to be.

I didn't mind the quiet time. I thought about yesterday and the fear I'd felt for Ryan and everyone else in the group. And how I'd felt hearing Drav's roar. I loved that man completely. A world filled with infected and hellhounds didn't seem so scary with him at my side. In fact, it seemed darn right survivable because of him.

Each hellhound death meant a better chance of a future for the remaining survivors. I thought about what that future might look like. Moving to houses where families could live...a family with Drav. It would be hard. This world would never be what it once was, at least not in my lifetime. Yet, the world not returning to the way it was might not be a bad thing.

Out of potatoes, I filled a pot with water and started quartering the spuds. Once I had three pots going, I scooped the peels into another pot and went outside. Mom had mentioned they planned a garden in the back field next year, and I figured the peels would make a good start for compost.

Mom stepped out of the laundry building when I passed and waved at me. Carrying a basket of clean sheets, Shax stepped out behind her.

"Where are you going, Mya?" he asked.

"I'm going to start a compost pile with these peels."

"That's a good idea," Mom called. "Set it up just on the other side of the walking path by the field we started turning."

"Ok."

Shax hesitated to follow my mom.

"I left potatoes boiling on the stove. I'll be right back."

Those words must have reassured him because Shax continued on with Mom. I shook my head and kept going, saying hello to the people I saw on the way. I'd forgotten how far away the back of the base was from the kitchen and wondered if Mom would keep an eye on the potatoes. My arms started to get tired as I walked. The peels weren't bad on their own. The pot weighed a ton, though.

When I saw a lone fey walking toward me from the back of the base, I smiled widely.

"I'm so glad to see you," I called.

He looked surprised that I'd spoken to him. Maybe because he looked like a mess. He had to have just gotten back from one of the group missions. His shirt was torn and filthy. He probably wanted to go to the showers, and I felt guilty for stopping him. But, my arms were screaming for relief.

As we drew closer to one another, I noticed the deep scarring on his face and his throat. Scars made from a hellhound attack by the look of them. Although his long hair covered much of the scarring, I felt bad for him. The fey already had the odds stacked against them because of their grey skin and eyes. Adding scars would make it even harder for the poor guy to meet girls.

"What's your name?" I asked.

"Merdon," he said, his voice a rasp.

The name sounded vaguely familiar.

"Would you be willing to help me carry this pot to the back field? It's okay to say no if you'd rather go clean up first."

He blinked at me for a moment then took the pot from my hands.

"Thank you," I said, smiling. "I'll show you where it can be dumped."

He waited for me to lead the way and fell in step beside me. I could feel his gaze on me and glanced at him with a kind smile, wondering how long it would take before the fey stopped being so curious about women.

"Did everything go well on the mission today?" I asked. "It looks like you ran into a little trouble."

He grunted in the non-committal way they liked to communicate, so I tried a different topic.

"Have you seen any girls you'd like to meet? I'd be happy to introduce you."

I stepped off the path and pointed to an area between us and the field.

"I think we can dump the peels right there."

He continued walking right past where I'd pointed. I frowned and hurried after him. The fey had farmed a long time in those caverns and had probably picked up a few tricks. If he wanted to place the peels somewhere else, it was fine with me.

Just a few yards from the fence, he set the pot on the ground and turned toward me.

"Don't you think putting the peels this close to the fence is a little dangerous? I mean, I know there aren't many animals out there now. But once the hellhounds are gone, I think having a compost pile here might attract them."

He tilted his head and studied me for a moment.

"What's your name?" he rasped.

"Mya," I said automatically. How could he possibly not know that by now?

Between one heartbeat and the next, I realized my mistake. The scars. The dirty clothes.

This wasn't a friendly fey from Ernisi. One of the exiled criminals stood before me.

I opened my mouth, ready to scream for help, when he crouched forward, knocking the wind out of me with his shoulder to my middle as he picked me up. In a familiar move, he took a running start at the fence before I could catch my breath. The ground fell away underneath me. A second later, we landed with a thud on the other side of the fence, and he took off running.

Every time I opened my mouth to scream, Merdon bounced me on his shoulder, cutting off my air supply. My stomach wanted to heave as the world sped past beneath his feet.

Drav.

What would he think? I'd promised them all that I wouldn't leave.

The scenery changed. The once dense forest thinned, and Merdon ran next to a road. The pavement blurred under his feet, changing to lush grass. Then, the ground got very far away again. My stomach felt weightless, and bile crawled up my throat.

The fey dropped to the ground and slowed his pace. I lifted my head as Merdon stopped and wood creaked under our combined weight.

My heart pounded in my chest at the sight of an untamed yard. Why would he take me to a house?

He stepped inside and flipped me off his shoulder onto the hardwood floor. I teetered, dizzy. His hands gripped my shoulders tightly.

"You will stay, Mya."

CHAPTER TWENTY

MERDON DIDN'T SAY MY NAME WITH RESPECT OR REVERENCE LIKE THE other fey did. I studied his iridescent yellow eyes.

"It would be best if I didn't stay," I said.

He released my shoulders and gave me a nudge further into the living room.

"You will stay. You will listen to us."

Us? Shit.

"Listen to you? What do you mean?" I asked.

"Maybe she is like the stupid humans," a gravelly voice said from the back of the house.

I pivoted toward the source.

A fey stepped down the darkened hallway, his gait unbalanced. His dim outline made him look bigger than any of the other fey. Big enough that his broad shoulders almost brushed the walls as he moved forward.

I took a step back, bumping into Merdon as the new fey stepped into the light.

His hair barely brushed his shoulders, but his body was riddled with scars. Bite marks, bullet wounds, and jagged lines from deep cuts...a map of the brutality he'd suffered since his last resurrection.

His eyes glittered with vivid yellow and dark green as he stared at me.

"So, human. Are you stupid like the others?" he asked.

"No. And, my name is Mya."

He turned his gaze to Merdon.

"Why did you bring her here?"

"She was the one in the woods, Thallirin. The one Drav protects."

Oh, that didn't sound good. I blinked as I realized what woods he referred to. The moment outside McAlester when I'd had my pants down in the trees and an infected almost found me. I'd kissed Merdon by mistake. I stepped away from him, my eyes rounding.

"Hmm," Thallirin said as Merdon stepped toward me, a slight smile on his lips.

"You remember." Merdon crowded me, forcing me backwards until I hit the edge of the couch.

"Sit."

I sat and turned my head so I wouldn't be staring at his waist. I really didn't want to know what he thought of the kiss in the woods. Clasping my hands so they wouldn't shake, I reminded myself that the fey at Whiteman had been checking on me at regular intervals. When they found an empty kitchen, they would start looking. Hopefully, they'd find the pot by the fence and figure things out.

Merdon stepped aside, and Thallirin stalked closer.

"We want our exile lifted," Thallirin said.

"What?" I said. I'd heard him just fine. However, I didn't understand why he was talking to me about their exile.

"We want our exile lifted," he repeated, crossing his arms over his chest.

The cold, empty look in his eyes made my stomach churn. I swallowed with difficulty and tried to keep my voice from shaking.

"I don't know how to do that."

"I saw you with Drav," Merdon said. "He watches you. Carries you. Protects you. You are of importance to him. Even Molev consults you."

Thallirin leaned toward me, his hands braced against the back of the couch on either side of my head. His piercing gaze pinned me, and I tried not to shiver in fear.

"Are you important, Mya?"

"Yes," I whispered, afraid to lie. I was important in the way they were implying. Drav would do anything to get me back. That these two knew that terrified me.

Thallirin's gaze shifted between my two eyes.

"I see why. Your eyes beg me for mercy. For protection." He lifted a finger and gently brushed my cheek. "So soft and fragile. I would want to protect you, too."

He straightened away from me suddenly.

"Breathe, Mya. We mean you no harm."

I exhaled shakily and tried to muster some courage.

"I'm not sure I believe you. Molev exiled you because you killed someone. I don't think he's going to change his mind."

When Merdon growled something in their language, I wished I'd kept my mouth shut. Thallirin, however, didn't seem upset. He sat in the stuffed chair near me, the furniture creaking under his weight.

"That is why you are here. To listen when they would not." His gaze never wavered from mine. "Will you listen, Mya?"

I nodded jerkily. I'd listen to whatever he wanted and give the fey time so they could find me.

"We are not the dangerous criminals they think us to be," Thallirin said. He leaned back in the chair and considered me for a moment. "Merdon saw Drav take you to the entrance of our home.

You saw the glowing rocks in our world, yes?"

I nodded again.

"They give light and life, like this one." He lifted his wrist and showed me his crystal bracelet. "My first memory is of the caves and holding this crystal I now wear. I knew how to speak but didn't know my name or where I was. None of us did. That was our beginning.

"We started with nothing but the crystals we held and the seeds in our pouches. We worked hard, tying the crystals to our wrists to free our hands to help the plants grow. We spread out, working in small groups in the caves with the brightest crystals. We hunted to feed ourselves and wasted nothing because we had nothing."

He leaned forward, his gaze intense. "We planted. We hunted. We moved on. We did not know the monsters we were creating. You cannot imagine the confusion and desperation when the first hounds found us. We did not know what they were, only that they hunted us."

He exhaled heavily.

"It took time, and many deaths, to build the wall around our city. I was not the first reborn to the pool. But, I was the first to wonder how it worked. Why my clothes and hair did not return with me while my crystal did. No one else cared. The hellhounds were our priority."

"I tried not to care. I fought with the others to defend the wall and drive back the hounds. But with each death, I could not stop wondering why only the crystal always returned with us.

"After the wall was finished, Merdon, Oelm, and I went to the source where we harvested the larger crystals to keep the hounds away. As I worked, I kept wondering about the crystal on my wrist. I crushed my crystal, needing to see what would happen to me. Nothing happened. I felt no different. I cut myself and still healed quickly."

He looked down at his arm, lifting it enough to turn it to study the scars covering his skin. After a moment, he leaned back in his chair and focused on me again.

"Discouraged that I had been wrong about the crystal's importance to our rebirths, I went to retrieve a new one from the source. It gave me another, freely. It also filled my head with a vision of this world. Of killing a deer and waiting for it to come back to life."

"I saw that, too," I said, believing him. "When Drav brought me to your world, he wanted me to have a crystal. He thought it would work for me like it did for you, but the source didn't give me a crystal when I touched it. It gave me your history."

"And what did you see?"

I repeated the story the source crystal had shown me. He said nothing when I finished. His gaze stayed locked on the floor.

"What I don't understand is, why did it show me something instead of just giving me a crystal?"

"Because of our mistake." The anger in his eyes turned to bitterness.

"The crystal did not give me our history. Only the vision of the deer. And, I shared what the source crystal had shown me with Merdon and Oelm. All of us wondered what the vision meant. Oelm thought that the nearness of the crystals swayed the time it took to be reborn. He removed his crystal and told us to test his idea on him," he continued.

"And we did," Merdon said from behind me.

"When his body didn't leave, we tied the crystal back to his wrist. Still, his body remained. We carried him back to the city and placed him in the pool, but nothing happened. Oelm never returned, but we learned how important our crystals were. We were foolish to test the truth of the vision on our friend, and we were exiled because of it."

I couldn't deny that I felt a whole lot of pity for them. They'd made a huge mistake and had paid for it for a very long time. Why had the crystal shown Thallirin anything? Why had it shown me what it had? I looked at the floor, thinking.

"The crystal had been trying to warn you," I said, once again meeting his gaze. "At that time, you still didn't know the hounds were from the deer you ate, did you?"

"No. I believe the same as you. It was trying to tell us to stop killing the deer. We were too slow to understand that."

"I think the crystal was trying to warn me, too. My people are dying up here because of the hellhounds the fey accidentally created. The crystal changed you, giving you an immunity from the curse that created them. Humans don't have that immunity. I think the crystal was telling me that humans need the fey.

"It would have been easy for me to hate the fey for what'd been unleashed on my world had the crystal not shown me the truth. Now, I understand the fey had no choice about living in the caverns. I understand that none of you knew about the deer. I don't hate any of the fey for what's happened to my world."

I studied Thallirin for a minute, wondering what he would think of my next words.

"And while I agree that you made a mistake in killing your friend and have suffered long enough for it, I can't help but wonder if I should hate you for what you've done recently.

"You've been shooting out lights and letting the hellhounds and infected inside the fence to attack my people. Not just at the base where you stole me from, but also the first place we stayed."

Merdon growled, his fangs showing in his anger.

"They pierced our skin with their loud guns. They challenged us. It was our right to accept."

I considered both of them for a moment. They had no one to explain things to them. The other fey still wanted to remove heads when they were angry. Yet, they didn't because of me. These two had done no more than Drav had in the beginning. I could still remember the feeling of terror when the lights at the gas station had been broken the night I met Drav. Was I stupid to consider giving these two a chance to start over?

"Our ways are different. Gunfire isn't a challenge," I said. "It's a warning to stay away. We humans are just trying to survive, and we are afraid."

"Ah," Merdon said, calming.

"Yes. Ah. The rules are different up here. You can't behave the same way you did in the caves. What would you do if you were no longer exiled? What do you hope for?"

"To no longer be alone," Thallirin said.

"We miss our brothers," Merdon added.

The fey didn't have traditional families like humans, but they'd always had each other. Drav seemed to know each fey from his world and not just in passing. They were each other's family. I'd gone crazy trying to get back to mine. Why wouldn't it be the same for Thallirin and Merdon?

I studied the pair. Merdon stood by Thallirin's side. Both wore the same serious, forsaken expression. Both had more scars individually than I'd seen combined on all the other fey. They were fighters. Survivors. Like the rest of us. And, we humans needed as much help in this new world as we could get. Trading in an adversary for an ally made sense. Would Molev and Drav agree after I told them all of this?

They knew these men better than I did.

"You will speak on our behalf?" Thallirin asked, breaking the long silence.

"I will. But, you didn't help your case by stealing me. Drav is going to go crazy."

"But you will speak on our behalf," Merdon insisted. "There was no other way for us to speak with you."

"I will, but I can't guarantee it will help. Will you take me back to the base?"

"No. We will wait. Our brothers will come to us."

"That's probably not a wise plan. Your brothers would be more forgiving if you took me back."

Thallirin shook his head. "They would find us before we reached the fence and remove our heads before you could speak."

Given Drav's reaction when he found me at the school, Thallirin had a valid point.

"Fair enough. We'll wait. You wouldn't happen to have anything to eat, would you?" I asked.

"I do not know. We have not been here long."

"Mind if I look?"

Merdon extended his hand in the direction of the kitchen.

Nodding my thanks, I stood and went to check the cabinets. Merdon and Thallirin followed, watching me. Finding nothing significant in the cupboards, I opened the fridge before quickly closing it. The power had obviously gone out long ago.

"Don't open that," I said with a gag and a cough.

Moving around the room, I opened a plain door and found the pantry. Inside, cans of pork and beans, tuna, and little snack packs of mac-n-cheese sat on the shelves.

"Jackpot," I called, grabbing the tuna for the fey and a can of pears and a tin of chicken for me.

"Take a seat," I said, re-emerging from the pantry. I gestured at the table when they didn't move. "It's okay to sit."

Merdon and Thallirin sat and only glanced at the cans I put before them.

"You guys aren't hungry?" I asked, already moving to find the can opener.

Neither answered. When I glanced up from my search through the drawers, they were frowning at the cans. They didn't know what the cans were.

I found the can opener and grabbed some spoons from the drawers before joining them at the table. I reached over, picked up Merdon's can, and slowly opened it for him.

"It's tuna," I said. "A kind of meat that we've preserved." I started opening Merdon's can. "Most cans have something edible inside of them, but not all cans are meant for humans."

I set Merdon's can before him then gave them their spoons.

"I know you guys have rules about eating first based on the length of your hair. It's not like that here. You can go ahead and eat," I said, peeling the lid back on my chicken. After I took my first bite, they did the same.

"So, what have you been doing up here?" I asked after swallowing.

The two exchanged looks.

"We have been exploring," Merdon said.

"And killing?"

"We did not know there would be no rebirths," Merdon said, frustration lacing his words.

"You saw our home," Thallirin said. "You saw the safety the wall provided. Without that wall, the hounds hunted us. Merdon and I died countless times. Though we were strong fighters, stronger than those with longer hair, we were also tired.

"After the caves opened, we ran. We thought only of finding a place without the hounds. It was dark and strange. When we saw your people, they either wanted to bite us or use their guns. We accepted each challenge and removed many heads. But we never stayed to see their rebirth. Exile taught us to move. Fight. Stay alert."

"When did you realize we don't come back?" I asked.

"The birds in the sky killed many. No one returned," Merdon said.

"How did you learn English?"

"We watched and listened. One large, red home had a TV. We listened for one night and watched the men inside the fence shoot the stupid ones."

"They're starting to get less stupid," I said.

Thallirin nodded.

"We put something by the fence, and the less stupid ones climbed over the top. While the men were busy, we took the TV. It did not talk again, though," Merdon said.

"Yeah, TVs need electricity."

Thallirin nodded and set his spoon down by his empty can. I finished my chicken and started in on the pears.

"They come," Thallirin said, standing.

A moment later, a distant roar echoed outside.

CHAPTER TWENTY-ONE

MY HEART STARTED BEATING FASTER, AND I STOOD. MERDON wrapped his hand around my arm to stop me from rushing out the door.

"Will you speak for us?" Thallirin asked.

"I said I would."

"Then wait. If you leave, they will kill us."

"Mya," a voice yelled. Not Drav's, but one of the other fey's.

"I won't leave," I promised. "But they need to see me to believe I'm okay."

Merdon looked at Thallirin, who nodded. Merdon let me go, and I ran to the door and pulled it open.

"Drav," I called.

"Mya." The chorus of my name spoken by many voices spread out in the nearby woods.

"I'm here," I yelled. "I'm safe."

An infected stumbled out of the trees, its cloudy gaze finding me. It opened its mouth and moaned, sprinting toward me. Merdon pulled me back, and Thallirin rushed past us to meet the infected on the porch. The wet spray of its blood as Thallirin removed its head hit me across the face. I blinked and wiped the wetness away.

"I am sorry, Mya," Thallirin said, tossing the head to the side. "I could not allow it to harm you."

"No, it's okay. You can take the heads off the stupid ones. Just be careful with the infected blood around other humans. I don't know if the infection spreads in ways other than a bite."

He nodded and came back inside to stand behind me.

Further away, several big, gray bodies burst from the woods.

"Trust me," I said before stepping out onto the porch. The headless body of the infected lay not far from my feet when I stopped.

"I'm okay," I called again.

Molev ran at the front of the group, his expression a mix of anger and worry. More fey spilled from the trees as the first group passed.

From the other side of the clearing, another fey broke free of the woods and sprinted toward me. He ran so fast, he looked like a streak of gray, and I knew who it was before he reached me.

"Drav," I breathed.

Within seconds, he reached the porch and held me so tightly I could barely breathe.

"Mya," he said into my hair. "I will not let you out of my sight again. Never again, Mya."

"Too tight, Drav. I need to breathe."

His hold loosened, and he pulled back enough to cup my face and stare into my eyes.

"You gave your word."

I'd expected anger but not the pain in his eyes.

"I did, and I didn't break it. I swear. I want to tell you what happened, but first, I need you to promise me something." My gaze flicked to Molev and the rest of the fey who now surrounded the porch. "I need you all to promise me that you will listen and not do anything until I finish my story."

The hurt faded from Drav's eyes, replaced by worry. He released me and gently wiped my cheek. His finger came away with blood on it.

"Are you hurt, Mya?"

"No. I promise I'm not. That's infected blood. From that guy there," I said, pointing at its body.

Drav's gaze flicked to where I pointed. He frowned at the dead infected then focused on me.

"You did not do that," Drav said, softly. "Who is here with you?"

I shivered at the menace in his voice and looked at Molev for help.

"Do you promise to listen?"

Molev hesitated before giving me a single nod. I met Drav's angry gaze and put my hand on his chest. He shook beneath my touch.

"Do you promise?" I asked.

"I will listen. Then, I will react."

That didn't sound good. I took a deep breath and got to the point.

"Merdon and Thallirin are inside—"

Shouts filled the air from many of the fey who stood on the lawn. Molev and Drav looked murderous.

"—and I'd like you and Molev to come in with me so that I can tell you the story," I said loudly to be heard.

"No, Mya," Drav said.

"You promised."

"You do not understand."

"Maybe you're right. Maybe I don't. But, can you honestly say you understand when you haven't yet listened to what I have to say?"

He closed his eyes for a moment, exhaling deeply. I stood on my toes and gently touched my lips to his. His hands captured my head, cradling me gently as I lightly licked his lower lip.

"I need you to listen," I whispered against his mouth.

He sighed heavily and released me.

"I will listen."

I smiled and took his hand. He didn't budge when I tugged, though.

"I go first, my Mya."

He shared a look with Molev then led the way into the house.

Thallirin sat in the chair facing the door. Merdon stood beside him, leaving the couch empty. I quickly took the seat nearest Thallirin, ignoring Drav's growl, and patted the cushion beside me.

Drav sat. Molev stood. It was enough. For the next fifteen minutes, they listened.

"They made a mistake, and it cost a friend his life," I reiterated after I finished my tale. "They've paid for that mistake. We're in a different world now. A different world with different rules."

Drav's thumb, which had been exploring the back of my hand as I spoke, stilled.

"They stole you from me," he said, his voice dangerously soft.

"Only because you left them with no other choice."

"I will not lift your exile," Molev said.

"Hang on, Molev."

"No, Mya. We have heard your story, and I deny their request."

I glanced at Thallirin and Merdon, who hadn't yet said a word. The cold, emptiness in their gazes made me afraid for our future. If I couldn't find a way to end their exile, I knew that the hellhounds would no longer be our biggest threat.

Taking a settling breath, I focused on Molev.

"Justice has been served. Thallirin and Merdon took a life and have lost their own countless times. More than any other fey. Exile for life, when your lives never end, is not justice. It's cruel," I said.

"You would have us welcome them back? Men who callously

disregarded the safety of their closest friend?"

"No," I said.

Merdon growled in frustration.

"If you welcomed them back now, you would resent them and never trust them. What I'm asking is that you give them a chance to redeem themselves in your eyes. A chance, that's all."

"What do you suggest they do that would make up for the life they took, Mya?"

I looked at Merdon and Thallirin, taking in their scars and battle-hardened expressions, and hated what I was about to say.

"They each have to kill ten hellhounds. If they want to rejoin the fey and live with humans, they need to show they are willing to fight to protect us. They need to help give humans a chance at life."

Molev remained silent. He glanced over at Drav then at the two exiles.

"The fey are the only ones who can kill the hellhounds," I continued. "Each dead hound is one less threat to the humans who still live. These two would be saving lives as well as risking their own."

I could see the moment I began to sway Molev. He wasn't happy about it, but he understood the challenge the two fey would face.

"Do you agree to these terms?" Molev asked the exiles.

Thallirin stood, his expression set.

"I agree."

Merdon scowled but nodded.

"I as well."

"Remove their hearts and bring them back whole. I will witness you destroy them and count each heart as one kill," Molev said.

My heart ached for Merdon and Thallirin as Molev turned and left. I'd thought ten hearts a piece harsh. Bringing the hearts back whole meant the hellhounds wouldn't be dead. The creatures would likely be chasing the exiles the whole way back to Molev.

The determination in Merdon and Thallirin's eyes spoke volumes, though.

"The hounds won't die until the heart is crushed," I said, making sure they understood.

"But, it is a chance for us to come out of exile. Thank you, Mya," Merdon said, inclining his head.

"Thank you, sister," Thallirin said.

I stood, Drav shadowing me.

"When will you two leave?" I asked.

"Now. We wish to rejoin our people, and yours, as soon as possible."

With a nod to Drav, they walked out the door and down the steps. The fey outside parted for them but did not speak to them.

Drav wrapped his arms around my waist and pressed his nose into my hair.

"Does this mean you're not mad at me?" I asked, hopefully.

"I thought I lost you again, my Mya."

"Never, Drav. I will never leave you if I can help it."

He sighed gustily. "When Shax told me you had disappeared again, I feared the worst."

I turned in his arms and looked up at him.

"When Merdon picked me up and jumped over the fence, I should have been more scared than I was. Do you know why I wasn't?"

He shook his head.

"Because you will never let anything happen to me. Because I'm yours, and you're mine. And because you really, really like it when I jiggle."

He grinned and scooped me into his arms, pressing a dangerously hot kiss to my lips.

I wrapped my arms around his neck and let him have his way. When we finally broke apart, I could only think of one thing.

"Drav, take me home."

EPILOGUE

I watched Molev, Kerr, and Drav work with Ryan to get the solar panel they'd raided onto the roof of our house. An ice storm two days ago had cut power to our little community away from Whiteman. Some folks had called it quits and returned to Whiteman on the following supply run. Not us. Not the fey.

Ryan and Dad had started going out with them to collect what we needed to be "off the grid." Not that there was much of a grid anymore. Power failures were happening all over the place. Lack of people to maintain it, I supposed. And there were more infected to wreck things.

But, not here. It seemed that the infected had gotten smart enough to avoid the fey because they no longer wandered the area around our community. Or maybe they just didn't like the "wall" the fey had constructed around us. However, the scarcity of nearby infected meant that the fey went further afield on their hunting parties to kill infected and search for hellhounds.

"When's the next hunting party?" I asked.

"Tomorrow," Molev answered. "You will have heat before we leave."

"Go inside, Mya and Mom. It is too cold for you," Drav called down.

"That's why we have winter jackets," I called back. "We're fine."

Mom chuckled.

"He is such a sweetheart. Do you know he wouldn't let me drive the tractor around the field because I was too jiggly on it? He didn't think your father would like the attention it was drawing."

I shook my head without taking my eyes from Drav. He wore jeans and a jacket like the rest of the fey, looking fairly human except for the grey skin still exposed on his hands and face.

"They sure do get fixated on body parts," I agreed.

"Just the girl ones."

I glanced at Mom, caught her wide grin, and got suspicious.

"What happened?"

"Ghua came to talk to me after I got off the tractor and said you told him to go away."

"Oh, God." I already knew where this was going and why I'd told him to go away.

"He was lamenting that fact when your father came up from behind him to hear, 'When will I get to see some pussy for myself?'"

I covered my face with my hands.

"Your father's reaction wasn't so mild. He got right in front of poor Ghua and hit him in the face. Then he lectured every fey within earshot about how it's inappropriate to talk about the p-word with a married woman."

I looked at Mom. "And they listened?"

Mom's smirk told me they hadn't. She opened her mouth to say something, but her gaze shifted to someone approaching behind me. I looked over my shoulder at Ghua. His face looked remarkably unscathed.

"Good morning, Mom. Is Dad's hand feeling better?"

"It is, sweetie. Thank you for asking."

He nodded and looked at me.

"Mya, may I ask you something?"

"Sure. What's up?"

"Is every vagina the same or are they slightly different like our cocks?"

Mom busted out laughing.

"Fixated," she managed between hoots of laughter.

"Ghua, you need a hobby," I said.

"I did not use the p-word," he said, worriedly.

"You're fine, honey," Mom said with a pat on his arm. "Why don't you show me how your solar panel looks?"

Our roof wasn't the only roof getting a solar panel and some new wiring. Not only were the fey working to kill the hellhounds and infected during their rotations at Whiteman, they were also settling in to stay. Each fey had his own home that he was preparing in hopes of one day sharing it with a female.

Mom and Ghua walked two houses down to look over what Ghua had done. I could hear Mom's praise for his hard work.

The fey had a hard path before them, like the rest of us. During the day, the infected still caused a very real threat for any human away from the fey. At night, the hellhounds roamed, threatening both human and fey. But, I held onto hope, like the rest of the survivors.

It would take time and effort to rebuild a world together. But, with Drav, the fey, and my family at my side, I didn't fear the future. I welcomed it.

Thank you for reading the first three books in the Resurrection Chronicles! Want to know what happens next to Drav and the other fey? The series continues with Ghua and Eden, in Demon Escape.

AUTHOR'S NOTE

What a ride! We loved writing this trilogy and continued the journey for humans and fey alike. Interested? Check out Eden and Ghua's story, *Demon Escape*. We don't recommend reading this next one in public. Or at night. (You're welcome!)

Remember how we mentioned that your support keeps us writing! Well...that hasn't changed. Go tell a friend that you're reading about hot dark fey who love killing zombies and eating p—peanut butter (yep, we were going to say that all along).

And don't forget to subscribe to MJ's newsletter at mjhaag. melissahaag.com/subscribe. She likes sending out teasers, random facts about herself, and the occasional newsletter-only short story for side characters you love. (She only sends periodically, so you won't be overwhelmed.)

Until next time!

Melissa and Becca

SNEAK PEEK

Demon Escape

For Eden, surviving alone proves more difficult than she ever imagines. While running from zombies and hellhounds, a new creature emerges who wants so much more than her body. He wants her heart and trust. Eden must decide who the real devils are between man and demon. Choosing wrong could cost her life; choosing correctly could lead her to the haven she's been searching for.

I clawed my fingers into the dirt.

"Eden, what are you doing?" a male voice said from right behind me.

"Digging for carrots, asshole; what do you think?"

"Aw, don't talk like that. There are so many nicer things a pretty girl like you should do with your mouth instead."

"Yeah, like bite your dick off." I pulled a carrot from the cold, hard ground and threw it over my shoulder.

Van chuckled, and I knew he'd caught it.

"Good find, Eden. This is why you're our favorite."

I said nothing. Instead, I crab walked forward, looking for the wilted remains of another carrot top.

"You know you don't need to be out here," he said. "You could be warm and comfortable back at the bunker."

"No thanks."

I used my trowel to scrape away the dead weeds, then my

fingers to dig up the carrot. Using my fingers meant an undamaged root and more food. It also meant my hands were numb already. I tossed the new find over my shoulder, too.

"One of these days, you'll change your mind," he said. "And, I bet it'll be sooner than you think."

I listened to Van's steps as he walked away, and I tried to quell the dread consuming my stomach. What did he mean sooner than I thought? What did he have planned?

Turning my head, I watched him walk toward the work truck where four of the other gunmen kept an eye on the eight of us. My fellow workers, who were also looking for missed carrots in the abandoned field, didn't bother to look at our protectors. Most of their attention wasn't on the ground but on the trees around us.

At the first sign of an infected, they would scramble back to the truck and likely run right into the line of fire. I'd seen two workers die that way already in the two weeks I'd been here. It seemed like a lifetime ago, though. How many weeks had it been since the quakes had caused everything to go to shit?

"Keep digging," one of the men in the truck said. I couldn't be sure which of the men was speaking, but I got back to work anyway. I didn't want to draw unwanted attention.

We worked for another hour as the sun passed its zenith.

"Back to the truck." Van nudged my shoulder with the point of his rifle to punctuate his words.

I picked up my basket of carrots and headed toward the truck. When I reached it, I waited in line as Van collected what we'd found. Like most of the gunmen, he looked cleaner than the workers. Non-greasy blonde hair, baby-blue eyes, and a classically handsome face didn't make him appealing, though.

"Were you even digging?" he said to the first person. I didn't look to see who he spoke to but kept my eyes on the ground.

Van moved down the line, muttering complaints about the lack of food each person had found. What did he expect? We'd picked over this field three times already, and that was after the field had already been harvested at the end of the growing season...before the hellhounds started turning people into flesh-eating infected.

"Eden, look at you," Van said, stopping in front of me. "This is what I'm talking about, people. There's a full two dozen carrots here. Pat them down. Anyone stealing loses tonight's ration." His fingers touched my chin, forcing my gaze up to meet his. "What about you, Eden? Trying to steal?"

"What do you think?" We both knew I wouldn't dream of trying to keep something for myself. Just like we both knew that didn't really matter.

"Oh, sugar, I think I need to check." He took the basket from my hands and passed it off to one of the grinning idiots behind him. Then he unzipped my jacket and groped me under the pretext of a carrot search.

After a minute, I wacked the back of his hand with my trowel.

"If you can't tell the difference between a breast and a carrot by now, maybe I should be the one with the gun."

He grinned at me as he shook out his hand.

"I think you're safer with your little shovel. Get in back."

I wasn't safer with my trowel. He was.

Now Available!

THE
RESURRECTION
CHRONICLES

Humor, romance, and sexy dark fey!

BOOK 1: DEMON EMBER
In a world going to hell, Mya accepts help from her new-found demon protector to find her family as a zombie-like plague spreads.

BOOK 2: DEMON FLAMES
Mya is taken to Ernisi, an underground Atlantis and Drav's home, where she learns that the shadowy demons are not what they seem.

BOOK 3: DEMON ASH
Returning to the bomb-ravaged surface, Mya seeks to stop everything that's trying to destroy what's left of the world.

BOOK 4: DEMON ESCAPE
While escpaing her captors and struggling to survive the zombie apocalypse, Eden encounters a new creature in her search for safety.

BOOK 5: DEMON DECEPTION
To gain protection and save her children, Cassie accepts the help of a certain dark fey and experiences the unexpected.

BOOK 6: DEMON NIGHT
Pregnant and trying to hide it, Angel agrees to coach Shax on how to win the girl of his dreams and loses her heart instead.

BOOK 7: DEMON DAWN
In a post-apocalyptic world, Benna is faced with trading her body and heart to the dark fey in order to survive the infected.

BOOK 8: DEMON DISGRACE
To gain protection and save her children, Cassie accepts the help of a certain dark fey and experiences the unexpected.

THE
RESURRECTION
CHRONICLES

The apocalyptic adventure continues!

BOOK 8.1: DEMON DESIGN

Driven by hunger, Brooke propositions the fey she's been sketching from afar for weeks and ends up with way more than a simple meal.

BOOK 8.2: DEMON DISCORD

After Terri's husband leaves her, she finds refuge with a fey who offers so much more than the familiar hate and bitterness she'd been clinging to for years.

BOOK 9: DEMON FALL

Struck by an unexpected loss, June turns her attention to making the Tenacity a better place with Tor's help.

BOOK 9.1: DEMON KEPT

A woman seeking to escape her past accepts refuge from two fey warriors determined to keep her safe and make her their own.

BOOK 9.2: DEMON BLIND

In a post-apocalyptic world, an optically impaired young woman makes the mistake of a lifetime and discovers glasses are just as hard to find as birth control.

BOOK 10: DEMON DEFEAT: PART 1

Andie is "sacrificed" for the betterment of humanity, only to discover risking her life isn't nearly as dangerous as risking her heart.

BOOK 11: DEMON DEFEAT: PART 2

In the epic conclusion, Andie and Molev work together to find a way to stop the hounds and evolving infected from destroying the community the survivors have built.

THE BEASTLY TALES

Beauty and the Beast with seductively dark twists!

BOOK 1: DEPRAVITY

When impoverished, beautiful Benella is locked inside the dark and magical estate of the beast, she must bargain for her freedom if she wants to see her family again.

BOOK 2: DECEIT

Safely hidden within the estate's enchanted walls, Benella no longer has time to fear her tormentors. She's too preoccupied trying to determine what makes the beast so beastly. In order to gain her freedom, she must find a way to break the curse, but first, she must help him become a better man while protecting her heart.

BOOK 3: DEVASTATION

Abused and rejected, Benella strives to regain a purpose for her life, and finds herself returning to the last place she ever wanted to see. She must learn when it is right to forgive and when it is time to move on.

Be careful what you wish for...

PREQUEL: DISOWNED

In a world where the measure of a person rarely goes beneath the surface, Margaret Thoning refuses to play by its rules. She walks away from everything she's ever known to risk her heart and her life for the people who matter most.

BOOK 1: DEFIANT

When the sudden death of Eloise's mother points to forbidden magic, Eloise's life quickly goes from fairy tale to nightmare. Kaven, the prince's manservant, is Eloise's prime suspect. However, when dark magic is used, nothing is as simple as it seems.

BOOK 2: DISDAIN

Cursed to silence, Eloise is locked in the tattered remains of her once charming life. The smoldering spark of her anger burns for answers and revenge. However, games of magic can have dire consequences.

BOOK 3: DAMNATION

With the reason behind her mother's death revealed, Eloise must prevent her stepsisters from marrying the prince and exact her revenge. However, a secret of the royal court strikes a blow to her plans. Betrayed, Eloise will question how far she's willing to go for revenge.